The Defiant Heir

I scrambled up on the low line of rocks with the others and saw what they'd been looking at.

It bobbed against the rocks, caught there by the rising tide, black water lapping against brilliant scarlet wool. I caught a glimpse of dark hair spreading like floating seaweed, bloated white fingers, and the gleam of gold trim on a too-familiar uniform jacket. Then I had to look away, clasping my arms across my lurching stomach.

"Grace of Mercy," I whispered.

"He's one of ours," Marcello said grimly. "A Falconer."

Praise for
The Tethered Mage

"*The Tethered Mage* is a riveting read, with delicious intrigue, captivating characters, and a brilliant magic system. I loved it from start to finish!" Sarah Beth Durst

"Charming, intelligent, fast-moving, beautifully atmospheric, with a heroine and other characters whom I really liked as people. (I overstayed my lunch break in order to finish it.) I would love to read more set in this world" Genevieve Cogman

"Intricate and enticing as silk brocade. Caruso's heroine is a strong, intelligent young woman in a beguiling, beautifully evoked Renaissance world of high politics, courtly intrigue, love and loyalty—and fire warlocks" Anna Smith Spark

"One of the best first novels in a brand-new high fantasy series that I've read in ages . . . *The Tethered Mage* is the book you need right now. Absolutely recommended" *The Book Smugglers*

"A beautifully written political fantasy drama full of courtly intrigue, powerful enemies and phenomenal magic potential. I raced through this exquisite debut in three days and adored it" *Fantasy Book Review*

"Engaging and entertaining with intrigue, a good pace, and strong characters. Zaira and Amalia are bright, bold heroes in a smartly constructed world" James Islington

"Breathtaking...Worth every moment and every page, it and should make anyone paying attention excited about what Caruso will write next" *BookPage*

"An enchanting voice and an original world you won't want to leave" RJ Barker

"A brilliant novel that delivers on all its initial promise...I was entertained from beginning to end" *The Eloquent Page*

"A rich world, political intrigue, and action that keeps you turning pages—*The Tethered Mage* is classic fantasy with a fresh voice" Jeff Wheeler

"*The Tethered Mage* is the best kind of fantasy: intricate world-building, the most intriguing of court intrigues, and a twisty plot. But while readers might pick it up for those elements, they'll stay for the engaging characters and the unlikely friendships at the story's heart" Rosalyn Eves

"It's a pleasure to journey with shy and slightly awkward Amalia as she puts her scholarship in magic and puzzle-solving skills to good use...Charming" *Kirkus*

"A gorgeous, fresh fantasy debut filled with political intrigue and ethical quandary...Highly recommend." *Girls in Capes*

By Melissa Caruso

Swords and Fire

The Tethered Mage

The Defiant Heir

The Defiant Heir

Book 2 of the
Swords and Fire trilogy

MELISSA CARUSO

www.orbitbooks.net

ORBIT

First published in Great Britain in 2018 by Orbit

1 3 5 7 9 10 8 6 4 2

Map by Tim Paul

A CIP catalogue record for this book is available from the British Library.

ISBN 978-0-356-51062-0

Printed and bound in Great Britain by Clays Ltd, St Ives plc

Papers used by Orbit are from well-managed forests and other responsible sources.

Orbit
An imprint of
Little, Brown Book Group
Carmelite House
50 Victoria Embankment
London EC4Y 0DZ

An Hachette UK Company
www.hachette.co.uk

www.orbitbooks.net

To Jesse
for always supporting my dream
and for putting up with me while I wrote this book

A Current and Accurate Map of
ERUVIA
The Winter Ocean
The Sunset Ocean
VASKANDAR
Tira
Elowan
Kosenia
Urshul
Asral
Roskoth
Vilskafar
Markova
Atruin
Let
Sevaeth
Eyrie Lake
Kazerath
Kar
Alevar
Mt Whitecrown
Mt Enthalus
Ordun
Gened
Morgrain
Highpass
Durantain

Callamorne
Ardence
Loreice
Trevelle
The River Arden
Palova
The Serene Empire
Raverra
The Tranquil Sea
Idrante
Valisia
Calsida
Celantis
The Imperial Ocean
The Ostan Sea
Osta
N
W
E
S
The Summer Ocean

Kazerath
Atruin
Sevaeth
The Witchwall Mountains
Highpass
village
castle
village
Durantain
Marcello's camp
Terika's village
armies and fortifications
The River Arden
The Serene Empire

Chapter One

It seemed a shame to burn a place so green.

The tiny island interrupted the path of the prevailing current from the Serene City, and trash collected along its curving inner shore. It was a mere mound of rock and sand, a navigational hazard without even a name. But flowering bushes edged the narrow strip of beach on which we stood, giving way to an improbable clutch of young trees and brush in the center. A salty breeze off the lagoon coaxed sighs from leaves that had so far escaped the encroaching yellow of autumn.

The whole place appeared far too flammable. Not that it mattered much, with balefire.

I calculated angles and took three steps across the sand. It couldn't hurt to stay upwind. This might be a training exercise, but it could still kill us all if things went wrong.

Zaira lifted her brows beneath the windblown tangle of her dark curls. "Are you done dancing around? We're not here to practice the minuet."

I judged the space between us. Three feet, perhaps. Not nearly enough for me to make it to safety if she lost control. But then, thirty feet might not be enough either.

I nodded, heart quickening. "All right."

"I won't set you on fire," Zaira promised. "This time."

"I trust you." I didn't add, *when you're you*. There was no trusting what she became when the flames took her.

She glanced at Marcello, who waited a good fifty feet away along the gray stretch of sand. He stood at apparent ease, his black curls loose against the collar of his scarlet-and-gold uniform, the Mews looming watchfully over his shoulder across the calm lagoon waters. But his hand, hooked so casually into his belt, touched the grip of his pistol.

Not that it would do him much good. The only thing that could stop Zaira's fire was the word I could speak to seal it. However, in this exercise, I wasn't supposed to; Zaira was practicing control. Which meant that if I made a tiny error in judgment, waiting a second too long, people would die.

I much preferred my university days, when failing a practical lesson would have meant nothing worse than a stern lecture from my professor.

"Are you ready?" Zaira called.

Marcello nodded.

Zaira held out a hand to me, palm up, as if she expected me to put something into it. The jess gleamed golden on her stick-thin wrist.

My mouth went dry as blown sand. "Are you sure you want to do this?"

"No, I came out here for a picnic. Of course I want to do it. Release me."

I drew in a breath of damp sea air, then let it go again, shaping it into the most terrible word I knew.

"Exsolvo."

Zaira closed her hand. When she opened it, a pale blue flame licked up from her fingers.

It was a small thing, for now, but wicked as a hooked knife, lovely and fatal. It clawed the air with hungry yearning. *Balefire.*

The slim twist of flame leaned toward me, against the wind. I took a step back.

"Hold your ground, Lady Amalia." It was Balos's voice, deep and firm. He stood twenty feet down the beach in the opposite direction from Marcello, along with Jerith, his Falcon and husband. "You need to get used to it. You can't let it distract you in an emergency."

"It's hard not to get distracted by something that wants to kill you," I muttered.

"It's nothing personal." Zaira grinned, but the tightness around her eyes betrayed her strain. She was afraid, too. "It wants to kill everyone."

"Now light something on fire," Jerith called. Somehow, he sounded more like a child daring a schoolmate to cause trouble than an older warlock instructing a young one.

Zaira flicked her wrist at a squat bush with shiny, round leaves. A spark leaped from her hand, searing a bright path through the air, and landed inside it. Blue-white flames sprang up from within the bush, crawling hungrily up its blackening branches, withering every leaf to ash.

"Keep it contained," Jerith said. The mage mark gleamed silver in his eyes as he watched Zaira's face. "Don't let it spread."

"I know what I'm doing," Zaira snapped. Sweat gleamed on her temples.

"Oh? Then what's that?" Jerith jerked his chin at the fire.

Only a jutting charred stick remained of the bush. But the blue flames reached higher than ever, straining for the tree branches above. Thin lines of flame meandered outward, searching, following the bush's roots under the ground.

One slithered along the sand's edge—thin, powerful, and rapid as a snake—heading toward Marcello. Memories of figures writhing in an agony of blue fire and the stench of charring human meat seared my mind. I sucked in a breath but held back the word to seal her power again, though it strained behind my teeth.

I had to trust her to handle it. That was half the point of this exercise.

Zaira reached toward the racing line of fire, as if to gather it back, but it only leaped higher. A faint blue gleam shone in her eyes. Marcello took a hasty step backward, but the flame was faster; it would reach him in seconds. I opened my mouth to cry out the word that could save him.

"Zaira!" Jerith called sharply.

Zaira sliced a hand through the air. The balefire winked out, leaving a smoking black smear on the ground.

"See? Fine." She tossed back her mane of dark curls. "Completely under control."

But her hands trembled ever so slightly, before she shoved them into her skirt pockets.

"*Revincio,*" I sighed, sealing her power. My knees felt ready to buckle with relief.

Jerith shook his head, a diamond glittering in his earlobe. "Control will be much harder when it's a company of Vaskandran musketeers or some Witch Lord's pet chimera coming at you with venomous claws."

I shifted my feet uneasily. "We're not at war with Vaskandar."

Jerith laughed. "Oh, don't be coy, my lady. Your Council secrets are safe with me. Anyone who's heard of their troop movements knows they're preparing for an invasion. It's only proper we afford them the same courtesy in return." He jabbed a finger at Zaira. "And that means improving your control to the point where Lady Amalia can release you without worrying about getting set on fire along with the enemy."

Anger flashed in Zaira's eyes. "So the Empire can use me as a weapon."

"No. So you don't kill anyone you don't mean to." Jerith's smile was bitter. "The Empire will try to use you as a weapon whether you've got good control or not."

Balos slipped a thickly muscled brown arm around the storm warlock's slim shoulders, and I wondered if Jerith spoke from experience.

Marcello approached, a frown marring his brow. I couldn't help but appreciate the flattering lines of his uniform doublet. Never mind all my efforts to remind myself over the past weeks that we weren't courting—*couldn't* court—at least not yet. I wasn't ready to throw away the power of political eligibility.

"That was better," he said.

Zaira flicked a glance down the beach to the ashy remains of last week's practice. I'd had to seal her, that time. "Damned right it was. Do you think I'd put up with any of you if this weren't working?"

"We should try again," Marcello suggested. "For longer, this time."

I eyed the tangle of brush and overhanging branches surrounding the charred stump of the bush Zaira had burned. "Maybe in a place where it won't spread quite so easily."

Marcello's eyes caught mine for a moment. Their corners crinkled with wry amusement. "Good idea. I won't deny my heart got some exercise at the end, there."

I smiled back, but an uneasy flutter stirred under my breastbone. In the weeks since we'd returned from Ardence, he'd been friendly and courteous, professional to a fault; it was as if we'd never shared that desperate kiss, at what I'd thought was our final farewell. I wasn't sure anymore, when he smiled, whether I glimpsed an undercurrent of hurt beneath it.

His gaze slid away, scanning the beach. "How about over there?"

He gestured to a line of barnacle-crusted rocks that extended into a thin spit a short distance down the beach, at the point of the tiny island's crescent. Balefire could burn on stone—or water, for that matter—but at least a chance breeze wouldn't dip a tree branch into the flame.

Zaira shrugged her indifference, so we started over in that direction. She seemed in no hurry, and though I'd worn breeches, my city boots turned awkwardly on the soft, sliding sand; we soon fell back behind the others.

It was just as well. There was something I needed to ask her, a gnawing unease I had to face.

"Jerith's right," I said quietly. "It's no feint, this time. Vaskandar is preparing for war. And you know what the Council will ask you to do."

"Yes, I heard. Musketeers, chimeras." She tugged gently at the jess on her wrist, as if testing whether it might come off at last. "Should be easier than burning some scraggly old bush, frankly. Small is harder."

"Are you..." I tried to think how to phrase my question. "How do you feel about this?"

"Why does everyone ask about my feelings? Graces' tits, you and Terika..." She clamped her mouth shut.

"Perhaps we care about you."

Zaira snorted. "Must be nice to have the luxury to worry about bilge like that. In the Tallows, you learn feelings are worthless. They're what drunkards piss away the morning after."

Some things were worth arguing with Zaira about, and some weren't. "I don't want to see you put in a position where you're forced to use your fire to kill."

"As opposed to what? Roast meat skewers in the market? There's not much else it's good for." She shook her head. "You heard Jerith. To the Empire, I'm a tool for killing, nothing more. And they're not half wrong. If I stay in the Falcons, I'll leave a wake of ashes through Vaskandar. Your pretty little qualms and niceties won't change that."

That *if* bordered on treason. Imperial law gave the mage-marked no choice, compensating them with riches and lavish comforts for their mandatory conscription into the Falcons. But I had no doubt Zaira could successfully run away anytime she chose; it was only knowing she could leave that had reconciled her to staying. For now.

"I wish I could get my Falcon reform act passed before war breaks out." I kicked at a rock, sending it skittering across the sand. "So every mage could choose whether to become a soldier. But my mother says there's no way I'll get the support I need in the Assembly with Vaskandran armies at the borders."

Zaira gave me a sideways glance. "That thing, still? It'll never pass."

"Once the Vaskandran threat eases, it might," I insisted. "I have a few dozen members of the Assembly willing to back it already. I just need time."

"A few dozen. Out of a thousand. Forgive me if I don't wait like a good little girl for you to free us." Zaira stopped, hands on her hips. "You don't think that's why I'm still here, do you? Because I've got hope for your stupid law?"

"No." I raised my brows. "I assume you stayed for Terika."

"I like Terika," Zaira admitted. "But if you think I'd let her chain me to the Mews, you don't know me."

"I suppose not," I sighed.

"I'm here for one reason." She leveled a finger at me. "To learn to control my power well enough not to hurt anyone. Well enough to hide. Because now the world knows I exist, and there's nowhere I can run where they'll ever leave me alone."

"Ah." I didn't know what else to say; it was true.

"They might swallow your law for artificers or alchemists. Devices and potions don't make people wet their breeches the way balefire does. But they're too afraid of warlocks." She shook her head. "No sane person wants someone who can single-handedly destroy a city on a whim to wander around free. The whole continent of Eruvia wants me locked up safe in the Mews—or better yet, dead."

"I don't want you locked up or dead," I protested.

"Oh?" Zaira lifted a skeptical brow. "If I decided to run away and take my chances in hiding, what would you do?"

It was an uneasy question I'd worried at frequently over the past weeks. Not least because it was hard to imagine any future where Zaira would be content to stay cooped up in the Mews for long. "I'd try to find a way for you to do it legally. To convince the doge and the Council to let you go."

"They'd never let me go, and you know it."

"Well, then, I'd use my influence to do what I could to stop the Empire from coming after you. To keep you safe." My heartbeat quickened at the inherent rebellion in that declaration; my duty as a Falconer would be to help them find her.

But then, I was more than just a Falconer.

"Safe?" Zaira let out a bark of a laugh. "I make everything unsafe. I'm danger salt—add me to anything, and I make it more interesting."

"I can't deny that seems an apt assessment. But if you ran away, where would you go? What would you do?"

Zaira kicked at the sand in silence, scowling. "I don't know," she said at last. "If I knew, I'd already be doing it. But this is the first step: getting my fire under control. After that, I can figure out what to do next."

"So you're only remaining with the Falcons until then?" My throat felt strangely tight. Of course I wanted Zaira to be free, and my life would certainly be quieter without her in it. But it would be a lonely sort of quiet.

"That depends." Zaira's voice dropped low. "After that idiocy in Ardence, I made myself a promise. If the doge orders me to burn down people who don't deserve it, that's the line. I'm gone."

I nodded. "I understand. But if he orders you against Vaskandar? What then?"

"If they invade us, that's different." She brushed off the thought of war with the Empire's most powerful neighbor as if it were an annoying insect. "I've heard the stories of the Three Years' War from the wrinkled old relics in the Tallows. Grandfathers strangled in their beds by bramble vines, children fed to bears—the Witch Lords don't know mercy. If they come across our borders, I'll show them they're not the only demons in the Nine Hells."

Ahead of us, Marcello stopped at the crest of the rocky spit as suddenly as if the wind had slammed a gate in his face.

"What's that in the water?" Fear bleached all the color from his voice.

Jerith and Balos hopped up beside him and looked down on the other side of the rocks. Balos clapped a hand to his mouth; Jerith swore.

Zaira and I exchanged glances and ran to catch up with them.

Zaira crested the rocks first, her skirts whipping behind her. She took one look down into the water and gave a decisive nod, as if confirming a suspicion.

"Dead," she said.

I scrambled up on the low line of rocks with the others and saw what they'd been looking at.

It bobbed against the rocks, caught there by the rising tide, black water lapping against brilliant scarlet wool. I caught a glimpse of dark hair spreading like floating seaweed, bloated white fingers, and the gleam of gold trim on a too-familiar uniform jacket. Then I had to look away, clasping my arms across my lurching stomach.

"Grace of Mercy," I whispered.

"He's one of ours," Marcello said grimly. "A Falconer."

I couldn't bring myself to help as Marcello, Zaira, and Balos hauled the body out of the water. When Zaira called me a wilting pansy, I merely nodded, lips tight, and kept my eyes averted.

At least I'd kept my dinner in. Jerith staggered back from the woods to my side, wiping his mouth, even paler than usual.

"Oh, that poor bastard," he groaned.

"Who is he?" I asked, throwing a nervous glance to where the others bent over the corpse. "Did you recognize him?"

"No. He'd been gnawed on too much. But his name should be on the uniform." Jerith sank to the sand and rested his forehead on his knees. "I don't have a problem with dead people. Seen dozens of them. Blood, terrible burns, I don't care. But not in the water. Not days in the water like that."

I nodded an emphatic agreement. Thank the Graces the wind blew across my face, carrying away the death-tainted air.

The others rose from the corpse. Balos remained over the dead man, his head bowed. Marcello walked past us to the water's edge, his face drawn and haunted, and swished his hands in the clean salty lagoon. The pain pulling his handsome features taut cut me like a knife. I started toward him.

Zaira stomped up to us, wiping her palms on her skirts.

"Well," she said, "that's a bloater if I ever saw one. A week in the water, at least."

Jerith lifted his head, swearing. "A week? Verdi!"

Marcello straightened. "I know. It's too long. His Falcon must be dead, too."

"Oh, Hells." I hadn't thought of that. When Falconers died, their Falcons had several days to get new jesses, or the innocuously lovely golden bracelets leaked deadly magic into their veins, slowly killing them.

It was never supposed to actually happen. Or at least, Marcello believed the intent was preventive only, to remove the incentive for criminals or foreign powers to murder Falconers. I, however, suspected that the doge considered it well worth killing a Falcon to keep them out of enemy hands.

"Who was it?" Jerith asked, his voice strained.

"Anthon. He became a Falconer a year after I did." Marcello stared out across the lagoon at the Mews. "His Falcon was Namira, an artificer from Osta. They were on leave, to visit her family. But they must never have made it to their ship."

"What happened?" I glanced over to where Balos stood, solemn and still; I couldn't see the sad scarlet bundle beyond the low line of rocks. "Did he drown?"

"His throat was cut," Marcello said curtly. "He was murdered."

Chapter Two

A pall hung over our table at Lady Aurica's dinner party. Marcello barely spoke, and the servants whisked away his plates almost untouched for the first two of the fourteen planned courses. Zaira, on the other hand, attacked her food with even more ferocity than usual. Marcello's sister Istrella bent over a small pile of fiddly artifice bits she'd brought in her silk purse, a worried frown creasing her brow as she twisted a slip of wire. An old dowager at the next table gave her a disapproving sidelong glance and a sniff for this behavior, but it was just Istrella being Istrella.

I didn't have the heart to try to support a conversation on my own. I hadn't known the murdered Falconer or his presumably deceased Falcon well enough to do more than put faces to their names: Anthon had been growing a beard, and rubbed it self-consciously when he talked. Namira had been my mother's age, with bright sharp eyes and an iron-gray frost upon the tight curls of her close-cropped hair. But it still seemed wrong to be at a party the day after we found a body.

The servers laid a nut course before us, a bountiful harvest of several kinds piled artistically with flowers and greens on a silver platter. Zaira plucked up a walnut; the harsh crunch as she cracked the shell jabbed at my nerves, and I could stand the silence no longer.

"Do they have any idea who did it?" I asked Marcello.

He lifted his head. Shadows beneath his eyes suggested he hadn't slept much. I hated to see his clean-lined face so tired and worn. I wished I could reach out and smooth the worry lines from his brow.

"No," he said. "It doesn't make any sense. Namira was an artificer. She designed protective wards and taught new Falcons. There's no reason anyone would want to kill her, or poor Anthon either."

Zaira scowled at her plate. "I'd love to get my hands on the bastard who did. Namira was all right." A sharp crack punctuated her sentence, and she popped another nut into her mouth.

"My mother suspects Vaskandar." I cast a glance three tables over, where the Vaskandran ambassador lifted a glass with a pair of wealthy importers. "Only because they keep moving troops to the border, even with autumn upon us, and they're clearly planning *something*."

Marcello frowned. "I fail to see how murdering a single artificer and her Falconer would give them an advantage."

"Namira was a highly skilled designer specializing in runic artifice," I said. "Maybe she was working on some project Vaskandar was worried about, like a new kind of weapon or battlefield trap. We could look through her notes for clues."

"You always have good ideas, Amalia." Marcello smiled wistfully. "That's one of the things I love about you."

The word struck me like lightning, despite his casual tone. *Love.*

He hadn't used it since that moment in Ardence, when I was dying of poison and we'd parted with little hope of seeing each other again. *I think I might love you.* I'd tried to forget;

circumstances had been desperate, after all. And it would be foolish to dwell on whether he loved me, or I loved him, when I'd made the political decision to remain unattached, at least for now.

Which made me a fool, because naturally I'd thought of it nearly every day in the weeks since.

"Namira was working on adapting some of the lovely spiral runework you find in ancient Ostan tomb murals," Istrella said unexpectedly, without looking up from her project. "She was going to do more research in Osta. I was quite jealous; I want to go see the wirework artifice filigree in their royal palace someday."

"Maybe we can go together," I suggested, and Istrella flashed me a smile.

"I should have known they were missing." Marcello dropped his voice so low I could barely hear him. "They were due to arrive in Osta days ago. But because Namira was on leave, I didn't expect them to report in." He shook his head, his mouth set in a grim line.

I let my voice soften more than was perhaps wise. "Don't blame yourself."

"Who said I'm blaming myself?" He tried a rather unconvincing smile.

"Anyone who knows you."

"The Falcons' safety *is* my responsibility." He rubbed his forehead. "Especially since the promotion."

"Promotion! You didn't tell me you got a promotion." I'd noticed some extra braiding on his collar, and fancier falcon's-head buttons, but had just assumed it was a new dress uniform.

He hadn't told me. The realization pinched and twisted inside my chest. Perhaps he had simply been too busy; or perhaps he was keeping me at a distance.

Istrella glanced up from the wire she was coiling, beaming proudly. "Yes, he's Captain Verdi now. Second only to Colonel Vasante at the Mews. He can approve funding for my projects himself! I'm quite excited. He doesn't ask too many questions about safety precautions."

Marcello's eyebrows lifted in alarm. "Maybe I should fix that."

"Congratulations," I said, lifting my glass to him, determined to show no hurt in my smile. "I know you've been working toward this for a long time."

Marcello shrugged, tugging at the gold trim on his collar uncomfortably. "Thank you. It's already not what I expected, though."

"Oh?" I raised an eyebrow. "More work? More politics?"

"More guilt." He grimaced. "Colonel Vasante seemed to feel our handling of the Ardence situation showed I was ready for greater responsibility. But I'm afraid I'm already letting her down. With Vaskandar preparing for war, I should have assigned extra guards for all Falcons traveling outside the Mews."

Zaira grunted. "Punch yourself in the privates about it if you really want, but I'm more interested in blaming His Oily Excellency, there." She jerked her head toward the Vaskandran ambassador, who had stood to greet a countrywoman, his head bobbing ingratiatingly. "He keeps going off to talk to people in a side room."

"Does he?" I craned to look. Graces knew I should have been watching him, too, and not letting memories of death and decaying flesh smother my awareness.

He was a middle-aged man, with the look of old muscle gone to seed. A robust blond beard provided a counterargument to the bald spot that flashed each time he bowed. Even his wardrobe struck a compromise: a Raverran-style brocade jacket in

Vaskandran forest green. I searched my memory for his name and dredged it up from my last visit to the embassy, when I'd attended a truly grueling tea party with Prince Ruven: Ambassador Varnir.

Zaira was right; Varnir gestured to a door across Lady Aurica's dining hall, and he and his companion—a tall, graceful woman in a long leather coat edged with jagged Vaskandran embroidery—began picking their way between the tables.

"I'd give a lot to overhear what they talk about," I said.

Istrella's head popped up from her work. Marcello had made her leave her artifice glasses at home, and the mage mark stood out bright gold in her eyes, giving them a feverish gleam. "Oh! Really? Let me see what I can do."

Humming, she produced a tiny pair of pliers and began coiling wire around her dessert spoon. Marcello and I exchanged affectionate glances; leave it to Istrella to come up with an artifice solution to any problem. She slid a few beads onto the wire, then pulled a pin from the unruly pile of her bushy hair and dipped it into a tiny bottle of ink among her supplies. Within moments, she'd scratched out a simple circle and a few runes on the back of the spoon.

"Is that an amplification circle?" I asked, impressed. We had a couple of those in listening posts in our palace, but I'd never heard of anyone knocking one out with the casual speed of a market quick-sketch artist.

"Yes." Istrella beamed. "I made you a listening device!" She thrust the spoon toward me with the grand air of a favorite aunt offering a sweet. "It's a bit fragile, but it should work all right while it lasts."

"Istrella, you are a miracle."

Zaira grinned and pushed her chair back. "Right, then. Let's go see what's so secret it made a diplomat walk away from a free dinner."

Zaira led me to a hallway adjoining the private room into which our quarry had disappeared. She scanned the short, unremarkable corridor critically; it connected the dining hall to what smelled like the kitchens, adorned by nothing more than a couple of slim potted evergreens and a somewhat tarnished mirror in an elaborate silver frame.

"Right." She faced the mirror and began fussing with her hair, prodding the artful twists and jeweled pins my maid had spent half an hour arranging. "You lean against the wall like you're bored of waiting for me, and see what that crazy girl can do with a bit of cutlery."

I laid Istrella's spoon against the wall. Tinny voices emerged from it immediately.

"You understand, my situation here is delicate..." That sounded like the ambassador.

"Bored and waiting," Zaira snapped, without looking away from the mirror.

"Oh! Right." I leaned back against the wall, pillowing my head on my hands as an excuse to hold the spoon near my ear.

"I want all the information you can get me on these people." That must be the woman. Her voice was flat and cold, stripped of accent or inflection, utilitarian as a knife. "Their movements, their connections, their patterns."

"I see." Paper rustled, and the ambassador was silent for a moment. Then he sighed. "I'm so sorry, but I fear I can't help you with this matter. I am a diplomat, not a spy."

"You serve the Witch Lords." Even through the spoon, I could hear the warning in her voice.

"Yes, of course," the ambassador soothed. "But, forgive me—you are not a Witch Lord. And I dare not risk eliciting any more ire from the Raverrans. My position..." His voice faded. I shifted to bring my ear closer to the spoon, ignoring a glare from Zaira as she pretended to check her lip paint.

"The Lady of Thorns commands this," the Vaskandran woman snapped. "She will accept no refusal. More than your position is at stake."

The Lady of Thorns. There was something familiar about that name, but the memory eluded me, dancing just beyond my mind's grasp.

A long sigh vibrated through Istrella's device. "Very well, very well. I'll see what I can do. But I beg you to be circumspect, for both our sakes." Whatever paper he held crackled again. "Wait. Some of these people are here tonight."

"I know," the woman said. "Best you not think of it."

"Why is this one circled?"

A moment of silence. I held my breath, straining to hear the answer.

"That's between me and my lady," the woman said at last.

The ambassador muttered something I couldn't make out. Then, louder: "That's why you're here, isn't it? Don't you dare do anything at this dinner! You'll get us both arrested."

"You do not command me."

"You'll ruin all the deals I'm working on for the other Witch Lords!" There was a tearing sound, as if he'd ripped the paper in half. "You may have your orders from *one* Witch Lord, but I serve all seventeen. If you barge in to the middle of my negotiations and start causing major incidents, I'll have to answer to the rest of them for... Where do you think you're going? I'm still talking to you!"

Zaira let out a sharp sigh. "I *told* you, I'll be done in a minute!"

I jumped, startled. Istrella's spoon came off the wall. A server carrying a tray with bowls of fragrant seafood bisque passed by, hurrying from the kitchen.

"Graces wept. You're hopeless," Zaira muttered. "I might as well just kick you next time, if you're going to react like *that*."

"Sorry."

"Did you learn what you needed? I can't keep this up much longer." She nodded approvingly at her reflection.

I glanced past her, to the main hall, and saw the ambassador stalking back to his table, his face red with anger. There was no sign of the woman.

"We should get into that room, if we can," I said. "They talked about a list of names, and it sounded like he might have thrown it away. If we can find the pieces, it might tell us something."

"Should be easy enough." Zaira jerked her head toward the dining hall. "Come on."

She led me not to the side room door but to a table near it, which held a gilt-edged guest book for writing messages to our hostess. Zaira bent over it with apparent interest. I'd learned enough from our adventures in Ardence to play along, studiously avoiding glancing at the door, no matter how much I wanted to.

"Too many people watching," Zaira muttered. "Wait here and write in the guest book, to look busy, and I'll go get them to look the other way."

I bent dutifully over the guest book as she moved off, not without some trepidation at the thought of what Zaira might consider a suitable distraction. Lady Aurica was one of the backers for my Falcon reform act, and the last thing I wanted was to ruin her dinner party.

I dipped the silver-tipped guest book quill in the provided ink and began scribing a message thanking Lady Aurica both for the occasion and for her commitment to a better future for Falcons in the Empire. It couldn't hurt to leave that where other guests might see it.

"Ah, Lady Amalia," came a smooth, soft voice at my elbow.

"Still pursuing your noble dream of untethering the Falcons, I see."

I started, spattering fine drops of ink across the page. I'd had no idea anyone was standing so close to me. I turned to face the speaker and nearly dropped the quill when I saw who it was.

Lord Caulin, a mouse-haired slip of a man, officially advised the doge on Raverran law. But due to my mother's position on the Council of Nine, I knew his true role: the so-called Chancellor of Silence, an unofficial and highly secret post that oversaw the imperial assassins and liaised with the criminal underworld. He had a reputation for being quiet, efficient, and completely ruthless in achieving his ends. He radiated such nondescript diffidence that my eyes tried to slide off him, but I knew better than to underestimate him. The man was dangerous.

He also could be useful. Certainly his skills were more applicable to discovering the intentions of the ambassador and his lady guest than mine. But a memory flashed to mind: my mother, shaking her head at the Marquise of Palova after the latter had suggested enlisting Caulin's aid in gathering some piece of intelligence. *The man is competent, but whenever he gets involved in an endeavor, it acquires a body count.*

Perhaps it was best not to mention why I was lurking near this door after all.

"Of course I'm pursuing it," I said. "The mage-marked deserve the same choices as any imperial citizen."

"Oh, certainly they deserve it." Lord Caulin chuckled, as if I'd made a little joke. "But tell me, Lady Amalia, do you truly think the Assembly passes laws to give people what they *deserve*?"

"It's our duty to rule for the good of Raverra and the Empire," I said stiffly. I stopped myself before scanning the room for Zaira.

Lord Caulin inclined his torso toward me in a deferential half bow. "Precisely. And the mage-marked are powerful tools to secure that good. Are they not?"

"People aren't tools, Lord Caulin."

He lifted wispy eyebrows. "What a quaint notion. Ah, the idealism of the young." He shook his head. "You'll understand someday; you are your mother's heir, after all."

He was treating me like a child. A few months ago, perhaps I might have deserved that. But I'd done well enough in Ardence.

I lifted my chin. "Compassion isn't the same as naiveté."

"If you say so, my lady." Lord Caulin bowed deeply. "I pray you do not learn otherwise the hard way. Enjoy your evening."

I frowned after him as he slipped away, his black velvet coat and breeches remarkable for their simplicity among the colorful brocades and velvets of the dinner guests. But even trying to track him across the room, I lost sight of him almost immediately.

Then a great crash caught my attention. I spun to see a serving boy, flushed bright red, bending to pick up a fallen tray from an impressive spray of shattered pottery.

Zaira tugged my arm. "Don't *you* get distracted. Come on."

I barely had time to return the quill to its stand before she whisked me through a sliver of open door, then closed it neatly behind us.

The room was appointed for exactly the sort of private aside the ambassador had just indulged in, or perhaps for meetings even more intimate. A few chairs formed a tight, conversational cluster around a small gilt table. Luminaries glowed softly in niches on the walls, and an oil lamp on the table provided a warmer, less steady illumination.

I pushed uneasy thoughts about what Lord Caulin's subtle warning might mean out of my head. We might not have much time before the ambassador noticed we were in here—and I didn't particularly want to explain myself to Caulin, either.

"Look for the paper," I urged. Zaira dropped to the carpet and started peering under chairs.

My gaze strayed to a small fireplace with an elaborately carved mantel. A fire had been laid, but not yet lit, the wood arranged neatly in the grate.

Well, I knew what *I* would do with an incriminating document. I crossed for a closer look, and sure enough, a crumpled ball of paper lay fresh among the ashes.

I pulled it out and smoothed the two wrinkled halves of a list on the table, while Zaira peered over my shoulder.

A blunt hand spelled out perhaps twenty names. A rough line circled the third one.

Istrella Verdi.

"Oh, Hells," I breathed.

I dashed out of the side room, the list clutched in my fist, to find my worst fear waiting for me: Istrella's chair empty, her artifice supplies still spread across her place at the table. Marcello sat alone, poking his spoon into his seafood bisque without much enthusiasm. My stomach dropped as if I'd missed my footing on a canal edge.

"Where's Istrella?" I demanded.

"In the ladies' necessary. Why?" He stood. "Is she—"

Zaira and I didn't wait for his question. We ran through the crowded hall, Zaira's fluttering petticoats brushing against startled diners; I'd worn an ornate brocade jacket and breeches—the party wasn't quite formal enough to mandate a gown—and had more luck pushing through the narrow gaps between chairs. For once, I pulled ahead of her.

A dressing room served as antechamber to the necessary, its door painted with a quaint border of leaves and flowers. I threw it open on an airy room with tall windows, their gauzy curtains blowing in the pungent evening breeze off the canal. My heart froze to sharp-edged ice in an instant.

Istrella lay sprawled on the floor, like a wilted flower. A faint whiff of peppermint hung in the air.

The cold-voiced Vaskandran woman knelt over her, a dagger shining in her hand.

Chapter Three

The Vaskandran woman rose to her feet, drawing a second dagger to pair with the first.

"Lady Amalia Cornaro." Her eyes met mine with the readiness of a cat preparing to spring. "How convenient."

My pulse jolted, and I grabbed my flare locket. But at that moment, Zaira burst into the room.

Istrella's attacker cursed and bolted for the window in a swirl of dark coat and blond braid.

I didn't care. I threw myself down by Istrella and laid a hand on her neck. Warm and alive, with life pulsing and breath flowing. Dizzy relief washed through me.

Zaira bounded to the window, knife in hand. She threw back the curtains and leaned out into the night air. "Demons take you, coward!"

An oarsman called back something rude from the canal below.

"Can you still see her?" I asked, my chest tight. "Should I release you?"

"No." Zaira spat on Lady Aurica's rug. "She's gone."

Marcello arrived at the door, pistol out, and emitted a strangled cry, his eyes locked on his sister.

"She's fine," I assured him quickly. "Just knocked out with some sleep potion." I chose not to mention that I'd heard this was common practice among assassins who didn't want their targets' screams to give them away.

He came and cradled her head off the floor. "I should have gone with her."

"Into the ladies' dressing room?" I clasped his shoulder; his muscles were rigid under my hand. "She's all right. Nothing happened."

But it would have, in another minute. She might have been dead as poor Anthon, a week in the water. A shudder traveled down my spine.

I had no doubt Marcello was thinking the same thing. I'd never seen him so pale. He shook his sister gently. "Come on, 'Strella, wake up," he murmured. "I'm sorry."

A thin trail of drool trickled down her cheek, but she didn't stir.

I crouched down beside him, then hesitated. What was the appropriate thing to do to comfort an upset friend, when that friend was someone you'd kissed but declined to court? The space between us had once been charged with forbidden possibility; now any attempt to navigate those few inches presented a maze of complications.

I settled for patting his shoulder. "She'll wake up soon. She's all right. You're taking care of her."

He nodded, his lips thinning to a determined line. "Do you know who did it?"

"Vaskandar. And there's more." I uncrumpled the list I still clutched and spread it out on a nearby vanity. The plain, clear pen strokes spelled out name after name, some of them more than a little familiar.

Jerith Antelles. Terika. Istrella Verdi . . .

I swallowed. "You're on here, Zaira."

She crossed from the window to see. "What? Where?"

I pointed to her name. She couldn't read yet, but Terika had been teaching her letters and a few words, so I was reasonably certain she'd recognize it.

Zaira frowned. "Is that Terika's name, higher up?"

"Ah, yes."

She swore. "Nobody threatens Terika. I'll burn them till their teeth melt. Who else?"

"High-value Falcons. All the warlocks are here, and the Master Artificer. Marcello, you should check to make sure these people are well and accounted for."

"As soon as we get safely back to the Mews," he promised, a grim edge to his voice.

I scanned down the list, recognizing Falcon after Falcon, to the last name. My eyes stopped as if they'd hit a brick wall.

Amalia Cornaro.

Zaira must have seen something in my face. "What is it?" she demanded.

"I'll tell you later." I kept my tone as light as I could, despite the alarm singing its piercing song in my veins, and glanced meaningfully at Marcello. He didn't need more to worry about quite yet. Zaira grunted acknowledgment.

I folded the paper up and stuffed it in my pocket. "How's Istrella?" I asked Marcello. "Any improvement?"

He didn't lift his eyes from her face. "Maybe a flutter. She's still asleep. Whoever crafted this potion had some power."

"You stay with her, then." I straightened my jacket and checked the flare locket hanging at my throat. "I need to have a little talk with the Vaskandran ambassador."

Zaira and I stormed out of the dressing room, past our uneaten seafood bisque, between tables of diners craning their necks to see what all the fuss was about, and straight up to the ambassador's table. He faltered in the middle of telling his companions some anecdote as he saw us coming; the grins slid off their faces, and they inched their chairs back from him.

Good. Let him be afraid.

He attempted a strained smile and half rose. "Lady Amalia Cornaro! What a pleasure."

I leveled a hard stare at him. "Ambassador, we need to talk."

His features stilled to a wary blankness. Then his shoulders slumped, and he let out a long sigh.

"Very well, very well. Come, Lady Amalia; let us have this discussion in private."

I closed the door to the side room myself, to make sure he didn't slip an artifice seal on it. Ambassador Varnir bowed us toward the chairs, bending nearly in half.

"Please, my ladies. Make yourselves comfortable."

I put my hands on my hips. "I think I'll stand. What is the meaning of this assault on Istrella Verdi?"

"Why, I have no idea what you mean."

"Don't spout bilge at us," Zaira snapped. "We know you were chatting up that ice-eyed bitch in this room right before she attacked."

He grimaced. "Ah, *that* assault. Such a terrible thing. It failed, I hope? Yes?"

"If it hadn't, you'd be on fire now," Zaira growled.

"Of course." He swallowed. "I believe Lady Aurica keeps a bottle in here. Do you mind if I . . . ? Would you like some?" He turned toward a decorative cabinet and rummaged in it, coming out with a bottle and three glasses. His bald spot gleamed with sweat.

"Ambassador Varnir," I chided, "you're stalling for time."

"Of course I am, Lady Amalia. As would any gentleman contemplating how best to keep his head on his shoulders." He poured himself a glass of red wine, took a long draft, and then filled it again. "I did not endorse any action against your Falcon friend. In fact, I opposed it most vigorously. But you must understand, I have no power over what a Witch Lord sends her own agent to do."

"So you admit Vaskandar has stooped to assassinating Falcons."

"Vaskandar? Oh, no, not at all." He passed me a trembling glass of wine. I took it, pressing it against a certain ring wrapped in wire and graven with artifice runes; the ring stayed cool on my finger, and its central stone remained dark. No alchemy present, but that said nothing about mundane poison.

"Don't lie to me," I said sharply. "I know that assassin was sent by the Lady of Thorns."

"Ah." Varnir wiped sweat from his brow. "Such a bold accusation! I wouldn't dream of saying yea or nay to it. However, if you think the action of one Witch Lord represents Vaskandar as a nation, I fear you've fallen prey to a common misunderstanding about my country."

"I'm aware that the Witch Lords are each separate sovereign rulers of their own domains," I said icily. "You don't need to school me in the basics of Vaskandran government."

"Then perhaps you realize," Varnir said, "that every action you ascribe to our country—from the unfortunate and ill-advised attack on your friend, to trade deals, to the troops gathering on your border—is in fact the doing of one particular Witch Lord or another. Or a cabal of them, sometimes. But you cannot ascribe credit or blame to Vaskandar as a whole—or, thus, to its ambassador, I hope." He laughed nervously.

I frowned. "Wait, even the troops on the border? Are you telling me that's a single Witch Lord's gambit, and Vaskandar *isn't* preparing for war with the Empire?"

"Oh, my lady, as to that, I couldn't possibly say."

Zaira pushed back her lace-trimmed sleeves. "Say the word, and I'll light him up."

He raised his hands, wine sloshing out of his glass, eyes wide. "No, please! I'm not trying to be coy! I couldn't say because they haven't held the Conclave yet."

I exchanged glances with Zaira. "Conclave? Isn't that the Vaskandran ruling council?"

"No, no." Varnir pushed the idea away with both hands. "You Raverrans always want it to be like your Council of Nine, but Vaskandar *has* no ruling council. No one stands above the Witch Lords; their rule over their own domains is absolute. But when they need to resolve disagreements or band together for a common cause—such as war against the Serene Empire, for instance—the Witch Lords call a Conclave. Nothing will be decided until it takes place, about a month from now."

I set down my glass lest I squeeze it too hard. "So this Conclave might decide not to invade us at all?"

"Oh, no, no, no." He laughed politely, as if I'd made a dull joke. "There are a sufficient number of Witch Lords set on a course of conflict to render it inevitable, I fear, as I have tried to advise your doge. There are others who have asked me to assure Raverra of their commitment to peace; but each Witch Lord controls their own army. Those who wish war require no additional backing." He smiled indulgently. "You Raverrans seem to enjoy your certainty that Vaskandar cannot threaten you, but your Empire has never faced all seventeen of our Witch Lords at once. What you call the Three Years' War, that took place fifty years ago? That was three Witch Lords attacking on their own, with no support from the other fourteen."

A delicate chill tiptoed between my shoulder blades. Raverra had definitively won the Three Years' War, but it had wreaked devastation on the border lands that had lasted for decades. "And how many are bent on war now?"

Ambassador Varnir raised his eyebrows. "The Witch Lords do not include me in their councils, my lady. They merely each convey their will to me, and I do my best to fulfill their commands and negotiate their agreements without incurring anyone's ire."

"That's a rat's ass of a job," Zaira observed. "But don't expect mercy from us. One of your people just tried to kill our friend."

"Terrible idea, that. But I had no part in it."

"I can tell you were shaken up about it," Zaira said. "Fumbled that joke you were telling your friends. Barely had appetite for your soup. Forgot to warn us, even."

"I couldn't." He licked his lips. "Some of my masters are more reasonable than others. The Lady of Thorns would have me dragged back to her domain and impaled on a briar tree if I interfered directly with her plans."

I remembered where I'd heard of the Lady of Thorns, now. My paternal cousins in Callamorne, a client state of the Serene Empire, which bordered her domain, had kept me up staring sleeplessly into the darkness as a child with their grisly stories about what happened to children who strayed into her forests. I'd pulled the quilt of their guest bed up over my head and told myself that the Lady of Thorns wasn't real. But Ambassador Varnir apparently took orders from this creature of my childhood nightmares.

"Then I suggest some indirect interference now, if you wish to avoid being sent home in disgrace." I kept my tone reasonable, and refilled his glass for him. "Why would the Lady of Thorns target a fourteen-year-old artificer?" Istrella was an uncommonly strong artificer—one of the Master Artificer's rare apprentices, in fact, and one of only a handful who could craft the Empire's most powerful weapons—and her brother was now second in command at the Mews. But Vaskandar shouldn't know all that.

Ambassador Varnir accepted the glass gladly enough but shook his head. "I don't know. The Witch Lords don't confide their plans in me, my lady. I am what you would call a vivomancer, but I do not bear the mage mark; as such, they consider me beneath them. And I've found that a professional lack of curiosity into the affairs of the Witch Lords is a vital quality for a man in my position."

"You're lucky your position isn't in the dungeon," Zaira growled.

"My ladies, please. I have no power to stop the Lady of Thorns from carrying out her plans." He spread his hands. "I've given you all the information I can. That is the preferred currency in Raverra, yes? Was it not enough to buy me some consideration?"

"Enough that I'll permit you to walk out of here alive and free." That had as much to do with my urge to get back to Marcello and make sure Istrella was all right as any sense of gratitude, but let him think what he would. "The rest is for my mother to decide."

The ambassador paled. "La Contessa," he breathed. He groped for the wine. "Perhaps I'd better finish the bottle."

"Ambassador Varnir is a man with a great deal to lose," my mother told me the following evening, over a plate of buttery pauldronfish polenta. "It's making him both eager to cooperate with us and terrified to do so effectively."

Dinner with my mother had once been an uncommon occasion. She often stayed at the Imperial Palace late, coming home past midnight to find the artful meal our chef had prepared for her cold on the dining table under a silver cover. Or she'd eat while hosting some assorted handful of the most powerful people in the Serene Empire, making life-and-death decisions between bites of crab risotto or roast pheasant stuffed with mushrooms and herbs. Since I'd taken on more responsibility as her heir after last autumn's incident in Ardence, however, La Contessa had made dinner our near-daily information and strategy meeting, though it sometimes meant I had to eat at strange hours or join her at the Imperial Palace.

"So has he given you any useful information?" I tried to make my question casual, as if I didn't care what my mother thought of how I'd handled him.

"Some." She sipped her wine. "I am curious as to why you chose not to inform Lord Caulin that you had identified a Vaskandran assassin at the dinner party."

I supposed it had been too much to hope that she could have simply said, *Yes, you did well.*

"I didn't want to betray his identity to Marcello and Zaira. It wouldn't make any sense to bring in the doge's legal adviser." I hadn't actually thought of that until after the party, but there was no need to mention that. "Besides," I added, with more honesty, "I remembered what you said, about people tending to turn up dead when Lord Caulin involves himself in a matter."

"That's true." My mother set her glass down and regarded me across the table. "And in this case, I don't fault you for leaving him out of it. But you can't avoid getting blood on your hands, Amalia. Not once you join the Council of Nine."

"I know." I dropped my eyes to my plate so she wouldn't see my instinctive rejection of the idea. "I'd just like to put it off until it's necessary."

"Hmm. Well, Ambassador Varnir has at least agreed to set up meetings with some influential Vaskandrans who might be swayed against war during the Festival of Beauty next week." She sighed. "I'll take it. We don't get much intelligence out of Vaskandar."

I swallowed a bite of polenta. "Why not? I know we trade with them."

"And I assure you that a full third of Raverran merchants in Vaskandar are spies," La Contessa said. "But the Witch Lords have little use for those without magic, save as serfs toiling in their fields. Our people can't get close to the centers of power."

"What about actual Vaskandrans who are already in place? Can't you bribe existing servants for information, put pressure on nobles and advisers, that sort of thing?"

"You're learning." My mother lifted her glass to me. I fiddled with my fork to try to hide my flush of irrational pride. "But few fish in the Vaskandran pond will rise to such bait. Everyone is too afraid of the Witch Lords. Their power is absolute, and their whims are capricious and frequently cruel."

I remembered Ruven using his vivomancy to push a knife through his own guard's wrist as if it were butter, while the man stood paralyzed and silently screaming, and shivered. I could understand why Vaskandran servants wouldn't dare risk the wrath of their mage-marked masters.

I speared a piece of pauldronfish, thinking. "This upcoming Conclave Varnir mentioned..."

"I've been trying to get a spy into a Conclave since before you were born." My mother ran a finger along the edge of her glass. "What they decide there could determine whether this war lasts three weeks or three decades, and whether a hundred people die or a hundred thousand. We need to use every Vaskandran connection we have to influence its outcome."

Her voice had sharpened slightly on the word *every*. I lowered my fork.

"Surely you don't mean Prince Ruven."

She lifted an eyebrow. "He did give you a standing invitation to visit him."

"During our last interaction, we threatened each other with death," I pointed out.

"Nonetheless, he seems to hold you in high regard." My mother's mouth quirked. "I'm not saying you should drop in on him for tea. But your association is a card you have in hand;

whether you play it or not, it must factor into your strategy for the game."

"Fair enough." I had no desire to come near Ruven again, with his razor-edged smiles and magic that could melt bones or stop hearts with a touch. But that was doubtless no excuse, in my mother's eyes. If the good of the Empire required me to dance with him at the doge's birthday gala, she would expect me to pick out a dress that would look fashionable with long gloves and practice my minuet.

"Especially," my mother added, her eyes narrowing, "because Prince Ruven and his father, the Wolf Lord, appear to be the primary allies of the Lady of Thorns."

I nearly sprayed my mouthful of wine across the table. "What?!"

"The Wolf Lord and the Lady of Thorns rule neighboring domains. Their relations were uneasy back when I was courting your father, near their borders." She mentioned their famous courtship as casually as if he had been a country farmer rather than a prince, and their marriage a mere personal milestone instead of a historical event that brought the nation of Callamorne into the Serene Empire as a client state. "But in the past few years, thanks to your old friend Ruven's efforts, the two Witch Lords appear to be working together quite closely."

I stabbed my polenta with needless vigor. "If *that* snake is involved in this scheme, we'd best unravel it quickly."

He'd made more than one reference, when our paths had crossed last month, to not being ready for war with the Empire—yet. Perhaps after the Conclave, he would be.

"Indeed," my mother agreed. "And thus, caution in your dealings with him, for certain. Especially with your name on the list his closest ally gave her assassin."

I felt my way into a question that had been bothering me. "Mamma, every other person on that list is a Falcon." No other Falconers. No political or military targets. Just twenty or so carefully chosen mage-marked, and me. "I don't fit. Why is my name on there?"

For three ticks of the mantel clock, four, five, she said nothing. Old Anzo came and cleared away our dishes, then brought out a main course of tender beef medallions in blue cheese and tart-grass sauce, a dish my mother had developed a taste for during her time in Callamorne. Our plates sat gleaming and untouched between us, and still she stared at me, her expression gone pensive and brooding.

"Mamma?"

"I don't know," she said quietly. "And I don't like that at all."

Chapter Four

The grand ball celebrating the Festival of Beauty took place at the Imperial Palace the following week, and no mere threat of Vaskandran assassins could keep a Cornaro from one of the main social events of the season—even if the Cornaro in question would have preferred to curl up in the library researching Vaskandran history and politics. My mother had doubled the guards at the palace doors and stationed around the ballrooms, however, and for security reasons the heralds eschewed formal announcements of each guest arriving at the palace.

This might have allowed me to avoid attention and lurk peacefully in a corner, if I hadn't been glowing.

My gown of deep midnight blue shone with hundreds of tiny lights like stars: miniature luminary crystals enchanted to last the evening. More cascaded down from my hair. In case anyone might still somehow miss me due to a complete deficiency of eyesight, my maid Rica had also given me a symphonic shell pendant, so my own soft cloud of music surrounded me wherever I went.

It was an extravagant and nearly ridiculous gown, but then, this was the grand imperial ball; dressmakers and tailors worked all year to create the most outlandishly creative outfits possible for the occasion, just as artists, musicians, poets, and more competed to create lavish works in order to attract patrons, win prizes, and honor the Grace of Beauty on the last day of her festival.

And I was conservatively dressed compared to some. One lady had a cage of live finches braided into her hair, which seemed like a terrible idea to me on a number of levels. Another wore panniers so wide you could have seated eight people around them. I saw several truly unspeakable codpieces, stuffed to an aggressive size and complete with bells and ribbons, and one gentleman's collar could have plated a roast boar.

"Amalia," came Marcello's voice behind me. "You look..."

I turned from gawking around at my fellow guests to find him staring at me with a bemused expression. He wore only his new captain's dress uniform, with a rapier and flintlock pistol at his side, but he cut a far finer figure than any of the lords in rainbow-hued wigs or jeweled waistcoats.

"Ridiculous?" I suggested, my hand going to the crystals in my hair. "Absurd?"

"Amazing," he finished.

I was glad Zaira had disappeared into the thick of the party, so she wasn't here to tease me. My face warmed. "You're only being polite, but thank you."

"If I were being polite, I'd say nothing, and leave you to your business." His mouth twisted into a rueful smile. "That's probably what I should do, if I knew what was good for me."

"Of course not! You're my friend. You can always talk to me." My voice came out high and false, and I hated it. Marcello was the one person I'd never needed to pretend for. But here I was, left with no idea how to respond to a simple compliment because I had decided, for reasons that slid from my mind when he smiled that wistful smile of his, not to court him.

"Everything is complicated, now." A shadow flickered in his eyes. "I'm trying to follow the rules, but I don't know what they are anymore."

"I'm sure there's some book of etiquette for precisely this situation." I dropped my voice nearly to a whisper, relaxing it with relief into something more frustrated and true. "But I never read that kind of book. I can tell you how to repair a broken courier lamp, or what Queen Belianne of Loreice said when she ordered her third husband beheaded during the War of the Handkerchief, but not how to..." I trailed off.

How not to hurt a friend. How not to kiss a friend. How not to hurt a friend *while* not kissing him.

"What did she say?" Marcello asked, lightening his tone. "To her third husband?"

I winced. "That it was nothing personal; she simply had no use for him anymore."

Marcello blinked.

"It was perhaps a bad example." My cheeks burned as if Zaira's flames coursed through them. "And I hasten to assure you, it has nothing to do with our present circumstances. Quite the opposite."

Marcello's dimples emerged as he struggled not to laugh at me. "So, it *was* personal? Or you still have a use for me?"

"I should have stayed home tonight," I groaned. "I've been in the door fifteen minutes, and I'm already doing everything wrong."

"May I suggest a way to make it all right again?" Marcello extended a hand to me, tilting his head toward the dance floor.

All the mad acres of silk and giddy laughter overflowing the ballroom faded. His warm green eyes, the clean line of his jaw, and his leather-and-gunpowder scent filled my senses, far more solid and real than the fanciful sartorial illusions swirling around us.

"A lady can dance with a man she's not courting. Can't she?" An uncertain hope lit his features, like muffled sunlight behind passing clouds.

My heart beat firm as a chaperone's knock on a broom closet door. Half the Raverran court packed the room, pressing close around us, greeting each other and plucking wine and crostini from passing trays. No one seemed to be watching us, but I had little doubt our prolonged proximity to each other had caught the corners of a few eyes already.

"You know I'd love to," I whispered. "But, Marcello—"

"Just one dance," he said. "After you've done your duty taking turns with half the bachelor princes in Eruvia. To celebrate my promotion, so at least one good thing can come of it."

One dance couldn't hurt, surely, if it was one of many. And Marcello was such a splendid dancer. "All right. *If* I can make it through the other dances first without breaking an ankle."

He grinned in return, and saluted. "The palace security appears to be well in order, my lady," he said more loudly. "You and Zaira should be well protected here tonight."

I gave him a grave nod. "Carry on, then, Captain."

I watched him move away through the crowd until a wall of feathers and brocade and sparkling jewels flowed between us.

Time to get to work. As my mother had reminded me while our boat brought us to the palace, for a Cornaro this sort of occasion wasn't an entertainment—it was an opportunity. I garnered a wineglass from a passing tray and, holding it before me as my weapon, set off with determination to win myself more backers for my Falcon reform law.

It quickly became clear to me, once again, that I was not my mother.

I didn't know how to do this. I smiled at people, complimented their outlandish costumes, nodded politely to their return greetings, and then had no idea how to steer the conversation to a useful topic. Hells, beneath all the makeup and towering hair, I barely recognized anyone.

"Lady Amalia?" a gruff voice greeted me.

I turned to find a retired army colonel I knew, dressed in a doublet of gray velvet tailored to look like old-fashioned plate armor. "Hello," I greeted him vaguely, realizing with a twinge of panic that I had forgotten his name.

"Wanted to let you know I've heard what you're working on. That Falcon act." He nodded stiffly. "Been telling them for years to put a stop to the mandatory conscription. Terrible idea."

"Really?" I tried not to sound too surprised.

"Of course." He blew a breath through his copious steel-gray mustache. "Last thing you need in battle is to wonder whether the mage holding your flank is going to break and run because they don't want to be there. Keep up the good work. I'll be voting for it."

He clinked his glass off mine, emptied it, and headed toward the nearest wine table.

Hope caught my heart in a sudden updraft. If support for Falcon reform extended into the military, that greatly enhanced my chances of passing this law.

Then I spied something less welcome: a crowd of hopeful fortune hunters preparing to converge on me, lured by the gleam of unwed Cornaro gold. It was time to move on.

I took a brisk tour of the seven rooms set aside for the ball, at a quick pace designed to shake off my would-be suitors. Different strains of music greeted me in each room, from lively minuets for dancing to the soothing strains of a trio sonata. In one, a pair of poets up on a low stage strutted in an epigram duel, circling each other with words sharp as swords. My footsteps slowed as a roar of laughter rose from the crowd at the end of one couplet, but I didn't dare stop and listen.

New paintings hung on every inch of space on the walls, and statues created for the occasion graced every tabletop and corner; the artists' names appeared on small cards next to them, so that discerning nobles could offer patronage to their favorites.

Tables of food lined the walls, little bites I sampled as I passed; all the recipes were new, too, developed in fierce competition in dozens of the finest kitchens in Raverra. It was all to honor the Grace of Beauty, whose gift to humanity was art.

I couldn't force myself to keep my pace up, with so many wondrous things around me. A strange sculpture, if one could call it that, caught my attention, and I stopped to examine it closer. A wooden platter displayed what resembled a pile of bones or twigs done in jewel-colored glass. Was it a work of art after all? Or perhaps a dessert?

"It's a game."

It was a tenor voice, loose and careless, but with a certain husky catch to it. I looked up, startled, and found myself facing a young man who frowned down in contemplation at the strange display from the other side of its little table.

He wore a black cloak with a feathered mantle, thrown back over a pale gray tunic of cloud-soft leather. Silver and black embroidery in the Vaskandran style edged his hem and sleeves, all asymmetrical angles. At first I thought he'd finished the outfit with some kind of feathered or furry headpiece, but then I realized it was his own unruly mane, pale enough blond to be nearly white, with the tips dyed black. I had to admit his monochromatic style was striking, if not what the Raverran elites would call fashionable.

"You take turns stacking the pieces, I think." He placed a bright green twist of branching glass on top of a red one, nestling it in place.

I had to admit that he and the game both intrigued me. But he was Vaskandran. I glanced around and saw several guards quite near, at least one of them watching us, and the room was full of witnesses.

All right, then. It couldn't hurt to play.

"What, like this?" I snagged a four-pronged blue piece and settled it on top of the other two.

He gave a pleased nod. "Yes. It's a balancing game. If you work together, you can build it higher than if you use your moves to fight each other."

I gave him a sharp look, but his eyes stayed fixed on the bits of glass. He selected a gleaming black piece like a miniature coral branch and fitted it onto the growing tower. "Don't you agree, Lady Amalia Cornaro?"

My pulse quickened, humming in my veins. "I do prefer building things to breaking them. And I am a great proponent of cooperation."

He chuckled. "I'm frequently willing to cooperate with people who'll play games with me. Especially when we can unite against mutual opponents."

Grace of Wisdom help me. This was my mother's sort of dance, not mine. He had to be talking about Vaskandar; and if he was here, at the imperial ball, he must have rank enough to negotiate with. I couldn't ruin this chance.

"We in Raverra do see opponents lining up across the board," I said. "We'd welcome more players on our team."

"Hmm. I'm not the type to join someone else's team. And besides, the balance is too delicate. We have to maintain a certain amount of tension."

We'd kept building our tower, and it had developed a slight but unmistakable lean to the left. He placed a piece at its apex that veered back to the right, but the angle was too sharp. I hesitated, every muscle in my abdomen locked rigid beneath my corset, unsure how to add a piece without bringing the whole thing down.

"One can work together even with a player who may not be wholly on one's side," I said at last, and, with trembling fingers, balanced a piece on top of his. A round medallion crowned it, precluding any possibility of further building and completing the tower.

He laughed, regarding our construction with apparent delight. "Oh, I like you, Lady Amalia. Well played. Yes, I think we can work together."

"I'm glad to hear it."

"However." He lifted a finger. "I'm not ready to make any open moves against our mutual opponents."

"Oh, that's fine." I waved a hand. "Raverrans prefer to keep our moves out of the open."

"Given the position of the pieces, I think simple suspicion that we've formed an alliance might give some of our adversaries pause." He tapped his chin. "But how to suggest an alliance without formalizing one?"

"Why *not* formalize one?" I asked.

He lifted a pale eyebrow. "Because, my lady, we should all be wary of traps."

A virulent yellow ring gleamed around his pupils. The mage mark.

My tongue turned to lead. But I forced it to move. "True enough."

"A symbolic gesture, perhaps," he mused. "We do place great weight on symbols."

I thought of my mother's wedding ring: a diamond and a sapphire, to represent the alliance her marriage had formed with Callamorne, bringing it into the Serene Empire. "Like a wedding."

"Rather less binding than that."

"Of course." A nervous laugh bubbled out of me. "Like a courtship, then."

He grinned, his eyes sparkling with mischief. "Is that an offer? But we hardly know each other!"

I took half a step back from the table, a flush creeping up my neck, ready to wave off the idea as the joke he seemed to make of it.

But my mother had said to make alliances in Vaskandar by any means we could.

I lifted my chin. "It could be. If it brought an allied player into the game."

He blinked. Then he blinked again. "All right," he said.

"All right what?"

"All right, I accept your offer." He shrugged, the feathers in his cloak rustling. "I'll court you. It will drive the Lady of Thorns mad as a sick coyote, which is worth it by itself."

My world skewed sideways, leaning more crazily than the tower we'd built together. In another room, the dueling poets finished, and the crowd burst into distant applause.

"Ah," I tried to say, but my throat had gone too dry to speak.

He cocked his head. "Do you even know my name?"

"I'm afraid," I managed, "I have not yet had that pleasure."

"You can call me Kathe." The Vaskandran dipped in a courtly but modest bow. "The Crow Lord."

Grace of Love died laughing. I'd just agreed to court a Witch Lord.

Chapter Five

Kathe's lips twisted in a wry smile. "I've never courted a Raverran woman before. What comes next?"

I'd never courted *anyone* before, but I wasn't about to tell him that. I waved a vague hand, glad he couldn't see my legs trembling beneath my skirts. "At a ball like this, I believe dancing is customary."

"Ah." He considered that a moment. "I'm afraid I don't know any Raverran dances. You could teach me, I suppose."

I laughed despairingly. "I'm not much of a dancer myself. Certainly not good enough to teach anyone. I always thought it was a bit silly, and never learned half the steps."

"Hmm. Perhaps not dancing, then."

The humor in his tone calmed my nerves somewhat. It was commonly held that the Witch Lords were mad, and the majority of them cruel monsters; but if a man could laugh at himself, he couldn't be all bad. "What do you do in Vaskandar?"

He tapped his chin. "Well, when you begin courting, it's traditional to go on a long walk and have a conversation, to get to know each other better."

"I can walk and talk perfectly well," I said.

"I see you're quite accomplished." He proffered a hand, grinning. "Shall we?"

I hesitated, my skin prickling as I recalled how dangerous it would be to accept such an offer from Prince Ruven. But Ruven was a Skinwitch, whose powers worked best on human flesh and bone; it was highly unlikely that Kathe shared that rare and unsettling specialty.

I took his hand, cautiously as if it were a live spider. It was slim but surprisingly rough, at least compared to the baby-soft skin of Raverran courtiers; these hands spent time outdoors, doing things and making things. Or breaking them.

He tucked my arm through his. The feathers on his cloak brushed my bare shoulder. I could feel a humming energy in him, even through his sleeve, of magic or some inner tension. *Like Zaira.*

We strolled off through the ball, leaving our improbable glass tower behind us. I tried without much success to force my muscles to relax, my speeding heart to slow down. Our fellow revellers parted before us, plumed hats dipping and mountainous skirts swaying, giving way to the combined presence of a Witch Lord and a Cornaro. The sea of fantastical gowns and rainbow-hued jackets closed again behind us with a growing murmur, passed behind fluttering fans and discreetly lifted palms, as gossip ran through the crowd faster than spilled wine.

I know, I wanted to tell them. *I'm fairly shocked, myself.*

"What shall we talk about?" I asked. "War and diplomacy? Magical theory? That elderly gentleman's outrageous codpiece?"

Kathe glanced at the garment in question and then lifted a hand to cover a cough. "Well, that's... ambitious. But no, I have an idea. Let's play another game. We'll take turns saying two things about ourselves, one truth and one lie. The other person has to guess which is which."

I supposed it was too much to hope he'd want to talk about magical theory. "I think my cousins played this game in Callamorne when we were younger," I said. It had usually ended with them punching each other.

"It's an old Vaskandran game." Kathe stopped by a broad, round column of caramel-veined marble, the first of a row of them holding up the vast and distant ceiling of the main hall.

This was the pounding heart of the celebration. Half the Assembly seemed to be packed into the center of the great room, swirling on the dance floor in ensembles themed after everything from a basket of fruit (the bodice appeared to be trimmed with real grapes) to a fiery phoenix (complete with a fluttering train of scarlet and gold ribbons). The troupe of musicians played with more than enough life and passion to keep everyone dancing; I had little doubt they'd win a patronage from their efforts tonight. Chairs and small tables lined the edges of the room, populated by those exhausted from dancing or more inclined toward conversation, and dozens of servers kept up an efficient circuit of the room with trays of food and drink. This spot Kathe had chosen might well be the quietest in the main ballroom: not close enough to the center to get swept up in the dancing, but distanced enough from the chairs to avoid interruption by a well-meaning acquaintance seeking to join us.

He leaned against the column, long and wiry, his feathered cloak ruffling up around his shoulders. "I'll begin."

"All right." I stepped in closer, to hear him better over the murmuring crowd. It wasn't often one got the chance to learn personal details about a Witch Lord, after all.

"Let's see..." His face lit with an idea. "I don't have any brothers. I love my brothers."

"The first must be the lie, and the second the truth," I said immediately. "You do have brothers, and you love them. After all, you can't fail to love brothers you don't possess."

Kathe clicked his tongue, a scolding sound. "Not quite. I feel no love for my *dead* brothers, despite no longer having them. Your turn."

I stared at his composed face, his mocking half smile, and

his unsettling yellow-ringed eyes. His irises were gray beneath the mage mark, almost pale enough to fade into the whites and disappear.

Was he such a monster he'd felt no affection for the brothers he'd lost? Or had *they* been the monsters, and he was well rid of them? For all I knew, baby Witch Lords murdered each other in the cradle to determine who would inherit their parents' domain.

"I don't suppose you'll explain that further?" I asked.

He cocked his head. "That depends. Do you want to fully explain all of *your* answers?"

"Perhaps not." I swallowed. "All right, my turn. I, ah..." Curse it, I had to think of something clever. "I never met my father's father. I've never seen my father's father."

Kathe raised his brows. "Unless you're older than you look, the first must be the lie. I happen to know your paternal grandfather died when your father was a child. How is it that you've seen him?"

My spine prickled. It wasn't entirely strange someone might know about my grandfather, since he after all had become King of Callamorne when he married my grandmother. But Kathe had responded so quickly, without thinking through the chain of royal lineages and political marriages to get there, as if the knowledge had already been at the forefront of his mind.

This game was far less creepy when I played it with my cousins.

"His portrait," I said. "I see it every time I visit my grandmother."

"Of course." Kathe nodded. "You have so much art in the Empire. I admit I'm jealous. Very well, my turn."

He reached out and snagged a little cake from a passing tray without looking; the server, who hadn't seen him, jumped in surprise and scuttled off through the crowd, eyes wide. It seemed word had passed among the servants about the Witch Lord.

If Kathe noticed, he didn't care. "Let's see," he said. "Here you go: I don't hold grudges. I take care of my own."

He popped the cake in his mouth and waited, eyes sparkling, for my response.

I gave it more thought this time. The Raverran assumption was that Witch Lords cared for no one and abused their own people. That was certainly true of Ruven, the only other Vaskandran royalty I knew. And Kathe seemed too impulsive to nurse a steady grudge. But the way he'd spoken about the Lady of Thorns suggested bad blood between them and a certain intensity lurked in the shadows of his eyes, belying his light tone and casual stance.

"I think you *do* hold grudges," I said.

He chuckled. "All crows do. Well done. Your turn."

I tried to focus, over the laughter and chatter and music around me. The lady with the finches in her hair passed by, coiffure twittering; on the dance floor, I spied Zaira dancing a gavotte with a young baron.

This game mattered. If I lost Kathe's interest, I might lose his alliance. But everything I could think of was either too boring (*I prefer Muscati's theories of artifice to Da Bardi's; I like coffee*) or too easy to guess (*I've killed a man with my hands; I've killed a man with a word*). It was hard to think with him watching me, the corner of his mouth crooked with amusement.

There was one interesting detail about me he might not guess, but it risked revealing a secret. He might be my ally for now, but I had no desire for him to know my greatest weakness.

He raised an eyebrow. "Well?"

One thing was already clear. With Kathe, if I played it safe, I lost the game.

"I was poisoned earlier tonight," I said. "There's poison in my veins right now."

He lifted his eyebrows. "You lead a dramatic life, I see."

"The Serene City is many things, but never dull. Do you have a guess?"

He tilted his head. "You were poisoned, but got a cure. The second statement is the lie."

"No."

He blinked. "No?"

"You guessed wrong." I licked my dry lips. "Your turn."

Kathe straightened from his casual slouch against the pillar, a puzzled frown pinching his brows, as if I were a strange new creature and he couldn't decide whether I might be dangerous or perhaps edible. "Curious," he said. "I don't suppose you're going to explain."

"You will note that I chose to avoid that requirement."

"All right, then." Mischief kindled in his face. "My turn, indeed."

He leaned in close, until his lips were near my ear. I could feel that wild energy in him, charging the air between us.

"I know about a dangerous legacy you don't realize you've inherited," he whispered. "I have no hidden motive in courting you."

All my words withered on my tongue. I stared at him, struck silent.

He straightened and laced his hands behind his head, mussing his black-tipped hair. "Too easy, I know. I can see in your face you've guessed right." He sighed dramatically. "I'll have to concede this round."

"What?!" The word burst out before I could stop it, borne on a wave of outrage. How could he stop *there*, dangling that kind of knowledge in front of me and then withholding it?

But I knew exactly how. He was good at this, damn him. Now I burned to discover what he knew, and what he was up to.

I tried to rein my expression back under control, but I could tell by his damnable grin that he'd seen how he'd gotten to me.

"Conceding, truly?" I asked. "Surely you can't admit defeat so easily."

"I can when I've met my match."

Hells. He hadn't lost, and he knew it. He'd angled his cards to show me his winning hand and then declined to play it down. "You are a maddening individual, Lord Kathe."

He bowed modestly. "Thank you, my lady. One does one's best."

As he straightened, his eyes went past my shoulder and his smile widened. "Ah! La Contessa Lissandra Cornaro."

I whirled, my heart spasming as if it might burst. Sure enough, my mother stood there, resplendent in an amber gown worked with subtle embroidery to turn the skirts into a stylized map of the Serene Empire. Her auburn hair cascaded artfully over one shoulder, secured with an elegant golden comb that wrapped a tiny globe in jeweled artifice wirework. Her calculating gaze took us both in as she dipped a brief but gracious curtsy to Kathe, which was more than she afforded most royalty.

"Lord Kathe, of the Domain of Let. I'm pleased to see you honor Raverra with such a rare visit."

He returned a cocky bow. "The honor is mine. Thank you for inviting me to this most entertaining occasion. I nearly didn't come, but now I'm so glad I did."

I stared at my mother. *She* had invited him? Good Graces. I'd taken a blind leap into the middle of one of her schemes. I could only hope I hadn't done too much damage.

"I hear," my mother said with a sharp-edged smile, "you're courting my daughter."

Of course she knew already. Graces preserve me. I bit my lip to keep from blurting excuses for not consulting her first.

"It's true." Kathe spread his hands, as if it were a great wonder how this could have occurred. "Impulsive, I know, but think of the possibilities! Do we have your permission?"

La Contessa held his gaze a long moment, unflinching despite his mage mark. At last, she said, "Amalia is a Cornaro. She makes her own decisions and does not require my permission. But I'm delighted our family will have the chance to cooperate with you—and I assure you, we make formidable allies."

The steely note in her voice made clear the unspoken corollary that she also made a formidable enemy. Somehow, the knowledge that my mother would implicitly threaten a Witch Lord for me warmed my heart.

Kathe chuckled. "I look forward to discovering what our families can do together. And to the discussion you invited me here to have, Lady Cornaro." He tilted his head, as though listening. "In the meantime, I should offer my respects to the doge, and I'm sure you two have plenty to talk about." He bowed. "Until later this evening."

I dipped a curtsy in return. He'd hardly made it three steps away when my mother grabbed my arm in a companionable sort of way, if velvet-sheathed steel can be considered companionable.

"I'd invited the Crow Lord here to discuss the possibility of an alliance, on Ambassador Varnir's information, but it would seem you beat me to the negotiating table." Even pitched to go no farther than my ears, her voice retained its rich resonance. "What agreement did you make with him, exactly, Amalia?"

Hells. What *had* we agreed to? I tried to recall the details of our conversation, but it was a blur of balancing bits of glass and striving not to sound like an idiot. "Nothing, really, except to court each other. As a symbol of alliance only, to dismay our mutual foes."

My mother's elegant brows drew down. "Will he defend us if other Witch Lords attack? Allow us to move troops through his domain? Use his magic on our behalf?"

She always made me feel five years old again, as if I'd wandered into the middle of a Council meeting looking for sweets and any minute Old Anzo would come hustle me back out. "I'm afraid our conversation wasn't that specific. I'm sorry, Mamma. An opportunity came up, and I did my best, but I'm not as good at this as you are."

She sighed, rubbing her temples. "No, it's all right. From what I understand of him, there was never much chance he'd commit to anything. I'm surprised you got as much as you did."

I couldn't tell if that was praise or just low expectations. I gave a tiny nod.

She glanced around, checking to make sure no one was in earshot. "Don't trust him," she murmured. "He's not known for cruelty like some of the others, but he might leave you dead in a ditch if he thought it was funny."

I caught her sleeve. "Is this a terrible idea? Did I make a mistake?"

My mother hesitated. "We need him. His domain borders those of the Lady of Thorns and Ruven's father; if they're concerned about having the Crow Lord at their backs, they can't bring their full strength to bear against us." She let a breath pass her lips, releasing some hope or worry she didn't care to shape into words for her daughter. "But it's a risk. I wouldn't have asked you to do it. If you ever feel you need to end this charade, for your own safety or happiness, don't hesitate to do so. As to whether it's a mistake . . . Well, we'll see."

I nodded, apprehension knotting my throat.

My mother touched my cheek with a gentle, perfumed hand. "Be careful, Amalia. The Witch Lords play politics by different rules than we do. If you lose this game, you could lose your life."

Chapter Six

"You're joking," Zaira said.

I'd found her sipping wine at the edge of the room, still flushed from dancing. She narrowed her eyes at me in suspicion, setting her glass down on a nearby table.

"I'm afraid not," I replied.

"But the Witch Lords are all crazy as a sack of vipers."

I shrugged, stirring the trails of shimmering lights in my hair. "In wartime, we all must make sacrifices."

Zaira shook her head. "And all they want *me* to do is kill a few thousand people. I don't think I'd trade."

"Thanks." I wished I were as calm as I sounded. A bubble of panic was slowly growing in my chest, now that what I'd done had had time to sink in.

Zaira glanced across the ballroom to where Marcello stood, talking business with one of the soldiers on duty. "Have you told Captain Loverboy yet?"

My ears warmed. "It would hardly be appropriate to run and tell him directly after accepting the Crow Lord's courtship proposal. And besides, Marcello and I aren't... Well, he's only a friend."

Zaira delivered me a witheringly skeptical look.

"All right," I admitted, grimacing. "I'm putting it off."

"He's not going to like it."

"Well, we were never courting, so he doesn't have to," I snapped. "I told him we couldn't court for precisely this reason. It's not my fault if he didn't listen."

Zaira's face spread to a knowing grin. "Oh, I don't see how he could ever have gotten the wrong idea, given how you keep giving him these long meaningful glances and staring after him like a moon-eyed maiden."

Now my entire face burned. "I shouldn't be doing that."

"But you doooooooo," Zaira sang.

At that moment, like a gift from the Graces, Terika appeared through the crowd.

She wore a gown in all the colors of the sea, and a crown of shells and pearls sat on her honey-brown hair. Her Falconer, Lienne, escorted her, somehow resembling an indulgent aunt even in her uniform; few would guess she could best most of the Mews with a rapier. Terika's eyes sparkled with mischief as she laughed at something Lienne said.

Zaira stared at her as if she'd never seen her before. "Hells have mercy. We need to take her to more fancy parties."

"That can be arranged." I didn't try to rein in my smile; this was exactly why I'd gotten Terika an invitation. "You should ask her to dance."

Zaira glared at me. "Why would I do that?"

I blinked. "Aren't you courting?"

"No," Zaira said. "What made you think we were courting?"

"Oh, I don't know." I tapped my chin. "You're together all the time. You flirt shamelessly. You like each other a great deal. You were just staring at her like she was the Grace of Love incarnate..."

"You can be friends with someone and like how they look and flirt with them and not be courting."

"I suppose." It seemed best to concede the point, given what

I'd just said about Marcello. "But *why*? I'm fairly certain she *wants* to court you."

Zaira scowled. "Because we're Falcons, you idiot."

I stared at her blankly.

Zaira threw up her hands. "Because we don't have our own lives, or our own futures. Because I'll be damned to the Nine Hells before I tie myself to the Mews that way. Maybe even because you might have noticed that everyone I care about tends to burn to death."

"Not anymore," I said softly.

Zaira turned her wrist; the red crystals gleamed in the golden wirework of her jess like beads of blood. "True. Not anymore. That's the one good thing about this cursed chain you gave me."

"I can't say you're wrong about the difficulties," I admitted. "But she cares about you."

Zaira groaned. "Feelings again. You know my opinion on feelings."

I nudged Zaira's ribs. "She's beautiful. And smart. And funny. And puts up with you, which has to be a rare quality."

"She's too good for me," Zaira said dourly.

"She's also coming up behind you."

Zaira spun to face Terika, her back rigid, petals fluttering as her skirts swirled.

"Zaira!" Terika greeted her gleefully. "Did you see the Marquis of Valisia's doublet? His entire chest is on display, down to his navel, and I swear he's oiled it."

Zaira glanced around. "Oh, I can't miss that. Where?"

"He was dancing with Lady Brame, last I saw him."

Zaira cleared her throat. "If the view on the dance floor is that good, I suppose we'd better go take a closer look."

Terika laughed. "I thought you'd never ask. Come on!"

She grabbed Zaira's hand and pulled her off toward the dance floor, grinning. Zaira threw one last glare over her shoulder at me that sent a message clear as a printed page: *If you say anything, I will set you on fire.*

I waved, laughing, and watched them for a moment, a smile stretching my cheeks. Zaira didn't know any courtly dances, but she didn't seem to care much either. Their skirts spun together in a mesmerizing swirl of colors, and with each little touch Zaira's steely guard visibly relaxed.

She made bawdy comments about people we saw in the street all the time, and flirted with whole crowds at once at parties; but with Terika, Zaira seemed almost shy. I accepted a glass of wine from a passing tray and lifted it in a toast, silently wishing Terika luck.

Then the air around me seemed to go warm and soft, and I suddenly became aware of Marcello at my side.

"They're good for each other," he murmured, smiling across the ballroom at the two Falcons.

He stood close enough that in another world, where my only consideration for courtship was how much I liked a man, I could have snaked an arm around his waist.

"They are," I agreed. But the peace of the moment was gone. Dread of what I had to tell him sat in my stomach like a stone.

He turned to face me, lifting wistful eyebrows. "I don't suppose we could join them? Or have you still not gotten in your requisite number of politically mandated prior dances?"

"Marcello," I blurted, "I'm courting a Witch Lord."

He blinked. "What?"

Grace of Love forgive me. Those eyes. "It's political, of course. It just happened. I... I'm sorry."

His face hardened from bewilderment to anger. "We can't let them do this to you. Who arranged this madness?"

"I did." Too many people pressed around us, skirts rustling, glasses clinking, forced laughter rising to the frescoed ceiling in the shadows above. I dropped my voice until I wasn't sure he could hear it, between the noise of the crowd and the faint tinkling music of my shell pendant. "Marcello, *I* set up the courtship. To help win the war, or perhaps even avoid it. It was my decision."

He stared uncomprehendingly. "With a Witch Lord? But Amalia, they're mad tyrants! Why would you do that?"

This was going to be as hard as I'd thought. I grabbed a couple of wineglasses from a passing tray, shoved one into his hand, and steered him by the elbow to the least crowded corner I could find. No one stared openly, but I could feel eyes on us. I opened a wider space between us.

"This is how I can fight," I told him, my voice low and urgent. "This is a weapon in my arsenal, to protect Raverra and all the Serene Empire. I'm doing it to save lives, Marcello."

"But... Courtship..." He took a swallow of wine, then glowered at his glass. "I'm used to the idea I might have to kill an adversary to protect the Empire. It seems worse, somehow, to have to kiss one."

"It's for show, to present a sign of alliance to the Witch Lords preparing to invade us. I doubt there'll be actual kissing involved."

But as the words left my mouth, I realized I had no idea if they were true. Good Graces, how did I feel about that? Courting a Witch Lord was one thing, but kissing him entirely another. Though Kathe was handsome, in his strange way.

I took a long drink.

Marcello drew in a ragged breath. "I suppose it's none of my business. Whom you kiss, or whom you court."

I didn't want to do this to him. Or to myself. I squeezed my eyes shut for a moment, then opened them again.

"It *is* your business, at least a little," I said softly. "It's not as if there's nothing between us. But this is a temporary thing, a necessary thing, and not a matter of the heart. It doesn't change anything in the long run. And now you know."

"Now I know." He ran a hand through his hair, stared at his drink a moment, and then set it aside on a table. "Doesn't it bother you, though, Amalia? Even a little?"

"I don't mind going through this charade of courting him." I sighed and lifted a hand to my own cheek, since I couldn't touch his. "But I'll admit I wish I didn't have to keep you at arm's reach. I wish…"

I trailed off. I didn't really wish I were some commoner girl, able to court anyone I wanted. I traded freedom for power, and I could use that power to keep the people I cared about safe. To wish for both freedom *and* power would be selfish; there was a reason everything came with a cost.

"I wish I were some Ostan prince, or the doge's nephew," Marcello said. "I hate not being good enough for you."

"You *are* good enough." I curled my hand into a fist before it could reach for his. That was his horrid father speaking through his voice, telling him he was a failure—and now I'd made it worse. "Better than any foolish prince. Graces, Marcello, if I were courting based on personal merit, we'd be out there dancing right now. This is a move on the board, nothing more."

"Then I hope it's a winning move." He tried a smile, but it came out more like a grimace. "I do feel a bit like a sacrificed pawn."

"Never sacrificed." I caught his eyes. "We just have to move you across the board and crown you."

He managed a more natural smile. But a certain stiffness remained. "I'd best get back to work. I'm here to help with security, after all."

We never did dance that evening.

The next morning Ciardha, my mother's alarmingly competent aide, brought me a package at breakfast.

"From your suitor, Lady." Her face remained perfectly composed as always, but her dark eyes shone with mirth.

The irregular bundle lay beside my half-finished roll and cup of steaming chocolate, wrapped in what appeared to be a daily gossip sheet tied with silver thread. I'd put together more convincing gift packages from random bits in my maid's sewing basket when I was a small girl.

With some trepidation, I picked apart the messy knot and spread open the paper. Great blocky print at the top shouted: *WITCH LORD COURTING SERENE CITY'S MOST ELIGIBLE HEIR*. Lovely. They must have worked all night to set the type.

I folded back the crumpled paper to reveal a necklace, of sorts: a leather cord adorned with carved wooden beads and black claws.

I lifted it dubiously in the air. "I have to wear this, don't I."

"I fear it would be impolitic not to, Lady."

"There's a card." I laid the crude necklace back in its paper, trying not to despair over how it would look atop lace and brocade, and flipped over the rectangle of fine, creamy vellum.

For your protection, should you visit my country, it read.

"How wonderfully foreboding." I set the note down and examined the gift.

Vivomancers, such as the Witch Lords and most Vaskandran mages, used their powers to control and shape living things. In Vaskandar, they called them either Greenwitches, specializing in plants, or Furwitches, specializing in animals, but all vivomancers could affect both. They couldn't imbue objects with magic, though, like artificers did, or call out the latent magical properties in substances, like alchemists. I doubted the necklace was magical. The claws, however, seemed entirely real.

We do place great weight on symbols, he'd said. I sighed resignedly and lifted it over my head. Talons clattered on my chest.

"How do I look?" I asked.

"Your reputation as an eccentric will doubtless be enhanced, Lady."

"Lovely." A terrifying thought struck me. "I need to send him a return gift, don't I?"

"That is the custom, Lady," Ciardha confirmed. "You'll want something to give him on your outing this afternoon."

The implications of her words cascaded onto me like cold, rattling pebbles. "My outing this afternoon?" I asked faintly.

"With Lord Kathe." Ciardha's face and posture remained perfectly composed, but somehow, I knew she was silently laughing. "La Contessa pressed him to formalize terms of an alliance when they spoke at the end of the ball last night, and he said he preferred to discuss such matters with you, since you were now courting. So naturally, La Contessa arranged an outing for the two of you at once."

I swallowed. "What sort of an outing?"

Ciardha inclined her head in a short bow of what I chose to interpret as sympathy. "A picnic, Lady."

Chapter Seven

"So I'm going on a picnic with a Witch Lord in five hours," I finished breathlessly. "I've never even courted before. I need to get him a present. Help me—I have no idea what to do."

Zaira stood frozen on the grassy lawn of the Mews courtyard garden, one arm cocked back to throw a stick she must have ripped off a mangled-looking ornamental bush nearby. Her dog, Scoundrel, bounced impatiently at her feet, his entire back end squirming ecstatically.

"And you're coming to *me* for advice? What am I, your matchmaking granny?" Zaira hurled the stick, and Scoundrel tore after it, pink tongue trailing.

"You're the only person I can ask." I spread my hands. "Venasha's in Ardence with Aleki, visiting family."

"If I'm all you've got, you need more friends."

That stung more than it should have. My voice took on an edge. "I believe you are aware of the difficulties of making friends when everyone around you always wants something from you."

Zaira sighed and turned to face me at last. "I know."

"So, help me!" I spread my hands. "What do I do?"

Scoundrel caught up to the stick, shook it vigorously, and dropped onto his belly in the grass to chew on it. Zaira shrugged. "Damned if I know. I've never courted anyone either."

"Really?" I immediately wanted to curse myself for the surprise in my tone. I spotted Terika approaching up the garden path, her brown curls disheveled by the wind and her face flushed, and modified what I'd been about to say. "I mean, you're always so, ah, confident with your admirers at parties and such. I assumed you must have courted *someone.*"

Zaira snorted. "If you don't know the difference between flirting and courtship, you need more help than I can give you."

Terika joined us, tossing an amused glance at Zaira. "Yes, some people are a master of the first and hopeless at the second. Hello, Amalia."

"Oh, quiet, you." But the welcoming smile Zaira gave her was more free and easy than I'd seen her with anyone else but Scoundrel.

"I just don't know what one does, on a picnic with a person one is courting." I waved a vague hand.

Terika grinned. "That depends. Will you have a chaperone? Because if not, well, all *sorts* of things."

"He's a *Witch Lord.*" My voice rose nearly to a squeak.

"Should have thought of that before you agreed to court him," Zaira said.

Terika tapped her lips thoughtfully. "If you want to keep him at a distance, you could try flirting with him."

"Wouldn't that have the opposite effect?"

"Some people have been known to use flirting as armor." Terika didn't look at Zaira this time, but mischief shone in her eyes. "Some people are surprisingly skilled at not letting others get close to them, in fact."

Zaira rolled her eyes. "Some people are pushing their luck."

Terika clasped my shoulder, with an air of great seriousness. "But you have to be careful. If you seem to welcome a person's advances, and then keep them at a distance, they might become confused and hurt."

Zaira snorted. "Or they might tease you incessantly. That could also happen."

I knew full well Terika's remarks were directed at Zaira, but I couldn't help but think of Marcello, with a pang. "So what would you advise?"

Terika patted my arm with a show of sympathy. "You must be understanding. Your would-be suitor may have been through a lot and needs time to learn to trust you." She paused, unable to repress the laughter pressing against her lips. "Like a stray dog."

"Like a—why, you!" Zaira burst out laughing. "A dog, am I? Like *this*?" And she licked Terika's cheek.

"Down, girl!" Terika wiped the drool off her face with her sleeve, then glanced back at me. "Have you gotten him a gift?"

"No," I groaned. "I have no idea what to get a Witch Lord. A bucket of bones? Some creepy, rare, flesh-eating plant?"

"Perhaps an artifice device?" Terika suggested. "They don't have many artificers in Vaskandar."

"Good idea," I approved, relief rushing over me. "I'll go see if Istrella has anything she might be willing to part with."

As I left, I heard Zaira bark teasingly at Terika, while Scoundrel came bounding back to caper around them.

I climbed the stairs to Istrella's tower room but found her unwilling to open her door more than a sliver because she was working on something "extremely volatile" and the slightest disruption could be "catastrophic." By the smoke that wafted out through the door crack, I took her seriously.

"Do you have any ideas for an artifice device that would make a good present for a Witch Lord?" I asked her.

Behind the colored lenses of her rune-circled artifice spectacles, Istrella blinked. "Why would I ever give anything to a

Witch Lord?" she asked, with slow care, as if examining the bewildering question as she spoke it.

"No, no, *I* have to give a present to a Witch Lord."

"Oh! Well, in that case..." She shut the door in my face.

I stared at the sign that hung there (*Please Knock, or I Cannot Be Held Responsible for the Consequences*), wondering if I'd somehow offended her. A rustle and a cascading crash sounded from inside her room—but then, that wasn't unusual with Istrella.

The door eased open a crack again at last, and her skinny arm reached through, something shiny swinging from her hand.

"Here!" she said happily. "Spyglass pendant. Made it to pass the time while Marcello was rambling on about how I need to get out of my tower more often. Ten times magnification, and terribly stylish, I'm sure! Speaking of which, I like your necklace."

I touched the cold, smooth claws at my throat. "Ah, thanks."

Istrella shook the pendant at me, as if trying to tempt a cat. "Now, I should get back to this project before the fire spreads."

I took the clear, round crystal wrapped in gold wire. "Do you need any help?"

"Oh, no, I think I have it all figured out," she said vaguely. "Tell Marcello I talked to you, which makes at least two contacts with the outside world this week. So he should stop nagging and let me work."

"Tell him yourself," I laughed. "I'll see you soon, Istrella."

As I tucked the pendant into the pocket of my chocolate-and-gold brocade coat and started back down the stairs, it occurred to me that I had time to visit Marcello. A strange, fluttery apprehension replaced my usual delighted warmth at the thought of him. *Oh, hello, Marcello, I have a couple of hours to spare before going on a potentially romantic picnic with the man I'm courting. You know, the one who isn't you. Would you like to engage in some painfully awkward conversation?*

I shook my head. I couldn't start avoiding him out of misplaced guilt. He was still a good friend, and the last thing I wanted was to let this political courtship put a wall between us.

Crossing the courtyard garden, I veered toward the patch of lawn where I'd left Zaira, hoping to thank Terika for the gift suggestion and ask if they'd seen Marcello about. There was no sign of them on the open grass, but Scoundrel's wagging rear end protruded from behind a hedge.

I peeked around it, lifting my hand in a cheery wave.

Terika and Zaira leaned against a tree trunk together. Terika's eyes were closed, so she didn't see me, which was for the best, since she and Zaira were engaged in a rather passionate kiss. Their curls twined into each other, and Zaira's head tipped back, baring her throat, her hand firmly between Terika's shoulder blades.

Zaira didn't spare me a glance but did use her free hand to signal with a crudely eloquent gesture her annoyance at my interruption. I quickly ducked back out of sight, my cheeks warming. But I couldn't help grinning as I hurried off.

It seemed as if Terika had gotten through Zaira's armor at last.

I'd made it nearly across the garden when I spotted Marcello heading toward me, his face pale, seeming on the edge of breaking into a run. That couldn't be good. I hurried to meet him.

"Amalia. Thank the Graces you're all right." The words burst out of Marcello with the urgency of ill tidings piling up behind them. "I've been on the courier lamps since the reports started coming in, so I didn't know if you'd..." He pushed a hand through his hair. "If you were safe."

I sucked in a breath through my teeth. "I take it there's bad news?"

He nodded grimly and pulled a paper from his pocket: a copy of the Vaskandran assassin's list of names. It trembled in his hand as he jabbed a finger at it. "Lamonte Clare. An artificer, in his twenties. He was supposed to arrive at his family's home in Loreice yesterday. I granted him leave to go ask his parents for permission to marry the woman he was courting."

I could hear the strain in his voice. *Oh, Marcello.* "He failed to arrive?"

"He and his Falconer vanished on the road, along with the additional guards I assigned to escort him; their horses made their way back to the post station last night, saddles empty. The soldiers at the post station are looking, but they haven't found the bodies yet."

I searched for words, at a loss for any comfort to give him. But he wasn't done. His finger moved to another name.

"Parona da Valisia. An alchemist. Smart and meticulous in her work; you would have liked her. She was stationed in Callamorne, providing cures and elixirs to the people there. The inn she and her Falconer were staying at on their way to her next call burned to the ground before dawn this morning. The proprietors and all six guests failed to escape the blaze."

"Grace of Mercy," I breathed.

He moved on to another name, speaking more quickly, forcing his way through. "Halim of Osta, an elderly alchemist. He was attacked while visiting the lace festival in Palova today. His Falconer and guards successfully fended off the attackers, though some were wounded. And Harrald Callo, a quiet artificer with a passion for baked goods. He was visiting his elderly parents at their farm near Ardence when he and his Falconer went missing last night. Their bodies appear to have been dumped in the farmhouse well." He folded the list with unnecessary vigor. "Not to mention the attack on Istrella a week ago, and Namira's murder."

I let out a low whistle. "That's four attacks in the past day. Six, if you count the two earlier ones."

"Yes." Marcello met my eyes. "All across the Empire, people on this list are dying. The extra guards I assigned to them weren't enough. Vaskandar has made a list of the Falcons most key to our military preparations, and they're expending enormous resources to kill everyone on it."

A spike of raw, wild energy jolted through my veins—half fear, half anger. "Have you warned the others?"

He nodded. "That's why I was on the courier lamps. I'm on my way to a meeting of officers now. Colonel Vasante said you should come, too."

That struck me as odd, but I fell in by his side, and we strode off toward the colonel's quarters. If the problem hadn't been so serious, I would have been grateful for the distraction; it kept me from worrying about how much distance to place between us.

"It doesn't make sense," I said. "This must have taken an enormous amount of planning and effort. Advance setup to get their people in place, coordination to strike around the same time, sufficient force to overcome the extra guards. All that to kill a handful of artificers and alchemists?" A thought struck me. "Could they be killing them to steal their jesses?"

Marcello shook his head. "Someone tried that a couple hundred years ago, and the artificers came up with a solution. Once they're bonded to a Falcon, jesses destroy themselves if they're removed. The only way to steal a jess is to get one that hasn't been used yet."

"Then this must be part of some larger plan we're not seeing."

"If the Lady of Thorns has a plot this big and well thought out, I'm worried," Marcello confessed. "One of our advantages against Vaskandar in the past has always been that Raverran strategy is superior; the Witch Lords we've fought tended to act impulsively and without coordination, rather than carrying out long-term plans or working together. If we're now facing different Witch Lords with more of a mind for the long game, we could be in trouble."

Ruven. This was his sort of twisted cunning. I'd thwarted his attempt to steal books of dangerous magic from the Empire a month ago, but I should have known he'd have other plans. He wasn't the type to sit quietly and accept defeat.

We'd come to the door of Colonel Vasante's study, where she called her officers for their most important meetings. Marcello reached for the handle with the surety of familiarity.

"I think we're already in trouble," I said quietly.

And then he opened the door, and I saw how right I was.

Maps, books, and antique weaponry lined the walls of Colonel Vasante's study, and draperies in Falconer scarlet swathed the windows. Most of the officers gathered around the scarred mahogany table also wore uniforms bright as blood. But one man, seated at Colonel Vasante's left hand, stood out ominously in his impeccably tailored black velvet coat despite the nondescript droop to his shoulders and his attitude of quiet deference.

Lord Caulin, the Chancellor of Silence. Hells, what was *he* doing here?

Colonel Vasante gestured us in with a curt wave of her hand, scowling. But as she met my eyes, I could tell her irritation wasn't for us. She knew, as commander of the Falcons, what Lord Caulin truly was. And she wasn't happy to have him in this meeting, presiding over the room like the Demon of Death with his obsidian ax.

"Glad you could make it, Lady Amalia." She bit off the words as if annoyed we'd arrived last, but her intent gaze carried another message. "I want you here for this."

Ah. So she'd invited me as her ally: the only other person in the Mews who would understand the disturbing implications of Caulin's presence.

"I appreciate the invitation," I murmured, and settled into a chair beside Marcello. Lord Caulin gave me a respectful nod.

Colonel Vasante flipped her iron-gray braid over her shoulder and swept the assembled officers with her gaze. Most of them straightened; Jerith, always contrary, slouched deeper into his chair. "You all know why we're here," she said. "Vaskandar has launched an assault on our Falcons, working down a list of targets that Lady Amalia intercepted last week." She turned to Marcello. "Verdi, have you accounted for everyone on that list?"

Marcello nodded sharply. "Yes, Colonel. Aside from the losses I've already reported, the rest are confirmed safe, either in person or over the courier lamps."

"Perhaps," Lord Caulin suggested in a silky voice, "it would be best to keep all Falcons under guard in secure fortresses until such time as we are certain the threat has passed."

A muscle jumped in Colonel Vasante's jaw. "Lord Caulin, I understand that the doge has placed you in charge of his investigation into the murders. However, I'll thank you to leave the running of the Falcons to me."

"Of course," Caulin murmured. "His Serenity merely wishes to be certain such valuable resources are well guarded."

Jerith sneered at that, and a few of the other officers stiffened. Some of them were Falcons, and I rather doubted they appreciated being called resources.

"We'll follow standard procedure for a known, active threat against Falcons," Colonel Vasante told her officers, ignoring him. "But there's another concern. Any of you notice a pattern in the attacks?"

"They were all traveling," Marcello said immediately. "Three on leave, and one on assignment."

"But the assassins knew when and where to strike," I realized, the implications pouring in like cold lagoon water. "They had people in place already. They knew where those Falcons would be before they arrived."

Jerith frowned. He leaned forward, putting his elbows on the table. And then he spoke the words I hadn't wanted to say, for fear of making them real.

"You're saying we have a traitor."

Chapter Eight

Silence fell over the table. The officers exchanged worried glances. I wanted to deny Jerith's conclusion, but no matter how I turned the pieces, it was the only way the puzzle fit.

"Who would have had access to the records of planned leave and traveling assignments?" I asked.

"Any Falcon or Falconer can access those records," Marcello said, shaking his head. "They get referenced all the time—to schedule leave, check who's available for assignments and training, or even just to see who'll be around next week for dinner in the city. They're not circulated outside the Mews, but they're not secret, either."

"Perhaps they should be," Lord Caulin suggested.

"The point is," Colonel Vasante said, without sparing him a glance, "someone inside the Mews provided those records to Vaskandar. Either one of our clerks, which I find unlikely given how closely we vet them, or some Falcon or Falconer."

"That's impossible," Marcello objected.

"And yet," the colonel said dryly, "it happened."

"I *know* our Falcons and Falconers. They're good people." Marcello's jaw set stubbornly. "They wouldn't set up their fellows to get killed."

Oh, Marcello. I wasn't sure if I wanted to shake him in frustration until he accepted the inevitable disappointments of reality, or shelter him from them so he could stay unspoiled forever.

"I can understand what a shock this must be." Lord Caulin laced his fingers on the table, his voice calm and soothing. "It's unpleasant to contemplate a traitor in our midst. Yet it can't be a complete surprise; there are those among the Falcons who have made their disdain for the Serene Empire clear."

He turned unperturbed eyes upon Jerith as he said it. Half the table stared at the storm warlock.

Jerith shrugged. "I've been known to compose the occasional satiric verse. Call it disdain if you like."

I'd pay a purse full of ducats to read those. Though I supposed some might pertain to my mother; I couldn't decide if that made me want to read them more or less.

"Hardly appropriate for an officer of the empire," Lord Caulin chided.

"There are reasons I haven't advanced to a higher rank in the Falcons." Jerith grinned, but there was an edge to it. I expected Balos to come to his defense, but then remembered his husband wasn't an officer, and thus wasn't present. "If you think making fun of the personal vices of our leaders is in the same league of offense as betraying my friends to Vaskandar, you have a rather poor understanding of human nature."

Lord Caulin's smile remained fixed. "I did not personally assemble the list of potentially rebellious Falcons I was given. I am merely here as an agent of the doge, to pass on his recommendations for how to handle suspects in this serious matter of high treason until such time as we catch the culprit."

I didn't like the sound of that at all. Especially given that expedient murder was high among Lord Caulin's favored ways of handling problems. I pressed my lips tight against the objection I wanted to voice.

Jerith's eyes narrowed, and his fellow officers stirred uneasily. One clasped his shoulder, a touch that Jerith shook off.

"Recommendations?" the colonel grated.

Lord Caulin unfolded a list of names and smoothed it on the table. Two columns of small, precise writing covered the page. I glimpsed Zaira's name near the top. "These are all new recruits within the past year, plus those who have expressed, ah, disgruntlement against the empire. A reasonable list of starting suspects, no?"

"No," Jerith said, crossing his arms.

Caulin ignored him. "We recommend simple precautions. Investigating their activities over the past month, and watching them closely until the traitor is caught. Reading their mail, both incoming and outgoing, and forbidding courier lamp use. Confinement to the Mews—"

Marcello stood, his chair scraping the floor. "Absolutely not."

"You are out of order, Captain Verdi," Lord Caulin said pleasantly.

Colonel Vasante leaned an elbow on the table. "Verdi is my second at the Mews, and responsible for much of its daily operation. Carry on, Captain. But respectfully."

"Thank you, Colonel." Marcello bowed stiffly. "*Respectfully*, then, Lord Caulin. Even setting aside that these are good soldiers who've done nothing wrong, they have jobs to do. They can't perform their duty to the Empire while they're locked up in the Mews."

Lord Caulin sighed sympathetically. "I see the difficulty, Captain. But I am merely a messenger. My orders—"

"Yes," I interrupted, affecting a tone of curiosity to cover the anger churning in my gut. "It does seem a little odd for the doge to convey orders to the commander of the Falcons through his legal adviser. Isn't the Marquise of Palova the usual point of contact between the Council of Nine and the military?"

Appreciation flashed in Colonel Vasante's eyes. She adopted the same contemplative tone and turned to Lord Caulin. "She has a point, Caulin. Perhaps we should get on the courier lamps to the good marquise, and bring her into this conversation?"

"I'm not here as an emissary of the Council of Nine, of course." Lord Caulin lifted his hands. "The doge has placed me in charge of his investigation into these murders and the security response to it."

"Ah." I nodded, as if this cleared matters up. "Then certainly you can be part of the discussion. But any actual orders for Colonel Vasante from the doge should come through the proper military chain of command, should they not?"

Lord Caulin smiled a broad, fixed smile. "Of course. Forgive me; I am but a mere civilian and ignorant of military protocol."

"Right." Colonel Vasante nodded. "Then unless I receive orders directly from the Marquise of Palova or the doge himself, we're going to focus on protecting the Falcons and finding the traitor, not on punishing good soldiers who've griped about the Empire a few times when they're off duty."

Lord Caulin's smile thinned. He remained silent for the rest of the meeting but watched with shrewd, calculating eyes.

As my oarsman rowed me home along the Imperial Canal, between the looming façades of palaces with their spun-sugar stonework and gilded frescoes, I fumed silently over Lord Caulin's interference. Clouds had gathered overhead, gray and sullen, draining color even from the bright hues of the flower garlands and festive bunting that still decked the palaces in celebration of the Festival of Beauty. By the time my own palace came into sight, dominating the final curve of the Imperial Canal with its broad rows of graceful arches and the courier lamp spire rising from the roof, rain had begun to patter against the silk canopy my oarsman extended over my head.

Rain. Good Graces. I'd nearly forgotten my picnic with the Crow Lord.

"You have a very different notion of picnics in Raverra than we do in Vaskandar," Kathe observed.

I glanced around the glass garden. Muted light gleamed on the delicate, hand-blown curves of orchid petals, the bright explosions of shining daisies on translucent stems, the undulating waves of emerald-green seaweed standing frozen in a moment of imagined time. Rain pattered against the wall of windows that overlooked the busy Canal of Two Maidens, bathing the room in a gentle music to match the soft gray light. The Glass House was a shop, technically, but its private solarium was a popular neutral meeting ground for delicate conversations, and with the help of Cornaro gold, it was even available on decidedly short notice.

After I'd given Kathe the spyglass pendant, which seemed to please him enormously, a servant spread our picnic on a little wrought-iron table ringed by glass flowers, laying out an assortment of pastries, cold meats and cheeses, and crostini on a fine cloth. The bottle of white wine between us had come from my mother's vault. The Crow Lord looked strikingly out of place with his gray tunic and black-tipped hair, monochromatic and wild in this sea of crafted color. I might as well sit down opposite a real crow, or a piece of the silver-bellied sky itself.

"To be fair, we do usually have them outdoors, when the weather is more cooperative." I tried a charming smile, but my nerves twisted it into something more like a grimace.

Kathe peered out at the canal below, where a richly dressed merchant and her wife whispered to each other and pointed up at us from their sleek-prowed boat. "We do seem to be stirring up gossip. They're probably wondering what we're talking about." He turned a grin on me. "Shall we live up to their expectations?"

My shoulders tensed. I was determined not to let him run away with the conversation this time. I had to hold my own. "I'm all in favor of skipping the pleasantries," I said lightly. "It's the substance of words that matters, not how prettily they're dressed."

"What shall we talk about, then?" He rubbed his hands. "The rise and fall of empires? Vengeance and betrayal?" A thought seemed to strike him. "Or is that insufficiently romantic? I could pay you empty compliments, I suppose, or cobble together an improper proposal."

Now he was trying to make me blush. "The purpose of courtship is to get to know one another, is it not?" I spread fig jam on a slice of cheese to keep my hands steady. "Why don't we go straight to the essential questions: who are you, and what do you want?"

Kathe placed a hand on his chest in pretended shock. "My lady! We can't give ourselves away so easily. I thought you Raverrans were supposed to be masters of subtlety."

"My mother would tell you I don't always measure up in that regard," I said. "But I find the direct approach can sometimes prove refreshing." And it was worth a try. I could hardly talk to a Witch Lord about the weather for half an hour.

"I have an idea." Kathe grinned. "Instead of telling you about myself, I'll tell you about *you*. Stop me when I go wrong, and we'll switch. We'll see whose guesses are more on the mark."

I raised an eyebrow. "Getting a straight answer out of you is like getting a ribbon back from a cat, isn't it?"

"Let's see." Kathe leaned back in his chair, contemplating me across the table. "Your mother, the great and terrible La Contessa Lissandra Cornaro, married your father, Prince Embran Lochaver, as part of an agreement to bring the country of Callamorne into the Serene Empire. You visit your grandmother the queen at least once a year, ostensibly for political purposes, but it's dreadfully boring and you've spent most of your time there sneaking off with your cousins."

"Have you been talking to my family?" I demanded. He knew far too much about me for my comfort.

"No, but I've been to Callamornish court functions. But surely I can do better than that." He tapped his chin thoughtfully. "Your father passed away when you were quite small, on a visit to his home country. You have no idea how he died."

I lifted a finger. "Wrong. His horse bucked him off, and he broke his neck. My mother was never one to skip details to spare my feelings."

Kathe inclined his head graciously. "Your turn, then."

By the smile lingering on his lips, he'd gotten something from that exchange. He seemed awfully interested in my Callamornish family; did he know something about them I didn't?

I had to turn this game to my advantage. I slid my chair an inch closer. "The brothers you mentioned yesterday, dead but unmourned—you don't love them because you don't remember them." It was a guess, but if I was wrong, it would tell me something vital about his character.

Kathe nodded. "They died before I was born. I know very little about them." His voice softened. "I might have liked a brother. Most people give the mage-marked a wide berth, in Vaskandar, and it can be lonely."

Unexpected sympathy caught in my throat, sharp as a fish bone. A memory surfaced from some forgotten vault in my mind, blurred and faded with years: the crushing mortification when I had summoned the courage, at last, to ask my parents to get me a little sister at the market, and they burst into gales of laughter at the question.

"But," Kathe continued with a sigh, "the wisdom among Witch Lords is to have only one heir at a time."

I wanted to ask why, but I might be able to find that answer through research, while books seemed unlikely to hold the secrets of the Crow Lord's intentions. I needed to ferret out information for the good of the Empire, not to satisfy my personal curiosity.

It was hard, however, not to be curious about Kathe. Everything from the mischief in his yellow-ringed eyes to the black-dyed tips of his hair invited questions—and promised enticingly unsatisfying answers in return.

"You have a grudge against the Lady of Thorns," I said at last. "That's part of why you're willing to entertain an alliance with the Serene Empire. But it's not the only reason."

"Go on," Kathe said, his face still and watchful.

I licked my lips. "You're trying to seem like you agreed to this courtship on a whim, but it's all part of your plan. This gambit is far more important to you than you're letting on, and you'd give more than you're willing to admit to see it succeed."

Kathe fingered the spyglass pendant I'd given him, which now hung around his neck. "You are perceptive, my lady. I should know better than to try to deceive a Cornaro. Please, continue."

Time to take a risk. I leaned forward, the table's edge pressing against my jacket buttons. "In fact, you are sufficiently eager for my cooperation that you might give me information about the murders of Falcons by Vaskandran agents in return."

Kathe's eyebrows flew up. "I had no idea your Falcons were being murdered. I'm sorry to hear it."

That was good to know, I supposed, though I couldn't help a twist of disappointment. "Go ahead, then. Your turn."

"You can't help but be dubious about this courtship." Kathe set his elbows on the table; I was still leaning in, and the shift brought his face close to mine. His voice dropped, confidingly. "You don't know if you can trust me. There are all those terrible stories about the madness of Witch Lords, after all."

The yellow rings in his eyes gleamed. Too short a distance separated us now. I could feel the silent hum of his power in the air around him. But I didn't draw back.

"So far, so good," I said, my voice barely above a whisper.

"But you need allies for Raverra. You need a way to influence the Conclave, to ensure that as few Witch Lords lend their might to the war as possible." A clean, wild scent clung about him, like the air after a lightning strike. "You'd give a great deal for the chance to attend the Conclave as my guest."

I swallowed. "You have my undivided attention."

"The prospect might well be enough for you to continue this courtship despite your understandable lack of attraction to a strange bird like me."

"I have to stop you there." I sat back in my chair, willing myself not to flush.

Kathe blinked. "Because you wouldn't continue, or because you've fallen prey to my questionable charms?"

"That's an interesting question. It's a shame we Raverrans are so subtle and despise giving direct answers easily." I folded my napkin in my lap.

Kathe's mouth opened, then closed. But I had barely a second to relish catching him speechless before some shift of pressure or deepening of silence warned me to look up, and I found Ciardha standing beside me, my best coat draped over her arm.

My heart dipped in my chest. If my mother had sent her here

now, disrupting my picnic with Kathe, the news couldn't be good.

"Ciardha? What is it?"

She inclined her head in a short bow. "Lady Amalia. My profound apologies for this interruption, but the Council of Nine requires your presence at the Imperial Palace. La Contessa sent me to escort you there at once."

The Map Room at the Imperial Palace had hosted innumerable councils of war. Vast, detailed maps of Raverra and the Serene Empire adorned the walls, and the floor inlay spread out all the continent of Eruvia beneath the Council's feet. Every time I crossed its threshold, I could feel the scope of the Empire's history pressing down on me. I'd sat in on strategy sessions before, where the Council crowded around the table with generals and admirals; this meeting had a more spare and urgent feel, with only the Council of Nine and the doge himself gathered to peer down at the marker-covered map before them.

I paused inside the door after Ciardha gestured me through, held back by the sense that my summons must be a mistake. I had no place in this room right now. But Ciardha didn't make mistakes.

"It could still be a feint," the Marquise of Palova was saying. Her white hair had partially escaped its knot, straggling around her face. But she was a veteran of the Three Years' War and one of the best military strategists in Eruvia, so everyone listened with grave respect. "We know Vaskandar wants Loreice, after they failed to get it twice in the last century. If we focus too much of our strength on Callamorne, at the other side of the Empire, we won't be in a position to defend if they come across the Loreician hills in number."

"So we use the minimum force we're certain will hold the border, and keep much of our power in reserve but ready." The doge glanced up as he reached for a marker on the map. His glittering, deep-set eyes caught mine. "Ah, Lady Amalia. Join us."

I approached the table, my boots tapping across Osta and the southern coast as I crossed to my mother's side. Dozens of markers covered the map: blue for imperial forces, and green for Vaskandar. There were far fewer of the latter, but I suspected that had more to do with our limited intelligence resources across the border than it did with the forces at Vaskandar's disposal.

"I hear you secured us an alliance with the Crow Lord of Let," the Marquise of Palova said approvingly. "Best news I've had all day."

I touched the claws hanging on my chest and dipped my head in a bow of acknowledgment. "I'm glad I could help."

"But that is not why we've called you here." Niro da Morante, the doge of Raverra, was not a man to waste time tossing around compliments. He gave me a narrow, assessing look, as if estimating the heft of a weapon he might take to hand. "We have two tasks for you. The first is a matter of diplomacy."

I shifted uneasily. There was too much tension in the air. My mission to Ardence had been a matter of diplomacy, too, but with the city's survival at stake if we failed. "I am always pleased to serve the Serene Empire."

"Good," my mother said. "It's time for you to pay a family visit."

"Ah." I glanced at the map; a great many of the green markers clustered along the western end of the Witchwall Mountains, at Vaskandar's border with Callamorne. "You mean my grandmother."

La Contessa nodded. "For several reasons. The most straightforward being the diplomatic one: to show our commitment to defending Callamorne and stopping Vaskandar at the border."

"I still think we should dispense with diplomacy and strike across the border first, while they're fussing about waiting for this Conclave." That was Lord Errardi, an elderly council member notorious for dozing off during Assembly meetings. "Why give them time to make their infernal preparations, when we can crush them with overwhelming force before they're ready to invade?"

"Because it would be stupid," the Marquise of Palova replied bluntly. "Setting aside the fact that the snow could come down and close the passes anytime in the next six weeks, trapping our forces across the border—we've never won a battle on Vaskandran soil."

That got my attention. "What, never?" Military history wasn't one of my primary areas of study, but as I mentally reviewed what I knew of the Three Years' War, it did seem all our key victories had been defending our own lands, not pressing into theirs.

"That's what makes the Witch Lords so dangerous." The marquise's voice went deep and hollow as an old grave. "Every living thing in their domains bends to their will. In the Three Years' War, we tried making attacks across the border at first. But you might as well mount a sortie into the Hell of Carnage. An entire platoon of soldiers with their eyes pecked out by birds. A forest of men hanging impaled on branches, sometimes six to a tree, stretching as far as you could see. And you've never watched someone die badly until you've seen them swarmed by a hundred furious rats." She shook her head. "I could keep going, but I won't."

"I see," old Lord Errardi muttered weakly, looking ill. I had some sympathy; my stomach fluttered uneasily at the scenes she'd conjured.

"If they take territory and hold it for more than a few weeks, it starts to become *theirs*." The Marquise of Palova planted her fists on the table. "We don't dare cede them an inch. No one has ever taken back land from a Witch Lord once they've put their claim on it."

"So you can see why Callamorne is nervous," La Contessa interjected, pulling my focus back from wild images of corpses dangling from trees like hideous fruit and rivers of furry backs heaving over picked-clean bones.

I eyed the map. There were a lot of green tokens on Callamorne's northern border, more than anywhere else. "I'd certainly be worried if I were them."

"And they've only been part of the Serene Empire for twenty years." My mother said it casually, as if she hadn't been the one to bring them into the Empire by marrying my father, but I caught the faintest lift of pride in her voice. "Callamorne suffered near-constant raids from Vaskandar when they were an independent country, even with the mountains acting as a natural defense. Protection from their northern neighbor was one of the primary enticements that persuaded them to join the Empire." The same had been true of Loreice; one could argue that Vaskandran expansion had gained the Serene Empire more client states than any other force in history. "They need reassurance that we can and will keep them safe, if we want them to remain our staunch ally and loyal subject."

"I can do that." It made sense. And I liked my grandmother and cousins, even if the Callamornish court was overly fond of ceremony for my taste.

I took a closer look at the map. The two domains bordering Callamorne across the Witchwall Mountains were Sevaeth and Kazerath. I knew the latter was Ruven's father's domain, so the former must belong to the infamous Lady of Thorns. Green markers clustered in the major passes through the mountains, ending at the western flank of Mount Whitecrown.

I recalled another gathering of forces on that same mountain last month, and frowned. "Mount Whitecrown again," I murmured.

"Which brings us to the other and more urgent reason we called you here." The doge's voice sharpened. "I am told you have some familiarity with Prince Ruven's research into volcanoes."

A chill struck me like a sudden icy rain. I caught my mother's eyes.

She nodded gravely. "We've just received a report from the Witchwall Mountains. Our scouts have found a newly graven artifice circle near the base of Mount Whitecrown, barely on our side of the border. The artificer at the local garrison says he's never seen anything like it."

No. I gripped the table edge. We'd stopped Ruven's plot to trigger a volcanic eruption. Hadn't we?

"That could be Ruven's doing," I said slowly. "If he studied the book he tried to steal long enough to replicate the design."

"Do you think it has a chance of working?" the Marquise of Palova asked, her dark eyes bright and piercing.

"Perhaps. I don't know." I shook my head. "It was highly experimental, combining vivomancy and artifice." Vivomancy was nature magic, wild and raw and personal, originating in the shadowy forests of Vaskandar; artifice was a precise magical science, working through patterns and rules, developed by the scholars of ancient Osta at the other end of Eruvia. "There's been very little research done into combining the two types of magic, since they're so different. But the theory in the book seemed sound enough. Like taming a wild river through irrigation canals." I heard the mounting excitement in my own voice and forced my mouth shut before I could launch into a dissertation that no one here cared about but me.

"We can't take the chance that it might work," the marquise said grimly. "An eruption would wipe out our defenses in some of the key mountain passes. Even a moderate one could destroy major fortresses, artifice weapons, and wards, and slaughter the thousands of troops we have stationed there. It would be a catastrophic loss and would open the border wide to their invading forces."

"That's not even including the civilian losses," my mother added grimly. "There are towns and villages all along the border that might be wiped out entirely. The land for miles could be buried in ash, the rivers choked with it. Countless homes destroyed, people killed, families displaced and starving. A large enough eruption could endanger nearby cities with populations in the tens of thousands, like Ardence."

"And then Vaskandar would sweep in behind," the Marquise of Palova concluded, "like an army of demons from the gates of the Nine Hells. We'd stand no chance of holding them back. The whole north of the Empire would fall, giving them a clear route down the River Arden to the Serene City itself."

I swallowed. "So we need to make sure that doesn't happen."

"I want you to examine the circle during your visit to Callamorne," the doge said. "You've studied this book, you're a scholar of magical theory, and you know Prince Ruven. You're the best chance we have to unravel this design. I want to know whether it's truly the volcano enchantment, how likely it is to work, how immediate the threat is, how we can stop it—anything and everything you can tell us."

I nodded, feeling vaguely queasy at the thought of a man as unscrupulous and impulsive as Prince Ruven with access to that kind of power. "Can I bring an artificer, to help me counteract whatever I find?" I asked.

"Naturally." The doge waved his assent. "We need to send

artificers to the border to reinforce our magical defenses anyway. Take whoever you need."

The Council was giving me more backing than I would have expected. And they were taking me seriously, as well. When I had faced the Council of Nine in this room last year, I'd been glared at for speaking; whether it was what I'd accomplished in Ardence, my increasing involvement in my mother's duties since, or my coup of sorts with Kathe, they seemed to accept my voice as one worth listening to.

Unease mingled with my surge of pride. If no one listened to you, no one remembered when you were wrong. The more power you had, the more terrible the consequences of your mistakes.

The doge leaned across the table, fixing me with his gleaming eyes. "We have one more purpose in sending you to Callamorne. A military purpose." He tapped the Callamornish capital, which lay near the foot of the Witchwall Mountains, not far from the Serene Empire's northern border. "Your Falcon will accompany you. You will remain in reserve in Durantain until we have a better idea where Vaskandar will strike first and hardest. Then you'll move to defend the most critical pass with balefire."

I'd known this was coming. It was a good plan, and the best way we could help in the war. But I couldn't look forward to unleashing Zaira's fire on hundreds or thousands of people—even enemy soldiers—with anything but dread.

"Very well," I said, trying to sound businesslike and confident instead of afraid.

"This mission may prove dangerous. The attacks on Falcons have occurred when they were traveling." The doge's tone grew stern. "Neither you nor your Falcon are expendable. We will be sending a full military escort with you. You must take no chances with your safety or your warlock's. Do you understand?"

"Of course." My cheeks heated. One adventure in Ardence and my reputation seemed to have changed from retiring bookworm to reckless thrill-seeker.

The doge gave me a slow, assessing nod. "Good. I see no reason to delay, then. You'll leave tomorrow. And may all the Nine Graces go with you."

Chapter Nine

I had my oarsman row me to the Mews at once, to tell Zaira the news in person. I couldn't help but notice the increased activity at the Mews docks, with larger naval vessels tied up alongside the sleek cutters the Falconers normally favored, and soldiers hustling up and down the planks to load provisions. The Serene Empire was deploying her Falcons for war. Dread settled over me with the growing shadows of sunset.

I found Zaira in the cavernous mess hall, having just finished dinner; Scoundrel was curled up at her feet, and I passed Terika leaving on my way in. She gave me a broad, triumphant grin, and my heart panged with the news I couldn't yet tell her.

But Zaira accepted our new assignment with a shrug, barely pausing in her scratching of Scoundrel's ear.

"Be nice to get out of this chicken coop for a while. I've never seen Callamorne. Who else are you bringing?"

I pulled out the notes I'd made and spread them on the table between us. It was empty, aside from the two of us, though a murmur rose up to the arching ceiling of the mess hall from the half a hundred Falcons and Falconers still lingering over their plates. "Well, I need a skilled artificer to help me examine the circle, so I thought I'd take Istrella."

Zaira gave me a knowing look. "Mmm. And I'm sure the

fact that her brother will have to come along as her Falconer has nothing to do with it."

My face heated. "Actually, she has exactly the right sort of mind to come up with innovative solutions for unexpected artifice problems." Never mind that I'd feel much better on this volatile mission with Marcello's stable, steady presence at my side. "I'm thinking we'll also bring Terika."

Zaira straightened. "Terika! Why?"

"Well, she's from Callamorne, and she might like to visit her family. And we want a skilled alchemist at hand to concoct cures for any venoms, poisons, or plagues the Witch Lords might employ against the Empire." Zaira's skeptical stare demanded the truth, so I added in a low voice, "And she knows how to make my elixir. My mother wanted me to have an alchemist along who could do it, in case something happened to my supply."

Zaira grunted. "Can't blame her, after last time." Scoundrel nosed her hand insistently, and she went back to scratching his head. "Aren't you worried about bringing Istrella and Terika into a country that's about to be invaded? They're not exactly fearsome warriors."

"Neither am I." I folded up my notes and tucked them away. "I did consider it, especially given that their names are on that list of targets. But we'll have a sizable escort of soldiers, and they shouldn't need to go anywhere near the border."

"Unlike us." Zaira's eyes narrowed thoughtfully. "If war breaks out, they're going to put us right in the thick of it."

"Most likely." My stomach fluttered at the thought. "If Vaskandar attacks, you could have to unleash your fire on hundreds or thousands of soldiers. Are you . . ." I swallowed. There was no good way to ask this. "Is that all right?"

Zaira raised an eyebrow. "You're asking me if roasting hundreds of people alive is *all right*?"

I grimaced. "Not really. More whether *you're* all right."

"I'm always all right. If something will make me miserable, I don't do it."

This was no more than half true, but I nodded anyway. "I just wanted to . . . Well, I didn't think you'd done anything like that before."

Zaira snorted. "The empire would damned well have noticed if I'd murdered a small army. So no, I haven't. And no, I don't really know what it'll be like, or whether I'll bounce up afterward all chipper and ready for cakes and tea. So you can stop asking me about it, before I twist your tongue off to stop you from talking."

I couldn't help lifting my fingers to protect my mouth. "Sorry."

Scoundrel nudged at Zaira again, and she hunched down to fondle his ears with both hands. He closed his eyes in ecstasy.

"If you must know," she said after a moment, still staring at Scoundrel, "I'm actually glad to have the chance to let loose this Hell of fire inside me to *protect* something for a change." She sent a fierce glance sideways at me. "So stop trying to make me feel bad about it."

I put my other hand over my mouth as well, and nodded.

The problem with Raverran books on Vaskandar, I reflected, weighing Imoden's *Rise of the Witch Lords* in one hand against Lavier's *Chronicle of Vaskandran Expansion* in the other, was that they were written by Raverran historians. I rather doubted the authors had ever set foot in Vaskandar. Most of these books had been published immediately after the Three Years' War and focused almost entirely on military history; they traced Vaskandar's expansion from a small clutch of territories in the north as they swallowed up forest clans and petty kingdoms, raising a new Witch Lord over each, and culminated in Vaskandar's wars with the Serene Empire. The few details they contained about Vaskandar itself were hearsay and folklore, full of contradictions and omissions.

I laid them both in my trunk anyway. Kathe had told me, before saying good-bye at our picnic, that Callamorne was on his way back to Let, and he might see me there; I wanted to come to our next meeting armed with more knowledge.

I ran a finger along a line of spines on my shelf, their leather bindings warm and smooth like the touch of old friends' hands. I added *Principles of Vivomancy* and *Origins of Magic* to the trunk, and then somehow wound up lying on my stomach on my silk-curtained bed, with Orsenne's *History of Eruvia* spread open to the early Vaskandar chapter, just for a quick overview.

A familiar rap on my door startled me into slamming the book shut; by the time I'd sat up on the edge of my bed, my mother had swept into the room.

"Are you done packing, Amalia? Your boat leaves for the Mews to collect Zaira in half an hour." Her gaze took in my trunk full of books. "I am asking rhetorically, of course."

"Almost, Mamma," I lied.

Her eyebrow was insufficiently impressed to lift more than a hair's width. "I'll have Rica see to your clothes. But make certain you bring plenty of elixir, and pack it in multiple places this time."

"Of course, Mamma." I pulled a one-dose vial halfway out of my inner coat pocket, to show her that I could, in fact, learn from near-death experiences. "I've got more in my satchel as well, so I can take it with me on excursions, just in case."

"Good." She came and sat down on the bed beside me, her face serious. "Be careful on the road. I'm hoping there's been no time for news of your trip to leak to the Vaskandran spy in the Mews, but only fools make assumptions."

I straightened, remembering what I'd been burning to ask her earlier today. "Speaking of fools and the traitor in the Mews, what is Lord Caulin up to?"

"He's no fool," my mother said sternly. "Whatever else you may think of him, don't make that mistake."

"You know what I mean." I waved an irritated hand. "Why did the doge send him to interfere with the Falcons?"

My mother regarded me a long time in silence. Finally, she said quietly, "Most likely, because of you."

I stared at her, wondering if she was joking. But there was no humor in her piercing dark eyes. "What do you mean?"

"I know the doge better than almost anyone. And if Niro loves one thing, it's control." She turned her gaze to the window, where the clear morning light set the warm-hued façade of the palace opposite to glowing. "He is well aware that the Falcons are the keystone of the Serene Empire's power. And what do you think it looks to him as if you are doing?"

"You mean, with my Falcon reform act?"

"Not just your law. Your acquisition of the Empire's only fire warlock. Your cultivation of key officers in the Mews."

"I didn't *acquire* Zaira." Warmth flooded up my neck. "And I'm not cultivating anyone."

My mother did not dignify my protests with a response. "Even if your law comes to nothing, it's a shrewd move to earn the loyalty of the Falcons."

"That's not why I'm doing it!" I protested. "I just want to give them a choice."

"That doesn't matter." She turned her gaze back to mine, raising an eyebrow. "He can't afford to lose the Falcons to you. Especially not now, with Vaskandar at the border. So he's asserting control over them."

"He's using the murders to play political games?" I couldn't keep the outrage from my voice.

"I'm certain that catching the traitor and preventing more murders are his chief priorities." La Contessa waved away my ethical concerns. "But Niro da Morante is a man after my own heart in this at least: he rarely does anything for only one reason. Why not catch the informant *and* consolidate his political power?"

"But Caulin is going about this in the wrong way!" I bunched the lace of my cuffs in frustration. "He's not going to catch the traitor by harassing Falcons."

"I don't trust Caulin's investigation either, frankly." My mother's eyes narrowed. "He's the one pushing the doge to tighten his grip on the Falcons; he's hardly coming at this from a neutral perspective. This could all be part of his play for the Council seat."

"He's putting himself forward for Baron Leodra's old seat on the Council of Nine, then?" That might explain some things.

"He stands a good chance of winning it, too, more's the pity." My mother shook her head. "He's competent, and I respect the work he does for the Empire. But he lacks the vision to lead it. He's too focused on his own ploys and machinations and not on the larger picture. And he sees you as a threat."

I glanced down at my own hands, soft and unskilled, worrying at my cuffs. "I don't feel very threatening."

My mother raised an eyebrow. "Two months ago, no one in Raverra thought of you as anything more than a marriage prospect. You hid in this palace and fiddled about with books and artifice projects, and you were barely politically aware enough to know who the doge was. But after what you pulled off in Ardence, thwarting experienced schemers and installing your own hand-picked new duke, everyone is paying attention. And now that you've stepped out on the political stage, your first act is to try to pass a law that rewrites one of the key provisions of the Serene Accords, tampering with the very foundation of the Empire."

"I wouldn't say it rewrites the Serene Accords. Appends to them, maybe."

"Suffice to say there are few who'd have the gall to introduce such a measure. But you can do it, because you're only eighteen." A spark of something that could have been admiration entered my mother's voice—or more likely, bemusement at my foolishness. "If the law fails, they'll shrug it off as youthful idealism, and there'll be no permanent damage to your career. If it passes, though..." Her lips curved in a wry smile. "If it passes, everyone will consider you brilliant and dangerous. We have a limited window of time remaining to ensure they're not wrong."

"I don't feel brilliant and dangerous," I muttered.

"The Lady of Thorns thinks you're dangerous." Her tone went hard. "She put your name on that list."

I caught her hand, suddenly excited. "Mamma, I've been thinking about that." An idea had come to me late last night, as I lay awake dwelling on thoughts of war and courtship, volcanoes and murders. "I think all this Vaskandran interest in me must have to do with the Witch Lord blood in the Callamornish royal line."

It was no secret; royalty quickly ran out of sufficiently high-ranked marriage prospects, so half the great families in Eruvia had a splash of Vaskandran royal ancestry somewhere, and that meant Witch Lords. Border states like Callamorne had more than a splash. My father's father had been of royal Vaskandran blood, well connected enough that his marriage to my grandmother put a stop to an ongoing invasion of Callamorne. If there was some political significance to his line, that might be enough to explain both my name on the assassin's list and Kathe's secret intentions.

"I suspect you're right." My mother tucked a loose lock of hair behind my ear, studying my face. "Wars and weddings twine Vaskandar and Callamorne together, in a long and personal history. You are part of that history, and it will give you diplomatic advantages on this mission that I never possessed. But it also exposes you to dangers I never faced."

I hugged my book to my chest. "Did you ever meet my grandfather's family?"

"No, and neither did your father, so far as I know. But I believe your grandfather was a Witch Lord's son." La Contessa frowned. "There are bound to be enmities and alliances that he left behind him, beyond the Witchwall Mountains."

"But now Vaskandar is dragging them across the mountains into Callamorne." I sighed. "I'll be careful, I promise."

My mother's mouth crooked toward a smile. "I'm not certain I believe you. But I have high hopes you'll be clever, which is better."

She embraced me, then, holding me in a circle of warmth and delicate perfume. I closed my eyes, wishing for a moment that I were small again, and would spend this trip doing nothing more important than running up and down the stairs in the royal castle in Durantain with my cousins.

"Clever it is, then," I whispered.

For the first few days of our journey by coach to Callamorne, we traversed the endless green-gold fields at the heart of the Serene Empire, past red-roofed villas girdled with flowers and lonely lines of cypress trees. As we approached Callamorne, the flat land wrinkled into gentle folds and rolls; the shallow valleys and hollows collected mist in the mornings, and the high places held on to the lingering golden light at sunset.

Terika stared hungrily out the window of the coach, gazing over the heads of our mounted military escort for the first sign of the shadowy hills of her homeland on the horizon.

"Wait till you see," she told Zaira cheerfully. "The hills in Callamorne are much bigger than the rolling little bumps you get here in the central Empire, rugged and covered in lovely woods. And soon we'll get snow, and the fields and meadows will turn sparkling white, all the way to the mountains."

Lienne, Terika's Falconer, shivered. "Yes, and cold to freeze your blood, with icy footing. I prefer Raverran sunshine and a cup of mulled wine, thank you."

Zaira shrugged. "I'm there to wait around until it's time to set things on fire. If it makes you happy, I can look at some muddy hills in the meantime."

"So charming." Terika sighed. "That's what I like about you."

She slipped an arm around Zaira's shoulders. Zaira gave her an alarmed glance, then relaxed against her. Lienne turned her face to the window to hide a smile.

The coach should have felt like a rolling target, with four people in it on the Vaskandran assassin's list, but we'd taken enough precautions that I wasn't worried. Zaira was back to wearing her artifice-worked corset stays and hairpins, which protected her from musket balls and blades alike; unfortunately, they required her innate magic as fuel for the powerful shield, and none of the rest of us could use such protections. Marcello rode outside the carriage with our escort of a full two dozen soldiers, training a wary eye on every fold in the land, line of trees, or farmhouse. No band of attackers large enough to threaten us could possibly escape his scrutiny, in the unlikely event they could penetrate this far into the Serene Empire at all.

No, it wasn't fear that weighed on me as we traveled northwest toward Callamorne. It was the heavier, duller burden of expectations.

If I couldn't figure out what to do with Ruven's circle on Mount Whitecrown—if it was even the volcano enchantment at all—thousands of people could die. If Vaskandar invaded and the doge called Zaira to the border, thousands of people *would* die. And there was the old guilt I always felt when visiting Callamorne, wound queasily through it all—that an entire nation trusted in me to secure and uphold their place within the Empire, including my own family, and I only visited once a year and rarely thought of them.

They must have hoped for more when they gave up their prince to marry my mother and swore allegiance to Raverra. And this time, I had to give them more, so they would know the Empire would uphold its half of the bargain my birth had sealed.

I wished I could just sneak off with my cousins again, and perform no more complicated diplomacy than talking to Roland about Callamornish history to distract him while Bree stole apples from the castle orchard. But I had stepped up to take my place in my mother's shadow, and there was no stepping down now.

Istrella rode in the coach with us, tinkering away on some experimental modifications to her brother's powder horn, which I'd insisted she empty and clean first. The last thing we needed was to make exciting new discoveries about the interaction of artifice and gunpowder while locked in a moving carriage with a fire warlock. I couldn't help but notice that Terika and Zaira seemed physically closer than they had before their kiss—small touches and glances passed near constantly between them, and no sliver of space divided them on the carriage bench.

When we stopped at a roadside inn on our fourth and last night before crossing into Callamorne, I took advantage of a moment alone with Zaira at our table in the inn's crowded, candlelit dining room to lean in and murmur the obvious question.

"So, are you two finally courting now?"

Zaira glared at me, then flicked her eyes to the stairway leading up to our rooms on the second floor. Terika and the others hadn't come down to dinner yet, though we expected them to join us shortly; I only had a few minutes to get in as much teasing as I dared.

She picked up her cup, realized the server hadn't filled it yet, scowled into its emptiness, and set it down again. "It's none of your pox-rotted business, but let's just say Terika is the only person I've met who's more stubborn than I am. You can tell she grew up on a goat farm—the spiky-headed bastards must have given her lessons."

"That's a yes." I leaned back in my chair in satisfaction. "And good for Terika. You're allowed to be happy, you know."

"I don't know what she's thinking." Zaira shook her head. "She's sweet as a summer peach, and I've got a fair bucket of blood on my hands. Besides, what future does she think we have together?"

"Well, if I get my Falcon reform act passed—"

Zaira snorted.

"All right," I sighed, "forget my act. Purely theoretically, if you could have any life you wanted with her, what would it be?"

"Do I look like some moon-besotted idiot who sits around dreaming about a charming country cottage and a bunch of babies to you?" Zaira flicked her cup with a fingernail.

"I have no idea. Which is why I asked." I shrugged. "If I could pick my own fate, I'd like an extensive library, a circle of good companions, and . . . and someone to share it with." Marcello's smile and warm green eyes filled my imagination; by the gleam in Zaira's eyes, she knew it. "What about you?"

"That's a dangerous question."

"Dangerous? How so?"

Zaira's eyes narrowed. "If you waste time thinking about everything you want and can't have, it'll eat you up from the inside, like you swallowed a cup of bloodworms. If you can't reach out and take it, brooding about how much you want it only makes you wretched."

"That's a rather grim philosophy."

"Growing up in the Tallows, you have to focus on staying alive moment to moment. You don't think about the future, beyond making sure you have one at all."

I traced a curving scar on the tabletop, where someone had carved their initial. "I never dreamed much about my future either, to be honest, for the opposite reason. Mine's already been laid out for me. I can't choose what I'm going to be or do." Even in that dream of a well-stocked library and Marcello at my side, I had to vaguely imagine my mother still scheming away in the background, filling her seat on the Council of Nine. Once she retired, any last vestiges of freedom I possessed would vanish into the depths of the Imperial Palace.

Zaira grunted. "Maybe you're the one who should run away."

A server finally arrived with a wine pitcher to fill our cups; I welcomed the reprieve from needing to find an answer. An old, sullen anger had stirred half awake at Zaira's words, left over from the last time I'd seriously considered running from my fate: when I opened my mother's letter that called me home from the University of Ardence, just when I'd finally found a place to be myself and not the Cornaro Heir.

I raised my glass to drown the bitter memory.

"Took you long enough," Zaira grumbled at the cringing server, and reached for her own cup.

As the wine tilted toward my lips, a spark flared on my hand. A sharp prick of heat pierced my finger, and the wire-bound crystal on a certain ring glowed gold.

Alchemy. Someone was trying to poison us. Fear lanced through me, jagged and white as lightning.

I slammed the cup down, splashing red across the table. "Zaira, don't drink it! It's poisoned!"

Zaira froze, her cup halfway to her lips.

The server lifted her bowed head, her face emerging from curtains of blond hair. Cold, deadly resolve burned in a face I'd seen before: the Vaskandran assassin who'd attacked Istrella.

I barely had time to recognize her before she drove the knife she'd held hidden under her tray into Zaira's side.

I let out a shriek of panic and despair, but the air in front of Zaira rippled as if someone had dropped a stone into a still pond. The assassin's knife rebounded from Zaira's rune-scribed corset stays.

All this during the time it took me to leap to my feet—I was moving too slowly, and the assassin was too fast, and the desperate energy flooding my body made me clumsy. But I lunged at the assassin anyway, the impact jarring my hip and shoulder with bruising force, and I knocked her away from Zaira before she could strike again.

The assassin immediately recovered her balance, slipping out of my reach. She moved with deadly grace, efficient and lethal as a striking heron. Alarm spiked up from my lungs; I knew my limits, and I wasn't good enough to stop her.

Zaira cursed and drew her dagger. The assassin cast her tray aside; it hit the floor with a room-silencing crash, shards of pottery skittering everywhere. All over the tavern, heads turned, voices exclaimed, and chairs scooted back in alarm.

Hells. The tray had hidden a pistol. The assassin leveled its gleaming barrel at Zaira. Time seemed to slow down, all the light in the room focusing on that fateful cylinder of polished wood and metal.

But then the assassin narrowed her eyes, seemed to think better of chancing Zaira's shields again, and swung the muzzle around to point at me.

It stared at me like the cold eye of the Demon of Death. The hammer clicked back.

"Ex—" I caught the release word halfway out of my mouth, clamping my lips on my own panicked cry. Frightened faces pressed back behind the assassin; a mother thrust a crying child behind her.

Too many people. I couldn't do it.

An earsplitting crack filled the dining room, followed by a sharp-smelling haze of gunsmoke.

Chapter Ten

I flinched, but no pain came.

The assassin stumbled backward, blood blossoming on her side. She discharged her pistol in my general direction, her eyes glazing, and the crowd screamed at the second sharp bang; an oil lamp on the wall behind me shattered. It took me a long instant of frozen terror to realize the second shot had missed, and the first one hadn't been hers at all.

Marcello thundered down the stairs, his pistol smoking, Lienne at his heels with her rapier drawn. My heart leaped at the sight of them, even as I pressed back into the table as if I could somehow merge with it, one hand on my flare locket. Grace of Mercy, that had been close.

"Please clear the room," Marcello called, his voice full of calm authority. The inn patrons scrambled to oblige, some still swearing or crying. The innkeeper hustled to help them out to the garden, murmuring soothing words and apologies. I had to admire his ability to gently tease order from the chaos.

The assassin knelt on the floor, one arm clamped to her bleeding side. Her other held a dagger, but the point wove and dipped. Lienne strode over and flipped it out of her hand with the tip of her rapier, then lifted the edge to the assassin's neck. Marcello reloaded his pistol, scanning the room for any sign of further danger with infinitely reassuring competence.

Zaira let out a shaky sigh. "I should have seen that coming. Damn it, I've gotten soft."

"Any questions for this vermin, Lady Amalia?" Lienne asked.

That's right. I was in charge here. I didn't have the luxury of sinking into a chair and downing half a bottle of wine while other people took care of things, no matter how much I wanted to.

My pulse still sang in my veins, keen and nearly painful. I stepped forward; my knees trembled, but the assassin was too busy coughing up blood on the gleaming wooden floor for me to worry whether she noticed.

"What is the Lady of Thorns planning?" I demanded. "Why is she murdering Falcons?"

The assassin's lips, pale and bloodstained, moved. "Can't believe I missed," she whispered. A cough racked her, and more blood hit the floor. She sucked in a wet, ragged breath. "But it doesn't matter, Amalia Lochaver Cornaro. You're already rushing toward your own death."

"Answer the lady's questions," Lienne snapped.

But the assassin couldn't have answered if she wanted to. She swayed and collapsed, blood still flowing from her side, her breath gurgling in her throat.

Marcello swore. "I know her."

I nodded. "She was the one who came after Istrella, back at Lady Aurica's party."

"No. I know her from years ago." Marcello bit his lip and turned away, his shoulders hunching.

"Should we..." I trailed off. I couldn't bring myself to look at the assassin; she might have tried to kill me, but her blood was red as any human's, and her struggles to breathe tore at my sympathies. We all needed air, and we all knew pain.

"She's not going to talk, and she's not going to survive," Lienne said grimly. "Captain?"

"Yes," Marcello said.

I turned away from Lienne's quick, brutal mercy.

While our escort removed the body, I found the innkeeper, apologized with a handful of ducats, and told him to treat the rest of the inn guests to the best wine in his cellar and let me pay for their rooms. The man's eyes lit with reflected gold—it was probably more than his inn normally earned in a month—and he hurried about taking care of his guests with renewed vigor.

One more innkeeper who will speak well of the Cornaro family to anyone who passes this road. I wouldn't have thought of it, last year, but it was all part of my mother's training. Generosity bred goodwill; generosity *and* goodwill meant people brought you information; and information was the elixir that powered politics in the Serene Empire.

And besides, I did feel bad about ruining dinner for everyone.

I returned to the dining room to find the body gone, Terika examining the poisoned wine cups with Zaira and Lienne, and Marcello slumped by himself at a table in a corner. I headed straight for Marcello, but Terika waved me over before I could get there.

"There's Black Malice in this wine," she said, her tone serious. "You and Zaira would have been dead within the hour if you'd drunk it."

It was oddly reassuring to find ourselves attacked with such mundane weapons as guns and poison. I'd far rather that than vivomancy.

"I'll have to thank my mother again for this ring." I ran my thumb over the stone, which was now cool to the touch.

"Black Malice takes a mage-marked alchemist to create," Terika said. "I'm not sure Vaskandar has any alchemists strong enough; their mage-marked tend to be vivomancers. So there may be another child out there who the Falcons didn't find in time, forced to make poisons for someone unscrupulous enough to sell them to Vaskandar."

Anger compressed her brows, and determination hardened the round, freckled face I usually saw lit up with laughter. She must be remembering her own childhood, when her father had sold her to an assassin's guild that had forced her to mix poisons for them—possibly including the Demon's Tears that still ran in my veins.

"We'll find them," Lienne promised, putting an arm across Terika's shoulders. "We rescued you, and we'll rescue this one, as well."

Marcello lurched to his feet, fists clenched at his sides. "I know who it is."

We all turned to stare at him. "Who the alchemist is?" I asked.

"Yes. Grace of Mercy protect him." Marcello ran a hand through his hair, as if he could push memories away. "The boy."

Lienne clicked her tongue. "Ah. I heard about that."

"What?" I asked.

Marcello started pacing. "Four years ago, when I was a new Falconer, I stumbled across a mage-marked boy whose family had been hiding him. Emmand, his name was. He was ten years old, an only child of minor gentry; his parents told everyone their son was sickly, and kept him shut up in their house." He shook his head. "I was off duty, and since he seemed perfectly safe, I saw no reason to rush him straight to the Mews. But when I came back to check on him the next day, his parents were dead, and Emmand was gone."

"How do you know this was him?" Terika swished the poisoned wine in Zaira's cup. "It could have been anyone."

"I recognized her." Marcello jerked his chin toward the bloodstain on the floor. "I took the village militia with me and followed their trail. We caught up to the kidnappers, but there were a dozen of them, and we only had six. That woman was one of them. I'll never forget her face—she was the first person who ever shot me." He absently rubbed his thigh.

Lienne let out a surprised snort. I took a half step toward him, lifting my hand instinctively before I let it drop. "I never knew you'd been shot."

"I healed well enough." Marcello's voice grew taut and raw, like brittle leather stretched too far. "But I was too hurt to follow. I took a last shot at the kidnappers as they dragged the boy off, but he thought I was shooting at him and started screaming." He swallowed. "That was the last I heard of him—screaming that I was trying to kill him as they led him away. I never knew if he lived or died."

I crossed to him and squeezed his shoulder, my heart aching in sympathy. "You did everything you could to save him."

"Well, if they were capturing them years ago, they've moved on to killing now." Terika's voice was oddly cheerful as she poured the poisoned wine out the window. "Black Malice is invariably lethal. The Lady of Thorns didn't intend for you to survive."

When we finally headed up to our rooms, I drew Zaira aside on the stairs to murmur an apology.

"I'm sorry," I said. "I should have released you as soon as I saw you were in danger."

Zaira's brow contracted. She glanced at the handful of people who'd timidly reentered the dining room, then up at Terika, who'd preceded us to the landing.

"No. It was too crowded in here." She shook her head. "I would have burned that bitch, faster than you can blink. And like as not, half the unlucky bastards standing around her. You did the right thing."

"I did?"

"Don't let it go to your head."

"I want to learn to get this right," I said. "To release you immediately when you want your balefire, before you even have to ask. Like Jerith and Balos."

Zaira's eyes narrowed. The dim light in the cramped stairwell made them black as obsidian. "When I want it? Or when you think I need it?"

"When you want it," I said firmly. "It's your fire."

"You're not going to sit on your hands and have the vapors for half an hour first, like you used to?"

"That was different." Shame heated my cheeks. "I was afraid."

Zaira snorted. "You're still afraid."

"Of course I am!" I said defensively. "Anyone in their right mind would be scared of a fire warlock."

Zaira's face closed like a slammed door.

"Of balefire," I corrected myself quickly. "I meant your balefire. Not you personally."

"I know what you meant," she said.

And she turned and followed Terika up the steps.

The next morning, I couldn't tell whether Zaira was ignoring me more than usual. My own guilt over my words on the stairs made it hard to meet her eyes; between that and the stiff, cheery awkwardness of my exchanges with Marcello as we prepared to resume our journey, I was ready to hide my nose in a book as soon as I got into the coach.

We stopped at the first post station for Marcello to report the assassin incident over the courier lamps. By the tautness of his features as he emerged, shaking his head, the conversation had not been reassuring. The courier lamp relay spire loomed behind him, its paired mirrors reaching above the trees to catch the signal from the previous post and send it on to the next one.

"What is it?" I asked anxiously, hurrying over to meet him in the post station yard as the station soldiers worked with practiced efficiency on switching out our carriage horses.

"No one had access to that list of our stops on this trip besides Colonel Vasante and the people traveling with us. Even the rank-and-file soldiers in your escort don't know the details."

I stared at him, unease coiling in my belly. "That can't be right. What about the clerks at the Mews? The Council of Nine? Lord Caulin?"

"Certainly the Council would have access to the information, but we were really careful about not letting it out this time." Grave lines pulled at Marcello's face, making him look older. "So far as I know, aside from the colonel, it's you, me, Zaira, Istrella, Lienne, Terika, and the officer in charge of our escort."

I glanced at the officer in question, Sergeant Andra, a no-nonsense woman with close-cropped hair who'd been a Mews soldier for twenty years. It was no easier to picture her as a Vaskandran agent than any of the others.

"Someone must have overheard us talking about the trip." I grabbed at the idea. "Zaira and I were discussing who to bring in the mess hall. Anyone could have heard us."

"Did you read off the list of stops the assassin had in that letter?" Marcello shook his head. "I suppose someone might have written it down, and a spy could have seen it. But otherwise, it looks as if the traitor is traveling with us."

The impossible knowledge settled over both of us, a burden too heavy to carry alone.

"We should have gotten Terika to mix up a truth serum for the assassin," I muttered. "She probably wouldn't have lived long enough, but it would have been worth a try. It's a pity Lienne killed her."

Lienne. I flicked my eyes to where she stood talking to some of the post soldiers, her hands going even faster than her mouth, making a friend by the smile on the young soldier's face as she shook her head. It had never occurred to me think Terika's Falconer might be the traitor; she seemed so warm and kind, and so protective of Terika. But I didn't know her well, and she'd certainly ensured that the assassin didn't give up any knowledge she might have had.

"The worst part of this," Marcello said in a low and troubled voice, "is that now I have to suspect people I've trusted for years."

I nodded. But I thought, *No. The worst part is that someone you've trusted for years has already betrayed you.*

The hills of Callamorne first appeared as a blue haze in the distance. They could have been low stormclouds resting at the ends of the earth. As we drew closer, blue transformed to green and gold: the deep, rough green of pine woods and the dry autumn gold of fields and meadows, making a welcoming patchwork across the soft ridges thrust high against the cloudy sky.

Then we crossed a river on a sturdy wooden bridge, and we were in Callamorne. The hills reared around us, rocky and familiar, the trees forming sloping secret halls beneath their branches.

Immediately the houses were different: peaked roofs to slough off the snow in winter, and log walls rather than whitewashed plaster. They tucked into whatever pockets of level ground they could find, spreading out fields like tablecloths around them. Woodsmoke rose from their fieldstone chimneys.

I drank in the scent. It brought back a flood of memories: visiting my cousins for the Festival of Bounty at the autumn harvest, when the long tables in the great hall of the royal castle overflowed with the hearty fare Callamorne favored. Red and gold leaves and clusters of purple grapes decorated the scant spaces between the platters, and the warm smells of roasted meat and potatoes filled the chill-touched air of the castle. My cousins and I crawled under the tables, in the long caves made by the fine white tablecloths. Roland pretended to be a Queen's Musketeer, stalwart and brave; Bree was the monster hunting us through the tunnels. I wanted to be an artificer, full of ideas for magical traps I could set to catch the beast.

You can't, Roland had insisted, with the superior air of a ten-year-old explaining the ways of the world to his foolish young cousin. *You're a princess. Princesses can't be mages.*

Yes they can, Bree had retorted hotly. *Princesses can be whatever they want.*

I couldn't remember if that particular argument had ended in a fistfight, but they often did, when Bree and Roland were young. Thank the Graces they'd stopped doing *that*, anyway; it had been terribly awkward to sit by, an outsider to their squabbles, waiting anxiously for them to laugh and be friends again.

This time, I couldn't hide under tables. The Callamornish people, unlike Raverrans, were not content to allow diplomacy to occur behind closed doors. They preferred grand public gestures and heartfelt speeches.

Shrines to the Graces stood beside each house we passed, and more of the tiny wooden niches with their simple statues, weather-worn ribbons, and melted candle ends seemed to mark every other mile by the roadside. Callamorne took religion far more seriously than the more secular Raverra did. I'd have to remember to watch my tongue. I tried to think of a good way to suggest to Zaira that she do the same but decided she'd only take that as a challenge.

Zaira. Graces, I needed to talk to her. I didn't think I was imagining things; she was deliberately ignoring me. At first I thought I'd offended her; then I realized the last thing Zaira would do when she was offended was sulk in silence. She'd rip me up one side and down the other like a ruined seam.

So I'd managed to actually hurt her, which was worse.

It was hard to find a moment alone with her; I couldn't precisely bring up a delicate personal matter when we were crammed into the coach with three other people. But when we stopped to water the horses at a stream, and Terika was engaged in chatting with Lienne, I saw my chance.

Zaira had wandered a short way down the bank, then sat down and started chucking rocks into the current. I followed after, and plunked down awkwardly at her side.

"I'm sorry," I said.

She gave me a weary glance. "You say that all the damned time. I'm getting tired of it."

"All right then, let's just say I wish I could take back what I said last night." I threw a pebble into the stream, too; it disappeared into the rush without a splash. "About being afraid of you."

Zaira grunted. "Apologies aren't worth the spit used to speak them if you don't mean it."

"I do mean it," I protested.

She turned skeptical eyes on me. The sunlight caught in their deep, murky brown, bringing out the black circles of the mage mark around her pupils. "Don't make yourself a liar. You *are* scared of me. Everyone is." She frowned, and tossed another stone into the river. "Except Terika."

"She's good for you," I said softly.

"She *should* be afraid of me. One way or another, I'm going to break her heart, if I don't kill her first." She said it in a matter-of-fact tone, as if she were talking about the common inevitability of rain.

"Give good things a chance to happen."

Zaira's eyebrows, I had noticed over our time together, had a lot to say about my judgment, none of it positive. "You're a history scholar. Tell me, do your books talk about fire warlocks?"

"Of course." Fire warlocks tended to leave broad, ashy holes in the pages of history.

"I bet the fire warlocks in those books always live happily ever after, surrounded by friends and family." Zaira's voice dripped sarcasm.

They did not. I dropped my eyes to my mud-spattered boots. "Still..."

"Let's say I don't blame you for being scared," she said abruptly, "and leave it at that."

"But I'm not scared of you," I insisted. "Not of the *real* you. It's the way you get when the balefire takes over that's..." I trailed off.

"Terrifying?" she supplied.

"Well, yes."

Zaira fell silent. I looked up and found her weighing a rock in her hand, staring off across the water. "I don't know her," she said in an odd, quiet voice.

"Who?" I asked uncertainly. I searched her words for some sarcastic bite or blunt mockery, but I couldn't find any.

"I never remember a damn thing, when the fire takes me. Only the burning, and the joy." A shiver shook her. "But I think it's me."

I stared at her, transfixed, not sure what to say. "You," I repeated at last, in the barest whisper.

"Just like it's still me when I dream." She looked at me, and I was unprepared for the raw honesty in her bottomless dark eyes. "That balefire that makes you wet yourself—you might like to pretend it's not a part of me, but you're wrong. It's *me.* That burning girl is me, even though she's a stranger." A bitter-edged smile crossed her lips. "Like a drunk who gets mean and then forgets it in the morning. With as much of a headache, like as not."

"More like the Grace of Victory, with her flaming sword," I said, my voice coming out hushed and husky.

"No, not a Grace. The Demon of Death." Zaira stood, brushing dirt off her skirts. "And nobody in their right minds would court the Demon of Death. So Terika must be mad as a magpie."

"Oh, I don't know," I said lightly. "If she can put up with the things that come out of your mouth on a daily basis, balefire must seem a small matter by comparison."

Zaira laughed, loud enough to startle a pair of crows in a nearby tree. They cawed in protest, amplifying the harsh sound of her mirth. Then she grabbed my elbow and hauled me companionably to my feet.

"Oh, she likes my mouth right enough," she chuckled. I felt my face go scarlet. "Come on, back in your coach, before you pass out from all that blood going to your head."

For the next two days, as we wended through the steepening hills, rain sheeted down from leaden skies; our outriders dripped miserably, hoods up and hunched against the weather. I invited Marcello into the carriage, but he shook his head, water dripping from the curling tips of his hair.

"It's best that I remain out here, my lady," he told me through the window. "I'm on duty."

Thoughts of traitors and volcanoes kept me from entirely settling to my reading as the coach clambered and bumped up into the hills. Istrella seemed distracted as well, frequently looking up from her project and frowning as if there were something she wanted to say, but each time she sighed with apparent frustration and returned to her work.

At last, Istrella lifted the finished device from her lap. It appeared to be a necklace, bounded with great lopsided chunks of obsidian.

"For you. It's a flare locket." She held it out across the coach to Zaira, with a bit of a resigned shrug, as if accepting its flaws. "So you'll have something other than your balefire to fall back on. Though I hear you're quite good at stabbing people with knives, too."

Zaira took it, bemused. "Uh, thanks."

"It seems to use an awful lot of volcanic glass for a flare locket," I said, trying to sound casual and not at all alarmed. "Is there a reason it needs so much power?"

"That's a good question." Istrella tipped her head, as if thinking it over. "I suppose you could say I made some enhancements. I wouldn't open it if you don't need to."

Zaira's grip on the locket chain became more cautious. "I'll keep that in mind," she said.

I was about to ask what sort of enhancements when something caught my eye through the coach window: a lone figure standing on a boulder at the edge of the bluff that fell off beside the road. He gazed out over the fog-cupping valley, with its ragged pines catching shreds of passing clouds against the dark hills. Wind ruffled the feathers at his shoulders and the black tips to his pale hair, and a crow perched on his shoulder.

"Stop the coach," I called.

Zaira glanced out the window. "Oh, *him.* Stopping for a tryst in this weather?"

Terika climbed half over Zaira to peer at Kathe. "Mmm, nice view, though."

Zaira laughed and put an arm around her waist. "Might be worth getting your dress muddy for, eh?"

"I'm going to go see what he wants," I said loudly, pushing open the carriage door before we had completely stopped moving.

"Oh, I'll bet you are," Zaira chuckled.

I picked my way across the muddy road toward the rock on which Kathe stood. I could feel the eyes of our escort on me, Sergeant Andra's hard stare, even the curious horses—and especially Marcello, who sat still dripping on his bay mare. The crow on Kathe's shoulder watched me approach for a moment, then gently nipped the Witch Lord's ear and took off. Its wings beat the air with ponderous grace as it sailed to a nearby pine tree.

Kathe turned to face me, the yellow rings in his eyes standing out as one bright splash of color in the gray landscape.

"There you are. Come on, there's someone you should meet." He hopped down from the rock, his cloak rising about him like wings.

I glanced back at the two dozen soldiers staring at us. "Is it far? And hello, I'm delighted to see you, too."

Kathe grinned. "Far enough to make your guards worried, but I'm afraid you have to come alone."

He certainly knew how to reassure a lady. "And who would I be meeting?"

"It's a surprise." He held out his hand. "This isn't a trap, I promise."

I regarded his slim, elegant fingers dubiously. This was a terrible idea. My Callamornish cousins used to make up grim and gruesome stories about children coaxed off into the wilderness by Witch Lords in disguise; it had probably never occurred to them to invent a heroine foolish enough to follow one into the woods without the need for any trickery.

Kathe knew it. The gleam in his eyes dared me to come with him anyway.

I sighed. "If this ends with my bones carved into necklaces for foxes, I'm going to be very put out."

"Never fear. Foxes don't like jewelry."

I turned and waved cheerily over my shoulder. "I'll be right back," I called. "Sorry to make you wait!"

Even from fifty feet away, I could see the whites of Marcello's eyes as they widened in alarm. But I took Kathe's hand, feeling the tingle of power under my fingertips like unspent lightning, and let him guide me down a short rocky slope to a path that vanished into the gloomy forest.

"This is the part where, traditionally, I am eaten by wolves," I said lightly, to mask the racing of my heart.

"Crows, in my case," he corrected me. "Though I get along reasonably well with wolves."

The air under the pines was cool and damp, but it held a faint trace of woodsmoke from nearby houses, reminding me that this was Callamorne, not the wilds of Vaskandar. I let my shoulders relax a little. "I've read that vivomancers tend to favor a particular animal or plant they identify with most closely, even though their powers work on all of them. Is that how Witch Lords get their titles?"

"Of course. It's always easier to work with your preferred animal—like speaking in your native language, even if you know dozens of them fluently."

"What do you do if there's already a Witch Lord with your animal's name?"

Kathe's teeth gleamed in the shadows. "I imagine you'd have to kill them."

I couldn't tell if he was joking.

Soft gray light poured through the trees, and we stepped out into a forest of charred black trunks, rising like picked-over bones against the cloudy sky. A sloping hill of green stretched beneath them, knee-high trees and grasses rising up to fill the gap left by an old fire.

A woman stood among the blackened spires. A green velvet gown with cape and train flowed from her shoulders, strikingly out of place in the forest; it swept a half-circle through the coarse brush and ashy twigs behind her as she turned to face us. Her hair fell in three pale braids down to the backs of her knees, crowned by a delicate golden circlet shaped into a pattern of artfully woven briars. The mage mark shone venom green in her eyes.

"You're late," she said to Kathe in a silken voice, rich with resonance and power. Then her gaze fell on me, and her lip curled. "And what is *this*?"

I stiffened. Before I could retort, Kathe squeezed my hand and released it, offering the lady a slight bow. "Forgive me. I couldn't pass up this opportunity. My lady, may I present the Lady Amalia Cornaro. Amalia, meet the Witch Lord of Sevaeth—the Lady of Thorns."

Chapter Eleven

Kathe might as well have hit me in the face with a tree branch. I stared, stunned, the damp air crystallizing to frost in my lungs. What was an enemy Witch Lord, the dreaded Lady of Thorns herself, doing in Callamorne, half a day's ride from the capital?

The lady's eyes narrowed to poison-green slits. "Amalia *Lochaver* Cornaro? Is this a gift you bring me, Crow Lord?"

Dozens of tiny green shoots sprang up around the hem of her gown, curling skyward in graceful spirals. They sprouted thorns as they grew and began leaning in my direction.

Kathe laughed. "Hardly. Lady Amalia and I are courting. I thought you two should meet." He sounded completely, infuriatingly at ease. But then, he didn't have a Witch Lord glaring murder at him.

"Charmed," I said, clipping the word off like a withered rose.

The Lady of Thorns gave no acknowledgment that I'd spoken. "You're courting a Lochaver?" she demanded of Kathe. "What is the meaning of this? I come to discuss a deal with you in good faith, and you flaunt my enemy in front of me?"

"I can leave, if my presence is unwanted," I said. Curiosity and alarm mixed a pulse-quickening elixir in my gut, but no amount of mystery would compel me to stand here and let my adversary insult me to my face.

"I won't blame you either way," Kathe muttered, "but there's advantage to be had here, if you know how to take it." Then he raised his voice as he turned to the Lady of Thorns. "If you think a moment, I'm sure several reasons will occur to you why I might bring the Lady Amalia to our meeting. None of them involve you being rude to my guest."

"I can indeed think of several motives you might have, and they all come down to either an offer or an insult." The slim tendrils of briar vines around the Lady of Thorns' feet began slithering across the ground toward me. "Surely you would never presume to the latter. As for rudeness, if you wish, I can be entirely polite while I eviscerate her."

My legs strained with the urge to run, but I held my ground. I had to get some measure of control over this conversation before it became unrecoverable.

"I'll grant that we are enemies," I said, forcing the edge in my voice to be stern rather than afraid. "But you are alone, outside your domain, and one word from me will unleash a fire straight from the Hell of Death itself. I came here for a civil conversation, not a violent conflict. Did you not do the same?" I hoped she would answer; the question was far from rhetorical.

"You dare threaten me, you powerless worm?" the Lady of Thorns hissed. Her bramble vines reared up like cobras. My heart stumbled in panic, but I held my ground, desperately hoping Kathe would do something and not merely watch with curiosity as I was ripped apart by angry flora.

Kathe looked back and forth between us with apparent amusement. But when he spoke to the Lady of Thorns, his voice cracked like a whip. "Do you truly think this is the best way to help your daughter?"

The thorny tendrils froze, a few feet from my boot tips. "What do you mean?"

Tension crackled in the air between them. Kathe wound it

tighter with a slow, wide grin. "Why risk your purpose here in Callamorne? Besides, I could hardly overlook a grievance so significant as an attack on the woman I'm courting—and you know what I have to offer you."

Twin circles bright as poison flicked in my direction, then back to him. "If you came here to trade, then do it."

"Ah, ah." Kathe lifted a finger. "I'm not sealing any bargains until the Conclave. You'll have to wait till then if you want my cooperation. In the meantime, I know you came here to pay a call on the Queen of Callamorne—and I doubt she'll receive you if you murder her granddaughter."

The Lady of Thorns regarded him for a long moment. I watched them both narrowly, searching for any further clue of what understanding might pass between them.

Finally, she let out a sigh. The briars she'd sent toward me collapsed, withering, with her released breath. "Very well. You've made your point. We can finalize our deal at the Conclave."

"Oh, good." Kathe rubbed his hands together.

"And you, upstart Lochaver." The Lady of Thorns sneered as she turned toward me. "I'm letting you live now only out of respect for the Crow Lord. If you show such brazen cheek to me again, know that I'll send you to meet your father."

She spun with a swirl of velvet train and stalked off between two twisted black trees. A latticework of branches spread in sudden, groaning growth between them, like the slamming of a door.

My father. I felt as if I'd swallowed a coal: cold and hard for now, but harboring the potential to burst into flame.

"We'd best go quickly, before she changes her mind," Kathe murmured. "I'm not certain I can beat her if it comes to a fight."

He offered his elbow as we turned back toward the forest, but I didn't take it. "You implied you'd sell me to her," I accused.

He glanced back over his shoulder, then hurried faster

through the crunching brush. When the sound-swallowing pines engulfed us once more in their dripping shade, he said quietly, "You're Raverran. I trust you understand the principles behind letting someone think you can give them what they want."

"Like you've been doing with me," I said pointedly.

"Well, yes." He flashed me a smile. "But I've already delivered something of value to you."

"What, death threats?" I demanded. Graces, he could be infuriating.

"The best currency of all, of course. Information." He assumed a pedantic expression, spoiled by the mad yellow rings in his eyes. "Tell me, what did you learn today?"

"I learned to always ask you where exactly we're going before letting you take me anywhere!"

"Quite a valuable lesson." He nodded. "What else?"

"That the Lady of Thorns is incredibly rude and disrespectful."

"That's because you're not mage-marked." His tone grew heavy with some buried emotion. "I'm afraid there are some among my peers who believe those without magical ability to be beneath those with it. Property, not people. The Lady of Thorns is the worst of the lot."

"Lovely woman," I said through gritted teeth. The path inclined upward toward the road, but my anger drove me up the hill with far less effort than it would usually have taken me. "I also learned that she apparently wants to kill my family."

"See?" He spread his hands. "I could have told you that, I suppose, but I feel direct personal experience is the best teacher."

"Forgive my reluctance to sign up for practical lessons when the subject is powerful mages trying to murder me," I said.

"Anything else?" Kathe asked brightly.

Yes. Several things. Like what Kathe had said about her

daughter, and how it had stopped her cold. Or that she had plans to visit my grandmother, which seemed ominous given her apparent animosity for Lochavers. But we'd broken out of the trees, and Marcello waited as tense as a leashed hound by the coach, surrounded by mounted guards. I only had time for one question, and the coal smoldering in my belly demanded an answer.

I stopped and faced Kathe. "Did she kill my father?"

The animation and mischief drained out of his face, leaving his eyes bright and somber. "I don't know," he said quietly. "But I suspect she did."

A hot flood of emotions threatened to break through me in a boiling wave. I stuffed them down, for now; he might be wrong. And I couldn't do anything about it at the moment.

Still, it took me a moment to force my jaw to unlock. "You're right," I said. "It was useful information."

He bowed, with only a hint of his usual mockery. "Glad I could help. I'm sure I'll see you again soon, Amalia Cornaro."

I nodded, my neck stiff. Then I turned, smoothing my face out into a mask of serenity, and picked my way around mud puddles to the coach.

Thoughts and feelings about my father and the Lochaver family and the Lady of Thorns rattled around in my head like a handful of pebbles, shaken by the motion of the coach. Nothing had settled when, a few hours later, we first caught sight of Durantain.

The Callamornish capital spilled from a blocky stone castle at the crest of a hill down to the narrow twist of river valley at its foot, washing partway up the side of the next hill. The gray slate roofs and square construction of the houses gave it a businesslike look from afar, as if every shop and home might at any moment disgorge grim-faced warriors armed with whatever implements came to hand—and there had been times in Callamorne's history when that wasn't far from the case. The only signs that the city had changed in the past two hundred years were the tall poles of courier-lamp relay posts scattered about the hill, sending signals away from the spire that now ruined the symmetry of the castle's towers. Another sending spire jutted up from a large house near the crest of the hill: the Serene Envoy's palace, where the Empire's adviser to the queen kept his residence.

This was my father's city. He'd grown up here, in that castle on the hill, as a prince. I had few memories of him, but my time-hazed impression was that he was both more playful and more soothing than my mother, a calm presence full of bubbling good humor. It was hard to connect this rain-drenched place with my warm, faded memories of the man who'd held me on his knee and told me the story of the Dark Days, with gravelly booming voices for the demons, and rich lovely ones for the Nine Graces who taught humanity how to drive them back.

I could conceive of no reason why a Witch Lord would want to murder him. A Raverran, surely, to get at my mother. Perhaps even some misguided Callamornish patriot seeking to break the treaty that bound their country to the Empire. But a Witch Lord? My father had been the kind parent, the quiet one, full of wry compassion and threatening nobody.

When we arrived in the open square before the castle gates, a grand public reception awaited us. Ranks of royal guards stood in smart attendance, cuirasses gleaming and muskets on their shoulders. A curious crowd filled the square, children riding on their parents' shoulders in hopes of a glimpse of the royal family; the people of Callamorne adored the Lochavers, in no small part due to my grandmother's legendary heroics in conflicts with Vaskandar in her youth.

My grandmother and cousins came out to greet us. The queen cut a regal figure in her stiff leather doublet with ornamented bright steel scrolling, halfway a cuirass; a fur-trimmed mantle hung from her shoulders. Her long silver hair fell over one shoulder in a thick braid from beneath her simple circlet crown. She looked every inch a warrior, as always, ready to draw the more than ornamental sword at her side and cut down the enemies of her kingdom at any moment despite her advancing years.

As I descended the coach steps to meet them, Roland gave me a serious nod, doing his best to look suitably princely in a military-cut burgundy velvet doublet with a hundred tiny buttons down the front. Bree, by contrast, seemed poised off-balance, as if she might lunge suddenly into action at any moment—which, knowing Bree, she might. She'd pulled her hair into a messy knot at the back of her head and wore a gorgeous copper-and-russet brocade half-cloak slung off one shoulder, over a simple cream-colored tunic dress with split sleeves and sides, leaving her limbs unencumbered. I suspected she could move in it quite freely.

"Amalia!" Bree called, and ran to give me a fierce hug. "It's good to see you." Roland clasped my shoulder, with more decorum.

My grandmother swept piercing gray eyes across my companions; they lingered on Zaira, who stretched and yawned as she climbed out of the carriage, her jess catching the light.

"Welcome home," she said in a deep voice that rolled out like thunder over the crowd. Cheering greeted this pronouncement, and I felt an odd, guilty pang: Raverra was home. Callamorne, with its straightforward blocky grayness, was a foreign country.

Under cover of the crowd's cheering, I murmured to my family, "The Lady of Thorns is in Callamorne and intends to pay you some sort of unspecified visit, Grandmother."

The queen's eyes narrowed. "Come inside, then, and we'll talk."

"... So she's a short distance from Durantain, and the Crow Lord said she'd come to 'pay a call,'" I concluded urgently, after telling my family everything from our suspicions that she'd planted a traitor among us to my unexpected meeting with the Lady of Thorns. We stood clustered in the castle courtyard, while grooms bustled to take our horses and those of our escort off to the stables for a well-earned rest.

My grandmother exchanged glances with Roland. "That's not as unusual as you might think. Our relationship with Vaskandar is... complicated. Since their personal power makes them virtually invulnerable, when a Witch Lord takes it into their head that they have something to say to us, they often just walk right up over the mountains and say it."

"Given that she's preparing for war, I don't like it," Roland said, his brows drawing a line of concern across his forehead. "Vivomancers don't have many offensive options in stone cities, but she may have brought hidden forces with her."

"I'll increase the guard and arm them with defenses against vivomancy, just in case," my grandmother said. "And tell them not to let her in if she shows up unannounced."

Roland gave Zaira a small smile. "At any rate, I suspect even a Witch Lord would hesitate to start a fight with a fire warlock in residence."

Zaira curtsied. "All-powerful murderous mages deterred. Free service with room and board."

We barely had time to settle into our guest rooms and bathe before dinner, which was always a grand and disquietingly public affair in the royal court of Callamorne. The whole castle broke bread at the same time in a great, high-arched hall hung with banners and tapestries that fell the full three stories from ceiling to floor.

Callamorne's meticulous attention to rank and precedence put me at the royal table with my family. They'd seated Zaira with me; whether because she was my Falcon or out of deference to her ability to destroy entire cities if she became vexed, I couldn't guess. Marcello and the other Falcons and Falconers had been placed at the high tables that flanked us at right angles, too far away for conversation.

Roland, as the heir, sat at the queen's right hand. But my grandmother was deep in discussion of defense planning with the Serene Envoy, which left him and Bree free to converse with Zaira and me.

"So, how have you been?" Bree asked. "We've heard some wild rumors here. That you murdered the Duke of Ardence—"

"You've heard that *here*?" I exclaimed, dismayed. "I didn't kill him! I was framed."

"—and drove Prince Ruven of Vaskandar out of the Empire with balefire—"

"I would have loved to," Zaira grumbled. "But no, she just threatened him."

"—and that you're courting the Crow Lord." Bree laughed and shook her head.

I shifted in my chair. "Ah, well, as to that..."

Bree and Roland both stared at me, eyes gone wide as wine cups.

"It's true." Zaira sighed. "There's no accounting for taste, but maybe his options were limited in Vaskandar."

"You're joking," Roland said, shock or disapproval flattening his voice. "You can't be serious."

"Is that going to be a problem here?" I asked, worried. "I didn't think of the political ramifications in Callamorne. I know there can be a certain, ah, animosity toward mages here."

Zaira raised an eyebrow. "Oh, *really*?"

"Only among idiots," Bree grumbled. "But every country has a fair number of those."

"It's why our father had to abdicate as Grandmother's heir, and never comes to Durantain." Roland kept his voice low, glancing at the nobles seated at the other high tables. "Everyone accepted Grandfather as king because he was only Grandmother's consort, but neither our people nor Raverra would be pleased to see a ruling vivomancer on the throne."

Bree scowled and stabbed her table knife into the slice of roast on her plate. "If he cared about his family, he wouldn't let stupid politics keep him at the far end of Callamorne. He'd be here, with us, and if anyone was nasty to him we'd make them choke on it."

Roland cleared his throat. "Be that as it may, I think you'll be all right, Amalia. The people remember that Grandmother's marriage stopped a war. They'll understand."

"And are your people going to say things to me that make me punch them in the face?" Zaira growled.

"Oh, no." Roland waved his hands. "The prejudice in Callamorne is only against vivomancers, because we've suffered so much at their hands in war. Everyone loves warlocks."

Zaira blinked. "That's a new one."

"The first known storm warlocks ruled Callamorne over a thousand years ago," I explained. "It was the height of Callamorne's power, before the rise of the Serene Empire or even the Witch Lords. The Storm Queens of Callamorne ravaged every coastline in Eruvia and were responsible for the fall of ancient Osta."

"I don't think anyone outside Callamorne looks back on them

fondly," Roland admitted. "But no one should give you trouble. Given what the Witch Lords have waiting for us across the border, everyone feels much better with a fire warlock on our side."

"What *do* they have waiting?" I nudged my glass, as if shifting its angle might magically cause it to be filled with wine rather than the beer they seemed to prefer in Callamorne. "I've only seen markers on a map."

"Chimeras," he said darkly. "All manner of creatures twisted to new forms by the Witch Lords' magic."

Bree spread her hands with evident relish. "Picture venomous bears the size of horses. Wolves with rat tails and porcupine quills. Leopards with lizard skin and rows of teeth like a shark. Great clouds of razor-winged moths that suck your blood."

"You haven't seen anything like that!" Roland said.

"Oh, how would you know?" Bree turned to me. "He hasn't been to the border. He's not expendable, like some of us."

"Go on, rub it in, that you get to lap up the glory while I'm stuck at court," Roland said tartly. "But you *still* haven't seen all that."

"So," I asked Roland tentatively, "are you saying the chimeras *aren't* like that? My reading suggests that what Bree describes is possible for a sufficiently powerful vivomancer, but I'm dubious anyone could create enough of them to fill the ranks of an army."

"Not whole armies of them, no," Roland said. "Individuals and small packs. It doesn't take many to cause a lot of chaos, especially when they're backed up by musketeers and pikemen. They break your lines with the chimeras, or get them over the walls of a fortress, and then the human troops come behind to clean up."

Bree turned to Zaira and me, assuming a pompous expression. "You'd best listen to Roland. He is the Anointed Heir, and he Knows Things."

Here they go. Hopefully they were old enough not to wind up hitting each other this time.

"Hmph." Roland crossed his arms. "You'd know things, too, if you didn't skip strategy meetings to go drinking and carousing in the worst parts of town until all hours of the night."

"I must correct you, Roland," Bree said haughtily. "Those are the *best* parts of town."

Zaira snickered and clinked her glass against Bree's.

After the last apple cakes were cleared away and half the great hall emptied, those who lingered milled about and talked with each other. Bree grabbed a pitcher of beer from a passing server and descended to the lower tables, throwing herself into the thickest crowd with the excitement of a dog leaping into a duck pond. Zaira went to join Terika, while Roland and I remained at the high table.

"I can't believe they're letting *you* go to the border, but not me," Roland muttered, taking a sip of beer as he watched the people below greet his sister with unmistakable enthusiasm.

"Only because they have to. No one wants to let the heir do anything," I commiserated.

"It's supposed to be different in Callamorne. A Lochaver is supposed to put their life on the line for their people." He gestured toward our grandmother with his mug, dropping his voice. "Like she did at the Battle of Ironblood Bridge. There's a song about that, you know."

"I know." Roland had sung it to me first, when we were both small, with great seriousness and passion, before we played a game acting out the battle. He was the queen, and Bree and I were the charging Vaskandran invaders.

"I'm never going to prove myself worthy to my people if

Grandmother keeps me safe in Durantain all the time." Roland's voice held a faint trace of uncertainty that I knew too well. It wasn't his people he had to convince of his worth, I suspected; it was himself.

"There are other ways to be worthy besides in battle," I said. "Otherwise, I'd be hopeless."

Roland sighed. "Battle is my *best* hope. I'm not good with people. Not like Bree is."

Below us, Bree already had half the hall gathered around her, Raverran officers and Callamornish castle folk alike, holding mugs and engaged in some uproarious conversation. Everyone was smiling and laughing.

"Look at her," Roland murmured. "She can walk into a room and make everyone love her within five minutes."

"It's not a talent I have, myself," I admitted. "I'm lucky if I can leave a party with one or two people thinking I'm somewhat pleasant."

Roland gave me an understanding glance. "You're a step ahead of me. All I can manage at parties is to stand in a corner and try to look princely."

"Maybe we should go down there and mingle, too," I said, with some trepidation. I was supposed to be here to reassure the Callamornish people, after all.

Alarm flashed in Roland's eyes. "Or we could sit here awhile longer. We have so much to discuss."

I raised an eyebrow. "You're scared of them, aren't you?"

"No! Of course not." Roland grimaced, and pushed his napkin away from him on the table. "Well, yes."

"Of your own people?"

"*Any* people," Roland said. "If I went down there, I wouldn't know what to do. I'd feel stiff and stupid, and everything I did would be the wrong thing."

"Not to them, it wouldn't," I said.

"But it would to me. And then I'd beat myself up for it for days or months, running through in my head again and again everything I did wrong."

"Ah, I see." I nodded sagely. "You're expecting yourself to be a fine, majestic Lochaver prince, and so you're upset when you're not as perfect as you think you should be. Do what I do: expect yourself to be a complete disaster, and then if you manage not to trip over your own bootlaces you can count it a resounding success."

Roland laughed. "You might be on to something."

Still, he made no move to descend from the high table.

I sat with him until the crowd in the great hall thinned and Roland got drawn into conversation with the queen and a handful of lingering advisers. Then I rose from the table at last and wandered through the shadow-hung hall to the spot my eyes had been avoiding all through dinner.

I stared up at my father's portrait. Candles burned at a small shrine beneath it, flanking a single fresh remembrance lily. It had been easy not to glance this way, since I was seated facing another direction, but a part of my mind had never forgotten his portrait was here, watching. It felt inevitable that I stood before it now, as if my father had been waiting patiently for me to finish what I was doing and come visit.

The painting didn't look like him. His pose was too stiff, with one hand resting on a scroll and the other on the hilt of a sword—which itself was ridiculous, since so far as I knew, my father had never fought anyone in his life. His expression was too wooden and distant, almost bored. Time had blurred my memories of him, like water spilled across an ink painting, but I was sure his face had always been in motion: smiling kindly down at me, laughing, winking at some mischief we were getting into of which my mother might not approve. Grimacing when she inevitably caught us. This still, flat image wasn't right. It wasn't him.

Boots rang on the stone floor. My grandmother, Queen Galanthe Lochaver, the Hero of the Ironblood Bridge, blessed of the Grace of Victory, strode toward me, her face grim as if she went to face the Witch Lords in battle once more. But then she looked up at her son's portrait, and her face softened.

"I miss him every day, you know," she said.

I squeezed my eyes shut, remembering how I used to run giggling toward the closed drawing room door when my mother was having some dreadfully serious policy meeting just so my father would scoop me up in his warm arms and tuck me under his chin, scolding me gently. *We can't disturb your mother now. Come on, let's go to the library and pick out a book . . .*

I opened my eyes to find my grandmother watching me. "I wish I remembered him well enough to miss him every day."

She clapped a hand on my shoulder with gruff sympathy. "You do, you know. With the way you smile, the way you look at something that makes you curious, the way you slouch in your seat when you think no one's looking. You remember him in a thousand little habits and actions and expressions."

Graces, I was *not* going to cry. I swallowed. "Thank you."

She looked away, giving me a moment. Her eyes fell on Roland, where he sat talking with the Serene Envoy at the high table, and softened with fondness. She let out a long breath. "I overheard a few words of what Roland was saying to you. I wish he understood why I'm holding him back from danger."

"He wants so badly to show you he's good enough," I said softly. It was a feeling I understood far too well.

"Of course he's good enough." My grandmother's voice went a touch indignant, as if I'd said otherwise. "I just can't risk losing him. He's the only possible heir."

"Bree isn't so bad," I objected. "I know she's not exactly a polished courtier, but—"

"That's not the problem." The queen turned grave eyes on me. "Brisintain is a vivomancer."

"Bree?!" The word burst out of me louder than it should have. I reined in my voice. "I never…" But I trailed off, remembering a few incidents when we were children. A trick she'd shown me in the castle orchard, hitting a tree just so to make a ripe apple fall into your hand; I'd never been able to duplicate it. The time she'd soothed a panicked horse in seconds by speaking its name gently, or how insects never seemed to bite her even when they swarmed the rest of us on muggy summer days.

"She's not mage-marked, like her father," my grandmother said, "so the Empire might not insist she abdicate, like they did for Carrogan; but the Callamornish people have fought vivomancers trying to seize our country for too long to hand the throne to one willingly. We've hidden her abilities all this time." She sighed. "I'm afraid your grandfather was too strong, and the magic in his blood has bred truer than I'd hoped."

"Grandfather." Everything seemed to come back to this man I'd never met. Bree's magic, the Lady of Thorns' enmity, Kathe's and Ruven's interest—and perhaps even my father's death. "He was a Witch Lord's son?"

The queen nodded. "His mother was the Lady of Eagles."

I searched my memory of the books I'd read. "That's the title of the Witch Lord of Atruin, the most central domain in Vaskandar."

"Yes." Pride straightened my grandmother's shoulders. "She's one of the strongest Witch Lords. When I married Vandrin, that put a stop to the attacks across our border. That's probably why you got the impression the Lady of Thorns doesn't like us; she and Vandrin used to be allies. She may have considered it a betrayal when he sided with Callamorne in the end. But no matter how angry she was at Vandrin, she didn't dare risk his mother's ire."

"But now she's preparing to invade again. And the Wolf Lord, too."

The queen pressed her lips together, then nodded. "The Lady of Eagles is highly neutral about everything and keeps to her own domain. After Vandrin passed, the other Witch Lords knew she wouldn't interfere on behalf of her more distant descendants, and Callamorne became fair game again. It's why we needed the Serene Empire's protection. And why the Lady of Thorns can target the Lochaver line with impunity."

I glanced over at Bree, in her crowd of friends, and then at Roland, who sat alone now, staring glumly into his mug. "You should let Roland go to the border anyway," I said, my voice low. "Maybe not into true danger, if you think you can't risk him. But he told me that a Lochaver puts their life on the line for their people. You should let him help."

For a long time, my grandmother didn't say anything. I thought perhaps I'd gone too far. But then she passed a hand over her brow. "I know," she whispered.

"Then why don't you?"

"I can't keep you all safe. I know that." The pain in her eyes was old, deep, and harrowing, and I shied away from looking at it. That was my father, shadowing her gray gaze. That was the shape of the empty space in our lives where he should stand. "But perhaps, just perhaps, I can protect one of you." She patted my shoulder, with brisk affection. "Now, go get some sleep. You have a long day tomorrow."

The queen wasn't exaggerating. With only one full day to show me off as a living token of the Serene Empire's commitment before I had to leave for Mount Whitecrown, she'd created a packed schedule for me. I met the nobles of the court, made public appearances before large crowds in the city, visited temples to the Graces, and met so many dignitaries they all blended together in an endless blur. At first it was terrifying, but I went numb quickly enough.

Everywhere I went, as I bowed and smiled and made variations on the same brief speech, I kept encountering reminders of my father. His memorial stele in the remembrance garden outside the Temple of Love caught my eye across the crowds as I made a public appearance in the Temple Square. The Lord Marshal sighed and told me how much I looked like him. I was introduced to a group of barons as "Prince Embran's daughter." And everywhere I went, I kept thinking how my father's eyes had fallen on the same scenes, and his feet had walked the same stones, and I wondered what he'd thought and hoped and wished for when he was my age.

By the time I returned to my room for a brief respite before a formal reception in my honor to be held in the castle that evening, I was feeling somewhat melancholy.

At least in Callamorne, a day of formal events didn't require a corset. I kicked off my boots and stretched on a divan in my sitting room, surrounded by faded old tapestries depicting violent and tragic Callamornish legends, and considered whether to distract myself with reading or go next door to see if Zaira might be willing to talk. Given how she'd grumbled about being dragged all over the city with me today, and the firm tones with which she'd stated her intent to take a bath and a nap, I rather doubted it.

A gentle knocking sounded not at my door, but at the floor-to-ceiling shutters that led to my balcony overlooking the gardens.

I rose, drawing my knife, and tensed to listen.

Nothing. Perhaps it had simply been a windblown branch, or a bird?

Knock, knock. "Lady Amalia?"

Graces preserve me. It was Kathe.

Chapter Twelve

I flung open the shutters, my dagger still in hand, and found him crouched on the stone railing of the little balcony, his feathered cloak hanging down behind him. The wind ruffled his black-tipped hair.

He broke into a grin. "There you are!"

I leaned on the door frame, a certain giddy weakness flooding my limbs that was not exactly relief. "Yes. Here I am, because this is my room. So it makes sense that I'm here. Whereas it makes no sense whatsoever that you're here."

He raised his brows. "I heard they're throwing a formal reception for you this evening, so of course I stopped by on my way back to Let."

"Of course you did." I glanced past him into the castle garden. Guards patrolled the battlements of the thick outer stone wall, and my balcony was a good twenty-five feet off the ground. I rather suspected my grandmother would have mentioned if she had a Witch Lord as an expected guest. "I'd invite you in, but I don't want to compromise someone else's wards without their permission."

I stepped out onto the balcony with him instead, to be friendly, but regretted it almost at once; there wasn't much space, and we were quite close. My pulse quickened—nerves, I told myself.

"Another thing we don't have in Vaskandar. But then, I don't need wards in my own domain." He leaped down from the railing, graceful as a cat. Now barely a foot separated us. His lips curved in a mischievous smile. "I'm glad you still trust me enough to meet with me alone like this. I was worried, after the Lady of Thorns was so rude to you."

"I'm a Cornaro. Our trust is always conditional." I lifted an eyebrow. "Though perhaps you're only interested in my Lochaver blood."

"My lady, I assure you that both sides of your legacy fascinate me. But what we two can do together is most intriguing of all."

I gripped the railing to keep my balance. I didn't know how to begin to peel back the layers on this man. "And what is it you hope we could accomplish?"

"Oh, all manner of things. The possibilities are wide as the sky and deep as the sea." He cocked his head. "I'd say you should come visit my domain, to know me better. But you'd have to pass through Kazerath or Sevaeth to get there, and you might not make it alive."

"Perhaps we could meet somewhere," I suggested, feeling daring. "Like at the Conclave."

He laughed, the feathers on his shoulders rustling. "The Conclave! Strike at the heart to slay the beast, eh? I'd love to see the stir if I brought you along. The Lady of Thorns would tear the mountains themselves with her rage."

"Is that an invitation?" I pressed. "You did imply you could bring me as your guest."

"You're far too eager to fling yourself into that nest of chimeras." Kathe shook his head. "Vaskandran politics are different than your little games of gold and poison. You don't even know the rules."

"I could learn."

He caught my hand in his, quick as a snake, and panic flashed white-hot through my chest. But he only turned it in his cold, graceful fingers, examining it as if it were a gem of some worth. "In Raverra," he asked thoughtfully, "what do people want from you?"

"Money," I said at once. Half of me wanted to snatch my hand back, and the other half hoped he didn't let go. His touch left a strange tingling in its wake, less unpleasant than Prince Ruven's twisted magic. "And influence. A shortcut to my mother's power, and the doge's ear."

He traced the scar on the back of my wrist, from an assassin's dagger long ago. "And what do *I* want from you?"

I stared into the vivid yellow rings around his pupils. "That," I said, "is a fine question."

"You don't know." He released my hand. "You can't win a game if you don't know the stakes your opponent is playing for. What do you think a Witch Lord wants?"

Graces have mercy. I didn't know what to do with him—his glittering eyes, the haughty planes of his face, the power that thrummed in the air around him, all far too close on this wretched balcony. It didn't help that I wasn't so certain I *wanted* more space between us.

"Power," I guessed, rubbing my hand. "But that means something different for you than it would for me."

"We're all fighting for the same prize." He tilted his head. "Do you know the secret of a Witch Lord's power? What makes us so much more than a mere normal vivomancer?"

I leaned in eagerly, my pulse quickening. "Tell me."

His eyes gleamed. "You tell *me*. When you can, I'll take you to the Conclave."

Of course he couldn't answer the question he'd posed himself. He had to make it a challenge—in this case, a magical theory challenge.

Good. That was my specialty.

"I'll hold you to that," I warned, smiling fiercely.

"Please do. I'd love to see what you might unleash there." He drew closer, bending until his breath stirred the hair by my ear. "Here's a hint for you."

His voice dropped to a whisper, taking on a mesmerizing, singsong quality.

"One lord, all alone
Ten spires made of bone
One realm circles round
All roots underground
Ten streams through it all
One wood growing tall
All things quick with life
One sharp, bloody knife
Ten drops fall on stone
One lord on the throne."

A delicate chill settled over me like mist. "Is that a riddle?"

"A rhyme the Yew Lord sang to his children." He drew back, his eyes shuttered and solemn. "And they to theirs, and my mother to me."

A nervous, breathless laugh escaped my lips. "It's hard to imagine you having a mother."

"Even Witch Lords are born, and even Witch Lords can die."

A knock sounded on the door to my rooms, far more diffident than Kathe's had been. "Lady Amalia," a servant called. "I'm here to help you prepare for the ball."

I turned and called to the door, "One moment."

When I swiveled back to Kathe, some word forming on my lips, he was gone. A breeze swept across the balcony railing, brushing away any invisible trace of him. He might have been nothing but a vision of madness.

Balls in Durantain were more ceremonial affairs than in Raverra. A herald announced arriving guests in order of rank, from lowest to highest, and everyone needed an escort. While the heralds worked their way through the lesser nobility, the royal family and honored guests gathered in a private antechamber with comfortable seats, a platter of fruit, and chilled beer (again, much to my dismay), attempting to work out who was escorting whom at the last minute.

"I'm with Terika," Zaira announced, wrapping an arm around Terika's waist. "The rest of you lot can draw straws for all I care."

Marcello was with Istrella, awaiting introduction in another antechamber, somewhere after the lesser gentry. Zaira's presence had occasioned endless argument among the court heralds over what her effective rank should be, since she technically had no title but clearly merited some special attention as the sole fire warlock in Eruvia and a person well capable of burning Durantain to the ground if offended. They'd finally decided that her close connection to a member of the royal family and her status as an honored guest from the Serene Empire meant she could be introduced just before the royalty without offending any but the stuffiest aristocrats.

"I'm stuck with *him*," Bree complained, elbowing Roland. "I wanted to bring a lad I met in a tavern last week, but Grandmother said no."

I eyed my grandmother, uncertain.

"I always enter alone," she said. "In your grandfather's honor." She frowned. "We need to find someone for you, Amalia."

I hadn't even thought of arranging an escort; I'd been too distracted worrying about the inevitable speech I'd have to give. I waved my hands. "I can come in by myself, too. It's all right."

"It's a custom," my grandmother said, with severe gravity. "It would show disrespect to my guest and my granddaughter to let you enter alone."

"Really, I don't mind."

The queen tapped her lips. "Perhaps one of the march lords, or a general. Anyone would be honored. I'm sure we can find someone."

"No need!"

We all turned toward the new voice.

It was Kathe. Of course it was Kathe, brushing off a flustered guard as he strode into the room, feathered cloak swirling, eyes dancing. "The Lady Amalia and I are courting, after all. There could be no more appropriate escort."

Bree and Roland gaped. Zaira appraised Kathe openly; Terika and she exchanged an appreciative look, and heat crept up my neck. *Grace of Mercy, don't say anything, Zaira. Please.*

My grandmother's stony gaze didn't waver. "The Crow Lord of Let. I was unaware we would have the honor of your presence at this occasion."

He bowed, forcing the queen to return a deep, respectful nod. It would take an expert at protocol to figure out which of them outranked the other.

"I'm gratified to hear it, Your Majesty. I do try to avoid being predictable."

"Announcing the Lady Amalia Lochaver Cornaro, Princess of Callamorne, heir to the Council of Nine; and her escort, the Crow Lord, Witch Lord of Let."

The herald's artifice-amplified voice almost cracked, and his eyes bulged as if he couldn't believe the words coming out of his mouth. Every face in the room turned to stare at us as we stood framed in the curtained entryway to the cavernous great hall, the sea of courtiers hushed to stunned silence.

I was used to having eyes on me, as La Contessa's eligible daughter, but a room of a few hundred people openly staring at me was a new experience. At once, I became paralyzingly aware of every part of my body.

Kathe's arm shook in mine from repressed laughter. "Look at their faces. This was a bit out of my way, but oh, it was worth it."

Most of the nobility and dignitaries in the crowd wore the more sober fashions and muted colors of Callamorne: deep plum and navy, forest green and chocolate brown and charcoal gray, all in fine wool or velvet with only modest touches of lace. Some, especially the younger set, sported the more flamboyant embroidered silks and brocades of Raverran fashion, in brighter colors, with a sprinkling of jewel tones like bright flowers poking up through a winter garden. But all of them wore the same expressions of open surprise and shock.

No one had warned them a Witch Lord would be attending the reception. I could sympathize.

I tried to school my expression into something calm, regal, and reassuring, as if of course I knew exactly what I was doing and was in complete control of the situation. It was my mission to give these people confidence that the Empire had their backs, and by all the Graces, I wasn't going to let Kathe's mischief undermine that.

I held up my skirts as we paced our stately way down the steps to the great hall floor. Just before we descended to the level of the crowd, I spotted Marcello and Istrella; the latter waved enthusiastically, grinning. Marcello tried on a wan smile, but it sat poorly on his strained face.

Good Graces. I hadn't meant to flaunt Kathe in front of him without warning.

Then the swirl of people pressed around us. The guests nearest us recovered admirably from their surprise and offered me words of welcome, not without alarmed glances at my escort, before opening a certain space around us. The heralds proceeded to announce Bree and Roland, providing enough of a distraction that I could move away from the densest part of the crowd, Kathe still chuckling at my side.

"This isn't funny," I murmured. "I'm here to help them not be afraid."

"That's perfect. You can help them not be afraid of me. It'll be like practice for more dangerous Witch Lords."

I couldn't tell if he was serious.

All around us, ball guests gathered and hesitated, like bees dancing around something they weren't yet sure was a flower. I was the guest of honor, so everyone wanted to talk to me, but with Kathe at my side, even the bold people of Callamorne had to gather up their courage before approaching us. Kathe's yellow-ringed stare and sharp grin didn't help put anyone at ease.

It was up to me. I tried on a gracious smile and extended my hand to the first noble I recognized. "Lady Maroc! So pleased to see you again!"

She broke into a tentative smile, and the atmosphere around us relaxed a little. Courtiers took turns stepping up to exchange a few pleasantries; Kathe nodded at them but said little. I did my best to project reassuring confidence, to offset his unsettling presence, approaching people with a warm smile if they hesitated to step up themselves.

My inner fuming at Kathe's interference was only stronger for the knowledge that without the need to counteract the nervous fear his presence fostered, I'd never have worked the room this actively or come across so confident. I wondered if he was doing it on purpose.

Finally, between greetings, Kathe let out a sigh. "This is dreadfully boring. How do you stand it?"

"It's my job. Do you not have a royal court in Let?" I asked, curious.

"Not like this. I have my Heartguard, who are advisers, guards, and companions; and I have my Seconds, who manage various aspects of my domain for me. But they don't hang about the castle going to parties and gossiping. We're very informal." He lifted his eyes to the banner-hung ceiling far above us. "I think my entire castle could almost fit in this room. Not quite, but nearly."

"That sounds..." I searched for the right word.

"Provincial?" He raised an eyebrow.

"Relaxing," I said.

Kathe laughed. "Oh, we find ways to keep busy. My Seconds tell me I need to stop trying to solve every problem in the domain with my own two hands."

Another guest angled his way through the crowd, approaching us; I turned to offer a courteous greeting and found myself face-to-face with Marcello.

Determination set his jaw in rigid lines as he stood before Kathe at last. Hells, I wasn't ready for this.

Chapter Thirteen

Marcello looked from me to Kathe and back again, and he bowed. "Lady Amalia. Lord Kathe."

"Ah," I said, my voice high and strained. "Kathe, allow me to introduce my good friend, Captain Marcello Verdi."

Marcello nodded, meeting Kathe's eyes unflinchingly. "I wanted to meet the man who's courting my friend."

"I see." Kathe's grin broadened. "I suppose you're wondering what my intentions are toward the Lady Amalia?"

"Perhaps," Marcello said. But his eyes flicked to mine, not Kathe's, a question in them.

Kathe put a dramatic hand to his chest. "Are you concerned for the lady's honor? Worried I might take advantage of her?"

I gouged his ribs with my elbow. He might be a Witch Lord, but there were limits.

But Marcello only laughed. "Not in the slightest. The Lady Amalia can guard her own honor, and I doubt very much anyone in Vaskandar has the necessary skills to take advantage of a Cornaro."

Kathe tipped a respectful nod in my direction. "At least, no more than she takes advantage of me."

I wished I shared Marcello's confidence in my political prowess. But his questioning gaze reassured me that he had no intention of starting a fight; he was checking to make sure I needed no rescue. I gave him a small nod and a flicker of a smile.

"When two parties take mutual advantage of each other, I believe it's called an alliance," I said.

"Then you see this as a political maneuver, Lord Kathe? It's only a game?" Marcello's spine relaxed a little as he asked it, as if this were a relief.

Kathe shrugged. "If a thing has rules, and players, and is entertaining, that makes it a game. But I might take exception at your use of the word *only*. Games are often deadly serious."

"Suffice to say," I said firmly, "that Kathe and I both understood the rules when we sat down to the table." I caught Marcello's eyes and tried to convey a message: *I'm fine. I can handle this.*

Never mind that in truth I wasn't at all certain I could handle Kathe. But here, in Callamorne, where he was out of place and I was surrounded by allies, I'd manage.

"And you, Captain?" Kathe turned glittering eyes on Marcello. "Do you consider yourself a player, or a pawn?"

Marcello snorted. "Lord Kathe, I'm a soldier. I signed up to be a pawn a long time ago. So long as I trust the one making the moves, I'm content."

"And do you?"

Marcello met my eyes. "Absolutely."

His faith in me pierced my heart with sweet pain.

I expected Kathe to respond with some quip, but to my surprise, his face fell into serious lines. "You are fortunate indeed, Lady Amalia, to be gifted with such loyalty."

"I know," I said, wishing I could tell Marcello with a glance how much I meant it.

Kathe lifted his head, suddenly, like a hound hearing barking in the distance.

"Is something wrong?" I asked.

A slight frown creased the space between his brows. "Such a

subjective word, *wrong*. Most people use it to mean something they don't like."

"Well, then, is something wrong by that definition?"

His gaze met mine, and sharpened, returning abruptly from a distance. He showed his teeth in a grin. "Oh, yes. Most certainly." He released my arm. "My apologies, but I should look into this. I'll return soon."

Marcello and I stared after his feather-cloaked back as he bowed and departed.

"I wonder what that was about," he murmured.

"I'm not certain whether I'm more concerned that we won't find out, or that we will."

That earned me a wry smile, and it struck me at once that we were alone together. If one could call it alone when we stood among a sea of Callamornish nobles, some of whom had already begun to look hopefully in my direction now that Kathe was gone.

Marcello noticed them, too; he grimaced. "Is there anywhere more private we can talk for a moment?"

I needed to talk to those people. But, I realized with a pang, I'd also put off talking to Marcello far too long. I cast around the crowded hall. "Short of hiding behind a banner, I think the best we can do is find a relatively empty corner. We can't exactly sneak off at a reception in my honor."

He sighed. "All right, let's see what we can find."

As we maneuvered through the crowd, nodding and smiling, I asked him, "Where's Istrella?"

"With Lienne," he said, waving toward a bank of narrow windows looking out over the gardens. "She felt the castle wards were below her standards and is designing improvements even now."

Lienne. I'd never mentioned to Marcello my suspicions that she might be the traitor; I had no evidence, beyond her dispatching the assassin, which she'd done on his orders. But she and Istrella stood in full view of the hall, Lienne nodding as Istrella gestured and pointed. She seemed safe enough. And I couldn't run away from this conversation any longer.

When we reached a corner shielded by a couple of empty tables from the worst of the crowds, Marcello stopped. He regarded my face for a long time, as if committing it to memory, and let out a long sigh.

"What?" I asked, fighting embarrassment.

"Your Crow Lord isn't like Prince Ruven." Relief colored his voice.

"I should hope not! I wouldn't court a murderous lunatic."

"I understand that you need to do this." He ruffled a hand through his hair, as if he could scrub away his own discomfort. "It's part of your duty, and it's your choice. I wanted you to know that I respect that, and I'll wait."

A pang struck deep in my chest. I'd almost hoped he would argue with me; that would have been easier. "I don't know how long this will go on. Or if there'll be another political courtship after. Some suitors might not mind if I had another lover, but I can't make that assumption and close off a potential alliance."

He nodded. "I'll wait," he said again, grimly. "Months or years. You're worth waiting for, Amalia. But..." His throat jumped in a swallow. "Can you promise me something?" he whispered.

A knot tangled in my stomach. "There are very few promises I can make in this life, Marcello."

He stepped closer, his green eyes catching gleams from the luminary on the wall beside us. "Take however long you need, to do what you must to protect the Serene Empire. But when it's over—when you've danced all your dances and the music is done—promise me we can be together. Promise me there's a future for us, and I'll wait for that future, even if it doesn't come until I'm an old man."

For a moment, bittersweet joy flashed in my heart, brief and bright as lightning. I hadn't lost him by agreeing to court Kathe. He would wait.

It would be so easy to promise. It was what I wanted: to escape this political courtship and any that followed it unscathed by serious commitment, and finally hold Marcello in my arms without worrying about the political ramifications. To let myself simply love him, rather than carefully picking out any affection that seemed too romantic while trying to keep the warmth of friendship. To kiss him again, without the desperation that came with the approach of death; to confess my worries to him, and to hear his, and to protect each other from the cruel turning of the world.

But making that promise would be a lie.

"I can't," I breathed.

He winced, as if I'd struck him.

"I want to, but I can't." I closed my hands into fists, so I wouldn't reach for him. "My *plan* is to use courtship as a tool and a weapon while I can—while I must—and then to follow my heart once I can lay that weapon down. But I don't know what the future holds, Marcello." I shook my head. "What if I need to make a political marriage? To annex one of the island kingdoms, perhaps, or to secure the support to make my Falcon reform act into law and save thousands of future children from conscription? Would you really tell me to put what *I* want ahead of those children's freedom?"

"No. Of course not. But..." He took a moment and rubbed his forehead, eyes averted. When he turned his face to me again, shadows seemed to cling to the hollows of it. "Where does that leave me, Amalia? I don't know what to feel. If you tell me to give up hope, I will. If you tell me to just be your friend, I will, gladly. But this—not knowing whether to hope or not—I don't know what to do."

It struck me like a punch to the gut that I could lose him. He said he would wait, and I had no doubt that he would; but nothing waited forever. The tide changed, the sun set, and love faded. A man could only hold his breath so long before he had to let it go.

Or even if he waited for years and years, what then? An image came to mind of the Temple of Love in Raverra, all decked out in flowers for a royal wedding, and me standing crowned in roses at the altar. And Marcello, staring from the shadows at the back of the temple with broken green eyes for a moment before he turned his back and walked out the temple doors, throwing his long shadow behind him.

If I refused to make a choice, if I drew this out for year after year, it could destroy us.

"You're right," I said softly. "I have to decide." Either I was willing to sacrifice my chance of happiness with Marcello for the Serene Empire, or I wasn't.

"Not now," he said hastily, lifting his hands. "I don't need an answer right now."

"I understand." I gathered my velvet jacket more tightly around me, feeling the chill of autumn in the drafty stone hall. "I need time, Marcello. But one way or another, I..." I forced the words out, knowing full well what they could mean. "I won't make you wait forever for an answer."

He smiled, relief breaking over his face like a sunrise. As if I hadn't just uttered a terrible thing, a dream-breaking thing, opening the door to an ending for all that lay between us.

"That's all I ask," he said, and bowed with graceful precision.

It took a full glass of beer before I was ready to dive back into my duties at the reception. But I was here to reassure the leadership of Callamorne of the Serene Empire's commitment to defend their country, and now that Kathe and Marcello were done disrupting my evening, I was going to do that, by the Grace of Majesty.

I circulated through the party, talking with as many people as I could. Yes, the Empire was dedicated to the defense of Callamorne. Naturally I would ensure that Raverra kept its promises, as a Lochaver myself. Of course Zaira would unleash her balefire if Vaskandar tried to push through one of the mountain passes. I *had* seen it, in fact, and it was as effective as the legends said. Why, yes, I was courting a Witch Lord. It was all part of the plan. Everything would turn out well.

As I leaned against the cool stone wall, glass in hand, taking a brief break before plunging back into the diplomatic fray, Roland approached. He let out a long sigh and put his back against the wall beside me, raising his own glass to his lips.

"Crowd getting to you?" I asked him, a sympathetic smile pulling at the corner of my mouth.

"A bit," he admitted. "But *some* of us are working hard anyway." He glanced meaningfully across the great hall at Bree, who stood on a bench, reaching up with great showmanship to balance an overflowing tankard on her head. A crowd gathered around her laughed and cheered; I spotted Zaira among them, her arm over Terika's shoulders.

"Yes, well, that's Bree for you."

"She does everything she can to destroy her own royal dignity." An edge of envy crept into Roland's voice. "But it doesn't matter. She can get away with anything, because she's not the heir. She makes a clown of herself like this, and the people *love* her."

I thought of Zaira, and how she always had a great crowd around her at parties. "I don't think sober responsibility is the most charismatic of personality traits, alas. She's doing her part in her own way."

Bree now hopped on one foot, the tankard sloshing over her

hair but remaining upright on her head thus far, while the crowd around her clapped. The older and more conservative members of the Callamornish court gave her a wide space, but they shook their heads with affection, not disapproval.

"Do you know who her patron Grace is?" Roland asked, irony suffusing his voice.

In Callamorne, at a baby's naming ceremony, they performed a ritual where the parents carried the baby around in a circle past shrines of the Nine Graces until some sign occurred—the baby laughing, a bird singing, the sun coming out from behind a cloud, anything really—to indicate which Grace would be the child's patron for life. Bree had taken great delight in telling me that *my* sign had been making a grab for the candle at the shrine of the Grace of Wisdom, and suggested that such an unwise act shouldn't have counted.

"She never told me," I admitted. "I know yours is Courage, but I don't know Bree's."

Roland snorted. "That's because she's embarrassed, and rightly so. Guess."

I ran through the Graces in my head. "Bounty?" She might be unwilling to admit that, given that Callamornish folklore said the chosen of the Grace of Bounty had large numbers of children, among other assets and advantages best not discussed in public.

"Majesty." Roland gestured grandly across the room. "Just look at her. Absolutely majestic."

The tankard had fallen off Bree's head, drenching her. Someone was passing her another one.

"Oh, dear." I frowned. "That's a bit awkward as a patron for a younger sister, isn't it? You're the heir."

"Thank the Graces. Can you see her as a queen?" He shook his head, but there was admiration in his tone when he continued. "I think the Graces got us mixed up. She's braver than a cornered badger."

The queen murmured a word to one of her attendants, who nodded and crossed the hall toward Bree, a look of determination on her face.

Roland straightened from the wall, grimacing. "Back to work for us. It's time for the speeches, unless I miss my guess."

Of course there were speeches, because this was Callamorne, and there had to be speeches before there could be dancing. I'd prepared something brief; making speeches was far from my favorite part of politics, but I told myself that after having to do so in front of a council of Ardentine nobles who thought I was a murderer, a friendly Callamornish audience should be easy.

My grandmother's speech came first, delivered in a great ringing voice to a rapt audience. She welcomed me formally back to Callamorne and spoke of the strong bond her son had forged between his own country and the Serene Empire. It was novel hearing the alliance phrased as my father's political coup, rather than my mother's, and I wished with a pang that I could ask him for his side of the story.

The queen gathered momentum to a stirring conclusion. "We stand now in the face of a storm we have weathered many times before." Her voice reverberated in the very bones of her listeners, with a power that had cut across the chaos of battlefields. "You know the legends that say when the Witchwall Mountains turn red at sunset, it is with the blood of our mothers and fathers and grandparents: all those who laid down their lives to stop the Witch Lords in the passes. Again and again, through great sacrifice we have prevailed—barely." She held up a hand. "But this time, at last, we do not fight alone."

It took a while for the wild, enthusiastic cheering to die down. Roland went next, reading his dry speech from handwritten notes, sweat beading on his temples. They applauded him anyway, and he smiled out over the crowd, but when he returned to my side at the back of the royal dais, he groaned, "I think I'm going to throw up."

Bree led the hall in a rousing rendition of the Ballad of Ironblood Bridge instead of a speech, which my grandmother suffered through with admirable composure, though her jaw twitched at the more extravagant descriptions of her heroism. And then finally it was my turn.

Raverran politics tended more toward backroom deals, so I hadn't had to make formal speeches often. But my mother had told me that the shortest speech was always popular. I'd scribbled out a few lines earlier in the day, when Roland had warned me I wouldn't escape the tradition; after seeing Roland's lukewarm reading, however, I decided to say something from the heart instead. It might not be very Raverran, but after all, I was here because I was Callamornish, too.

I stepped to the front of the dais. A sea of faces looked up at me, expectant, anxious, hopeful. Waiting to see what the Empire had to say.

I took a breath and pushed my voice out from deep in my belly. "You know me as Amalia Cornaro. But I am here today as a Lochaver."

Enthusiastic cheers rose up at once from the crowd. My grandmother's popularity ensured that the mere mention of the name *Lochaver* was enough to start most Callamornish folk waving flags. I swallowed, emboldened, and continued. "Twenty years ago, Callamorne honored the Serene Empire with a great trust, by placing its future in Raverra's hands. Today, I am here to repay that trust." More cheering. A warm, giddy feeling rushed up within me. "The Falcons stand with you, with their cunning and their fury." Wild cheers. "The Serene Navy sails with you, with all its speed and power. The imperial army stands with you, with its might and muskets. And I stand with you." The cheering swelled to a roar.

I was ready to go on, but my grandmother caught my arm. "That will do," she murmured. "Let's let them move on to the drinking and dancing."

When the cheering began to die down, my grandmother lifted her hands to quiet the hall. Bree and Roland stepped up beside her, and we smiled out over the sea of eager faces, everyone waiting for her to call an end to formalities and command the festivities to begin in earnest.

In a far corner of the hall, I spotted Kathe, returned from whatever business had drawn him away. A swirl of winter air might as well surround him, given how people drew back as he made his way through the crowd. He caught my eye, determination on his face, and mouthed something disturbingly like *Look out.*

The queen drew in a breath. But before she could make her declaration, a herald's voice cut across the crowd, faltering in the middle and coming to a hoarse finish.

"Announcing the Lady of Thorns, Witch Lord of Sevaeth."

Chapter Fourteen

Every head in the hall swiveled to stare at the Lady of Thorns. She stood framed in the archway beside the herald, an aloof smile curving her lips. She wore a robe of emerald velvet, trimmed with traditionally jagged Vaskandran embroidery in black and gold; its long train flowed behind her as she descended the steps, like a fall of water. Her eyes fixed on the queen, mage mark shining with poisonous virulence.

Marcello and Lienne moved to position themselves between the Lady of Thorns and their Falcons, hands near weapons; the royal guard shifted to close around the dais where we stood. A current ran through the crowd, like the receding tide drawing the water away by any channel it could reach, as the Lady of Thorns swept toward us. Callamornish dignitaries drew back from her with pale faces and stony stares. The force of her presence ran before and around her like a great wave, the pressure of it almost unbearable. Her boots rang sharply in the silence.

Out of the corner of my eye, I saw Roland clasp Bree's hand. Ancient, animal instincts screamed at me to flee from the malevolent intensity of the Witch Lord's gaze as she stopped before us, but I held my ground.

"You are bold, Lady, to arrive here without notice or invitation when your armies are camped on my border." My grandmother's voice rang out, cold and forbidding.

The dais, her own height, and the crown sitting upon her pinned-up braids placed her above the Witch Lord of Sevaeth, and the radiance of the lamps and luminaries struck gleams from the metal accents set into her armorlike bodice. But the sheer malevolent energy pouring off the Lady of Thorns made her seem more real, somehow, more solid and sharp and dangerous, and I was suddenly afraid for my grandmother.

The Lady of Thorns spread her arms wide. "Consider this a day of great fortune, Galanthe Lochaver." Her voice held a silken sweetness but carried a power and menace that smothered the room. "For I am moved with uncommon mercy. I come to you with an offer of peace."

I found myself rather skeptical of both the supposed mercy and the offered peace. My grandmother must have felt the same, because her eyes narrowed. Murmurs ran through the crowd. Whatever they had expected, it wasn't this.

"If you wish peace," the queen said in a voice of iron, "all you need to do is refrain from invading us."

The Lady of Thorns smiled. "Such restraint does not come without a price." She held out an open hand, the motion rippling the fine dark velvet of her sleeve. "I will withdraw my forces from your border and leave your country alone. Even the occasional raiding parties and wandering chimeras to which you are accustomed will cease. But in return, you must cede to me the northern quarter of your domain, along the Sevaeth border."

I glanced at Roland, shocked. What kind of arrogance brought her all the way to Callamorne with an offer like that? He shook his head, face stiff with anger.

"*Will* you." The queen's hand rested on the pommel of the entirely serviceable sword strapped to her side.

"I will make this offer once." The Lady of Thorns' smile broadened, her eyes gleaming, as if she knew a secret. "Reject it at your peril, Queen of Callamorne. If you do, know that I will take your country anyway—but I'll destroy your family, first."

The muttering in the crowd took on an edge of anger, but no one dared raise a voice or take a step toward the Lady of Thorns. She stood with an insolent unconcern, holding in contempt the very idea that she should offer deference to her enemy while standing alone within her seat of power.

I glanced from the Lady of Thorns' serene smirk to my grandmother's face, hard as granite. She had to say no. I couldn't imagine her entertaining such an insulting offer. But the moment stretched on, dragging my nerves tighter with it.

At my side, Bree stared murder at the Lady of Thorns, her fists half-raised. Roland put on an impassive face, but the faint sound of his teeth grinding reached my ears.

"You dare," the queen said, her voice soft as death. "You *dare* come before me and make threats against my family in my own castle."

"Do you refuse my offer, then?" The Lady of Thorns sounded almost bored.

"I think so little of your offer I do not deign even to spit on it." The queen took a step forward, to the edge of the dais. "Callamorne does not fear you. Callamorne has withstood Vaskandran assaults for hundreds of years, and by the strength of our arms and the will of the Graces, we will continue to do so!"

A ragged cheer rose up from the crowd. Bree muttered, "Damned right we will."

"Are you certain that is your answer?" The Lady of Thorns' voice held a cold edge, like a knife to the throat.

"I have nothing more to say to you," my grandmother said.

"So be it." Her offering hand swept down with the finality of a scythe blade.

All the guards in the great hall leveled muskets and pikes at her. But she simply swirled a circle of shimmering green velvet and began stalking away, her three blond braids swinging behind her.

Then she paused and held out one hand, almost as an afterthought, as if waiting to be helped into a carriage.

"It's unfortunate we couldn't resolve this peacefully," she said sweetly. "But then, that's not really why I came."

A few tiny black specks dropped from her fingers to the floor.

"Damnation," my grandmother whispered, the color draining from her face.

Seeds. Hell of Disaster. Those were seeds.

The Lady of Thorns resumed walking. Behind her, green-black tendrils shot up from the floor, a whipping nest of bramble vines unfurling with terrifying speed. Stone buckled as the thorn tree put down roots, and barbed branches reached hungrily toward the dais where we stood.

I scuttled backward with a yelp, clutching instinctively at my flare locket. Guards leaped forward, hacking at the rapidly growing thorns with their pikes. My grandmother drew her sword and stepped up to meet the writhing branches, cutting a couple off with capable ease.

"Zaira?" I asked sharply.

She shook her head in clear frustration. "With that thing flailing around, I'd light up the whole room and everyone in it."

The desperate energy of fear and anger pounded through my blood, demanding action, but there was nothing I could do. My flare locket was useless against an enemy with no eyes, and I didn't have the skill with weapons to help fight off the swelling tangle of vicious black briars.

Bree and Roland had joined the fray, and I could see across the hall that Lienne and Marcello had backed into a corner with Terika and Istrella, the better to keep them safe; Istrella was pointing at the runic wards circling the hall windows and yelling something, trying to get her brother's attention, but he had his hands full deflecting branches with his rapier. The Lady of Thorns had vanished in the confusion. The bulk of the proliferating thorns reached for the royal dais, building above and around us like a breaking black wave of a thousand arboreal claws. It was huge, and horrifyingly *wrong*, and everything in my sensible Raverran soul rebelled against it in shocked disbelief.

One snaking tendril arced toward me over the guards' heads, dagger-sized thorns whistling as they cut the air. I flinched from it, raising my arms in a futile effort to protect my face.

Kathe hopped up on the dais, lightly as a landing bird, and reached casually for the oncoming branch. He looked nearly bored; he might as well have been getting a jar of jam down off a shelf.

All it took was a brush of his fingertips. The branch withered to a crumpled nothing, coming to rest at my feet.

I stared at its curling brown emptiness, then up at Kathe, my heart still racing painfully in my chest. He shrugged, feathers rustling.

"I came to warn you that the Lady of Thorns had gotten into the castle, but I see you already know."

His words fell into an unexpected silence, where a moment ago there had been yelling and crashing and the clang of weapons. Past his shoulder, the great thorn tree had gone suddenly still. Then, with a tremendous clattering like a spill of bones, it shuddered and collapsed all at once. Its sprawling tendrils covered half the hall.

The crowd stared, for a moment, harsh breaths scraping at the silence. Then a few guards stabbed at the branches with their halberds. It didn't move.

"Did you kill it?" I asked Kathe. It came out half a gasp. I realized I was clutching Zaira's sleeve, and let her go.

"The Lady of Thorns declined to keep it alive. She got what she came for," he said ominously.

"What, to piss on the queen's floor?" Zaira snorted her contempt.

"No." Kathe's gaze slid sideways, to where my grandmother wiped sap off her sword with the corner of a velvet drape.

Bree and Roland stood with her, faces grim; the guard captain reached toward a cut on the queen's cheek, but she twitched out of the way as if avoiding an annoying fly.

"The cut... it's not poisoned?" I turned desperately to Kathe, already running through alchemical antidotes in my mind.

But he shook his head. "She needed a taste of Lochaver blood. Like giving a scent to hounds. Now she can set every living thing in her domain against your grandmother and her heirs."

The queen heard that and came striding over, drawing Bree and Roland with her. Meanwhile, the other Falcons and Falconers had hurried to the dais; Lienne still had her sword out, while Istrella shook her head in something like disgust.

"I'm grateful for your assistance, Crow Lord," my grandmother said, her curt tone suggesting a certain grudging quality to her gratitude. "What can we expect?"

"Oh, some manner of mayhem, I presume." He shrugged. "Suffice to say I wouldn't get too close to the Sevaeth border if I were a Lochaver. Everything from wasps to wolves will try to murder you."

"But I have to," I protested. The artifice circle I'd been sent here to investigate was on the Kazerath border, but near its intersection with Sevaeth.

"The roads might still be safe. At least, they're guaranteed safe for travelers by our own agreements, so no one can cut off the inner domains from trade." Kathe seemed to consider the matter. "I'm not certain you'd want to bet your life on it, though. So if you come visit me in Let, I'd take the long way around."

"How did she get in?" my grandmother demanded of her guard captain. "We attuned the wards against her. Did someone let her in through the front door?"

"Oh, about that." Istrella waved a hand, as though trying to get the queen's attention from far away, though she stood at the edge of the dais with Marcello. "I was just telling Lienne, before everything got so noisy, about your wards. Whoever designed them clearly missed the Master Artificer's class on closing gaps in your designs with auxiliary patterns or filler runes." Istrella's expression could hardly have conveyed more distaste if the nameless artificer had left dirty socks hanging on bushes in the garden.

Everyone else stared at her with varying degrees of incomprehension. But my heart sank. "Someone tampered with the wards," I translated. "Added runes to change the meaning, or altered the design."

The queen turned to her guards. "Check the wards on every window and door in the castle. Find where they've been altered."

"Istrella, can you help them?" Marcello asked.

"I'd better." Her thin brows lowered in determination. "Otherwise they'll never notice anything. Come on."

She grasped her brother by the hand and pulled him off, a group of guards in tow. More had already divided to secure the entrances to the hall, and I could hear commotion echoing through the castle.

Bree and Roland drew protectively close around our grandmother. Bree kicked at the withered remains of a thorn branch.

"What do we do now?" Roland asked, eyeing the massive sprawl of tangled branches. "We can't let this keep us from fighting back."

"Roland." My grandmother's voice took on a hard edge of command. "Take the royal guard and ensure that the castle is secure."

Roland nodded sharply. "Yes, Your Majesty!"

"Brisintain." The queen turned to Bree. "Reassure the people. Quash any wild rumors and make sure the truth is known. Show them that we have nothing but scorn for this petty attack."

"I can do better than scorn." Bree grinned fiercely. "I'll get them ready to fight."

"Good." My grandmother turned to me, and for a moment my heart jumped, ready for any task she might give me. But she only offered a stiff nod to Kathe, Zaira, and me. "If you'll excuse me. I have much to attend to."

A great bustle ensued, with each of the three of them heading off to take command of different groups of people. I watched with an odd loneliness unfolding in my chest.

"Well!" Kathe dusted his hands together. "It looks like you've got this under control. I should get back to Let before my Heartguard drains my beer cellars."

"Wait." I wasn't going to let him slip away so easily. He'd helped us, and I was grateful, but he was holding back far too much knowledge behind that charming smirk. "You knew she was coming, didn't you?"

"Of course. You met her on the road yesterday, yourself." He backed half a step, as if he might turn and leave, but I angled to put myself between him and the edge of the dais.

"Did you come here to stop her?" I asked. "Is that why you invited yourself to this ball?"

He shrugged. "Who can say why I do anything?"

"*You* can!" I took a step toward him, propelled by my own frustration; we stood a hand's length apart, and I glared up at him from close enough to feel his breath stirring my hair. "Why does the Lady of Thorns want my family dead?" I demanded. "And what does all this have to do with her daughter?"

"Excellent questions." He held my gaze, and his voice dropped, going soft and serious. "Find the answer I asked you for earlier today, and you'll find those as well. But I'll tell you this much: the Lady of Thorns' daughter is dying."

"Dying?" I could almost see the truth in his yellow-ringed eyes. "Of what?"

"The same thing that kills everyone, eventually," Kathe said with a grin.

"Are you *capable* of simply answering a question?" I demanded.

He laughed. "Where's the fun in that? But you touch on deep mysteries and ancient secrets, old as stone and red with blood. I'm certain your Empire has its own hoarded truths that you wouldn't pass out like spare handkerchiefs, even to friends who ask you nicely." He swept into a bow. "Now, if you'll excuse me, I should go check to make sure the Lady of Thorns has truly left. I doubt she'd attack any of you in a hall full of guards, but a dark corridor is another matter."

He lifted my hand and placed a feather-light kiss upon the back of it, his warm lips barely brushing my skin. Every nerve in my hand kindled like luminaries at dusk. I swallowed and managed a quick dip of a curtsy.

And he was gone. My heart still raced from the tingling whisper of his lips, and my thoughts tumbled together like windblown leaves.

Chapter Fifteen

That night, as I got ready for bed, a ruddy light came flickering through the curtains of my bedchamber. I peered out the window and saw the shadow-strewn courtyard below illuminated by the red light of some great fire, but a jutting tower blocked my view of the source. The smell of smoke tickled my nose. Raised voices came from the same direction, but there was no alarm in them.

I hesitated, then slipped out into the hallway to see if I could get a better view from the balcony at the end of the corridor. I paced in stocking feet down the tapestried stone hall, between luminaries glowing a warm gold in their sconces. The mellow light gave way to a bloody glow that streamed in from the balcony doors, which stood wide open to the chill night air.

A figure already stood at the stone railing, gazing down at the courtyard below. The firelight flattened her to a black silhouette, but I'd know that stick-thin frame and copious mane of curls anywhere; it was Zaira.

I stepped out beside her and gazed down at a scene straight out of Movari's paintings of the Nine Hells. Figures moved around a blazing bonfire, the unsteady light causing their shadows to leap and dance. Scarves muffled their faces, making their shapes bulky and inhuman. They hurled in armload after armload of what looked at first like human bones mixed with the claws and tentacles of some terrible beast.

But the scent that filled the air was the pitchy smoke of green wood, not burning meat. As I peered down at the sharp-edged jumble of dark tinder in the bonfire, I resolved the image to not bones, but branches. They were burning the remains of the monster thorn tree.

"It's such a tame fire," Zaira sighed. "Like a well-trained dog. There's no wolf in it."

A reflected orange spark lit her eyes. I repressed a shiver. "I'm not sure how effective it is, with the wood so green. You could probably get the job done much faster."

"They're having fun. If it's not ashes by morning, I'll offer to show them what real fire looks like."

We stood in silence for a time, side by side, watching the never-ending dance of the flames. Even with the wind taking the smoke mostly away from us, my eyes stung with it, but Zaira seemed unaffected.

"You ruin everything," she said at last.

I blinked. "I beg your pardon?"

"You've got me thinking about the future." She leaned her elbows on the railing. "I know better, damn it. But you keep asking these poxy questions, and now I'm fumbling around after answers like some idiot who knows there's nothing but mouse turds in the cupboard but can't stop themself from checking."

"It doesn't have to be mouse droppings," I said. Lightly as I could, so she wouldn't see how much it twisted my heart that she thought that was all life had to offer.

"It would be so easy to run," she muttered. "So long as I didn't loose my fire, no one would find me."

"You could do that." I tried to keep my voice carefully neutral, to hide the empty dropping feeling at the thought of Zaira leaving. Never mind what Lord Caulin or the doge would think of this conversation. "If that's what you truly want."

"I'm not one of those poor cosseted birds raised in the Mews, who keeps coming back to the glove because the meat is good." Zaira shook her head. "It's not that hard to shake one Falconer when you're out on the road. Most of them could fly away any time. But they won't, and those bastards who hold their jesses know it."

Zaira's own jess caught sparks of light from the fire below, its crystal beads gleaming bloodred on her wrist.

"The Empire counts on it," I admitted heavily. "They learned centuries ago that the Mews had to be a luxurious palace, not a prison. They need to be able to trust the Falcons' magic once they unleash it; an unwilling Falcon is no use to them. It's why I think I can get them to change the law, honestly. If they gave the mage-marked a choice, I'd wager nine out of ten would choose the Mews. Who wouldn't want to be rich and pampered and safe?"

"Me," Zaira said. "It's like a new Hell of Boredom. I can't stay there forever, and you know it."

Couldn't you? I wanted to ask. Graces forgive me, but somewhere in the back of my mind, I'd built an imaginary future where we traveled Eruvia together, doing astonishing things. Where she was the one friend no political necessity could take from me, since we were bound together by law and magic.

But that wasn't a future she wanted to give me. It wasn't mine, to ask for or to take. And my own future lay in the inner chambers of the Imperial Palace, cloistered in gilded rooms with the cynical old souls who ruled the Serene Empire. All other dreams must wither before the power of that fate.

"I suppose you can't," I sighed. "So where will you go?"

Zaira slouched over the railing, resting her chin on her arms, and stared into the bonfire. Another armload of mage-twisted wood went in, and a hissing cloud of sparks flew up toward the velvety darkness above.

"I don't know," she said. "In the Tallows, you always had to think of how you would scrape by into the next minute. Now I can see further, to a whole bucket of possible futures, and they're all bilge."

"And what will you do about that?" It was the question my mother always asked me, her tone without mercy, anytime I started to complain.

"Stop thinking about the future, of course." Zaira stretched, and turned her back to the night. "Your cousin Bree invited me and Terika out drinking when we get back from looking at this cursed rune circle of yours. You have to come with me and get drunk, too. You're my Falconer."

"I prefer to avoid getting drunk," I said, alarmed. "And I'm not certain it would be appropriate for me to visit some of Bree's, ah, preferred establishments."

Zaira grinned wickedly. "You're a scholar. It'll be a learning experience."

She clapped me on the shoulder and headed back into the warm golden light of the castle.

The next morning, we departed for Mount Whitecrown. Our full party from Raverra accompanied us, along with a hundred Callamornish soldiers. The latter would dwindle in number each day, as they were mostly reinforcements for fortresses along the way; but I still felt a bit ridiculous at first, traveling surrounded by a small army, with all the fuss and noise of a hundred horses rumbling around us, blowing steam in the chill autumn air like a host of dragons. The feeling faded, however, as we soon passed columns of infantry and chains of supply wagons on the road. This was daily business in a country preparing for war.

Bree had talked the queen into letting her accompany us as far as Highpass, the last fortress before the border. When Roland came to see us off, I'd caught him watching enviously as a cluster of castle children gathered around Bree on her dapple gray mare, handing her posies of flowers with admiration shining in their eyes.

"Ask Grandmother if you can go next time," I urged him. "She only sent Bree with us because she pushed for it. If you never ask, she'll never send you anywhere."

Roland sighed. "I can't help but feel childish for wanting to go to the border in the first place. I know I have important duties here. But I'd like to at least see with my own eyes what we're facing."

"If you put it that way, she won't say no," I said. "Especially if you're not asking to go into combat, or cross the border, but just to tour the defenses."

"Maybe I will." Some of the tension in his face eased. "Thank you, Amalia. And Grace of Luck go with you on your journey."

Now, with Bree and Marcello riding outside the carriage, Istrella absorbed in a project, and the others trading gossip too salacious for my taste, I delved into my books in pursuit of a matter I'd almost forgotten in the drama of the Lady of Thorns' visit: Kathe's challenge. I needed that invitation to the Conclave—the Serene Empire needed it—and it was a fascinating question in its own right. Why *was* the vivomancy of the Witch Lords so much more powerful?

Vivomancers normally needed to be in touching range to use their power, though with animals sometimes eye contact would suffice. But my books mentioned countless instances of Witch Lords controlling plants and animals from miles away in the Three Years' War. Every source agreed that only Witch Lords could break this rule of distance, at least on plants and creatures native to their own domain—but none had a credible suggestion for why.

I thought of the children's rhyme Kathe had given me. *Ten spires made of bone / One realm circles round*... My books on Vaskandar sometimes referred to boundary markers defining the borders of Witch Lord domains. Perhaps they formed some kind of vivomantic circle, using the same principles of patterned magical energy at work in artifice to amplify their power. I should try to get a look at one while I was near the border.

We traveled up through the steepening foothills on roads that wound through stately pines. A taste of snow came on the wind from the mountains looming in the distance. I wore my warmest fur-lined velvet jacket and soft leather gloves but still shivered in the carriage, my nose freezing, until Bree gave me a thick shawl of homespun wool to wrap around my head and shoulders. Zaira laughed at me, saying I looked like a country grandmother, but it kept me warm.

As we climbed higher in the foothills, the trees grew smaller, and the pines surrounding us occasionally gave way to broad meadows, lying open and waiting for the inevitable snow. We began to catch faraway glimpses of Mount Whitecrown. It towered above the other mountains, its glacier-mantled crest seeming to float against the distance-hazed sky, like some palace the Grace of Beauty had built out of clouds. It was hard to believe that this serene vision of snowy majesty could harbor a terrible fire deep within it, ready to rain destruction and death upon us all.

Late in the morning of the second day, we came to a crossroads where our way temporarily parted from Marcello and Istrella's. Istrella was to make a stop at a border fortress overlooking a major river valley pass to bolster their magical defenses, and she seemed disconcertingly excited at the prospect.

"I have the most lovely idea for a catapult." She clutched a pair of pliers dreamily to her chest as we said our good-byes. Her artifice glasses were already down, magnifying her eyes into great rune-ringed circles. "I think I can build one that will fling buckets of magical fog down into the valley below that will spread and ruin everyone's gunpowder."

"Perhaps wards first, *then* weapons," Marcello suggested, looking worried. "Besides, you might throw it on *our* troops as well."

But Istrella only let out a blissful sigh.

"Good luck with your endeavors, either way," I laughed.

"You, too! Don't get eaten by wolves!" Istrella waved cheerily, then turned to Bree. "And don't forget to fix those wards on your castle! Have a Falcon from the Durantain garrison take a look. They'll see what I told you about."

I pulled Marcello aside by the crossroads to say good-bye. On the ridge behind him, leafless gray branches wrote upon the sky in some arboreal language. The breeze sweeping across the meadow grass held a trace of ice as it teased locks of black hair into his warm green eyes. A crow cawed overhead, balancing gingerly on the wind.

What could I say to him? I had no words for the complicated territory that lay between us; I couldn't navigate it even to frame a simple good-bye. Seconds slipped by, and there I stood, staring at him like an idiot.

Marcello at first had the apprehensive look of a student called by the teacher to stay after class for a word. But then his shoulders relaxed, and his mouth twitched with suppressed mirth.

"Stop smiling!" I demanded. But my own lips had started to curve upward, too.

"What's wrong with parting with a smile?" he asked. His hand stirred at his side, as if it might lift to my face, but then he tucked it into his pocket.

"Nothing, I suppose. But I'll miss you. I'll miss talking to you about all of our terrible problems, and coming up with clever solutions together."

He glanced toward the waiting carriage and its escort of mounted soldiers. "Well, we have a few minutes. That seems like enough to cover a pending invasion, a traitor, a volcano, and a murderous Witch Lord. How are you going to fix everything this time?"

"The same way as last time," I said. "By relying on the efforts of my excellent friends."

"I'll have to meet them someday. They sound very capable." Marcello's smile faded, then, and his face fell into grave lines. "I won't ask you to be careful, because I know you won't listen. But here. Take this." Fumbling with sudden inspiration, he snapped a golden button off his uniform. He held it out to me, gleaming in his palm, a falcon in flight engraved on its face.

"Why are you mangling your uniform?" A loose thread dangled from his sleeve, and I itched to snip it off.

"I can sew another button on. Take this with you, and when you're thinking of doing something dangerous, I want you to hold this button and think what I would say to you." His mouth pulled to the side. "Then you can tell the button to be quiet and go and do it anyway, but at least you'll be thinking of me."

I laughed, and took it from him. The metal was still warm from his hand. "We'll see each other in a couple of days, you know, when you catch up to us. I'm not going on an expedition to the Winter Ocean."

"I'll still miss you."

The moment came when if I weren't the Cornaro heir, we might have kissed. I felt it settling around us, a brief lull in the wind like the blessing of the Graces, with the sun gilding our skin and a deep quiet between us.

And he knew it. A warm spark kindled in his eyes, and it was as if the space separating us meant nothing. Understanding connected us, sure and sweet as an embrace.

"I have to go," I said, and tucked his button in a secure pocket of my satchel, next to my elixir bottles and my artifice tools and everything else I wanted to keep close to me in case of trouble.

"I know. I'll see you soon."

I walked away, but the feeling of connection lingered, as if I'd left a piece of myself there with him in the cold, sun-drenched meadow grass.

The going became slow and precarious as we climbed up into the mountains, heading for Highpass, a remote fort that guarded a footpath through the Witchwall Mountains, and our last overnight stop before heading out to the suspicious artifice circle. I wasn't certain the coach would make it up the switchbacks and swerves, but Bree assured me she'd seen carriages complete the trip before; still, my bones seemed fit to rattle to pieces on the rocky track.

Terika, in fine spirits, spent most of the afternoon telling Zaira stories about her grandmother, who lived in a village we'd pass through on the road to Highpass.

"I can't wait for you to meet her." Terika grinned at Zaira, who looked alarmed at the prospect. "Baba likes people who speak their minds. She'll love you. Just don't get her started on the time she knocked out a Vaskandran musketeer with a post hammer."

Zaira glanced at me. "I don't know if Her Highness here can fit a stop into her busy schedule."

"I'd be glad to," I said.

Zaira gave me a *Why are you doing this to me* glare, and I responded with my sweetest smile. I wasn't quite interfering enough to push her and Terika together, but neither was I going to help her run away from what might well prove to be the best thing that ever happened to her.

Terika laid a finger on her lips, donning a thoughtful expression that failed to hide the mischief beneath it. "My baba might not appreciate it if I spring surprise royalty on her. I suppose Lady Amalia could wait outside, so it'll be only the two of us."

"I don't want to meet your grandmother," Zaira grumbled. A brief pause before *grandmother* suggested she'd barely swallowed some unflattering modifier.

"Why not?" Terika's sweet voice had taken on a dangerous edge.

"Because if you make a big show about introducing us, she'll get moon-mad ideas that we're thinking about getting married."

Terika grinned impishly. "Shall I tell her you're taking advantage of my maidenly virtue instead?"

Zaira snorted. "I can't win against you, can I?"

"No. No, you cannot." Terika ruffled Zaira's hair, which she tolerated with a mock scowl.

Lienne caught my eye, her cheeks round and bright with amusement. I smiled back, with an inner twinge of guilt that I'd thought she might be the traitor. How could she be, when she beamed with such affection at two of the Falcons whose names were on the Lady of Thorns' list?

"Oh, speaking of certain doom." Zaira dug in her skirt pocket and pulled out the irregular, obsidian-studded flare locket Istrella had given her. "Since we're going into danger and all that, take this. You need a way to protect yourself." She dropped it without ceremony into Terika's lap.

Terika took it up with great delight and clasped it around her neck. "Why, thank you, Zaira. Now I want to get you something, too."

"It's not a present. It's a weapon," Zaira said, with some exasperation.

"Weapons make the best presents," Lienne said, tapping the gleaming hilt of her rapier fondly. "This one was a gift from my sister. She knows what I like."

"It's all right, Zaira." Terika patted her knee. "I know you don't have a romantic bone in your body. I won't get the wrong idea. And neither will my grandmother."

The village nestled by a lake in a hanging valley, a picturesque scattering of slate roofs and red-painted barns, complete with a tiny temple to the Graces in the center of town. A scattering of goats surrounded the village, grazing among lichen-crusted rocks, with forested peaks looming above them. In spring, when the meadows blazed with wildflowers, it must have been idyllic.

But Terika, gazing out the coach window, frowned. "There's no smoke coming from the chimneys."

"Guess we'll have to skip it," Zaira said. "No grandmother meeting for me."

Terika ignored her, pressing her hand to the glass. "I don't see Old Arghad on her porch. And Lorran never leaves his goats untended. Something's wrong."

She opened the coach window and leaned half out of it, Lienne seizing her belt to make sure she didn't tip out onto the road, and yelled to the coachman to hurry. I glanced out the window, startled; the village did look eerily still.

"Maybe they all died, and I don't have to meet the withered old hag at all," Zaira muttered to me, her voice pitched low.

But Terika ducked back into the coach just as she said it. Her face went pale as paper, freckles standing out like flecks of blood.

"What did you say?" she demanded.

Zaira grimaced. I nudged her toe with mine across the coach, willing her to apologize. But she crossed her arms and said, "You heard me."

Terika pressed her lips together. Then she leaned out the window again and called, "Stop the coach! I'm getting out."

"Don't be daft," Zaira snapped.

Terika whirled and jabbed a finger into Zaira's chest. Her mage mark stood out boldly in eyes that shone with emotion, but her voice stayed calm. "I put up with a lot from you," she said. "But you do not disrespect my grandmother."

The carriage wheels squealed and rattled to a halt. Terika pushed past Zaira and clambered out the door without waiting for the driver to unfold the steps. Lienne shot Zaira a stern look and followed.

In a moment, they were up and mounted on horses, and the coach rumbled into motion again. Now it was just me on one bench, Zaira opposite, and the silence between us.

I didn't chew on it for long. "Go after her and apologize," I hissed.

"She should know I talk like that, and it doesn't mean anything," Zaira said sourly. "If she's got a wasp up her arse about it, that's on her."

"Why are you being so cruel to Terika, of all people? I thought she was the only person you—" I broke off. Zaira stared at the jess on her wrist, avoiding my eyes. "You did this on purpose," I realized. "You're trying to drive her away."

"So what?" Zaira looked up now, her eyes sparking with anger. "There's only two ways things can end between us. I get her killed, or I break her heart. I'd rather pick the latter and get it over with."

"You're right that there are two ways it can end," I snapped. "But one is that you find happiness with a wonderful girl, and the other is that you act like a fool and make both of you miserable for no reason."

"Believe what you want." Zaira leaned back, crossing her arms. "But I told you, I've been looking down the road ahead. And what do you think happens to Terika when Raverra's enemies figure out she's the fire warlock's weak spot? Or when that withered old bastard of a doge does, for that matter?"

She had a point. But that was the price for power in the Serene City.

"We *protect* her!" I threw my arms up in frustration. "I've been my mother's weak spot for my entire life, and it's been fine!"

Zaira stared at me in apparent disbelief. "You've been nearly killed or kidnapped half a dozen times in the few months I've known you, and you're only kept alive by a potion. You call that *fine*?"

Before I could form a reply, the coach lurched to a sudden stop. Zaira had to grab the edge of the window to keep from being thrown into my lap. I banged an elbow as the bench heaved beneath me and then was still.

We exchanged a frozen instance of a glance, then both stuck our heads out opposite windows to see what was happening. My heart thumped as if it still rattled around the inside of the coach.

The road ran through Terika's village, drawing a dusty line between a few houses and a small store that clustered along it. The rest of the farmhouses scattered across the valley like fallen gray stones, streaked with soot and weather. A thick silence lay across the road, somehow deepened rather than shattered by the blowing and stamping of half a hundred horses and the rattle of harness and coach wheels.

A deep cold settled in my belly. Terika was right. This large a party arriving in such a small village should draw attention. Curious children should be running out to greet us, and even the crankiest old codger should at least twitch back a window curtain to look. But the stone houses lay deathly still.

Except for the front door of the second house down the road, which swung loose and free, banging against the wall once, then again more softly, as if someone had just pushed it open.

The moment stretched longer than it had any right to. Lienne's hand fell to the hilt of her sword. A few soldiers slid nervous palms up the musket barrels on their shoulders.

Then a man staggered out of the house, lurched a few steps toward us, and fell face-first in the dirt of the road.

Chapter Sixteen

For a frozen moment, all I could think was that Zaira had somehow cursed the village, and everyone *was* dead. But the fallen man's back rose and fell with harsh, labored breath.

Terika slid down from her horse and ran to his side. Lienne drew her pistol and covered her Falcon's back, scanning every doorway and window, every barrel and stone.

Bree called to the Callamornish soldiers that made up half our escort, "Eyes out! Braegan, take your squad and search the houses for more people. Don't touch anything!"

I threw open the coach door and hurried over to Terika, who now knelt next to the man in the road. He seemed unconscious; his skin was pale and clammy. Terika peeled back his eyelid, smelled his breath, and touched deft fingertips to his wrists, throat, and forehead.

"Is he sick?" I asked, fear of plague roiling in my stomach.

Before Terika could reply, cries came from the houses the soldiers had entered, one after another.

"There's a family in here! They're alive, but they don't look good!"

"Found an old man... Argh, no, I think he's dead."

"Six in here! Two conscious, all too weak to move. They need water!"

The weight of my apprehension doubled with each cry of discovery. The instinct to flee, to get out of here and away from any possible contagion, pulled at me with strong hands, urging me to run.

Bree took command, dispatching a couple of soldiers trained in the rudiments of field medicine to triage the sick, and sending more to check the outlying houses, and still others to bring water and see what else the stricken villagers might need. Zaira stood back with a hand pressed over her nose and mouth, eyes wide, the stark dread on her face of one who has seen plague before.

But I didn't smell sickness. There was a different scent on the air, dissonantly sweet. Something very like . . . lilacs.

"Terika?" I asked, my voice betraying me with a slight quaver. "Is it poison?"

Terika rose, suddenly, and cried out, "No one touch the water!"

A pair of soldiers stopped in the act of hauling up a bucket from a well beside one of the houses. Fear whitened their eyes, and they dropped the bucket back with a clatter and a hissing slither of rope.

"Banebriar," Terika said, her voice tight and her face grim. "I've seen it before. The Lady of Thorns sends it creeping across the mountains from Sevaeth, its roots seeking drinking water to release its poison. We need to act quickly, or everyone here will die."

Zaira dropped her hand from her face and took a step toward Terika. "What can I—"

Terika ignored her, turning to Bree. "Please." Her voice scraped from her throat, hoarse and raw from strain. "Can you send someone to check on my grandmother? She lives in the farmhouse up on that hill, beyond the pine grove. I need to know if she's all right."

Bree nodded and sent a soldier immediately. Then she asked,

"I've heard of banebriar. Is there an antidote? Tell me what we need to do."

Terika closed her eyes for a moment, her lips moving.

This was her home. It sank in, like muddy water through a picnic blanket. Terika's grandmother had raised her; all these people were her neighbors and friends and family from before she came to the Mews, and from all her visits after. And now she had to try to remember alchemical remedies she might have learned five years ago when for all she knew, her grandmother could already be dead.

But she didn't break down with wails or shrieks, or go running off to find the people she loved. Her eyes flew open, and she nodded, with firm resolve.

"I can make the antidote. I have most of the ingredients, and I know where to gather the rest locally. But it'll take time to collect everything and brew it."

Bree leaped into action, commanding soldiers to search the town and bring Terika everything she needed. Purposeful bustling immediately replaced horrified staring. After a long string of commands, Bree turned to Zaira and me.

"Can you continue on to Highpass? Tell them what's happened, and have them send more help?"

I nodded. "Of course."

Terika was already pulling bags out of the coach, muttering about alchemical supplies. A soldier helped her heave out her things; Lienne called for the Raverran soldiers to find her a good worktable, untainted water, and candles.

Zaira took half a step toward her, then turned away, grimacing. She didn't say anything to Terika before climbing into the coach.

"If you won't apologize, aren't you at least going to say goodbye?" I asked her, as I clambered in after her.

"Didn't you see her? She's a bit busy right now." Zaira

slouched in her seat. "I won't deny I stepped right in a pile of dog dung, there, but I never did do anything by halves. Now she'll know she's better off without me."

Then the coach was rolling, and it was too late for parting words. Zaira stared out the window after Terika's back as she disappeared into a house, arms full of ingredient bottles, soldiers coming behind her with alchemical supplies.

"They're in good hands," I murmured.

"Damned right they are. Terika's the best." Zaira sighed, and touched gentle fingertips to the window glass. "I can't believe they were actually all dying. That old hag had better survive."

The coach bumped to another unexpected stop. I exchanged alarmed glances with Zaira; we were barely more than an hour out of the village, not even halfway to Highpass. Sergeant Andra rapped on the window, and my spine tensed. If she was the traitor, this could be a trap.

"Callamornish runner coming," she announced, in clipped tones. "Looks urgent."

Zaira and I descended warily from the coach, stepping out into a stiff, icy wind that cut along the mountain ridge we were climbing toward Highpass. The forested flanks of the ridge fell gently away on either side, and I could see the green cradle of the village fields below. A footpath intersected our road from the east, running along the mountainside above the village; it was along this narrow dirt track the runner came, waving desperately, one arm clutched to his side, with the frantic staggering gait of one driven to run past his own endurance.

Zaira swore. "He was one of the guards we left with Terika." We'd split our forces, both Callamornish and Raverran, leaving two dozen in the village to protect and help Terika and Bree, and taking two dozen to guard us for the remaining few hours to Highpass.

"But he's not coming up the road from the village," I muttered, frowning.

Our remaining escort gathered around us, some of them sliding off their horses to go meet the approaching runner. But he shook off their help, lifting his head to call out a ragged gasp of a message:

"The princess needs reinforcements!"

The Callamornish soldiers in our escort dismounted and began grabbing guns and powder horns at once.

"What happened?" I asked, hurrying toward the messenger, but Zaira practically bowled me over on her way past.

"Is Terika all right?" she demanded, her hands curling to fists at her sides.

The soldier struggled to catch his breath. Sweat drenched his temples, despite the deep chill in the air. A pale fuzz marked his upper lip; he seemed barely old enough to wear a uniform. "Princess Brisintain and the alchemist, Terika..." He sucked in a breath, even as his Callamornish fellows pressed a water flask into his hand. "They took a dozen of us and went to gather some ingredient from a place Terika knew." He pointed back over his shoulder, at a notch in the eastern slope of the mountain we were climbing. "There, up the mountain, right by the border. But we stumbled into a Vaskandran raiding party. The princess ordered me to run to intercept you, to ask for help."

Shame quavered in the boy's voice. She'd done it to spare him, and he knew it, and it was killing him.

Oh, Hells. *Bree.* She could be dead by now—and Terika, too.

Corporal Braegan and his squad were already slinging muskets over their shoulders. "How many?" he demanded.

"We took a dozen, and left the rest in the village." He pulled in a broken breath, bracing his hands on his shaking knees, bent nearly double. "There must have been... twenty of them?"

I scanned our two dozen soldiers, struggling to push aside the desperate worry clutching at my chest and think clearly. Highpass perched on the western side of the mountain, separated from the village and the notch above it by the long ridge we now climbed. We could reach Bree and Terika quickly from here, before the road left the ridgetop and swung left along the mountainside, but getting help from Highpass would require hours of travel there and back. We were the only hope they had.

"We can't leave Lady Amalia and Zaira unguarded," Sergeant Andra snapped.

"That's fine, because I'm going with them," Zaira said roughly, fury simmering in eyes that dared anyone to contradict her. "That should even the odds, and then some."

Andra regarded her analytically. "It certainly would. Lady Amalia? Shall we assist the princess and our Falcon? Most likely the raiding party will run at the sight of reinforcements, if they're still there."

I didn't hesitate. "Of course."

"We can't take the coach on that path," Andra said, frowning.

"You can't even take horses on it," the messenger reported, between gulps of water. "It gets rocky. We'll have to go on foot. Hurry!"

I turned to Andra. If she was the traitor, I didn't want her with us in such a dangerous situation. "Take the coach up to Highpass. Get reinforcements in case we need them, and an alchemist to assist Terika with the cure for the villagers." Or to replace her, if she was hurt or killed, but I wasn't going to say that in front of Zaira.

Sergeant Andra looked as if she wanted to argue, but she swallowed it and saluted. "As you command, my lady."

I ducked into the coach to grab my satchel. I dipped a hand in as I hurried back to the others, to make certain my emergency elixir bottles were in there—enough for three days, which my mother and I had deemed sufficient time to find a competent alchemist in any corner of the Empire—and my fingers closed on the cold nub of Marcello's button.

"Look," I muttered. "We're bringing a couple dozen soldiers with us. Are you happy?"

"Who are you talking to?" Zaira asked.

"No one." Even in a crisis, I had no desire to subject myself to whatever ridicule Zaira would devise if she learned I was talking to a button.

We jogged after the soldier boy along the narrow footpath. I puffed clouds of steam and kept my hands tucked into my sleeves against the chill air; there'd been no time to pull on the soft leather gloves tucked in my satchel.

The trail cut along the mountainside through low scrub pine, then began a rocky climb toward the notch we'd seen from the ridge. My city boots scrabbled and slipped on the stones, and I scraped my palms catching myself on my hands more than once. Zaira hopped from rock to rock more nimbly, though she had to tie up her skirt to keep it away from her ankles. Fear for Bree and Terika scraped like a clawed thing at the inside of my ribs, urging me faster despite my unfitness for mountain scrambling, but I couldn't help a sigh of relief when the path leveled out again.

Then we rounded a bend and saw bodies strewn across the trail, lying twisted where they'd fallen among the roots and rocks.

"Grace of Mercy! Watch the trees," Braegan shouted. Most of

the soldiers faced outward, muskets ready, covering the handful who ran to check the fallen.

I sucked in a breath sharp with horror. One of the corpses wore a scarlet uniform.

Lienne.

Chapter Seventeen

Terika." Zaira's voice had an edge of fury bordering on madness. I took one look at her face and was suddenly very glad for the jess on her wrist. I could almost see the flames writhing just beneath her skin. "Where is she?"

We moved cautiously closer to the fallen, musket barrels bristling in all directions. Most of the bodies wore Vaskandran green, but there were also two in Raverran blue, one in Callamornish white—and, of course, Lienne. Anguish wrenched my chest at the sight of her, bloodstained rapier still clutched in her hand, pistol fallen among the rocks nearby. The coil of her gray-streaked braid had come loose, and it trailed behind her, stiff with blood from the half a dozen gunshot wounds in her torso.

She'd been so alive just this morning, smiling over Terika and Zaira. And now here was all that was left of her, a bloody and empty thing, discarded on the path like a soiled glove. I'd thought she might be the traitor, but she'd died defending her Falcon. Graces keep her soul.

Out of sight up the trail, someone moaned.

We hurried toward the sound, muskets out, passing more dead Vaskandrans along the way. Dread of what we might discover weighed down my steps like cold, sucking mud.

The trail shortly emerged from the last traces of pine forest into a rocky saddle between two rearing peaks. Wind shoved at us, tugging hair and cloaks and skirts toward the gap. The far side of the notch fell away into a scree-choked, lichen-scarred old rockslide, which tumbled down to meet a swelling sea of ancient forest that cloaked the mountain's slopes in deep green shadow.

A woman sprawled among the rocks, her Raverran uniform stained with blood. A musket lay across her lap. Her hands were too weak to lift it, but her eyes glittered feverishly; she was alive.

"There you are," she gasped. "Took you long enough."

The boy who'd led us here ran up to her. "Thank the Graces, someone's alive! Where's the princess? What happened?"

Zaira strode up to the injured soldier with murder in every step. "Talk," she growled.

The soldiers had more mercy. One, a Callamornish woman in her thirties with a brown braid and powerful shoulders, pulled bandages and alchemical salves from her bag to treat the soldier's wounds. Another offered her water.

She took quick, grateful sips, but only between words. "Vaskandran raiding party attacked us. Saw a Falconer uniform and targeted the alchemist."

"Where is she?" Zaira demanded.

"I don't know." The wounded woman grimaced with pain, held up a finger, and took another sip of water. The soldier with the brown braid busied herself with the salve and bandages.

"How does it look, Grita?" Braegan asked.

"There's a good chance she'll live, if you let me do my work."

"Sorry." Braegan edged back, giving her more room.

The wounded soldier grabbed Braegan's sleeve. "You've got to hurry. They can't be far ahead. The alchemist used some artifice device to protect herself, but it was too powerful—it knocked everyone around her out. Put them right to sleep. The alchemist, too. I was rear guard, and the only one of us far enough back not to be caught in it."

Zaira paled at the mention of an artifice device. It must have been Istrella's flare locket. But it should have flashed a blinding light at her attackers, not put everyone to sleep. A queasy fluttering grew in my stomach; something had gone terribly wrong.

"And Princess Brisintain?" Braegan demanded.

"They grabbed the alchemist and looked like they were trying to decide what to do about all the sleeping people, so I shot one. That got them running, but they shot back, and here I am." Her eyes closed in pain, then opened again. "But then the sleepers woke up. A handful of Vaskandrans first, who'd been almost out of range, but I pretended to be dead and let them pass. Then the princess and the rest of them, ravening after like bloodthirsty hounds. They can't be more than ten minutes ahead. You can overtake them if you hurry."

I stared. "Bree went charging off into *Vaskandar*?"

"To get the alchemist back. Yes. She thought they could catch them just across the border, before they ran into anyone, since the Vaskandrans were hurt and dragging a prisoner."

I covered my face. Graces, that was so like Bree.

Unshed tears burned my eyes. *Later.* I had to hold together. Someone had to take command now, and decide what we were going to do—a decision that could lead to the deaths of everyone here, if things went wrong.

And I knew who that had to be.

"Lady Amalia?" a Raverran officer asked, tentatively.

Zaira stood poised at the apex of the pass, her hair wild in the wind, staring down the long slope into the rolling forests of Vaskandar as if she'd like to burn the whole country to ashes.

She looked back over her shoulder at me; rage carved her face into hard planes. "You heard the soldier. We can catch up if we go after them now." She slammed a fist into her thigh. "But if we let them go, she'll be gone. You take a look down there and tell me we have any chance of finding her if we let the trail go cold."

I stood beside her and gazed out across the rolling forest, spread out below over the skirts of the mountains. The knife-thin scar of a footpath zigzagged down the slope below the rock-slide, vanishing into the devouring darkness of the forest.

I was the Cornaro heir, the linchpin of the treaty that bound Callamorne to the Serene Empire, and the cornerstone of our alliance with the Crow Lord of Let. And Zaira herself was even more crucial to the Empire's defenses. We were too valuable pieces to lose for any reason. The doge had ordered me not to take risks, and I had no doubt that if my mother were here, she would forbid me to cross the border.

But Bree was a princess of Callamorne. She was also too valuable to lose. And imperial military policy was to take extraordinary measures to prevent the capture of Falcons. From what the wounded soldier said, they were only minutes ahead of us. We would barely have to cross the border at all.

"We have to send people after them," I said. "There's no doubt of that. The only question is whether you and I are going, too."

"Unless there's a Witch Lord hiding right across the border, there's nothing within five miles I can't handle." Zaira gestured out over the forested valley below. "If you send them alone, they could die and fail, and we'll lose Bree and Terika, and you and I will be no safer sitting here unprotected. If I go with them, nothing can stop us."

Past the foot of the mountain, some ways to the east, a cleared area of fields and a cluster of roofs broke the monotony of the forest. Wisps of smoke rose above the village. A castle reared black towers above the forest on a foothill farther to the east, but it was too far away to be a threat. To the west, smoke rose from a great gray swath of tents in a distant encampment of Vaskandran troops that filled a river valley below one of the major passes, but that was miles away. This section of the Witchwall Mountains was too rugged for war.

Kathe had said the roads were protected by treaty and should be safe even with the Lady of Thorns' word of death laid upon Lochaver blood. There might well be scouts patrolling the roads, or traders and hunters traveling them, but nothing more than that. Even if we left someone behind with the wounded woman, we had twenty fresh soldiers to add to Bree's remaining half dozen.

If we ventured a few minutes into the forest, no one would know. And Zaira was right; with a fire warlock along, nothing could stop us.

I slid a hand into my satchel, curling my fingers around Marcello's button. "I can't believe I'm considering this," I said.

"We don't have time to *consider* it, Hells take you."

I nodded, and spun to face the waiting soldiers.

"Two of you stay with the wounded and check for more survivors. The rest of us will venture a short distance across the border to see if we can catch up and get Princess Brisintain and Terika out of there. If the trees start trying to kill us, or animals attack us, or anything makes us think the Witch Lord knows we're there, we'll leave immediately. We will turn around before we reach the valley floor. Understood?" Salutes and grim nods met my order. "Let's go."

I scrambled down the rockslide with the others, picking up more scrapes, determined not to hold us back this time. The Vaskandrans must have lost a great deal of time trying to make their way down the rocks with an unwilling prisoner and wounded companions; if I had to fling myself down and bounce off every stone on the way, it would be worth it to gain ground on them. Soon we made it to the place where the cut through the mountains widened, and a dirt track broke away from the slide to switchback down a grassy slope and into the woods.

These were not the fig and olive trees of Raverran gardens, nor the stately cypresses of the imperial countryside. They even bore little resemblance to slender pines of the Callamornish hills. These were old, wild trees, with trunks broader than doorways and rough bark creviced deep enough to hide a hundred secrets. Moss crept up the trunks. Branches thick as a grown man hung above the path, gnarled and reaching, blocking out much of the light and filtering down green, shifting shadows.

They had *presence.* A dense, silent watchfulness hung about the forest; I could feel it palpably as we approached. All forests were alive, but this one was awake. I shivered.

Despite our headlong pace down the mountainside, we stopped when we came to the verge of the woods, without a word passing between us. The air wafting out of the forest was different. Colder, damper, and it carried a heady scent: mossy growth and moldering leaves, fresh pine and decaying wood, death and life wound together.

Zaira raised her fist. "All right, you rotten old wrecks. You may have swallowed my friend, but I'm going to shove my arm down your throat and pull her out so hard you'll cough up your own bollocks."

"Did you just threaten the trees?" Braegan whispered, as if afraid they'd hear him.

"Hells, yes. Bastards had it coming." And she strode into the forest. The rest of us followed, the soldiers quickly fanning out around her.

At once, everything went silent. Not the dead silence of an empty room, but a silence full of a thousand sounds too soft to break the threshold of hearing. The silence of movement only just stopped, and ready to spring into action again; the silence of a pause between bites, or a breath between screams.

The path widened when it entered the forest, from a narrow single-file track to the full breadth of a wagon road. Its width might be so that woodcutters could use carts to transport felled trees, but I had the feeling that in Vaskandar, they kept the brush cut back for another reason. When my steps wandered from the center of the road once, a tree branch creaked and strained toward me, twigs stretching and rattling.

"Stay on the path," I said, nerves cracking my voice. "Whatever you do. I've heard the roads are safe—or used to be, anyway."

Braegan nodded, drawing his pistol. "Aye. People live here, after all, and traders pass through. They say if you keep to the roads, it's not much more dangerous than a forest in Callamorne."

He didn't sound convinced.

The trail began a series of switchbacks down a steep, forested slope. I peered down through the trees, hoping for a glimpse of Terika and her captors farther below. I almost thought I'd seen something when the sound of crashing brush came from down the path, and a familiar voice issued blistering curses.

"Bree!" I cried, and broke into a run. Zaira and the soldiers quickened their pace around me.

But then the smell hit my nose. Blood, and worse. I threw a sleeve across my face, gagging.

"Amalia?" Bree called. "Graces' sakes, what are you doing here? Get out!"

I could make out a number of figures through the trees now. Only one was moving. The underbrush, however, heaved and thrashed like a living thing, and the pines swayed and groaned.

"Your Highness!" Braegan shouted. "Are you all right?"

"Fine." Strain stretched Bree's voice taut to the point of breaking. "But if you value your lives, don't step off the path."

The soldiers in front of me slowed their rush to an abrupt halt. In half a breath, I saw why.

One soldier hung from a tree branch that speared through his eye and out the back of his skull, body swaying gently. Another stretched in rigid, frozen agony across a tangle of briars that pierced his chest in half a dozen places. Others sprawled at the roots of burly trees with clearly broken necks or lay in scattered pieces with roots and vines still wrapped around their bloody limbs. The thorns that overran this part of the forest glistened red with blood.

My stomach lurched. Around me, the soldiers swore.

Bree knelt in the middle of it all, covered in scratches. The brambles grabbed at her from every direction, but she kept them at bay with her bare hands. Every branch she seized snapped off easily, and each tendril that touched her recoiled as if she were on fire. *Vivomancy.*

"Bree!" I started toward her without thinking, struck with deep horror at seeing her in such a place of blood and death. But Zaira grabbed the back of my coat, even as the tree branches overhanging the road strained in my direction.

"Oh, no you don't. Not unless you want to get gutted."

"Your Highness!" Braegan ran his thumb across his musket hammer, but guns would be useless against this enemy. "How can we get you out of there?"

"Stay there, and get ready to catch me," Bree commanded.

And with that, she staggered to her feet. Black briars caught and clung to her, straining to pull her down, cutting her tattered clothes.

Bree closed her eyes and let out a great, angry roar. The bramble vines clutching at her went suddenly limp, falling off her like wet spaghetti.

A couple of the soldiers gasped, and one backed away. Bree's secret was out.

Bree hurled herself toward the road, more than half falling. Thorns grabbed for her but withered when they touched her. She rolled through them on her shoulder until one reaching arm stretched past the edge of the path; Braegan caught her hand and hauled her the rest of the way to safety, trailing dead branches.

Bree lay in the road, gasping and pale. I dropped to a knee beside her, my gut still twisting in revulsion at the mangled bodies all around us, taking in gulps of relief that she was alive along with the terrible stench of death in the air.

Grita dropped down by Bree's foot, which was twisted in entirely the wrong direction. Hells, there was nowhere safe to look except Bree's face.

"Quickly," Bree gasped. "Those bastards who've got Terika are just ahead of us. We had them in sight when poor Alfrith got too clever and tried to cut across switchbacks to catch up. Then we all got tangled trying to save him."

"You're not walking on this ankle, Highness," Grita said firmly. "We're taking you back to Callamorne."

Bree sat up, agitated. "But they're so close! There are only five of them left, and three are wounded. There's no way they can make it to help before we catch them, if we go now and stick to the road!"

"Can you fix your ankle?" I asked her, making vague, wiggly magic gestures.

Bree shook her head. "I'm no Skinwitch. If I try to use my magic on a human, even myself, the power twists away and makes me queasy. It's like... like trying to stuff a bar of wet soap into a dog's mouth. Only you're also the dog."

"Get over your squeamishness so we can save Terika," Zaira growled.

"Go after her yourselves," Bree urged us. "I'm no good in a fight right now, but I can get the ingredients we collected to the Highpass alchemist to cure the banebriar poisoning."

"We'll go with you." I'd had enough. Corpses scattered among trees that drank their blood like rain—it was too much. "I'm sorry, Zaira. We have to get out of here."

Zaira's lips peeled back from her teeth. "Coward," she said.

"Not all of us can set everything on fire and blithely walk away," I snapped. "You're not the one who'd be at risk."

"Lienne is dead," Zaira said fiercely. "You know what that means. If Terika doesn't get a new jess within a week at most, she'll die. If we walk away now, we'll never get her back. We're killing her."

"Go after her," Bree urged, even as Grita and one of the Raverran soldiers helped her to her feet. "If you stay on the road, you'll be safe. You can still catch them!"

Zaira whirled and began stalking down the path, deeper into Vaskandar.

A wild, giddy panic seized my throat, and I spun on Bree. "Your impulses have killed a dozen good soldiers today," I snapped. "Are you so eager to add to the toll?"

Bree flinched. But then her brows lowered stubbornly. "No. I'm eager for their deaths to have meaning." She lifted her voice. "Braegan, go with Zaira. Keep her safe. That's an order."

Braegan saluted, then turned to Grita. "Get the princess out of here safely, no matter what. Don't come after us. *That's* an order."

"Oh, for Graces' sakes." Grita looked ready to throw Bree and Braegan both down a well, but she started half dragging my cousin up the road, grumbling about being surrounded by suicidal morons.

"Half of you with Princess Brisintain," I told my Raverran soldiers. "Half with me. We'll meet you at Highpass, Bree." I hurried after Zaira. To their credit, the guards sorted it out in a quick swirl of activity, nine of them falling in around me.

It didn't take long to catch up to Zaira. Shortly after the terrible grove of corpses fell out of sight behind us, I scurried around in front of her implacable stride and faced her. She stopped and crossed her arms, her eyes dark and intense. The soldiers fanned out around us, watching the woods, muskets ready. The trees loomed above us, bare branches stretched against the sky like patterns of bones.

"Zaira." I tried to keep my voice calm, but it was hard, with so much fear and grief and anger roiling inside me. "You're more sensible than this. We have a week. Listen, we can send in a team of spies to rescue her, or maybe get help from Kathe—"

"No. You listen." Her voice cracked across mine like a whip. "If I have this terrible fire inside me for a reason, this is it. So I can do things that would be madness for anyone else, like walk into Vaskandar and defy anyone to stop me." She swept an arm at the forest. "*This* is what I was born for. Not to destroy cities or slaughter armies, but to save people who are beyond saving. To win the day that's given up for lost."

An unearthly fury lit her face from within, like a candle shining against the shadows of the forest. She radiated the same power and grace she did when she unleashed her balefire, but her eyes were clear of its madness and piercing in their surety.

"Let's do it," Braegan blurted. "My lady, she's right, we can do this."

"Zaira . . ." I began, unsure how I would finish.

"Do you hear that?" one soldier asked suddenly.

A growing rustle tickled my ears, as if the forest gathered itself to scream. My scalp prickled.

"Oh, Hells," Braegan whispered. "Here it comes."

A handful of birds burst, startled, from a clump of ferns up the mountainside. The soldiers leveled their muskets at the spot.

And they came flowing down toward us, in great fluid bounds like leaping dolphins. Long and lean like weasels, but dog-sized, with three eyes and thumb-long, needle-sharp teeth. Rows of curving, silvery thorns gleamed on their backs like fish scales.

Chimeras. Three of them.

Chapter Eighteen

Gunshots cracked the air, impossibly loud, one after another. One of the chimeras stumbled, hit; a chunk of thorny armor flew off another, leaving a bloody patch on its back. But all three kept coming. The soldiers cursed and dropped their muskets, their one shot spent, to draw pistols and swords.

Panic burst white-hot in my chest and tried to fight its way out as a scream; I wrestled it instead into a ragged shout.

"Exsolvo!"

The lead chimera launched off a fallen log at us in a flying leap, claws flashing, maw full of razor-sharp teeth gaping—and burst into blue flame.

Our defensive knot scattered as it landed in the road, thrashing and screaming, splashing balefire around it like hot oil. I jumped away, yelping, and nearly crashed into Zaira.

"Watch out, idiot," Zaira snapped, lifting arms wreathed in pale, hungry flames.

I threw myself aside as twin lines of fire raced along the ground from Zaira to the two remaining chimeras, washing over them just as they were nearly upon us.

For a moment, only a thin ridge of bitter blue flame licked up from their sickly silver coats, and the chimeras howled and snapped at their own backs. But then they kindled all over, a thousand flowers of fire bursting into bloom on every inch of their bodies, and inhuman screams lifted into the air with the stench of burning fur.

"Pull back from the flames!" Braegan shouted, and we hurried some thirty feet down the trail. The chimeras lay still now, but the balefire leaped higher, fueled by their lives.

Zaira turned to me, holding out palms on which flames snapped and danced; they licked up from her hair, too, tasting the wind. Strain showed in her face.

"Seal it, quick," she barked. "I'm in control now, but it won't last."

"*Revincio*," I gasped, stumbling back from the flames as they leaned toward me.

All at once, the fires winked out, both on Zaira and up the trail.

She swayed. I held out my hand, but she shook her head, steadying herself on her own. "I'm all right. That much fire, I can handle."

It was just as well. My own knees were trembling so badly, I wasn't sure I could have held her up.

This was the limitation of balefire: so long as it kept consuming lives, it could rage indefinitely; but when it was done, it took a deep toll on the warlock. Zaira had come a long way in training, to be both conscious and in control now.

We couldn't afford to lose her to exhaustion, any more than we could risk being consumed by her flames. My heart thundered in my chest, and panicky energy shot along my nerves like lightning, but I had to stay calm.

Braegan turned to me, eyes white-rimmed, even as the soldiers hurried to pick up their muskets and reload. "Your Highness? Are you all right?"

"I'm fine," I began, "But we should—" I made it no further.

Six more chimeras came for us, charging straight down the path.

The soldiers cursed and fired their pistols; the sharp scent of gunpowder mixed with charred meat in the air, and one of the chimeras fell back, yelping.

I drew my knife and backed away. "Zaira?" I asked.

"Do it." She rolled up her sleeves.

"Exsol—"

Something struck me from the side, hard enough to drive the wind out of me. Suddenly I was rolling in the dirt with a seventh chimera on top of me.

I barely managed to fling an arm up between its teeth and my throat. Pain pierced my forearm, and three mad eyes stared at me from inches away. Claws tore at my coat.

I screamed in unabashed terror as I stabbed it again and again in the neck. My knife grated twice off thorny armor, but the third time hot blood spattered over my hand.

And then I was tumbling down off the edge of the trail, crashing through bushes and bouncing off tree roots, the thing still locked on to me and thrashing; its bloody teeth snapped near my face, and its claws raked my lower leg as we spilled down the hill together. I twisted my knife deeper into its neck as we fell, desperate to kill it, end it, make it stop.

We rolled out onto the next switchback below; I wound up on top. I drove my dagger into its third eye, but its hard, wiry body had gone still beneath my hands. It was already dead.

"*Exsolvo,*" I gasped, lurching to my feet. Pain lanced up my leg, but I ignored it, staring up the slope to the road above.

I spied a flurry of chaotic motion through the trees—shouting, cries of pain, swords flashing, scaly backs leaping—but I didn't have a chance to figure out what was happening, or if everyone was well. A silvery wave flowed down the slope toward me, third eyes gleaming, razor-filled maws gaping.

Four of the six remaining chimeras had plunged down off the road after me.

Grace of Mercy. This was my death, coming for me with eyes full of gleaming alien hatred and covered in thorns.

I raised my knife, falling into the stance Ciardha had taught me despite the certainty I couldn't fight four chimeras on my own. But a brilliant blue light flared through the trees.

A wave of balefire roared down the hill after them.

Flames devoured them, rearing up into the branches overhead and setting them alight. Near-white, starving fire flooded down toward me, engulfing everything in its path, a torrent of heat and radiance. The scent of death came in a hot wind before it.

"*Revincio!*" I shrieked.

The fire died at once. I blinked in the forest shadows. The yelling and clamor up the mountainside had diminished.

"Zaira!" I called, my voice raw and breaking. "Are you all right?"

"Lady Amalia!" That was Braegan, sounding panicked. "Thank the Graces! We're coming down."

I took a step toward his voice, unthinking. It brought me close to the edge of the road, and a tree branch swung down at me, as if a strong wind had stirred it. I jumped back, too saturated with fear even to shriek at this point. My leg and arm throbbed, and a few scratches and bruises made their presence known as well, but none of that mattered so long as I could still walk to get the Hells out of this forest as quickly as possible.

I started limping up the trail to meet Braegan and the others. The trees stirred around me, as if a wind blew through them. A gray shadow had fallen over everything, with no more glints of gold slanting through the leaves—the mountain peaks now blocked the sun. A haze of smoke hung in the air, from balefire and gunpowder both.

This was no place for me. Grace of Mercy, all I wanted was to be back in the Empire, where the landscape had the simple courtesy not to murder anyone.

Braegan came down the slope, sword in hand; Zaira leaned on him, head drooping, barely conscious. Five soldiers watched their backs, reloading their muskets.

"Where are the others?" I asked, dreading the answer.

Braegan shook his head, lips tight. My stomach dropped sickeningly.

In the distance, up the mountain, something howled.

"I know these now," Braegan said, his voice hard and grim. "Whiphounds. The Lady of Thorns' own hunting dogs. They're about twenty to a pack, so we've got more coming."

"More?" I clutched my flare locket; the claws at my neck rattled. "What about Bree?"

"I'm betting she made it to safety, because it sounds like they're all coming after us," Braegan said.

Zaira lifted her head. Exhaustion pulled at her face. "If I unleash again, I'm falling over. Or else killing all of you. Your choice. Graces forgive me, but I can't hold it back anymore."

The howl sounded again, much closer. More inhuman voices joined in, then broke into an eager baying, as if they'd caught the scent of prey. A chill like an ice shard pierced my spine.

"They're between us and the border," I realized. "And I'll wager they're smart enough to know we have to keep to the road."

Braegan looked at me, a grim reckoning in his eyes. "They're after you, Your Highness."

I swallowed and nodded. "Yes. I'm sorry."

He exchanged glances with the remaining soldiers. A bushy-bearded Callamornish man said, "I'm in."

"What?" I asked, uneasy.

"We're not making it out past more of those things," Braegan said. He pointed down the road. "I've read the scouting report for this area. We're almost to a junction, near the bottom of the mountain. You want the right fork, which heads toward the village. It's a bit deeper into Vaskandar, but the road crosses into Kazerath, the Wolf Lord's domain. The hounds won't follow you there; chimeras don't cross into another Witch Lord's domain without permission." He began reloading his pistol, with the swift ease of practice. "You should be able to find another woodcutter's trail up the mountains somewhere near the village, within Kazerath. All you need to do is stay ahead of the hounds until you cross out of the Lady of Thorns' domain."

"Oh, no. I know what comes next." Zaira put her fists on her hips, anger stirring some energy up from within her. "I hate last stands and dramatic gestures. None of this 'We'll buy you time' bilge. You come with us."

"There's no time to buy." Braegan turned to face up the path, where the baying grew louder. "They're coming. Get out of here."

Through the gathering shadows, through the tangled branches of the trees, I spotted movement high on the trail.

Braegan raised his pistol in one hand and drew his sword with the other. "Run," he urged us. "Get out of here, and boast to the rest of them for me that I died saving a Lochaver."

"They'll be jealous," Bushy Beard laughed. *Laughed*, with a light in his eyes. "Now, run!"

Zaira swore and grabbed my hand.

We ran.

At first fear drove me with blinding urgency. The baying sounded behind us, ever closer, and thorn branches strained toward me from the woods; but if I stayed in the center of the path, they couldn't seem to reach. Pain was something I set aside as irrelevant, a problem to deal with later, though I was aware on some level that my arm and leg were hurt, not working quite right, and complaining about it.

After a while, the sharp reports of gunfire came behind us. We faltered, but kept running.

I strained to hear more above my own labored breath and pounding footfalls. There might be distant shouting, and the scream of dying whiphounds; but I couldn't tell over the clamor of my own body and the phantom sounds that fear wove in my imagination.

Then the baying started again. Anguish twisted sharply in my chest, like a harp string snapping.

"Hells take them," Zaira panted. "Every one of them."

I didn't want this. I didn't ask them to die for me.

Twilight shadows took hold under the trees and deepened around us, turning everything gray and unreal. We came to where the path split and took the right fork without slowing down. But the baying was so close now, it seemed as if the hounds must be right behind us.

Zaira glanced back over her shoulder and swore. "I can see them."

The trail ran straight ahead; two standing stones flanked it in the distance, barely distinguishable from tree trunks in the dimming twilight. *Boundary markers.*

"I think," I gasped, "that's the border."

"We're not going to make it." Zaira spoke with ease, while I could spare no breath from running. She had been holding back to my pace. "If you release me, I can burn them all, but then you'll be dragging my unconscious body."

The stone pillars were so close. But a glance over my shoulder showed me eerily gleaming eyes and bounding silvery backs hurtling toward us.

I stopped and spun to face them; Zaira turned with me, lifting her hands, ready.

"Close your eyes," I warned.

I flipped open my flare locket. A blinding flash of light reddened my eyelids, and the whiphounds howled in pain and confusion. Without waiting, I sprinted for the stones, Zaira at my side.

"Good thinking," she called.

Something ripped in my injured leg. Pain speared up it with every stride. But I kept running, faster than I'd ever run in my life, until the standing stones loomed before us and I flung myself past the invisible line between them.

The road continued on through the forest, unchanged. But behind us, the hounds recoiled as if they'd met a wall.

I stopped, panting, and bent double, shifting my weight to my good leg. The hounds paced and growled on the far side of the stones—four of them, sniffing and slavering, their eyes all fixed on me.

This was a nightmare. It had to be a nightmare. But the air was sharp and cold in my lungs, and my eyes watered convincingly, and the pain was too real.

I wasn't going to wake up from this. Nothing I did could unwind what had happened. All those good soldiers were dead, and we were alone in Vaskandar.

"Let's keep going," Zaira said, her voice uneven. "I don't trust those rocks to stop them for long."

The boundary stones. A flicker of curiosity sparked through the murk of horror and guilt in my chest. I yearned to examine them, to trace the symbols I could make out in the fading light. But with the whiphounds pawing and pacing just beyond them, I didn't dare push the limits of their protection.

Too much had been given to get us this far alive. I couldn't throw it away because of a children's rhyme.

We started walking. But every step hurt, and a haze seemed to have fallen on me with the coming of dusk. I kept hearing the shouts of the dead soldiers in my head, and seeing the thorns stained with blood. I stumbled, and then stumbled again; the third time, I fell to my knees.

"Grace of Mercy, you're clumsy." Zaira grabbed my arm to haul me to my feet.

The wrong arm. I flinched, breath hissing through my teeth. Zaira pulled her hand back, swearing.

"You're wet. Hells, it's blood, isn't it?"

"It's not bad." I dragged myself to my feet.

Zaira went still. "Is that all yours?"

I looked down. I had one white stocking and one red one, hanging in tatters. The sight made it more real, and suddenly the pain stopped knocking politely at my door and came crashing through it all at once. I sat down, hard, in the dirt of the road.

"We should probably put something on that," I said. My voice came out detached and calm, seeming far away, but a high, panicked note sounded in my head, like a shrill flute.

"That might not be a bad idea, yes." Zaira knelt down beside me and peeled back what was left of my stocking. "Ugh. What a mess."

"It can't be too bad if I ran on it all this way." But I couldn't bring myself to look.

"I've seen worse," Zaira said, her voice carefully neutral. "Let me see if I can stop the bleeding."

She cleaned the claw wound with water from her flask, which stung enough to bring tears to my eyes, then drew her knife and tore strips off her skirt for bandages. I struggled to keep from slipping into a quagmire of hopeless misery, trying to focus on what we needed to do next. We had to keep going.

While Zaira wrapped my leg, I fished the first of my three small emergency elixir bottles out of my satchel—each a day's supply—and downed half of it. The last thing I needed now was to get weak from poison on top of blood loss.

Behind all the pain, and the fear, and the exhaustion, waited a great dark mass, like the ocean itself pressing against a sea wall. So many people were dead, and we hadn't even rescued Terika.

I had to know this, because it was important information. But I couldn't let myself feel any of it, even a little, until we got to safety. So it waited, a deep ache spreading quietly through me, like the poison my elixir held at bay.

"Well, we're neck deep in demon dung, aren't we?" Zaira helped me remove my jacket so she could get a look at my arm in the fading light. I shivered in the icy chill that had gathered under the trees as the sunlight drained away.

The coat had offered me some protection, and the bite was less serious than the wound on my leg, which I'd worsened with all that running; it had nearly stopped bleeding on its own.

"We just need to find a footpath through the mountains before it gets dark," I said wearily. "We can do this."

Zaira's hands paused on my arm. In the deepening twilight, her eyes were pools of shadow. "No, we can't."

The edge to her words pierced the numb fog in my brain. I took in the taut hollows of worry in Zaira's face, and the sunset-stained sky that bled through the branches behind her.

"We're not making it out of here tonight," she said, her voice low and rough. "It'll be dark as a demon's armpit soon. All that blood loss is making you loopy if you think you can climb up a mountain on an unfamiliar trail in the pitch-blackness with a mangled leg."

She had a point. I stared around at the darkening woods, the full depth of our peril pressing down on me. The roads might be safer during the day, but I had little confidence that limited protection would hold at night. And if the footpath wandered back across the border into Sevaeth, the forest itself might try to kill me.

But the forest didn't hate Zaira. The chimeras wouldn't hunt her. She was whole and healthy and nimble, and she could protect herself perfectly well. Especially if she wasn't trying to lug me around.

"You'll have to go without me, then," I said slowly.

Zaira shook her head. "Don't be stupid."

"It's not stupid. It's sense." I lifted a shaking hand to my temple; I felt a bit light-headed, but what we had to do was clear enough. "You're right. There's no way I can make it over the mountains with this leg. Any pass easy enough for me will be easy enough for horses, which means it'll be full of Vaskandran troops and guarded by Vaskandran fortresses. But you can scramble up some game trail easily enough. There's no reason for both of us to die if one of us can live."

"No."

"Zaira—"

"Shut up and listen to me." Zaira shook my shoulder with sharp, bony fingers. "I survived all those years in the Tallows by not getting close to anyone. Well, thanks to your meddling, now I finally have a few friends—only a few, mind you—and by the Nine Hells, I am not leaving two of you to die in this pit tonight."

I stared at her. *Friends.* And of course she waited until a time like this to say it.

A pale speck drifted down between us, and then another. One planted a tiny, cold kiss on the back of my hand.

Snow.

I shook my head as more soft white flecks of sky danced silently down the evening air. The cold of it bit deep into me, settling into my core, numbing my fingers and my cheeks and my aching heart.

"There's another reason one of us needs to make it back tonight," I said, my voice heavy with the awful truth I'd been trying not to think about.

"What?" Zaira demanded suspiciously.

"What do you think they'll do," I asked, "when Bree gets to Highpass and reports that they left us behind in Vaskandar?"

Zaira frowned. She didn't understand, yet. I pressed on. "The best-case scenario," I said, "is that they send a rescue party after us. But now the forest is all riled up, and they'll probably all get killed."

Zaira swallowed. "And what's the worst-case scenario?"

"They get on the courier lamps and tell my mother," I said.

"Sweet Hell of Death," Zaira swore.

"Yes."

Zaira crouched beside me, very still, for a long time. A dusting of snow began to gather on the outermost curls of her hair, where it was too far from her head to melt. I pulled my coat on again over my bandage, to try to stop my shivering, but somehow that only made it worse.

At last, Zaira stood, the hacked-up hem of her skirt swinging just below her knees. "We can't sit here in the road all night. Come on."

"Zaira..."

"Not another damned word about how valuable either of us is to the Empire. We're not counters in some game; we're people. You, too." She reached out a hand to help me up. "Let's head for the village. This close to the border, they must get traders passing through all the time. You can throw a bucket of that Cornaro gold at some brat to carry a message to Highpass, if you're so worried about what they'll do."

I was too tired and hurt to argue any more. "All right."

Zaira pulled me to my feet. Her jess hung on her wrist, catching the fading light. She followed my gaze, scowled, and pushed it up beneath her coat sleeve to hide it.

We hobbled off down the darkening road, deeper into the forests of Vaskandar.

Chapter Nineteen

By the time we staggered into the village, Zaira was half holding me up with my arm across her shoulders, and my leg had bled through the bandages. My torn stocking had frozen stiff with blood, and my fingers were numb with cold.

Little more than a dozen weathered wooden houses encircled the snow-dusted village green; a wide stretch of stubbly fields formed a buffer between the huddled cluster of lantern-lit buildings and the snarled darkness of the forest. Woodsmoke hung warm and welcoming in the air, and a dog barked at us through a barn window as we stumbled into town.

Not a soul was outside, not so much as a horse or a chicken. Light shone through the gaps in closed shutters, catching on bright snowflakes fluttering down in the air before them. Lanterns hung like ward sigils beside every door, but the village square lay still and quiet in its shroud of falling snow, as if no human or animal lived here at all.

But there was an inn: the largest house on the square, with bright lamps blazing beside the doors and hitching posts out front for hours when horses dared to be outside. A sign swung above the stout, iron-bound door, with a painted rooster perched on top of a pile of sacks and crates, declaring it *The Trader's Nest.*

I yearned for its warmth and light so much, it had to be a trap.

But these were normal people who lived here, regular Vaskandran folk going about their lives. They had no reason to expect Raverran heirs and warlocks to wander into their inn. Still, I took my own weight before we opened the door; there was no sense walking in looking like easy pickings.

A haze of sausage-scented woodsmoke and a wall of warmth enveloped us as we limped into the inn, trailing snowmelt. The dim, ruddy light came mostly from a massive fieldstone fireplace, around which a handful of old men and women in fur and leather clustered at a couple of tables. Two boys of perhaps fifteen years slouched at another table in a corner, playing some game with bone dice while a thin, stooped man with iron-gray hair and an apron set drinks down for them.

All eyes in the tavern turned to us; murmured conversations fell silent. A couple of traders paused in mid-deal, furs and herb jars spread on the table between them opposite fabrics and potion bottles. The innkeeper hurried over to meet us, wiping his hands on his apron.

"Come in, be at peace, and shut the door." He closed the door himself as he said it, barring out the icy cold and the snow-starred darkness. "Cutting it close, weren't you?" An accent sharpened his vowels and roughened his consonants, but he was understandable enough.

I swayed on my feet, too tired and numb to reply. Zaira said, "We want a room and dinner."

"Of course. I'll take your—huh. You don't have any bags, do you?" A puzzled frown creased his forehead as his eyes slid over my satchel and caught on my bloodstained leg. "Ah, saw some trouble on the road, I see. To be expected, at this hour. You're not the only ones today." He shook his head. "Sit down. I'll get you dinner."

I all but collapsed in the nearest chair. Zaira helped me put my leg up, then sank down next to me, her back to the wall. Everyone else in the tavern was still staring at us. Zaira glared at them, and a few looked away; after a moment, subdued conversation started up again.

"Be ready to release me," Zaira muttered.

"Here?"

"If you think no one ever gets murdered in an inn, I have some bad news for you." Zaira's fingers tapped the tabletop, restlessly. "I don't like how those brats in the corner are watching us."

The two boys flicked frequent glances our way, their heads together, talking. No one spoke much above a whisper, besides the innkeeper with his nervous chatter, and tension hung thicker than smoke in the air. I couldn't tell if it had been like this before we walked in, or if we were the cause of it.

"Maybe we should leave," I murmured.

"And go where?" Zaira shook her head. "These people might kill us in our beds, but this is still our best shot at living until dawn."

The innkeeper returned with plates of sausages and potatoes for us, cooked in the same pan, and tankards of weak beer. "I'll wager you'll be paying in imperial coin, from the look of you," he said, as he laid out our dinner. "That's fine. Half our business comes from across the border. Though it's been slow since the army came and rounded up all the young and able-bodied for Prince Ruven's war." He made a sign against his chest, fingers flicking out as if to brush cobwebs off his soul. "Avert misfortune."

My hand rose to my own chest, fingers tangling in Kathe's string of claws and the chain of my flare locket. The innkeeper blinked at me suddenly. "Oh! I'm surprised you had trouble on the road, with the Crow Lord's safe conduct on you. Did you step off the path?"

"Ah..." I wasn't quite exhausted enough to blurt out the truth, but too much so to think what to say.

"Something like that," Zaira said.

The two boys from the corner rose and approached our table. The foremost moved with the gangly swagger of a boy, in the midst of growing, trying to put on the airs of a man. The other had just begun to fill out the broad frame of his shoulders and rolled them as if eager to test their new power. There was a menace and a confidence to their stride that didn't match their shallow years; I checked their eyes, wary, but in the dim and flickering light I couldn't make out a mage mark in either of them.

The innkeeper's shoulders hunched in something approaching a bow, and he tried to leave with his empty tray, but the boys didn't move aside for him. Zaira slid her chair back an inch. I did my best to quell my shivers and look relaxed and confident, but mostly managed to lock every muscle in my body tight as an iron gate.

"And who are these?" the lead boy demanded. A wisp of blond beard clung stubbornly to his chin. His fur cloak bunched at his shoulders, likely calculated to make him seem bigger.

The innkeeper shrank from him minutely, his gaze dropping to the floor. "Guests, sir. She has a—"

"They look like runaway serfs to me," the boy interrupted, sneering.

If he thought we looked like Vaskandran serfs in our fine velvet coats, mine with thick golden embroidery at the admittedly bloodstained cuffs, I couldn't imagine he'd met many. More like it he was taking advantage of our ragged state to bully some coin out of us.

"We are most certainly not serfs," I snapped.

The innkeeper winced. The boy hovering like a guard scowled, his freckled face reddening. "Watch how you speak to him! Do you know who you're talking to? This is Grainor Greenhand!"

Zaira snorted. "Last I checked, having bilge slime on your fingers is no excuse to make an ass of yourself."

The innkeeper drew back at that, blanching. The freckled boy started forward, but Grainor stopped him with an idle gesture.

"You're not from around here," he said, "so I'll give you one last chance. The Green in my name is for Greenwitch. With my father away at the border, I now rule this village, and four others besides."

It seemed ridiculous that it had come to this, that I should be bullied by a two-bit vivomancer a few years my junior, but here we were. And we didn't dare draw attention to ourselves, with our situation so precarious. I had to smooth this over.

"Now apologize," the freckled boy demanded, looming over us. "On your knees."

Zaira pushed back her chair and stood.

"We're not from around here," she said, smiling to show her teeth, "so I'll give *you* one last chance. Look in my eyes, turdbiscuit, and say that again."

The freckled boy's hand dropped to his dagger. But Grainor whispered, "Wait."

He peered into Zaira's eyes. She stared back, still grinning, the hearth fire reflected in her dark gaze.

I slid my chair back and rose to my feet behind her, ready to run, or draw my knife, or speak the release word. I had to follow Zaira's lead—we were in Vaskandar; she was the one with the weight of status behind her words now.

Grainor went pale as milk. His hand flew convulsively to his chest, his fingers flicking out in the same casting-off gesture the innkeeper had made. He dropped to his knees, grabbing his taller friend to pull him down, too.

"My lady. Forgive me." He bowed his head nearly to the floorboards. "In the dim light, I didn't see your mark. Forgive me, I beg you."

The freckled boy stared at Grainor, aghast, and then at Zaira. He bowed his head, too, kneeling as if to a queen, making the same sign. "Avert," he whispered, almost too soft to hear.

Then the innkeeper dropped to his knees. And all around the room, there was a great scraping of chairs, as every patron in the inn threw themselves down to the floor, until only Zaira and I were standing.

"Oh, get up," Zaira sighed. "And bring me better beer than this."

Once they knew Zaira was mage-marked, everyone treated her as if she were something between a queen and the Demon of Death. The innkeeper brought her the finest food and drink in the inn, and bowed so deep he nearly touched the floor at the slightest provocation. Everyone else in the tavern averted their eyes, and cowered away from her if she made any sudden moves. Most of them fled either upstairs or to their homes as soon as enough time had passed to do so without insult.

"I could get used to this," Zaira said, grinning, as she tore into an herb-roasted chicken. "They know how to treat a mage right, here."

I nodded weakly. More than anything in the world, I wanted to be at home in Raverra, in my own bed, safe behind wards and under Ciardha's watchful eye. Really, a soft spot on the floor would do at this point. My leg throbbed, and I wasn't sure I'd ever been so exhausted.

But I had to find a way to get word to Highpass in time to avert disaster. I scanned the tavern for a likely messenger from the few who remained; my eyes lit on one of the traders, who was still packing up his wares in the corner.

My mother's words came back to me: *I assure you that a full third of Raverran merchants in Vaskandar are spies.*

"Zaira," I murmured, "Can you call that trader over? I want to try something."

She gave me a curious look, then shrugged. "You!" She called to him, across the tavern. The trader flinched. "Come over here!"

He hesitated, then approached our table with the air of a man called up before the executioner.

"My friend wants to talk to you," Zaira said, and ripped another bite off her chicken leg.

The trader's eyes flicked to me, taking in the blood on my sleeve. He relaxed visibly. "Ah, does my lady wish to purchase some imperial medicine? I have a fine selection of alchemical salves and potions, brought all the way from Ardence."

"I'll take the best salve you've got for healing deep cuts," I said fervently. "Also, forgive me, but I can't help thinking you look familiar. Do you perchance know Piero da Idrante?"

Recognition kindled in the trader's eyes. "Why, I believe I do. I met him once in Palova, during the Festival of Bounty."

He knew the pass phrases. Relief flooded me; it was as if the Serene City herself had thrown a line into the dark drowning water for me. If I recalled correctly from what my mother had taught me, the Festival of Bounty meant a low-level spy, but he would do.

I gave him my most charming smile. "Ah, I thought so. I saw him just yesterday. He asked me, if I saw you, to see if you could get a message to his Aunt Mirabella."

Zaira had stopped eating, and stared at us in fascination. The trader looked positively faint; Aunt Mirabella was a high-level emergency code he'd probably never heard outside of training, and indicated he should drop everything and act immediately.

"Of course," he said. "Where is Aunt Mirabella these days?"

"I believe she's staying at the fortress of Highpass. I know it's late, but I'm *really* hoping to get Piero's message to her tonight."

I dropped a fistful of ducats on the table, just to show him I meant business. "Do you think you could do that?"

The spy swallowed. "It's dangerous traveling through Vaskandar at night, but for Aunt Mirabella, I'd do anything. What's the message?"

"Tell her that my companion and I are fine." I gestured to Zaira, who grinned at the poor man in a most unnerving fashion. "Let her know we're running a bit late because we ran into a delay on the road and we've decided to stay here overnight, but we don't need any help and should be able to make it home without any difficulties tomorrow. Tell her we don't want any fuss, or it'll spoil the surprise."

The trader frowned slightly, clearly trying to work out what could be so urgent about this information. He took in the embroidery on my coat, the claws hanging from my neck, and finally the pile of ducats before him. The man was no idiot; he made the connection, and his eyes widened until they looked nearly ready to pop out of his head.

"My lady," he choked. But his expression became composed again almost at once, and he swept the money into his bag. "You can count on me, my lady. I'll see that Aunt Mirabella receives your message tonight."

"Thank you," I said fervently. "Grace of Luck go with you."

When he was gone, Zaira dropped her voice to a mysterious whisper and said to me, "The heron flies at midnight. The black dog craps on the palace floor."

"Oh, hush. It worked, didn't it?" I sank back into my chair, letting the haze of exhaustion and pain claim me again now that I'd accomplished my pressing task.

"I guess we'll know for sure when we wake up tomorrow and find out whether we're at war."

Not long after that, Zaira asked the innkeeper to show us to our beds. I paid him several times the worth of the room and dinner, which he took with wide-eyed horror, as if it were cursed gold from a ghost story. He then conducted us to the best room in the inn: it had a feather bed and down-stuffed quilt for Zaira, and a cot for me.

As soon as the innkeeper bowed his way out of the room, Zaira dragged the cot across the door. Then she checked the window and pronounced it not too high to jump from in a pinch.

I didn't care. I could barely keep my eyes open while Zaira helped me smear on the alchemical salve the trader had given us and change the dressing on my arm and leg. Chances were good they'd murder us while we slept, or chimeras would crawl in the unwarded window, but I was too tired to worry anymore. We were in enemy territory, in grave danger—but there was a bed here.

I fell into my cot like a drunkard off a bridge and sank into a deep lagoon of sleep.

I woke to something soft thumping onto my chest. I sat up spluttering and reached for my dagger, sure it was an attack; but instead Zaira stood over me, smirking in the thin rosy light of dawn.

She tossed another bundle at me. This one was warm and smelled deliciously of fresh-baked bread. The first, on a closer look, was a change of clothing.

"The innkeeper's up baking, so I got these for you," she said. "And an earful of blather. The man can't stop talking."

I blinked out the window at the stark black shapes of the mountains looming against the dusky apricot sky, Mount Whitecrown rearing behind them in dawn-ghosted glory. Reality sank in like snowmelt against bare skin, icy and unwelcome: we were still in Vaskandar. The dead soldiers, the whiphounds, our own terrible predicament—this was the hand we'd been dealt, and a new day wouldn't let us shuffle it back into the deck. We had to play it out somehow.

"Did you learn anything?" I asked wearily.

"A way home, maybe. Sounds like a smuggler's path. We have to slip past a castle to get there, but it's not close to the road, so that shouldn't be a problem." Zaira sat on the edge of her bed. Deep shadows under her eyes suggested she hadn't slept much last night; with a twist of guilt, I realized she'd probably kept watch. "How's your leg? Up for some climbing?"

"Let's see." I unwound the bandages from my leg and braced myself for the worst, but the salve had done its work. The bleeding had stopped, and the ragged gashes the claws had left on the outside of my calf seemed a bit smaller. It hurt far less, too. "Could be worse."

"Good," Zaira said gruffly. "I'd hate to have to put you down like a horse with a broken leg."

My lips twitched. "I've seen you with dogs. You'd never shoot a horse."

"Hells, no. I'm not a monster. But people are worse than horses."

A few heartbeats of silence passed between us. It was long enough for the sick ache in my chest to swell painfully, remembering blood and death and sacrifice.

"Thank you for not leaving me," I said at last.

Zaira shrugged. "It was one of your dumber ideas. You might be a blister on my arse sometimes, but you'd be even more worthless dead."

I smiled to acknowledge the compliment. From Zaira, that was all but a declaration of undying sisterhood.

We came downstairs to find a strange sight: three cradles sitting near the hearth in the gray morning light, and the innkeeper rocking one and shushing the thin wail coming from it. He sprang up at once when we entered the room, bustling over and bowing as the infant's cry gathered strength behind him.

"My lady, my lady. Sorry about the noise and the, ah, clutter."

Zaira stared in astonishment. "Why are there babies in your tavern?"

"They took everyone young enough and able-bodied for the army, you know." The innkeeper scuttled back a few steps and reached out a practiced foot to rock the cradle behind him; the baby's cry gentled to a discontented gurgle. "But the Wolf Lord in his mercy decreed that nursing mothers could stay home with their children. The Lady of Thorns made no such allowance for our neighbors in Sevaeth, so we are truly grateful." His hand flicked out from his chest. "But there's no one left to do the work, and we've got a lot to do to get ready for winter. So I'm watching the little ones while their mothers cut and haul firewood and make preserves, with help from the children old enough to walk and the grandparents. I'm sorry for the inconvenience."

A pang in my chest twisted so sharply it shut off speech.

"No, that's fine." Zaira waved off any need for apology. "Take care of the brats."

Graces preserve the families here. If Vaskandar's armies marched through the passes, it would be these babies' families facing Zaira's balefire and Istrella's weapons. All because their lord forced them away from their own homes and children.

A sick sympathy weighed down my gut. I wished I could stay here and help those poor exhausted mothers in the fields, or force out the petty bully whose vivomancy had given him power over these people. But too much depended on us making it back to the Empire.

Zaira and I stepped outside the inn to find the village just as deserted as it had been at night; from what the innkeeper had said, what few people remained must be working in the woods or the kitchens. The subdued morning light picked out details I'd missed in the darkness, like deep scores of claw marks on the doors of houses and broken shutters gnawed at the edges. Without all the warm lights that had driven back the darkness, the huddle of houses looked gray and desolate. A light dusting of snow covered the fields; not enough to drown them in pure white, but enough to make flecks of black earth show through stark and barren in the steep furrows.

Our breath frosted in the cold air, but water dripped from the eaves of the inn; the sun was warming up the world, and the snow wouldn't last. Back in Raverra, the leaves would just be falling, and fine ladies would complain of the chill forcing them to cover their arms; it wouldn't snow for another two months, if at all. I drew my soft leather gloves from my satchel and pulled them on.

Zaira didn't seem to feel the cold. She looked about her with bright eyes, her cheeks rosy. "It's pretty, isn't it?" Then her face fell. "I wish Terika were here to see it with us."

"We'll get her back," I murmured. But the sick feeling in my stomach and the memory of Lienne's bloodstained body belied my words. We would be hard-pressed to make it home alive ourselves, and Terika was running out of time.

The black castle loomed over the forested valley at the crest of a low foothill, rearing black towers like unsheathed claws against the cloudy sky. It crouched on the hill's uneven, rocky crest like a creature that had settled there only for a moment before springing down on prey below.

It bore no resemblance to the practical, efficient military fortresses of the Empire, with room for thousands of troops and battlements lined with cannons. Nor did it evoke the dainty façades of Raverran palaces, with their sugar-spun stonework, built as homes for wealthy aristocrats. Its towers were too slender and its windows too wide to be useful for defense, but its jagged lines shaped rather a forbidding profile for an inviting retreat built to entertain guests. And it wasn't large enough to shelter an army or an extensive noble court, but no town lay at its feet either.

It made no sense. Someone had built that castle not to serve a need or purpose, but because they felt like it. Someone who didn't need walls, armies, or wards to protect what was theirs.

As we came directly beneath it, the trees around us stirred in a nonexistent wind. A squirrel with black ear tufts stared down at us from a branch, unblinking. All the small sounds of the forest fell silent. My stomach tightened almost to the point of nausea, remembering the change that had come over the woods in Sevaeth before the chimera attack.

"Zaira," I muttered, "Do you get the feeling someone knows we're here?"

But she wasn't by my side anymore. She had stopped and was staring at the road that wound a scar up the side of the hill to the castle.

"She's up there," she said. "Terika."

"You don't know that," I protested, alarmed at the determined look in her eyes.

"Where else would they take her?"

"Zaira—"

"I know." She bit off the words. "We can't kick in the door and burn the place down to find her. It would start a war, I'd just get everyone killed, all that mealy-mouthed stuff you like to spit."

"Well, it's true."

"Demon's piss, I *know.*" She whirled on me, fury and pain mixed on her face. "But what sort of jellyfish am I if I walk past that place, knowing she's probably *right there* and needs my help?"

"A live one," I said.

A sound broke through the rustling of the leaves: hooves. Horses approaching on the road ahead.

"You there!" a commanding voice called.

"Bollocks," Zaira muttered.

Tendrils of panic unfurled in my stomach as a handful of uniformed and mounted soldiers rounded a bend in the road ahead. The officer in the lead spurred ahead to meet us, frowning, one hand on his pistol. Zaira straightened with the lazy grace of a cat rising from sleep; I could feel the dangerous readiness in her stance.

I forced a smile and waved. "Hello!"

The officer reined to a halt before us. "What is your business here?"

"We're passing through on our way to visit my friend Kathe, the Crow Lord of Let." I tapped the claws on my chest.

The officer straightened, eyes widening at the sight of Kathe's token. But then he frowned, examining us more closely. "You're going the wrong way. Who—" He broke off, paled, and saluted Zaira. "My lady! Forgive me. I didn't mean to show disrespect. I didn't see the mark in your eyes."

"Since it was an honest mistake, I won't kill you for it," Zaira said magnanimously.

The officer bowed, as best he could from horseback; the other soldiers followed suit. "You look weary from the road, honored lady. Let me escort you to the castle for hospitality and rest."

Something was wrong. The way the soldiers exchanged glances; the way the trees whispered to each other; the way a trio of sparrows gazed down at us from a nearby tree branch. We needed to get out of here. But we couldn't outrun soldiers on horseback, and the woods were no safe place to hide.

Zaira waved off the invitation. "That's quite all right. We've got places to be. On your way."

The soldier bowed again, almost touching his nose to the saddle. "Please, great lady. You would surely not risk offense by refusing my lord's hospitality. I must insist."

Zaira glanced up at the castle, and longing entered her eyes. I knew she was thinking of Terika. And she heard the steel in his voice as well as I did; if we didn't want to turn this into a fight, we had no choice.

"Oh, all right," she said airily. "I'll stop by for a quick drink, but then I must go."

The officer nodded with obvious relief. "As you say, great lady."

The mounted soldiers fell in around us, and we started up the road to the castle. I exchanged worried glances with Zaira. She mouthed, *Now what?*

I shook my head. "We keep bluffing," I whispered, "and hope the local nobility don't realize who's dropped in for tea."

The castle loomed above us, black against the muffled light of the clouds, magnificent with jagged asymmetry. Its balcony railings made me think of bones or antlers, and its battlements resembled teeth. The road curved before it to form a circular drive; at the center of the circle stood a tree with drooping, willowlike branches, its leaves the color of orchids. A garden of bushes and small trees spread out around the castle, some with sickly-sweet blooms in shades of deep violet, all twisted into clawing shapes.

What I had thought were statues flanking the castle steps moved, and I realized they were great gray wolves. Their yellow eyes stared at us, watchful, as we approached, and some deep instinct raised all the tiny hairs on my spine.

Wolves. The Wolf Lord of Kazerath. Oh, Hells.

I threw Zaira a panicked glance, but she frowned, uncomprehending. Then the soldiers escorted us up to the massive black doors, and they swung open before us, and it was too late.

A grand entryway swallowed us, all done in black and gray marble, with high, vaulted ceilings and a sweeping double staircase. The curve of the two sets of stairs and the balcony above framed an archway into a soaring hall, lined with tall, narrow windows and forested with slender columns—all focused on a throne at the far end, which dominated the hall in its spiky, asymmetrical glory. It might have been artfully crafted from a thousand real bones, so far as I could tell, if bones were jet black and bent to the hand like willow branches.

If you were a Witch Lord, maybe they did.

Our hosts stood waiting for us, framed in the archway. The one I assumed was the Wolf Lord of Kazerath wore a grizzled fur cloak that swept down to the floor, and had hair to match; if he shaved, he did so infrequently. A hard light shone in his eyes, which bore a mage mark white as winter. There was a broad power in his shoulders, and I had no doubt his scarred hands knew well how to use the broadsword sheathed at his side.

Beside him, holding a wineglass as if we'd just interrupted them over drinks, stood a genteel figure in a black leather coat with a high collar and jagged purple embroidery, his sleek blond hair pulled back in a long ponytail. A smile spread across his face at the sight of us, delighted and incredulous, as if we were the most wonderful thing he'd seen all year.

"Well, well. Welcome to my family's castle, Lady Amalia Cornaro," said Prince Ruven.

Chapter Twenty

Such a delicious surprise." Prince Ruven swept into a graceful bow. His wine barely tipped in its glass. "And Lady Zaira," he added. "What auspicious guests. We are honored to have you."

I returned a bow, stiff and formal, my heart and mind stumbling over each other to see which could race faster. "We were in the area, and it seemed rude not to visit."

At my side, Zaira's hands clenched and unclenched. Grace of Mercy, the last thing I needed was for her to punch Ruven in the jaw for stealing Terika. Especially when we had no surety whatsoever that he'd actually done so.

But she let out the breathless laugh she saved for people she held in the highest contempt and dropped him a curtsy. "Charmed. So very charmed, you have no idea."

Ruven gestured grandly to the fur-cloaked man at his side, who regarded us with the cold stare of a predator deciding whether we were dinner. "Allow me to introduce my father, the Wolf Lord of Kazerath."

A glib reply died on my tongue. There was old blood in his gaze, bound by those white circles. Rivers of it. I could feel the power coming off him like steam; it was different than the electric energy Kathe radiated—a deep, murky lake rather than a clear, bright stream, or thunder to Kathe's lightning. The stone floor beneath my feet felt insubstantial compared to his presence.

"Of all the scents the wind brought me this morning," he said, his voice deep and gravelly, "I did not expect the fire warlock and the Cornaro heir to be among them."

He took a pace forward, stalking, deliberate. His hand stirred in a lazy signal, and the soldiers swung the door shut behind us. The bar of sunlight it had cast on the floor narrowed and vanished. I willed myself not to step back, not to turn, not to show fear.

"And what shall I do with you," the Wolf Lord said, "now that you've wandered into my den?"

From side doors flanking us, lean gray wolves slipped into the foyer, moving like the breath of a wild night wind. I had always imagined wolves to be dog-sized, but up close, they were as big as deer. They prowled around us, forming a half circle, yellow eyes gleaming.

I locked my trembling legs in place but couldn't stop my hand from instinctively falling to my dagger. I barely heard Zaira whisper, "Hell of Nightmares."

Prince Ruven flashed a brilliant smile. "Why, we offer them hospitality, of course, Father. They are guests, after all."

"Is that so?" The Wolf Lord's eyes narrowed. "I see the Crow Lord's token on one but not both. Give me a reason to keep the warlock alive."

Zaira bared her teeth. "I'll give you one. I'll bet you prefer not being on fire."

"Zaira," I muttered nervously, "you may want to show courtesy to our host."

"Only when he shows some to me," she retorted.

The wolves circled closer, growling, until I could feel their hot breath when they passed. The Wolf Lord seemed unmoved by Zaira's challenge. The piercing white rings of his mage mark swiveled toward her. She visibly braced herself under his gaze, as if all the infinite stony mass of a mountain lay behind it.

"I know your kind." The Wolf Lord's words were soft, but they carried a full burden of menace. "We remember, in Kazerath, how dangerous you are."

I half expected Zaira's glare to melt the stone beneath his feet. "If I'm so dangerous, maybe I should see myself out through your castle walls."

Graces preserve us, Zaira. Why are you provoking them? A deep, wild rumble started in the throat of one of the wolves, and primal dread crackled down my spine.

"One good reason, Ruven," the Wolf Lord said again.

Ruven laughed, but there was an edge to it. "We would be poor hosts if we didn't at least offer our guests some food and drink before matters of business. Would we not?"

The Wolf Lord grunted. Ruven seemed to take that as a yes, and reached out an inviting hand. "Come, come. Let us sit and relax together, and speak of happier things."

"Like where you're hiding Terika?" Zaira demanded, taking half a step forward.

"Ah, you mean the alchemist?"

I froze in shock. So they really *did* have Terika here. Zaira let out a hiss, as if furious steam escaped her.

"She is your friend, then? Of course, of course you shall see her!" Ruven waved a dismissive hand. "Refreshments first. Come, sit and rest, and you can visit her after."

I didn't dare move. But then Ruven's father shook his head in disgust, and the wolves drew back, giving us space. "Very well, Ruven. We'll try it your way."

Zaira's smile was terrible as a finger bent to breaking. "Oh, yes, let's have a nice little tea party. No sense trying to murder each other on an empty stomach."

All three of them had the power to kill me easy as blinking. If we needed to resort to balefire, I had no illusions I'd make it out of this castle alive.

So I forced myself to step forward, though I ignored Ruven's proffered arm. At least there did seem to be some tension between Ruven and his father; perhaps I could salvage some advantage from this disaster.

"Thank you for your gracious hospitality," I said. "We'd be delighted to accept."

The Wolf Lord grunted. "I leave them to you, Ruven. Take care of them."

With that ominously ambiguous pronouncement, he stalked off, dismissing us without a backward glance. His fur cloak swirled behind him. The wolf pack cast us final warning glares and followed him on near-silent paws.

"Come, then, my lady." Ruven reached toward my cheek; I pulled away, heart pounding, far too aware of what he could do with a simple touch. He smirked, enjoying my discomfort. "Let us sit a moment and talk."

Ruven led us through one of the foyer side doors to a dining room with a long, gleaming black table, dominated at one end by a thronelike chair adorned with the pelts of wolves and leopards. Tall windows lined two of the dining room walls; woody vines grew over them, shaped into intricate patterns. I spotted the forms of howling wolves, running deer, and towering pines, all cunningly shaped from the living vines by the touch of a skilled vivomancer. I couldn't help staring, pulling more and more shapes out of the twisting vines, as we settled ourselves at the table.

Ruven noticed the direction of my gaze. "Ah, you like our little decorative lattice?"

"It's lovely," I admitted.

"My late mother's work. It was a hobby of hers." He sighed. "I spent many of my boyhood years here."

Liveried servants scurried in, eyes downcast, several with handprint-shaped scars on their wrists or faces. They laid before us plates of beef cooked with tartgrass and potatoes, and glasses of red wine, cringing whenever they came within Ruven's reach.

I found myself without much appetite for such heavy fare, when I could still hear the click of claws on marble as wolves paced the hall, and our hosts could decide at any moment that it no longer amused them to keep us alive. I was more than happy to reach for my wineglass, however.

I'd scarcely picked it up when my ring warmed on my finger, the stone glowing gold.

I set the cup back down, pulse racing. Zaira saw it and pushed her plate away.

"Forgive me, but there appears to be something amiss with the wine," I said, with cold politeness.

Ruven frowned. "That is unacceptable." He crooked a finger at the servant who had brought my cup, a flaxen-haired youth perhaps a few years my junior. "You. Come here."

The boy went pale as death; a burn mark on his neck stood out livid purple. But he stepped forward, even in his terror; the alternative must be worse.

"That won't be necessary," I said sharply. "I'm quite certain it wasn't your servant's doing."

Ruven spread his hands innocently. "Why, Lady Amalia, I cannot allow an inferior vintage at my table. If my own servants bring my guests something that displeases them"—his hand shot out, closing on the boy's wrist—"they must bear the consequences."

The boy screamed. The empty tray he held in his other hand crashed to the floor, and a terrible shriek of agony built in his throat. But before it could peak, the sound cut off, and he froze still as a statue. His breath came harsh and fast as he struggled to scream, still staring in horror at Ruven, unable to do anything else under the touch of his power.

I sprang to my feet. "Prince Ruven! I implore you to stop!"

The boy's sleeve tore, and the flesh beneath it. Sharp spikes of his own bone sprouted like thorns from his arm, the tips stained with his blood. His breath gurgled in his throat.

Zaira stood, throwing down her napkin. "That's it. Let's burn this place down."

"Now, now, please, sit down." Ruven released the boy, who collapsed to his knees, clutching his ruined arm, his body heaving with the attempt to scream. But he still couldn't do it. Whatever Ruven had done to silence him had left him mute.

Ruven snapped his fingers, and the other servants helped the boy to his feet, scrupulously avoiding his arm with its jagged spears of bloodied bone, and all but dragged him from the hall. His eyes strained wide, and his breath heaved like a dying man's. I couldn't tear my eyes away from him until they'd pulled him out of sight.

"I do apologize for displeasing you," Ruven sighed. "Our kitchen is not well versed in the palettes of Raverran aristocracy. I shall have the cook flogged as well."

"Please don't. Your cook isn't the one at fault." I forced my features to stern smoothness, or as close as I could manage. I couldn't let him see how much hurting his servants rattled me, or he'd do it again. "With all respect, I don't see why you're pretending to be hospitable if you're only going to poison us."

"Oh, that? It's not poison." Ruven chuckled. "My, Lady Amalia, why would I ever poison you? You know well enough I have other ways to end your life if I choose."

Zaira tugged at my sleeve. "Don't waste any more time talking to this pile of demon dung. Come on. Let's leave."

Ruven's brows lifted. "But what about your alchemist friend? Didn't you want to see her?" Zaira froze. Ruven sighed, shaking his head. "She'll be so disappointed when I tell her you left without saying hello."

Zaira slammed her fists down on the table, making the plates jump. "Hells take you! This isn't a game."

Ruven's violet-ringed gaze glittered. "Of course it isn't. I said you would see her, and you shall. Are you certain you won't have anything to eat, or even a sip of wine?"

"Quite certain," I said firmly.

Ruven rose, extending a hand. "Walk with me, then. Let us see if we can come to an amicable agreement through the power of civilized discussion."

Zaira snorted. "I don't promise to be civilized, but I'll go for a walk."

Neither of us accepted Ruven's proffered arm. We strolled out of the dining room and across the foyer to the great throne hall. I eyed the doors as we passed them, but I doubted we'd make it down the steps if we tried to run.

The throne stood empty, and servants scuttled along the edges of the hall, bringing in elaborately carved wooden chairs. A rotund woman and an elderly man, both in the livery of the household, argued about where to place them. All fell silent and bowed low when they noticed Prince Ruven.

"Forgive the mess," he said, and I realized with a jolt he was referring to the *people*. "We're preparing to host the Conclave soon, and I fear the castle is quite disrupted."

"I can disrupt it more for you," Zaira offered.

"Now, now," Ruven chuckled. "We do not need to be enemies. There is much we could offer each other."

"Oh, I think we need to be enemies," she said bluntly. "You have my friend prisoner."

"Do I? I assure you, she is less a prisoner here than at the Mews." We had drawn near his father's black throne, with its jagged fan of intricately interlaced points of bone or antler.

Ruven mounted the two steps of its simple dais to lay a hand on its arm. "You owe the Empire nothing, Lady Zaira. You are in Vaskandar now. And here, the mage-marked rule."

Zaira snorted. "That would be a fantastic idea if it weren't for people like you."

"You could join my father's court, as a member of the highest class of Vaskandran society. You would have as much freedom as I do, yes?" He ran his fingers along the dark curves of the throne, almost stroking it. "No tricks or traps. All you need do is become part of my father's domain. Then you would be a free woman, a great lady, set above all those without the mark. Is that not preferable to serving an Empire that only sees you as a weapon and uses you as a tool?"

If Zaira didn't hate Ruven so much, I'd have worried she might accept. And I might not have blamed her.

But she arched a skeptical brow. "And your father would welcome me into his court with open arms? The old bastard wants to kill me."

Ruven chuckled, as if the idea was delightful. "But of course he'd take you in! After all, he can still kill any of us at any time. This is *his* domain. The only law in Vaskandar is the will of the Witch Lords. Everything in Kazerath belongs to him."

"Even you?" I asked.

Ruven's eyes met mine; the violet ring of the mage mark gleamed around his pupils with a momentary intensity so stark it shocked me like an icicle driven through my heart. I couldn't tell if it was anger, hatred, or some twisted and desperate blend of more complex emotions.

Then he let out a long sigh and descended from the dais to stand on the hard stone floor with us again.

"For now, alas, yes." He shook his head. "It's why this war with your Empire is necessary. To rule my own domain is my birthright. To have my father set above me grows intolerable to both of us. But we have no unclaimed land left in Vaskandar, and thus must take it from you."

"Can't you just inherit your father's domain?" I waved a vague hand to soften the question, in case he thought I was suggesting patricide.

"Of a certainty, if my father ever takes it into his head to die." Ruven raised his brows. "You study history, do you not, Lady Amalia? You must have some inkling how long he has been the Wolf Lord of Kazerath."

"Actually, no," I admitted, embarrassed. "Raverran histories are singularly unclear about when a given title passes to the next heir in Vaskandar. They just keep talking about the Wolf Lord, as if it were..." I trailed off. *Demon of Madness.* "The same person," I whispered.

"There! Yes, you see my problem." He nodded, emphatically. "A Witch Lord is tied to every living thing in his domain, with bonds of absolute dominion. All that life, the great wild tide of it, is *his.* My father has lived two centuries already, and he is not even close to the oldest of the Witch Lords. I will be dust long before I could come into my inheritance." Ruven swept an arm at the throne. "If I wish to partake in such immortality—and who would not?—I require my own domain. And so you see, Lady Amalia, why Vaskandar is always at war."

"Grace of Mercy," I breathed. *Immortality.* My books spoke of vivomancers remaining healthy and young-looking into their seventies or eighties, but not living hundreds of years. No wonder Ruven wanted to invade the Serene Empire.

Zaira shook her head in disgust. "Eruvia needs you to live forever the way it needs me to set it on fire from end to end."

Ruven laughed. "If you take up my offer to join our court, perhaps we can arrange for you to burn it."

We stared at him. Even Zaira didn't seem to have any words left.

"No?" Ruven sighed. "I am disappointed. But perhaps you'll change your mind with further contemplation."

"Terika," Zaira reminded him, relentless. "Are you taking me to see her, or am I finding out how long it takes balefire to melt stone?"

Ruven's eyes narrowed. "I do not recommend testing my father's patience, Lady Zaira. I tell you this not as a threat, but for the sake of everyone in this castle. This is his domain."

"Then don't push me, either. Everything that burns is fire's domain."

"Very well," Ruven sighed. "I said you could see your friend, and you shall. I'll bring her to visit you in your room."

"Oh, we don't need a room," I said, politely as if of course no one had been threatening to murder anyone else. "We'll be on our way in a moment."

Ruven's eyes glittered. "Oh, no, you *must* stay the night. I insist. Vaskandar is a beautiful country, but I fear it's dangerous after dark." He snapped his fingers at a servant who cowered in a corner, one of the few who hadn't dared flee when the Wolf Lord entered; she flinched away from the sound. "Is our finest guest room prepared?"

The servant bowed. "Y-yes, Your Highness," she stammered.

"Good, good. Let me conduct you to your chamber, then, and you can take your rest there while I see about your friend." He extended a hand. I pointedly ignored it, but we had little choice but to follow him.

When we stepped out of the throne hall, two tall, lean chimeras slipped up next to us: built like long-legged hunting cats, but with smooth black scales and the reared-back heads of serpents. Their snakelike tails lashed behind them as they fell in beside us. One bent its head toward my injured leg, tongue tasting the air; I sucked in my breath and clutched at Zaira's arm, but it didn't touch me.

"Don't mind them," Ruven said. "My little pets. Quite harmless. Unless my father or I command them to attack, of course—then their venom is rather fatal."

Zaira's arm went rigid under my hand, and her face took on an almost greenish cast. "Everything about this place is ruddy charming."

Ruven smiled. "I'm glad you find it so."

His shining blond ponytail swung against the black leather of his coat as he led us back to the foyer and up the sweeping curve of stairs to the second floor. Zaira glanced longingly at the castle doors as we passed them, but there was no way we could make a run for it with the chimeras pacing at our sides. Oil lamps illuminated the windowless second-floor guest hallway, their warm light flickering off the curves of black wood that lifted the ceiling into a pointed arch, like a dead monster's rib cage. I had the uneasy sensation the castle was swallowing us.

Ruven threw open the door to a lavish, spacious room. More dark woodwork formed elaborate shapes over the lilac-painted walls, like the patterns of bare branches against the evening sky. Fur rugs scattered across the floor, some from recognizable creatures and others doubtless from expired chimeras. A fire burned in an arched hearth that made me think of a demon's maw, with chairs set before it covered in more pelts. Two canopied beds draped with excessive quantities of purple velvet stood at the far end of the room, side by side.

"Please, consider this your home," Ruven said. "I'll return shortly."

He bowed, a smirk pulling at his lips, and left. The two chimeras stayed in the hall, flanking the door, staring at us from slitted yellow eyes.

Zaira slammed the door on them, then put her back against it. "I want to burn his face off, then keep burning a path all the way to the border."

I sank onto a chair to ease my aching leg. A massive weight of postponed horror loomed above me, like the stony bulk of the castle and all its reaching towers. "It may come to that. But I'd like to try to come up with a better option first. This is an excellent chance to learn more about Ruven's plans, so long as we can get out of here alive."

"Plans be damned. I'd do it right now if it weren't for Terika." Zaira hunched her shoulders. "If they don't murder us before sundown, we can get her out of here tonight and leave this pit of vipers behind us."

I held little illusion it would be that easy. But I nodded, too weary to argue.

"Zaira," I asked, the words slow and heavy on my tongue, "do you want me to release you?"

She blinked. "What, right now? Given up on diplomacy already? That was quick."

"Graces, no." I held out my cold hands toward the fire, the one homey thing in this mad place. "But we're in Vaskandar. We're in danger every moment. I don't want us both to die because I couldn't say the release word in time. And more to the point"—I met her eyes—"the Serene Empire's laws don't reach here. It's your magic. There's no reason you shouldn't be the one in control of it."

"Damn right there's no reason." But then she bit her lip. For a long moment, there was silence, save for the crackle of the fire and the occasional skitter of claws on the floor outside.

Finally, she let out a long breath. "I'm going to be under a lot of temptation to violence in this place."

"You've got a lifetime of practice resisting that temptation. And if you lose control, I can always reseal you." I shrugged, trying to sound more casual than I felt. This wasn't what my mother would do; I could almost feel her disapproving gaze on me, across the miles. "It's up to you."

Zaira paced over to the hearth and leaned on the mantel, staring into the fire. Then she turned to face me, back straight, eyes shining as if the reflection of the flames still danced there.

"Hells, yes," she said. "Do it."

I closed my eyes. "*Exsolvo,*" I whispered.

I flinched from the word, bracing myself. But nothing happened. After a moment, I blinked my eyes back open.

Zaira stood there, her palms open as if waiting to catch rain. But they were empty. She flexed her fingers, and a grin spread over her face.

"Demons bless me, that's better. Like taking off a corset."

I grimaced as guilt pinched me. "I'm sorry I didn't do it sooner."

"Hmph. Well, the way things are going, by the time we get back to the Empire I'll be ready for a break from burning things for a while." She gave me an odd look, then, frowning as if something about me annoyed her.

"What?" I asked. "Is there something on my face?"

"No." She let out an exasperated sigh. "I caught myself being glad you could stop me if I lose control. I hate it when I have to admit you have your uses."

"Thank you," I said dryly.

I bent to give my injured leg a tender poke. The salve sped up healing considerably, but it still ached after all the walking I'd been doing. My arm hurt, too. If I'd been at home, I'd have felt terribly sorry for myself, and would have stayed in bed reading all day to rest. But now I was far more concerned with how much my limp might slow us if we had to flee from this place.

Claws scuttled in the hall, and a knock sounded at the door. I levered myself to my feet; Zaira rolled her shoulders, ready to fight.

I opened the door, stepping back and to the side, just in case.

Terika stood there, pale as paper, her eyes nestled in deep purple hollows as if she hadn't slept since we'd seen her last. Her curly hair was a dull tangle, and dirt streaked her clothes. Ruven stood behind her, one hand on her shoulder, smiling as if he'd given us a splendid present.

"Terika!" Zaira started forward, then checked herself. "Are you all right?"

Terika nodded, a stiff jerk of a motion. "I'm fine."

"Ah, such a happy reunion," Ruven sighed. "See? Your friend is well. We haven't been mistreating her. Have we?"

Terika shook her head. But her eyes stayed locked urgently on Zaira's, as if willing her to understand what she couldn't say.

"Then you'll allow her to leave with us?" I countered.

Ruven shrugged, his eyes gleaming. "If she wishes. Terika, do you want to leave with them, and go back to the Mews?"

Terika's lips tightened. She hesitated, then slowly shook her head again. "No. I want to stay here. I...like it here."

Zaira hissed, as if she were a snake chimera herself. "You can't possibly like this Hell pit. I'll believe you don't want to go back to the Mews, but not that you want to stay here."

Ruven laughed, as if it delighted him to hear his home called a Hell pit. "But you see, there are certain advantages to being my guest. Show them, Terika."

Obediently, Terika lifted her hands between us, as if to ward off harm.

Her wrists were bare.

Zaira caught one in her hand. "Demon's piss. He did *that* to you? Slid your jess off through your wrist? Did you ask him to?"

My stomach turned queasily at the memory of Ruven's knife pushing through his guard's wrist as if it were butter, when he showed Zaira how he could set her free. By the look of horror in Terika's eyes, she was remembering, too.

But she said, her voice flat, "He did it to help me."

Zaira swore and turned away, her shoulders rigid.

"Tell her," Ruven urged Terika softly.

"I'm glad to be free." The words fell from Terika's mouth like lead musket balls, lifeless and heavy. "You should let him remove yours, too. Then we could be free together."

From where I stood, I could see the corner of Zaira's eye. A faint blue light gleamed there, as if a spark had kindled deep within, and my stomach dropped. I'd picked the wrong time to release her.

I stepped forward but didn't take Terika's hand—not with Ruven's on her shoulder. I couldn't take the chance of giving his powers a bridge to reach me. "I'm glad you're well," I said, my voice bright and false. Terika's eyes pulled away from Zaira and caught mine, haunted and pleading. "We were worried about you. But you look as if you haven't bathed or slept."

Ruven sighed. "Alas, I fear she had quite a harrowing day yesterday. I'm sure she'll take better care of herself today. Won't you?"

Terika held my gaze. "If you wish it."

"Please do." I wished I dared hold her hand or give her shoulder a reassuring squeeze. "We don't want to leave here until we're sure you're safe and happy."

Terika's cheeks tightened, and her eyes shone with suppressed tears or fury.

"Never fear," Ruven assured me. "You can stay here as many nights as you wish. In fact, I am certain your stay will be a long and pleasant one."

He reached out, quick as a striking snake, and brushed a hand down my cheek while I was distracted by Terika. I jumped back; lingering magic prickled and burned my skin. I raised a hand to my face and felt heat there, as from a slap or a sunburn. But it could just have been my own red rage.

"Prince Ruven," I said coldly, "I had thought you a gentleman."

Ruven laughed. "My, my. So jumpy, Lady Amalia! I will not further offend your sensibilities. Now, Terika here is tired, and I suspect she'd love the chance to bathe and eat. Wouldn't you?"

Terika stared miserably at us. Her head barely moved in the requisite nod. Zaira spun back to face Ruven; the blue gleam was gone from her eyes, thank the Graces, but the look she gave him was no less lethal.

"By the Nine Hells," she said, biting off each word, "I swear to you, you'll answer for this."

Ruven placed a hand on his chest. "Me?" he protested. "All I've done, Lady Zaira, is set her free." He bowed. "Now, if you'll excuse us. Good night, my ladies, and pleasant dreams."

Terika stared with mute desperation at Zaira, but Ruven shut the door between them.

There came the unmistakable sound of a key turning in a lock. Then two sets of footsteps receded down the corridor.

Zaira snatched a candlestick off a nearby table and hurled it at the door. "Hells take you, you pox-faced bilge rat!"

A hiss sounded from the hallway. Claws scraped at the door, dragging into the wood.

Chapter Twenty-One

We waited for nightfall. I understood the need for the castle to settle into sleep, and for all the servants and soldiers who might otherwise spot us creeping around the castle to go to their beds; but every minute we spent in this place of madness and dread was a loss I felt in my bones. Soon, Bree and the captain at Highpass would realize something had prevented us from making it home from Vaskandar, and they would have to decide what to do about it. What's more, after I swallowed down an anise-scented evening dose of my elixir, I was halfway through my emergency supply; if we met more complications on the way to my luggage in Highpass, the few hours we delayed now could make the difference between life and death.

Zaira chafed at the inactivity even more than I did, pacing the furs and muttering curses on Ruven, his father, and their entire nation. Finally, she flopped down in a chair by the fire, staring broodingly into it.

"Look at us," she said. "Stuck in a Witch Lord's castle, with a dozen people dead to get us here, and for what?"

"We got Bree out," I said quietly. "And we'll rescue Terika, too." I hesitated, then added something I'd been thinking about over the past hour or two as I watched the colors fade from the world outside our window. "Also, this is an incredible chance to gather information. We should see if there's any spying we can safely do before we leave."

"I suppose we might as well. We're just as buggered either way."

"Well, at least we're together." I said it with an edge of irony but then discovered I meant it. I shifted my leg off the stool I'd propped it on, leaning toward her. "I'd be terrified if you weren't here with me."

Zaira snorted. "Always nice to have the 'set everything on fire' fallback plan."

"No, not because you're a fire warlock. Because..." I struggled for the words, and then couldn't keep the disbelief out of my voice once I found them. "Because for some peculiar reason, I find you reassuring. As a person."

Zaira blinked at me. "You're mad."

"Well, perhaps. But you keep a cool head in a crisis." I shrugged. "And you're good company, once one learns to overlook all the foul language and personal remarks."

She laughed. "And you're better than an infected tooth, I suppose. When I can ignore your rich brat airs and general obliviousness."

I tried a tentative smile. "We make a good team, you know."

"We do." Zaira lifted her brows, as if the discovery surprised her. Then she nodded decisively and surged to her feet, glancing out the window at the moonlit sky. "All right. It's late enough. Let's do this."

I rose, shedding the exhaustion that had overtaken me. My leg took my weight with far less pain than it had earlier. "I have no doubt you can pick the lock," I said, "but do you have a plan for dealing with those chimeras?"

"No." She threw open the window, letting in a blast of frigid air. Then she tied up her skirt and hoisted a leg over the sill. "But

I have a plan for *not* dealing with the chimeras. How good are you at climbing?"

I watched with growing alarm as she swung her other leg out as well, twisting to stand braced on something I couldn't see. "Ah, I've never really had occasion to try."

Zaira shook her head in disbelief. "Graces grant me patience. Never tried? Did you spend your entire childhood sitting in a fancy chair reading books?"

"Well—"

"Don't answer that." She sighed and shifted her grip on the window edges, seeming at ease as if she stood on flat ground. "You can either come with me and try to learn quickly, or you can stay there and rot. It's not far, it's not hard, and if you fall from this height you'll break both your legs but probably not die."

"You make it sound so delightful." I swallowed and pulled off my boots, stuffing them in my satchel. "I'll give it a try. I don't mind heights, at least."

Getting out the window was the scariest part. Zaira talked me through it with surprising patience, coaxing my bare toes down onto a curving woody ledge—the top of Ruven's mother's lattice. The arch of the vine gave slightly under my feet, but it was strong and smooth as polished wood.

I clung there, my freezing toes hooked over the vine, grabbing on to the edges of the window tight enough to make my fingers ache. A cold night wind raked my back and stirred my hair, and Kathe's claws rattled on my chest. I didn't look down, but there was only open air behind me, with none of the close shadows of looming pines. Stars teased at the corners of my eyes.

Grace of Mercy, what would my mother think if she could see me now?

The idea shook my shoulders with laughter. For a wild moment, I felt strangely free, as if I could leap away from the side of the castle and soar off into the night.

Then a howl rose from the forest, not far off. The wolf pack, hunting. I pressed myself against the cold stone of the castle wall.

Zaira guided me across to the next window, offering a hand to steady me for the last gap before I could grab the stone molding of the window frame. We peered in on another guest room, empty, its hearth dark. We inched along past two more windows, my bare feet aching in the icy air and my cheek pressed close against the castle wall, as Zaira muttered instructions and encouragement. Then we climbed into a third guest room, this one on a corner. I dropped to my knees, hands buried in the fur rug, arms trembling.

"Oh, get up. You're pathetic." Zaira nudged my ribs with her foot.

"Forgive me if my education lacked climbing practice." I heaved myself back to my feet. "I shall have to write a stern letter to the university."

Zaira listened at the door of the darkened guest room. "The chimeras shouldn't be able to see us from here," she said softly, "but they might hear us. I don't know how good their ears are. I'm betting on them following orders and staying by the door, and being too stupid to figure out we're not in there anymore. If they're smarter than they look, we could be in trouble."

"We could be in trouble anyway, I suspect." I pulled on my boots. "Let's see if we can spy on Ruven and the Wolf Lord. We won't have another chance like this."

Zaira grunted. "Only if it doesn't slow us down too much. I want to get Terika out of here."

"Out into the forest full of wolves, chimeras, and assorted other unknown horrors, where the trees themselves could start trying to kill us at any time?"

"Do you have a better idea?"

I sighed. "No. Very well. Lead on."

She eased open the door. I tried to step quietly as I crept

down the lamp-lit hallway behind her, but by the glares she shot back over her shoulder, I had mixed success at best. Every nerve in my body ached with the expectation that chimeras would bound after us at any minute, fangs dripping venom, but so far all seemed quiet.

"Where do you think Ruven and his father are?" I whispered near Zaira's ear, irrationally afraid the Wolf Lord would somehow hear. But then, with vivomancy as strong as his, he might well already be listening to the racing beat of my heart.

"With arrogance like theirs? The throne room," Zaira muttered, and headed for the center of the castle.

Soon, one wall of the hallway turned to a balcony railing ahead, and I recognized the high arching ceiling of the great throne hall. Sure enough, voices drifted up from below.

Told you, Zaira mouthed, smirking. Holding my breath, I crouched with her at the end of the wall to listen.

"... worked well enough with the others." That was Ruven's unmistakable tenor. "It matters little that they're suspicious. All living things must eat and drink, no?"

I edged forward until I could peer between the balusters. Below us, the Wolf Lord sprawled in his throne, regarding his son from under heavy gray eyebrows. Ruven leaned against a pillar, arms crossed, his black coat falling back from his shoulders.

"And then what?" Contempt laced his father's deep, rumbling voice. "If you think a potion will be enough to make that fire witch docile, you haven't looked in her eyes."

I could feel Zaira thrumming with anger beside me and had to agree with the Wolf Lord.

"Think of the advantage it would give us," Ruven pressed, stepping away from his pillar. "No one could stand against us—not the Serene Empire, not the other Witch Lords. You have nothing to lose by giving my plan a chance—"

"I did not become the Wolf Lord of Kazerath by giving people *chances.*" His tone froze Ruven where he stood. Even up on the balcony, a chill settled in my spine. "I judge your plans on their own merits, boy, and this one is folly."

"Folly?" Ruven's voice held an edge less smooth than I'd ever heard it. Fear? Hatred? Or merely frustration that his father couldn't understand his vision? I'd never thought what it must have been like for him, growing up in a Witch Lord's household. "When have my ideas served you anything but well? It was I who won you the alliance of the Lady of Thorns—"

"An alliance that is of little use." The Wolf Lord cut him off. "She intends to use you to get a domain for her daughter and cast you aside without one of your own."

Her daughter. A shiver of recognition raced across my shoulders. Kathe had said the Lady of Thorns' daughter was dying. That must be why she wanted land so badly—to get a domain for her daughter and grant her the immortality of a Witch Lord, so that she could live forever.

"I am giving you the measureless destructive power of a volcano," Ruven insisted. I strained closer. "Mount Whitecrown will cast your reach farther than any Witch Lord before you. No one else in Eruvia could have taken the magic of the Empire and wound our power through it the way I have. If you would only listen to me—"

"Enough." The Wolf Lord cut him off with a growl that set the stone of the castle to rumbling. I cringed beneath the force of that one word. But Ruven stood before it, hands in fists at his sides. "When you've carved out a piece of land from the Empire and claimed it with your own blood, you can make all the moon-mad plans you want. Until then, in your mother's memory, I may choose to allow your twisted schemes—but only when they'll get you out of my domain faster. Enough, Ruven."

Ruven must have heard the danger in his father's voice. But he stepped forward anyway, the mage mark flashing violet in his eyes. "You will win this war with the Empire because of my 'twisted schemes'! If you throw aside my plans simply because I choose methods more complicated than brute force, you're a fool."

Outside, wolves howled.

A rustling and groaning stirred along the castle walls, and a hundred black claws reached in through the windows—the vines of the decorative lattice, grown sharp as spears and creeping into the hall. The air thickened until my temples pulsed with the weight of power. Zaira sucked in a breath at my side. I flattened myself on the floor, filled with the sudden terror of a rabbit in a hawk's shadow, sure we'd been seen.

But the Wolf Lord didn't move from his relaxed slouch. The white rings of the mage mark in his eyes stayed fixed on Ruven.

"Are you challenging me, pup?" he asked, his voice deadly soft. "Here, in my own domain?"

"I?" Ruven laughed, a sound sharp as spilled nails. "I have not yet taken leave of my senses. You are the Witch Lord of Kazerath. I am merely your son."

The Wolf Lord held his gaze, unrelenting. Finally, Ruven bowed, his spine stiff, deep enough to bend himself nearly double.

"That's right," his father growled. "Don't forget it, Ruven. Not for a minute."

The pressure in the air eased. The vines slithered back through the windows, resuming their decorative shapes. Zaira caught my eyes and mimed wiping sweat from her brow. I blew out a nervous breath.

Grace of Mercy. And I thought my relationship with my mother was complicated.

We moved away from the balcony as swiftly as silence would allow. Zaira caught my gaze and shook her head, her own eyes white-rimmed. My pulse still carried a searing thrill through my body, the instinctive dread of a hunted animal.

We needed to get out of here. But we needed to find Terika first.

Of all the rooms along the shadow-girdled hallway, two showed the warm glow of firelight beneath. In a mountain castle without the benefit of artifice to heat it, I rather doubted any room without a fire would be occupied. Zaira and I crept closer to the first lit door; she applied her eye to the keyhole, and I bent down to peer under it.

The room within wasn't quite as fine or spacious as ours and held only one bed, though it was still draped in purple velvet and furs. A clutter of possessions suggested this room had a permanent occupant: an easel with a half-finished painting, shelves with jars of paint and brushes and all manner of art supplies, a bookcase, a pair of muskets with fancy engraving hanging on the wall. A red-haired boy of perhaps fourteen years sat in a chair by the fire, reading a book.

I frowned. His abundant freckles suggested Callamornish ancestry, but this was the room of a pampered young nobleman, not that of a prisoner. I exchanged glances with Zaira; she shook her head, I shrugged, and we moved on.

At the next door, I didn't even need to peek. Zaira had barely bent to glance through the keyhole when she straightened and nodded, lips pressed together. I watched for any sign of prowling chimeras, wolves, or Witch Lords as Zaira crouched before the lock and got to work—though I wasn't remotely certain what I planned to do if any showed up.

It must not have been much of a lock. I'd hardly taken three breaths when she pushed the door open. Terika's startled voice called, "Who's—oh!" as Zaira charged into the room.

By the time I stepped through, they were in each other's arms, Terika's head buried in Zaira's shoulder.

I closed the door softly behind me and glanced around the room, trying to give them a moment. It was half the size of ours, without the decorative lattice on the walls or the velvet curtains on the bed, but it was still finely appointed, in a hunting lodge sort of way. I couldn't help but consider it barbaric to use so many pelts as decor; the four bedrooms we'd seen must have held the skins of a few packs of beasts.

I was prepared to stare at the walls for quite some time, if necessary. But it was only a few minutes before Terika stepped back out of Zaira's arms.

"Lienne," she said urgently. "Is she..."

I shook my head. Terika pressed her lips together, tears gleaming unshed in her eyes. By the look in them, she hadn't held much hope.

"But Bree took the ingredients you gathered back to your village to give to the Highpass alchemist," I said quickly.

Terika let out a relieved sigh, her shoulders drooping. "He should be able to make the cure. I don't think he has the mage mark, but that shouldn't matter for a simple recipe like that." She put her hands on her hips, then, and glanced sternly between us. "And what are you two doing here?"

"Rescuing you, of course." Zaira grinned.

"You have to leave," Terika said urgently.

Zaira nodded. "Right. Grab anything you need to take with you."

Terika pressed her hands over her mouth. "I can't go with you."

"Can't, or don't want to?" I asked, eyeing the barely touched dinner and half-empty cup of water on the table in her sitting area.

"Can't." Her eyes flicked to the table, then back to me.

I closed my hand around her cup. My ring immediately glowed with golden light.

Zaira clenched her fists in her own hair. "Alchemy. Demons rot it, I don't know anything about alchemy. Did he give you a mind control potion?"

Terika shook her head. A bit of the usual spark came back into her eyes. "There's no such thing as mind control potion. Potions that muddy the mind, yes. Ones that make you suggestible, certainly. But no one's created a potion that bends someone else's mind to another's will."

I sank into one of the chairs flanking Terika's table, thinking. "Can you tell us what you think of Prince Ruven, Terika?"

"I hate him," she said immediately, with passion. "He's a terrible person. He's done unspeakable things."

"Like what?" Zaira clasped her shoulder. "What did he do to you?"

Terika shook her head. "Nothing. He's treated me well. I like it here." She kicked a chair leg, frustration clear on her face. "Damnation!"

"Hells have mercy." Zaira threw her hands up. "We don't need to do this dance. I get it. You can't tell us. Come with us, and we'll get you out of here."

Terika backed away, her hands lifted. "I can't! I can't go with you. If you try to take me with you, I'll fight you. Please, don't try." Real panic strained her voice.

I passed my hand over Terika's dinner and frowned as my ring glowed again. "How did a Witch Lord's son get his hands on so much alchemy?"

Terika pulled up a chair and sat next to me, nodding eagerly. She said nothing, but her eyes burned imploringly into mine.

"You wouldn't have made a potion to slip into your own food," I said slowly. "So there must be someone else."

"Everyone is very happy here," Terika said, leaning her elbows on her knees. *"Everyone."*

"Grace of Mercy," I breathed. "Everyone?"

Terika nodded, vigorously.

"What is it?" Zara demanded.

"The murdered Falcons." I gripped the arms of my chair as

the full implications settled in. "They weren't murdered at all. They're here."

"I don't know what you're talking about," Terika said triumphantly, squeezing my hand. "There are no other Falcons here."

Zaira started pacing. "Oh, I'm going to roast that wretch like a festival pig. So he snatched up Falcons, made it look like he killed them, used his flesh-melting trick to get their jesses off, and gave them some kind of potion to make them have to follow his commands. How many does he have here?"

Terika shook her hands out, making an annoyed sound behind her closed lips.

"There are some half dozen unaccounted for, I think," I said, trying to remember the particulars of the last report I'd heard. "We'll never sneak out of here with that many. Especially if he's ordered them to fight us." But that still bothered me. I leaned forward, tapping the table. "I don't understand how you're compelled. I've never heard of any alchemical potion that could force someone to follow commands against their will." There was the matter that he was exerting vivomancy upon her from afar, too, which wasn't supposed to work—except for Witch Lords.

"I'm not compelled. Why would you ever think that?" Terika bit her lip, clearly thinking. Then she said, casually, "Say, didn't you meet Prince Ruven in a library in Ardence last year, when he was conducting research?"

Zaira snorted. "We caught him stealing a book, if that's what you mean."

"*Interactions of Magic*," I recalled. "Domenic said there were sections in there about combining vivomancy and alchemy. Is this potion some mix of his powers and an alchemist's?"

Terika sighed. "I have no idea what potion you're talking about. That's quite an interesting theory, though. You might want to pursue it. But first, you need to get out of here."

Zaira's hands formed white-knuckled fists. "We came

through the Nine Hells to rescue you. People died to get us here. We can't just leave you."

Terika went to Zaira and clasped her hands, easing them gently open. "Please," she said. "I'll be fine. They're not going to kill me, or even hurt me. Get yourself to safety first, and *then* you can figure out a way to..." She struggled over the words, her tongue tangling on what she'd wanted to say. Finally, she settled on, "...for us to be together again in a good place. Ugh, this is impossible."

Zaira tried an uneven grin. "More impossible than me?"

"Nothing's *that* impossible."

Zaira swallowed. "Terika, about what I said on the road. Uh, about your grandmother."

Terika frowned. "That's right. I'm angry at you."

"I'm sorry."

Terika crossed her arms. "It was a rotten thing to say."

Zaira shrugged uncomfortably. "That's no surprise. I'm a rotten person."

"That's not true." Terika wagged a finger at her. "I've figured you out. You said that about my grandmother to drive me away, didn't you? Out of some foolish notion that you don't deserve me?"

Zaira gave her a guilty, caught-in-the-act grimace. But a pang of recognition caught my breath in my chest. Zaira had been right about one thing: her enemies were already using Terika against her.

I clasped Marcello's button in my fingers. It was easy enough for me to urge her to follow her heart, then blithely ignore my own advice. But nothing was simple for a fire warlock, any more than it was for the Cornaro heir.

Zaira spread her arms wide, with the dubious air of someone showing off a dress she had serious reservations about purchasing. "This is who I am, Terika," she said. "I'm a Tallows brat—crude and bitter. I'm like a flea-ridden dog that bites anyone trying to be kind to it."

A smile teased Terika's lips. "I seem to recall that we first caught each other's interest because we both have a soft spot for stray dogs."

"But you can do better than a grumpy bitch like me."

Terika tapped Zaira right on the nose. "Stop saying mean things about one of my favorite people."

Zaira blinked. "Me?"

"Yes, you. I like you. I don't care whether you think you deserve it. I like you, and you make me happy." She put her fists on her hips. "And unless you sincerely don't want me around, you're stuck with me. So there."

Zaira seemed to struggle a moment. Then she whispered, "I like you, too."

Terika lifted a hand to Zaira's cheek and leaned in, closing her eyes. For half a second, Zaira hesitated. But then she tipped her head and parted her lips, and they were kissing with the desperate tenderness of people who didn't know when they'd see each other again.

I looked away, thinking, *Tell her you love her, fool. Say it now, while you still can.*

She didn't say it. But it was a long kiss. Maybe Terika already knew.

"You have to go," Terika said, clasping both of Zaira's shoulders. Her voice was calm, sensible.

Zaira didn't look calm or sensible. She looked ready to dismantle the castle stone by stone with her teeth. "We could knock you out and drag you with us," she said desperately. "Or

I could force-feed that bastard Ruven balefire, and see how he likes the taste of it. Or—"

"Or you could leave, and get Amalia to safety, and come back here soon with a carefully picked team and a real plan," Terika said.

"We can't drag an unconscious or resisting person up the mountain," I agreed reluctantly. "Not with a Witch Lord after us. Zaira..."

"Shut up," Zaira growled. "I know all that."

"Ruven needs me. I'll be safe," Terika promised. "But you two won't." She hesitated, then, as if choosing her words carefully. "Please don't underestimate my ability to stop you if you try to take me with you."

"Fine." Zaira turned away, her voice strained. "We'll go. I hate big, stupid, dramatic gestures. But we'll get you out of here. Do you hear me?"

"I hear you," Terika said, with a tender smile.

They held each other for a long time, while I busied myself checking the contents of my satchel several times. Finally, Terika all but shoved us out the door into the dark hallway. Droplets of moisture stood like tiny diamonds at the corners of Zaira's eyes.

We crept through the castle corridors; flickering oil lamps cast wavering shadows against the walls. All that was left was to search what remaining rooms we could for useful information and find an unguarded window to climb out of.

We groped our way down a servant's stair. Without windows or luminaries, the steps were so black I couldn't see Zaira in front of me and had to keep my hand out to avoid bumping into her. We came out near the kitchens but had barely stepped through the door when the unmistakable sound of claws scraping the floor and heavy breathing approached us in the darkness.

Zaira mouthed a curse and pulled at my sleeve; we slipped around a corner, out of the cramped, hidden world of the servants and into the spacious corridors of the main castle. We ducked into the first empty room we came to that had an outside window. Zaira listened by the door, making sure the chimera hadn't followed.

I blinked in the darkness, letting my eyes adjust. This wasn't a bedroom; the shadowy shapes of furniture were square and blocky, bookshelves and desks, rather than soft-draped beds or mirrored wardrobes.

It was a study. I'd chanced on a vein of gold.

I scanned the room for any sign of papers; my gaze lit on a large scroll unrolled on a table under the window and weighted down at the corners. A map or diagram, from the look of it, and with the moonlight falling directly upon it. Perfect. I crossed to the table, peering at the great white rectangle shining in the darkness.

It was an artifice schematic. A dozen complex artifice circles, each layered with diagrams and runes, formed a greater ring, with a breathtakingly detailed control circle at its center. In the dark, it was hard to read the runes and follow the lines of the diagram, but it looked dreadfully familiar.

My pulse quickened. I'd seen that pattern of nested circles before, in *Interactions of Magic*, the book Ruven had studied and tried to steal. This was the enchantment to trigger a volcanic eruption.

"I hope you can make sense of that, because it's all pretty doodles to me," Zaira whispered.

"Too much sense." I pulled paper and a charcoal pencil from my satchel and bent closer, peering at the design. A crudely sketched map and a few notes suggested the location of each circle on Mount Whitecrown; I copied the information down as quickly as I could. "This isn't exactly the same as the design I saw in the book. Someone knowledgeable has helped him modify it."

"So he needs artificers to control the volcano, and alchemists to control the artificers." Zaira shook her head. "That bastard."

I peered at some notes scrawled at the edges of the diagram, hoping to learn more. It was hard to make out the writing in the dim light, but it seemed the control circle would allow him to direct the eruption and keep it from impacting his own lands. There were extensive notes about prevailing winds and how far away the ash might fall. Colored lines marked the extent of destruction from minor, middling, and major eruptions, with imperial fortresses, towns, and cities marked as to which would get caught up in each level of catastrophe.

Graces preserve us all. Even a minor eruption could kill thousands of people and open up the border defenses quick and brutal as a gull cracking open a crab. A major eruption that reached Ardence would kill tens of thousands of civilians and blanket half of Eruvia in choking ash.

"He's remembered far more than I would have imagined," I said. "And whatever artificer helped him knew their business. This might actually work. We have to stop him."

Golden light poured over us as the door behind us swung open.

"Well, well. I thought I scented you here. It seems my son can't even keep you contained, let alone controlled."

My heart spasmed painfully. I spun to find the Wolf Lord's shaggy silhouette filling the door, his presence building around him like a thunderhead.

"I'm out of patience with his schemes," the Wolf Lord growled. "It's time to end this."

Chapter Twenty-Two

I didn't wait to see what the Wolf Lord meant by *end this.*

"Zaira, eyes!" I cried, and flipped open my flare locket.

He let out a snarl of rage and threw up his arm to block the blinding flash of light, but he was too late. Zaira spun the instant the burst of brilliance ended and leaped out the ground-floor window, and I hurled myself through after. I crashed into a thorn bush, rolled to my feet, and started running after Zaira through the frost-silvered grass toward the looming shadow of the woods. Terror rendered the scratches on my face and hands as irrelevant as the dull pain that jolted up my injured leg with each step.

All around us, under the bold broken moon, the night came alive. Howls, hisses, and terrible cries I couldn't name rose up—from the castle, from the grounds, and from the forest we ran toward.

A primal cold tightened my lungs and slid up my spine, something ancient and electric. It ripped open wells of the blind, ragged energy of panic inside me; I ran faster than I ever had in my life.

We reached the tree line and plunged into the forest that covered the hill. Dry ferns swished against our calves, and the stark silver moonlight filtering down through the trees barely warned us of fallen logs to leap over. Slender giants towered above us, pines with shaggy boughs that didn't even begin until far above our heads; we dodged their night-blackened trunks as we careened down the hill in no particular direction, trying to get as far away from the castle as possible.

The trees swayed around us, branches reaching, but no wind blew through them. Ferns curled and snagged at our ankles. Zaira tripped and went sprawling with an angry yelp, but she tumbled to her feet and kept running, without losing much momentum.

Behind us, something let out a horrible cry, half hiss and half scream, far too close. Another answered it.

Ragged panting approached behind us, and the rapid thud of paws striking the ground. Any second, I expected knife-sharp claws to pierce my back.

Zaira cursed and whirled, balefire blooming on her hands. Its stark blue light caught in the reflective eyes of the two serpent chimeras that had guarded our door. For a brief moment their fangs gleamed in the glare, their serpentine bodies bunching to spring—and then a wave of fire consumed them.

I scuttled back across the forest floor, choking on a yelp. The flames reared up like a triumphant beast, climbing tree trunks with flickering blue claws.

Pale sparks kindled in Zaira's eyes as she turned to me. "Don't seal me," she said. "Let this cursed forest burn. Let my fire eat it and grow stronger."

I nodded, too short on breath and heavy with dread to reply. And we kept running, leaving the balefire raging behind us.

Something swooped past my face, and wings buffeted the back of my head. We barely fought our way through a stand of saplings that snatched us and struck at us with whippy boughs.

Needle-sharp teeth bit my ankles. Vines and brambles grabbed at us, slowing us down. And all around, howling lifted through the forest, rising to the belly of the night.

A stitch stabbed into my ribs like a stiletto, and my legs burned with the effort of running. I glanced back over my shoulder to see if anything was coming up behind us.

Backlit by the distant blue aura of balefire, shadows lumbered and bounded and writhed toward us. Dozens of them, from dog-sized to bear-sized, forming a wide and spreading arc as they closed in on us.

"Zaira!" I gasped.

She turned, planted her feet, and lifted her arms. I scrambled away from her.

Zaira drew a line of fire in front of her feet, eerie and beautiful: a thin, blue-white curtain that danced and twined and reached up hungrily toward the trees. And then it spread, racing forward across the ground, consuming all in its path.

Everything on the other side of that line was death, beautiful and unanswerable, a leaping garden of flames the color of lightning and bone. Cries of agony rose to the night, but they were swiftly silenced; horrible smells of scorching flesh filled the air.

Zaira laughed, with the free, giddy joy of a child, and raised her arms higher. Fire chewed its way up the tree trunks, turning the forest to a burning cathedral of blue light, revealing every stark detail with the bright clarity of day.

I cringed away from the flames and the stinking smoke, keeping some twenty feet directly behind her. "Zaira," I pleaded. "Enough."

She couldn't hear, or no longer cared. Balefire shivered down her hair and trailed from her arms like wings. She was a living flame herself, deadly and hungry, reveling in destruction.

Graces preserve us. I didn't dare go near her, let alone try to coax her into running with me. But if I sealed her power now, she'd drop like a stone, and I'd have to try to haul her through the forest with no way to protect myself.

A deep, furious snarl came from the forest, in the impenetrable darkness beyond the end of Zaira's line of fire. She spun to face it, and a liquid arc of balefire leaped toward the sound.

It struck a massive branch that leaned down to block it, trailing a cloak of moss. The branch sprang back up into position, burning and dripping fire.

Beneath its glowing arch stood the Wolf Lord of Kazerath, the mage mark glowing white hot in his eyes.

"You dare burn my forest," he growled. "You *dare*."

Lines of flame raced along the ground toward him this time, while I yelped and jumped out of the way. But roots buckled up out of the earth to catch them, shaking off showers of brown pine needles. The Wolf Lord stepped over the fire, slow and inexorable as time, swirling the edge of his fur cloak up to keep it from catching.

A terrible cracking and groaning sounded above us, loud as cannon fire.

"Zaira, look out!" I cried. I didn't dare grab her, but waved frantically as I scrambled to the side.

She hissed, cursing in the language of fire, and leaped out of the way just in time. With awful grandeur and a crash greater than thunder, a massive dead tree collapsed into the spot where she'd just been standing. At once, a cloud of sawdust enveloped us; I coughed on wood dust and smoke, my eyes watering.

The fallen trunk lay in pieces between us and the Wolf Lord, a decaying wall three feet high. I backed away from it, wishing desperately that Zaira would run. But balefire knew no fear.

A section of tree trunk wide as a door simply melted away, crumbling and vanishing into the ground in the time it took me to blink. The Wolf Lord stepped through the gap, never slowing his stride.

Something grabbed me from behind.

I shrieked and tried to twist free as branches caged me, and wiry vines snaked over my arms and waist, pulling me against a gnarled tree trunk. A twin-boled tree seemed to be giving Zaira similar treatment, pulling her—flames and all—into the crevice between the trunks in an attempt to crush her.

She flared up like dry tinder in a column of furious blue fire. A wave of heat struck me, searing my face; the twin trees shook and spasmed, whole limbs crumbling into ash.

The Wolf Lord approached, his pace regular as a clock ticking out the last seconds until midnight. He drew a sword white as bone, with edges that shone like diamond, and advanced on Zaira.

She stepped out of the flame-wreathed remains of the trees that had held her. I could barely make out her figure at all; she was a creature of fire, transcendent as the Graces themselves, moving with a dreamlike majesty.

Hells. I was stuck to a tree, with the forest burning around me, and she didn't even remember I existed. If the Wolf Lord didn't kill me first, her flames would.

I wriggled an arm loose from the vines and drew my dagger, then started slashing frantically at the branches that held me, desperate to get away from both of them. Sticky sap smeared my arms, and chips of bark flew. But it was too late.

The Wolf Lord raised his sword, and a great rustling roar filled the forest around us. In the shadows beyond and behind Zaira, where her fire had not yet reached, things with gleaming eyes coiled to attack.

Zaira sliced the air before her with her arm, and the Wolf Lord burst into flame.

There was no warning, no slow licking flames building to a grand crescendo. Her balefire was already stoked to an inferno with all the rich lives of the forest, drunk on what it had consumed. Fire burst up all around them both, an exhalation of violent light, like the blue breath of the Nine Hells.

The Wolf Lord staggered. His flesh began to char; the stench of ash and burned meat grew stronger. But even as his skin blackened and fell away, even as his hair sifted down as ash, even as his fur cloak turned to one of living flame, he did not fall.

"You fool," he snarled, his voice a tortured thing. He swung his burning blade at her; it clanged off the air an inch from her enchanted corset, shaking ripples from the air, and then began to push its way through. A line of light glowed white-hot at the edge of his blade as the balefire consuming his sword ate through Zaira's own protective shield as well.

Zaira slipped back out of his reach before the blade touched her, but the Wolf Lord stepped forward, closing the gap again. His hands had charred nearly to the bone, and the lines of his skull showed through his face; but still, terribly, he lived and moved. A scream of pure horror backed up in my lungs, but my throat was locked too rigid to release it.

"You can't kill me," the Wolf Lord rasped, with a tongue that blazed with balefire. "All the life in Kazerath sustains me. I cannot die."

I realized then that the chimeras that had been about to leap on Zaira had fallen dead. Even now, trees untouched by balefire withered, dropping needles in a rattling rain. Insects fell from the sky like snow, their lives expended to keep the Wolf Lord's going.

He raised his blade again, even as it burned away. I could only watch, knife still in hand; there was nothing I could do, no way to get close enough through the flames to affect what was happening. I was going to die here, a hapless spectator to this terrible duel, a mortal caught up in a war of demons. My fingernails scraped against rough bark, and hot ashes stung my eyes.

"Your magic is life, and that has sustained you," Zaira said, her voice distant and cold. "But my magic eats life and grows stronger."

She lifted her hand, as if beckoning the Hell of Death up from under the earth. And he became a great tower of flame. It roared up high and broad as one of the trees of his forest, white and wild and howling. A scalding wind blasted my face.

The forest screamed.

Every animal, every insect, every bird cried out as if it were dying. The trees thrashed and groaned, and the leaves rose up as if wind swirled through them; the ones too near the fire caught and became whirling showers of sparks, spreading the balefire farther.

I pulled myself from the tangling branches at last and ran a few steps away, choking on acrid smoke and ashes. I threw myself to the cool ground, covering my head as trees writhed and wolves howled and birds wailed around me, and sparks fell sizzling on my jacket. It was madness, a nightmare of fire and screaming, and I had to bite my own lip to keep from joining in.

Then everything fell suddenly silent, save for the crackling roar of the flames that raged through the forest.

I lifted my head. Balefire blazed on the ground, in the trees, everywhere, raising smoke thick and black as night itself to blot out the moon and the stars. I coughed, even lying on the ground beneath it; particles of wood and ash and gritty burning things coated my throat.

There was no sign of the Wolf Lord. There was nothing left for him to bind life into. She had obliterated him utterly.

Zaira stood triumphant, trailing a brilliant cloak of flames, pacing forward to meet the embrace of the conflagration like one transfixed. I didn't bother trying to call her name. She was lost to the fire.

"*Revincio,*" I croaked.

Everything went dark as a demon's soul.

Zaira hit the ground with a soft thud.

Chapter Twenty-Three

I dragged myself to my feet and limped over to where I'd heard Zaira fall, stirring up ash and rattling dry-seared ferns. The fire was gone, but smoke still hung thickly in the air; I coughed again, all the way down to the bottom of my chest. Wolves keened in the distance, but it was a mournful sound, not the bay of the hunt.

I nearly tripped over Zaira in the darkness. I dropped to my knees beside her and felt her throat just to make sure; her pulse beat quick and strong. Of course. *She* was fine. She got to sleep now, even.

I wanted to collapse over her and cry for a while, and then curl up among the ashes and sleep until dawn, myself. But we were still far too close to the castle. If the wolves came hunting vengeance, or Ruven came looking for his lost "guests," I couldn't do much more than bluff until Zaira woke up.

For all I knew, that might not be for days. I'd never seen her unleash on this scale before.

They'd taught me how to carry someone at the Mews, for exactly this reason. I slung her over my shoulders and stumbled through the night, with no sign of a path and no sense of direction other than *away*, aching from a dozen cuts and bruises, cold to the bone. Zaira's limp weight bore down on me like all the mountains of smoke piled above us.

It blended into one long, dark nightmare. I stopped a few times to put Zaira down, drink a few swallows of water, and rest, but the howling of wolves in the far distance always convinced me to struggle back to my feet and keep going. There was no part of me that didn't ache, but it didn't matter; hurting was better than being dead.

Finally, on one of my breaks, I laid Zaira down as carefully as I could on some moss and leaned against a tree to rest for just a moment. And when I blinked my gritty eyes open, it was dawn.

Grayish-pink light slid between the trees, falling softly to the rolling mounds of frost-silvered pine needles and yellowing ferns. Each sliver of sky between the looming tree trunks formed an empty pillar of air, holding up a world where dawn continued to happen in a miraculously ordinary way, as if this weren't the first day of some strange new world. Hundreds of miles away, that same rosy light touched the sky over the Imperial Canal, sliding down the façades of the palaces on the grand curve; it would be hours yet before it reached my window and fell on my empty bed. Perhaps my mother was up, already on her way to the Imperial Palace to manage whatever crisis the coming war presented her with today. Perhaps this same light kissed Marcello's eyelids open, in the officers' barracks of some border keep.

Or perhaps the captain at Highpass had gotten on the courier lamps to report my absence, and my mother and Marcello had been up all night, making Hells only knew what preparations to send troops into Vaskandar to get Zaira and me back.

I levered myself away from the tree trunk I'd slept against. Bark stuck to the back of my coat, and pine needles clung to my hair. My breath misted in the frigid mountain air, which had settled into every fold of my jacket and pierced deep into my weary bones.

Zaira stirred, wincing away from the light. "Too early," she groaned.

Then she searched the twig-scattered moss around her. She blinked her eyes open in bleary confusion, and sat up.

Her hand immediately flew to her temple, and she winced. "Ugh. My head hurts like a demon used my skull for a pisspot."

"You probably need to drink something." I handed her my flask. She started gulping down water, gratefully. "You may have strained yourself last night."

"What happened?" Zaira wiped her mouth on her sleeve. "Why did we sleep in the woods?"

I hesitated. "How much do you remember?"

Zaira frowned. "Uh...Running away from chimeras. I set them on fire, didn't I?"

"You set a few things on fire, yes," I said. I almost started laughing again but took my flask back and drank until the bubbling in my chest subsided.

"I'm starving," Zaira moaned. "I can't even think. Give me food, and then tell me how awful everything is after I eat."

I passed her the last of the bread. My own stomach rumbled emptily, but she needed what meager rations we had more than I did, after last night.

As Zaira devoured the bread, I felt in my satchel for my morning elixir, and my fingertips slid across Marcello's button. I imagined him shaking his head at me, at a loss for words at how far I'd strayed from what he would have advised.

"To be fair," I murmured, "this was only partly my fault."

"What?" Zaira asked, between bites.

"Oh, nothing. I've just lost my mind and am talking to a button."

Zaira grunted acceptance and kept eating.

I waited until she swallowed her last bite. Then I told her, "I think you killed the Wolf Lord."

She stared at me, eyes wide. "I don't remember that."

"I imagine you wouldn't. But it was memorable nonetheless, I assure you."

Zaira mulled that over for a moment, then sighed and clambered to her feet, leaning on a young tree to steady herself. "Well, what's done is done. Sorry if I mucked up politics or history or anything. Which way do we go?"

I shook my head. "We're completely lost," I said. "I'm a child of the city. I know how to find my way home following the canals in Raverra, or the temple spires in Ardence. I have no idea whatsoever how to navigate a forest."

Zaira glared around at the time-creased, moss-splotched trunks of the ancient trees as if they offended her on a personal level. She peered up at the scant glimpses of gray sky that the boughs overhead afforded us, but thick clouds entirely blocked the sun. "Then pick a direction, and we'll walk until we know where we are."

As we walked, it started to snow. At first, only a few flakes drifted down through the heavy pine branches, specks of bright wonder floating on the air. But soon it thickened, laying a dense silence upon us, transforming the world one tiny piece at a time to the stark white of winter. Snowflakes caught in Zaira's curls, glittering like jewels as they melted, but she never seemed to feel the cold. I clutched my coat around myself and shivered.

We came out of the trees in a scarred patch of bald rocks, slick with a quarter inch of fluffy white snow. My boots took wet, black bites out of the pristine white coating with each step. Through the soft haze of falling flakes, I could make out mountains rising on both sides of a long, wooded valley; their peaks vanished into low, thick clouds, and only the sweep of their forested flanks was visible in the gray distance.

The Wolf Lord's castle stood on its hill far behind us, black and jagged. Dark scars of burned trees marred the forest between. I could make out no sign of the village we'd stayed at; we weren't high enough to see that far, and the snow further choked our vision. The deep, wet chill sank into my bones. I yearned for a warm fire and a hot bath.

"Well, we've been walking in the valley between these parallel mountain ridges," I said. "One of them marks the border, and the other lies deeper in Vaskandar, but I have no idea which is which. Do you recognize anything?"

Zaira shook her head. "Just trees and white stuff. It all looks the same to me."

"Not to add to the pressure," I said, "but I've only got one day of elixir left. My life could depend on us choosing the right direction."

"Then choose it yourself," Zaira snapped. "You might be annoying, but I don't want your death on my hands."

I peered along the valley, first one way, then another. A crow called from a nearby tree.

"Oh, fine, laugh at me," I muttered.

It cawed again, then fluttered down to land on a branch nearly within grabbing range. It cocked a beady black eye at me.

Zaira let out a bark of a laugh. "See? It can tell you're going to die. Lining up for a bite."

"Thanks," I said dryly.

The crow lunged at my arm, as if to peck at me; I barely pulled my sleeve back in time. It steadied itself, wings half-spread, and then did a strange hopping dance, leaving claw prints on the snowy branch. It looked at me from the left eye, then the right, then muttered to itself.

A strange thought occurred to me. "Did Kathe send you?"

The crow cawed triumphantly, then flew to another branch twenty feet away. It looked back at me and cawed again.

Zaira gave me a half-lidded, level stare. "Tell me we're not going to follow the crow."

"Do you have a better idea?"

"This is the rock-bottom most idiotic piece of demon-begotten foolishness you've suggested yet, and that's saying something." Zaira shook her head. "But sure. Why not? I always let random birds make life-and-death decisions for me. Let's follow it."

The crow stayed ahead of us, fluttering from branch to branch. If we took too long to catch up, it cawed. When I slipped on the snow, it cawed. When Zaira cursed at it, it cawed. I couldn't be impressed at its vocabulary.

Within half an hour, it had led us to a road. Wagon tracks and hoofprints marred the snow, which had tapered off to occasional scant flurries. We made better time on the road's level footing, until at last the crow fluttered to land at the white-capped tip of a standing stone, one of two six-foot-tall menhirs flanking the road. It preened its glossy feathers, satisfied.

Boundary markers. A spark of excitement brightened my exhaustion.

"Does this mean we're heading back into the domain full of chimeras who want to kill you?" Zaira asked warily.

I frowned. "These stones look different."

They were older and more weathered than the ones we'd seen at the border between Sevaeth and Kazerath, the carvings half worn away. Snow blurred the edges, but the lines of the designs looked softer, forming waves and curls.

Something about those patterns seemed deeply familiar, compelling. I reached out to brush snow from the rough surface of one of the stones.

A ripple ran through me when I laid my hand on it, as if I touched a great bell and the vibrations of its deep tone shook through my body.

The boundary stone warmed under my touch.

There was no mistaking the change. It started cold, as stone standing in the snow should be; but within two breaths of laying my hand on it, I had to snatch it back from the uncomfortable heat. Water trickled down from the snow crowning the stone.

How very odd. I walked around to the other side of the standing stone, crossing the invisible line between domains, and laid my hand on it again, to feel its growing heat. What was it the Wolf Lord had said to Prince Ruven? *When you've carved out a piece of land from the Empire and claimed it with your own blood . . .*

"This isn't Sevaeth." I was certain of it, somehow. "That would make this Atruin, on the far side of Kazerath. The domain of the Lady of Eagles." My great-grandmother.

The crow suddenly took off from the top of the stone, cawing, its wings beating a breeze into my face.

Zaira froze. "I think someone knows we're here."

I pulled my eyes away from the strangely mesmerizing lines graven into the rock to find half a dozen elk staring at us. They formed a neat arc around us on the Atruin side of the line—not clumped together in a herd but surrounding us like predators. All six bore great, branching antlers; they watched us with shining brown eyes. Their breath formed clouds of steam around their velvet muzzles.

They were beautiful, with sleek fur, warm eyes, and graceful legs. But there was power in their broad chests, and they loomed above us. I doubted any one of them would find it a difficult matter to kick me to death, and their antlers spread sharp and proud above them.

I waited, not daring to move. But the elk simply watched. After several long moments, I took a tentative step forward, and then another.

The elk parted to let us through. Zaira drew in close by my side, and we advanced along the road together, carefully as if we walked on spilled nails. The elk fell in around us, three and three, like an honor guard, blocking out the cold.

"Now, this is just strange," Zaira complained. "Graces' tits, all I want is to be back in Raverra, where I can walk down the street without an escort of demon-cursed oversized deer, the only trees are chopped up in the fireplace, and the only things trying to kill me are human beings who have the basic decency to do it with knives and poison."

"I can't say I disagree," I said. But every step I took sent an odd, mostly pleasant vibration up my leg. This was technically the wrong direction, taking us farther from Highpass; but it somehow felt right, as if I'd been here before and knew the way. I wasn't normally a creature of instinct, but it made a certain amount of sense. At this point, the closest safe trail over the mountains was more likely to be ahead of us, in peaceful Atruin, than behind us in a Kazerath armed for war and roused against us.

The great beasts paced by our sides, watching us, pausing occasionally to rip a mouthful of tender pine needles off a branch in passing. The crow didn't follow us, though it cawed after us once, as if to say good-bye. I felt strangely uneasy leaving it behind.

Shortly we stepped out of the trees into an open stretch of neat fields, spread out in snowy white glory over the rolling land. These, too, felt familiar to me, like coming back to a home that had never been mine. A group of people pulling sledges heaped with firewood stared as we passed, but with interest, not hostility or fear. Rather than the furs and leather of Kazerath, they wore bright wool hats and mittens, and sheepskin coats with heavily embroidered trim in contrasting colors; and where the folk of Kazerath had been craggy and pale, here I saw shining dark hair and slighter builds. We passed well-kept farmhouses, and a pasture full of sheep spread out to forage for grass beneath the snow as if they had nothing to fear from wolves.

"Well, this is different." Zaira suspiciously eyed a shepherd who'd dozed off leaning against a leafless tree with his arms tucked around him, wrapped in a vivid red woolen scarf. "They're not flinching away from everything."

"I suppose not every domain in Vaskandar can be straight out of the Hell of Despair." I turned the thought in my mind, like a new artifice device of cunning design. "A Witch Lord has the power to keep everyone in their domain safe, comfortable, and healthy, if they choose to use it that way."

"And it's your own rotten luck if you're born on the wrong side of the boundary stones." Zaira shook her head.

After the last farmhouse, the forest swallowed us up again, the scent of woodsmoke and sheep fading behind us. Soon we came to a place where a narrow footpath branched off the main road, half overgrown and barely distinguishable. As we drew next to it, an elk stepped in my path and lowered his head, barring the way with the great spread of his antlers.

I stopped. "I think they want us to take the side path."

"Are we going to let ourselves be bullied by a bunch of poxy cows with branches stuck to their heads?" Zaira demanded.

Another elk nudged between my shoulder blades—a shove with its muzzle which it might have considered gentle, but sent me staggering a couple steps toward the side path.

Nothing in this land was afraid. Not of wolves, not of us, not of all the horrors their neighboring domains could offer. Something protected this place, hidden and unanswerably powerful.

"Yes," I said. "I think we are."

"Fine," Zaira grumbled. "Here I am, an army's worst nightmare, slayer of Witch Lords, prisoner of leaf-munching forest creatures."

We turned onto the overgrown path and began a long, gradual climb up the forested mountainside. At least we were heading in the right direction, toward the Empire; this might be the very trail we'd been looking for. The elk spread out through the woods around us as we followed the indistinct track. If we slowed, they closed back in.

I didn't dare stop even to take a sip of water. Zaira could have roasted them all easily enough, likely without losing control or consciousness, but I feared what would come after. The histories I'd read mentioned the Lady of Eagles among the titles of the first three Witch Lords, who founded Vaskandar over five hundred years ago.

The trail passed between a pair of old stones carved with designs similar to the border markers, but smaller—perhaps chest height, rather than reaching over my head. And then it ended at a mossy, dark opening: a fern-fringed cave mouth, gaping in the mountainside. More stones flanked it. The air wafting out of it held a trace of ice and smelled like old, wet stone.

Something in there set a thrumming deep in my bones, like a sound too low to hear.

The elk closed in around us, hooves stirring the snow, horns tossing.

"Oh, no," Zaira protested. "Absolutely nothing good can come of going in there."

I took a step forward, my pulse racing. The answer to Kathe's question lay in there. I was sure of it. "One good thing can. Knowledge."

Zaira shook her head. "You're mad. Knowledge of what? The kind of creatures that live in caves in Vaskandar and eat curious Raverrans?"

"The secret of the Witch Lords' power." I laid a hand on one of the stones beside the entrance. It grew hot to my touch, almost at once. One of the elk reared and snorted.

Zaira swept a hand at it. "You think the Lady of Eagles sent her pointy-headed friends to show you her secrets? To murder you if you learn them, more like it!"

What she said made sense. But something called to me from that cave, blood to blood. *All things quick with life, one sharp bloody knife . . .*

The elk knew. They could feel the connection, too. That was why they'd brought me here.

"To keep the Witch Lords out of this war, or to defeat them once it's begun, we have to know them. To thwart their power, we must understand it." Excitement stirred in my veins. Normally I hated dark, cramped places, but the ancient promise that exhaled from the cave's mouth enticed me with the prospect of discovery. What would my professors at the University of Ardence think of me if I walked away now?

"I'm going in."

I ducked under the hanging canopy of moss and stepped into the cold, rocky interior of the cave. Zaira swore and followed.

I blinked in the dimness, chasing shadows and leftover specks of sunlight from my eyes. The gurgle and rush of water surrounded me. I had expected the cave to be cramped, but it opened up into a domed chamber larger than my bedroom at home. The walls were too smooth; humans had shaped this place.

The back of the cave dropped off into a rushing underground stream, which flowed through the chamber and out the other side. At the center of the rough, uneven floor rose another stone, carved with the same flowing designs I'd seen elsewhere; this one had a shallow basin dug into the top. The air had the thick, hushed feeling of a temple.

An invisible tide of more than curiosity pulled me toward the stone. A channel ran from the basin down the back side of it, emptying into the stream. I ran a finger around the basin's rough edge. It warmed under my touch, pulsing slightly; a tingle ran up my arm, and a hum started in my bones.

"Ten streams through it all," I whispered. A dark stain marked the bottom of the channel. "Ten drops fall on stone, one lord on the throne."

Zaira hovered halfway between me and the cave mouth, her eyes wide. "All right, that's creepy. What in the Nine Hells are you talking about?"

"This is how Witch Lords claim their domains." Excitement unfurled in my middle. It all made sense; it was like finding enough key letters in a nonstandard artifice rune set that I began to be able to read the symbols and understand the magic. "A vivomancer's power is to control life, but normally they can't do it on such a grand scale, or from afar. But all life arises from water. Water is the web that binds it all together, like the central wire braid in a complex artifice weave. And blood is life and water both."

Zaira peered dubiously at the basin. "You're telling me they bleed into the streams and rivers?"

"To make themselves part of the land, and the land part of them. And they mark their claim with stones. They're not just boundary markers." I'd wager they formed a pattern, like an artifice circle. "The stones are the bones of the earth, and the rivers its blood. And once they've completed the binding, every living thing nurtured by that earth and that water would be part of their magic. That's why a Witch Lord's power over their own domain is so absolute."

"And that is why no one tampers with my blooding stones and lives." The new voice came from the cave mouth, sure and commanding, deep as the earth and fluid as the river.

I turned, slowly, to face the Lady of Eagles.

Chapter Twenty-Four

The Lady of Eagles' mage mark showed black against eyes golden as the sun. Her midnight-black hair fell straight and loose past her hips. She wore a mantle scalloped to mimic scales or feathers, each leaf a different shade of bronze, amber, brown, or gold, and each minutely edged in the spiky curves of Vaskandran-style embroidery. It draped from her shoulders like wings.

She was the mountain, ancient and still. She was the sky itself, bright and unreachable. She was the hunting cat who prowled the forest, lean and graceful, and the deer who bounded through it, fleet and free. And her eyes were an eagle's eyes: wild and fierce, piercing as the rays of daylight, and utterly without fear.

I bowed, holding it for a long time to give myself a moment to find my tongue. I half expected Zaira to leap into the silence, but she stood frozen, one hand reaching behind her as if searching for a wall to lean on.

"My lady," I said, when I found a way to shape words with my dry mouth, "I'm sorry if I've intruded. I didn't intend to tamper."

Her raptor eyes flicked to Zaira, then to the claw necklace on my chest. "Your intentions are dust to me. You woke the stones. I tire of intruders meddling with my domain; do not think my blood in your veins will protect you."

"I try to make a habit of not presuming anything, my lady." I swallowed. "If I may ask, when you say people have been meddling with your domain—Do you mean on Mount Whitecrown?"

Her eyes narrowed. "You know of it. And yet you claim innocence."

Graces preserve us all. Ruven had circles in place in Atruin. He would almost certainly have saved those for last, given the risk; his artifice pattern on the mountain might already be complete.

I stepped forward, too agitated to feel the fear I should have. "Have you found artifice designs around the mountain? Prince Ruven is trying to trigger an eruption."

She advanced across the cave and stared directly into my eyes. From this close, the sense of her power blazed like the sun itself. I felt small, helpless, and exposed, like a rabbit cowering beneath the eagle's shadow.

"You understand what this foolish pup is attempting?" she demanded. "This stolen Raverran magic? I have seen artifice many times before, but nothing like this."

I swallowed to wet my throat. "Yes, I think I understand it."

"Well enough to undo it?"

I reviewed the diagram in my memory—both the one I'd glimpsed in the dark study and the original I'd seen in a book in Ardence. It was almost ludicrously complicated and blended artifice and vivomancy in ways most of my professors would have called impossible. But I didn't need to understand the entire enchantment to sabotage one part of it. "I think so."

"Good enough." She whirled, her mantle swinging behind her. "Come with me."

We followed the Lady of Eagles along a game trail up the flank of the mountain. The narrow track climbed steeply, and I soon found myself panting, but she moved with springy grace, as if the earth itself lifted her up. Given what I'd learned, perhaps it did. The brush and branches bowed aside as she passed, strewing her path with shed snow like white petals, clearing the way for the great lady.

Soon, the Lady of Eagles stopped by a slab of bald rock—a place where the bones of the mountain showed through, with no earth, grass, or trees growing on the stretch of wind-scoured granite. She stopped and gestured with disgust to an elaborate artifice circle, perhaps ten feet across, carved into the stone. No snow had stuck to the circle or the area immediately around it. Her contempt rippled through the low bushes bordering the rock like a harsh wind.

This was it. One of Ruven's volcano circles. I stepped forward, a mix of eagerness and dread quickening my breath.

"I am no scholar of artifice," the Lady of Eagles said, "but this is not artifice alone. Another witch blooded this design, binding his power into it. My claim on my half of the mountain remains as strong as ever; however, this circle attempts to establish a competing one. It would be trivial to wipe it out, but this strange and complex magic is snarled around the mountain's heart, and disturbing it might unleash disaster. Tell me what this is, and I may let you live."

I knelt by the circle, tracing its lines with a trembling finger, translating runes in my mind. "There should be more like this, encircling the mountain."

"I know of others. Can you break it?"

"Let me think."

I ran my eyes along the complex lines of the diagram and the precise curls of the runes, searching for anywhere there might be room to work in an alternate meaning. The artificer had worked very carefully, chiseling each letter with clean edges my teachers would have praised, and measuring each line exactly. That usually meant a tightly woven work of artifice, with no room for meddling. But in some places the spacing between the letters was oddly irregular, opening gaps where there should be none; and there were subtle blank spaces in the design, spots where an experienced artificer should have put placeholder runes to avoid tampering.

"The artificer who created this was controlled, not willing," I breathed. "They worked in a back door."

"So you can sabotage it?" Zaira asked.

"I don't know yet. I can tell there are gaps where you could modify the design, but I need to figure out what the artificer wants us to do."

I studied the empty spaces, trying to read the shape they hinted at. As a whole, the artifice circle seemed designed to increase the pressure within the heart of the volcano while also keeping that pressure contained. But the containment could be dropped at any time with a command sent from a separate control circle. From what I recalled of the overall design, the control circle would also open a vent to release all the built-up pressure at the same time, triggering and directing the eruption.

I laid my fingertips on the center of the design. They tingled faintly, and the rock was warm under my fingers. A terrible weight settled in my stomach.

"This is already active."

"It's going to erupt?" Zaira stepped back in alarm, as if distance from the circle might save her.

"Not yet. All the circles around the mountain are combining their power to build up pressure, to prepare for the eruption and to make it more powerful when Ruven triggers it." I bit my lip, remembering those outlines of zones of destruction on the diagram in his study.

"I might be able to melt it with enough balefire," Zaira suggested helpfully.

"No! If you destroy it, that'll release the containment. We could have an eruption right now."

The Lady of Eagles didn't move, but I could feel her anger in the stone beneath my hands and knees. Far above us, a bird let out a harsh cry.

"He pushes my neutrality too far. He can do what he wills in his own domain, but this half of the mountain is mine."

I lifted my eyes from the graven stone and found the Lady of Eagles glaring in the direction of Kazerath. I could almost feel her gaze sizzling over my head and was grateful not to be its recipient.

"How will you, ah, respond to this intrusion?" I asked.

"At the Conclave." Her tone shut the door on any further questions. "It is where we resolve our grievances. You haven't told me whether you can remove this scar from my mountain."

I looked back at the design and licked my lips. "Once the eruption issue is resolved, an artificer can remove it, and I'll happily offer you the services of a Falcon to do so. But for now, I think I see how to at least stop this circle from building up any more pressure. We just need to add some cancellation and reversal symbols in the right places."

"And that'll stop the eruption?" Zaira asked.

"If we do it in most or all of the circles around Mount Whitecrown, and if no one triggers the eruption before enough pressure gets slowly and safely released. I can give you instructions for how to do the same with any other circles in your domain, my lady."

The Lady of Eagles nodded. "Do it."

I hadn't exactly brought any stone chiseling tools with me in my satchel. I dug away at the rock with my knife, slowly scratching deeper and deeper until I created a groove I could feel when I ran my hand across it. I was painfully aware of precious time slipping away from me as the sun settled down toward Mount Whitecrown's looming shoulder. As the shadows lengthened, cold settled over my bent back like a mantle of ice, but the stone itself warmed my busy fingers, and I kept carving away at the runes. Zaira yawned and settled on a rock to wait.

Finally, when my knife had lost its edge completely and my fingers were scratched and bleeding, I finished. A faint orange light flared in the design for an instant, and I felt a subtle shift in the mountain beneath me. It was done. I'd accomplished one vital task on this cursed mission, at least.

The Lady of Eagles stood watching, her golden eyes intent. Her presence pressed on me more heavily than Mount Whitecrown itself, looming above us in its ancient majesty with its heart of earth-shaking fire. After all, the volcano was only a small part of the domain she carried with her at all times, bound into her blood.

"Perhaps you are of some use after all," she said, "despite the disappointing lack of magical power in your branch of the line."

Zaira smirked at me and mouthed, *Disappointing*. But I rose and bowed to acknowledge the compliment. "I am honored to hear you think so, my lady."

"For this, I will forgive your tampering with the stones." The Lady of Eagles lifted her head then, as if listening. "Someone awaits you in the village below."

I swallowed. "My lady, with all respect, I need to get back to the Empire as quickly as possible."

"You will come with me and meet him." Her tone left no room for argument. "You must understand what you have done."

And with that ominous statement, she started down the mountain.

"Of course she meant you." I shook my head, but I couldn't suppress a smile.

Some private, foolishly hopeful corner of my heart had cherished the notion that the Lady of Eagles might have meant Marcello, come into Vaskandar to find us. But when the reverent villagers bowed us into the modest, thick-beamed village meeting hall, with its red-painted rafters adorned with designs of bright wildflowers, it was Kathe who waited for us.

He perched on the edge of a simple wooden stage that faced six double rows of benches with sky-blue embroidered cushions, his feet swinging idly. The place felt a bit like a theater or a temple, but there were no velvet curtains nor statues of the Nine Graces. The flickering light of several winged bronze candelabras warmed the dim corners of the room and cast interesting shadows in Kathe's black-tipped hair.

Kathe stood and bowed to the Lady of Eagles, who gave him a gracious nod in return. Then he grinned at Zaira and me. "You've been busy."

"Yes, they have. And we must speak of this." The Lady of Eagles didn't gesture or even glance at the first-row bench as she strode forward, but green shoots sprang from it, the wood wakening back to life in welcome; slim branches sprouted from it and twisted into elegant patterns, shaping a graceful throne. By the time her measured tread brought her there, it was ready for her, and she seated herself with regal poise. "The mountain's fiery heart is stirring, and in Kazerath you have unleashed chaos itself."

My steps faltered to a stop halfway between the two Witch Lords, as my insides lurched at her words. "By killing the Wolf Lord? Is . . ." I swallowed. "Is Ruven the Witch Lord there now?"

The Lady of Eagles nodded. "Kazerath is his. He is making his rounds as we speak, blooding stones to deepen his hold on the domain, but the land already knows him as its master." She turned the golden blaze of her mage mark at Zaira. "You have done Eruvia no favors by killing his father."

"It was that or let him kill me." Zaira shrugged, but there was tension in her shoulders.

"Ruven was the only heir, then?" Kathe asked resignedly, settling back down on the stage. "I suppose it was too much to hope he'd get embroiled in a contested claim. The Wolf Lord followed the old wisdom."

The old wisdom. What had Kathe said, during our picnic in the glass house? *The wisdom among Witch Lords is to have only one heir at a time.* If a Witch Lord's blood connection with the land was inherited, but only one could claim the domain, it made sense that a single heir would be the best way to ensure a smooth transition of power. I supposed having no heir would be even worse, since then the other Witch Lords might see one's domain as up for grabs in the event of one's demise.

"Followed it in one regard, yes," the Lady of Eagles said, her voice stern with disapproval. "But the Wolf Lord's heir is a Skinwitch. That flies in the face of all wisdom, old or new."

Zaira settled on the edge of the stage, a wary distance from Kathe. "I'd be more worried about his personality than his magic. Ruven's a rot-eating weasel."

"His charming personality is what *makes* him a Skinwitch." Kathe grimaced with distaste.

The Lady of Eagles nodded grimly. "The people who live in Atruin are mine," she said. "I do not own them; they are free to do as they will. But they are mine magically, part of my domain. In theory, there is no reason I could not twist their flesh as I did this wood, or bend their actions to my will as I do the birds in the sky. But if I tried, my power would balk. It goes against a deep and vital instinct recognizing other humans as my fellows—one that Skinwitches do not possess."

I recalled Ruven forcing his servant's bones to spike through his own skin, while the man stood frozen, wide-eyed, powerless to stop him or even to cry out.

I shuddered. "So Skinwitches by definition are those who don't respect or acknowledge the basic humanity of others."

Zaira snorted. "I could have told you that about Ruven without the lecture."

"But it's worse than that." My stomach twisted as I worked out the implications. "Before, Ruven had to touch someone's skin to work their flesh, or to control them. Now, every single resident of Kazerath is going to be his puppet, even if he's miles away."

Kathe nodded. "You see the problem."

"That's bad enough even without a volcano raining down fire and ash on half of..." I trailed off, feeling the blood drain from my face. "Hells. The ash."

Kathe whistled. "That explains some things."

"What?" Zaira asked, looking between us.

I cradled my forehead in my hands, stunned. "Half that mountain is Ruven's. On a deep, magical level. A large eruption could rain ash on a huge area, literally sprinkling his claim across the land."

"He would have power where the ash fell thickly," the Lady of Eagles confirmed gravely. "Another Witch Lord could easily brush such a weak claim from their domain, but in your Empire, there would be no one to contest it."

"Maybe he won't trigger the volcano, now that he has his own domain," I said desperately. "He's lost his motivation to invade, hasn't he?"

But Kathe shook his head. "He needs power more than ever now. It's common to have to fight off attempts by other Witch Lords to take your domain during the vulnerable inheritance period. Expanding his domain gets him more power to defend himself, and offering up pieces of the land he captures will garner him powerful allies. For Ruven, as a Skinwitch and a new Witch Lord, this invasion just became a matter of survival."

"Do not expect restraint from a man such as Ruven," the Lady of Eagles said. "Holding the destructive wrath of a volcano in his hands, he will not hesitate to unleash it." A deep, forbidding resonance filled her voice. "The sky will darken with his power. People and animals will breathe in his dominion with the ash-choked air. Plants will drink it up through their roots. He will take the lands the ash covers from your Empire as easily as walking into them; they will leap into his hand, already his."

My stomach twisted with revulsion at the idea of half the Empire under Ruven's control. "We have to stop him," I whispered. "My lady, will you help us?"

The Lady of Eagles turned her gaze to me, and it hit me in that moment how ancient those eyes were. She was one of the first three Witch Lords, older than the Empire itself. How many wars had she seen? How many petty power struggles?

"I will bring my grievance against him to the Conclave. I can mind my own domain. You must mind yours. Whether he invades the Serene Empire is none of my concern."

"So you'll just let him become a full Witch Lord?" Frustration sharpened my voice more than I meant it to. "You're one of the few people who might be able to keep him from taking over Kazerath!"

"And that is why I must not interfere. If I begin picking and choosing who becomes a Witch Lord and who does not, it will cause far more chaos in Vaskandar than a mere Skinwitch ever could." Her voice grew stern as old stone. "You are the ones who have brought this upon us by killing his father. It is your duty to deal with the consequences and prevent further disaster."

Zaira's face twisted in disbelief. But, with some apparent struggle, she held her tongue. Apparently her disregard for consequences did not extend to insulting the Lady of Eagles.

The Lady of Eagles caught her gaze and held it for a long time. Something built between them in the silence—some understanding or communication, from one mage who held life and death in her hand to the other. Neither of them looked away.

Finally, the Lady of Eagles said, her voice softer than I'd yet heard it, "You haven't found your place yet, child. If you seek a safe haven, Atruin is open to you and yours."

Zaira's eyes narrowed. "So you can have your very own fire warlock?"

The Lady of Eagles didn't so much as blink. "I need no fire warlock." Her voice resonated softly all through the building, and the ground beneath it, and the forest and mountains around us, and I had no doubt it was true. "I offer you peace within my borders, for as long or as short a time as you wish. That is all."

I held my breath. It was as close to freedom as Zaira was likely to find in Eruvia. The offer must be far more tempting coming from the Lady of Eagles than it had been from Ruven.

Zaira glanced at me, her eyes dark and thoughtful.

Hells. My duty to the Empire was to put a stop to this; we couldn't lose our only fire warlock. I could almost feel my mother's stern glance, urging me to do something—some subtle comment that would manipulate Zaira to choosing what I wanted her to choose, perhaps, without damaging our valuable relationship.

But if you thought of all your friends as assets, then you didn't have any friends.

The lady rose, her mantle falling about her. "In this matter, you have all the time you need; my offer stands. But your time for other matters grows short, so I will leave you."

"Wait." The word burst out of me before I could stop it, and I hopped down from the stage. I could feel Zaira and Kathe staring at me. "Did you ever meet my father?"

She went still. I couldn't read her ageless face. After a long moment, she said, "Yes. Once, briefly."

"Did you..." I floundered, uncertain what I wanted to say. *Did you love him? Did you care about him at all? Are we family?*

"Many Witch Lords ultimately find they cannot bear immortality." The lady's voice went soft and powerful as an evening breeze, the warm summer kind that swept the heart clean. "They cannot stand loss after loss, and they resign themselves to death. I have found it best to remain distant from the lives of my descendants, unless they manage to secure a domain of their own."

"Ah." A strange disappointment clogged my throat. "I see. Thank you."

The Lady of Eagles nodded. Then her eyes fell on my claw necklace, and she cast a piercing glance at Kathe. "I see this one wears your token." She raised a brow at me. "Do you know its significance?"

"It indicates his protection?" I hazarded.

"It is a piece of his domain," she said. Kathe winced at the revelation. By the gleam in the lady's eyes, his discomfort amused her. "It does signal to anyone in Vaskandar that harming you will incur his wrath. But it also allows him to know where you are, generally speaking, while you wear it."

"Does it, now." I glared at Kathe.

He shrugged. "I like everything I do to have multiple purposes."

"You could have told me." I tried to keep my tone light and neutral, as if I were merely pointing out a fact, rather than holding back anger.

"My lady, if I'd told you, you wouldn't have worn it. And if you hadn't worn it, you'd be dead by now." He shook his head. "You have no idea how many domain defenses in both Sevaeth and Kazerath left you and Lady Zaira alone because of that necklace."

"A good thing to know about crows," the Lady of Eagles said, "is that they can be relied on—but never trusted."

She turned away, her winglike mantle sweeping behind her. An owl glided in through the meeting house window to land on her shoulder; she inclined her head as if to listen to it as she left. We had already fallen beneath her notice once more.

Kathe cocked his head at me once she was gone. "Do you know your way home?"

"About that. I don't suppose you have a way to get a message to Highpass quickly?" I asked. Outside the meeting house windows, the sun was descending. Even with my message, they would have expected me at Highpass last night; it might already be too late to avert disaster. "I'm concerned the Empire may respond rashly to Zaira's and my continued absence."

Kathe clicked his tongue. "We can't have that. A war now would scuttle all my plans. Write your message, and I'll send it with a crow."

"Thank you," I said fervently, and dug in my satchel for writing supplies.

"How will you return to Highpass yourself? If I'm not mistaken, you have personal reasons to hurry, as well." Kathe eyed me keenly, and my stomach dropped. He was smart enough he might well remember what I'd said about poison at the ball in Raverra and make certain connections.

I tried not to look as if I had anything to hide and immediately felt my face twisting into uncomfortable positions. "I might," I said.

"The quickest way is back through Kazerath and Sevaeth," he

said. "But for you, it might prove too dangerous. Those domains are raised against you, and it's hard to arrive at your destination on time when you're dead."

I took a risk and answered honestly. "If I arrive late, I may be dead regardless."

"Well, then." Kathe rolled his shoulders, ruffling the feathers on his cloak. "I'll simply have to escort you."

Chapter Twenty-Five

"Please tell me you don't trust him," Zaira whispered to me. "Even your grandma said not to."

Kathe walked ahead of us, whistling. A light flurry of snow had begun to fall again, sifting down through the trees, and a scattering of snowflakes glittered on his feathered cloak in the moonlight. We had crossed into Kazerath, but the road was peaceful in Kathe's presence; the trees stood still and quiet, as trees should, and only the occasional calls of owls and night animals came from among them.

"No," I said, wrapping my arms around myself to keep out the cold. I'd found my last elixir bottle frozen, and had to tuck it into my shirt to warm it before I could drink my evening dose; only one swallow now remained. "But I don't think he wants to kill us, at least."

Zaira grunted. "Well, that's something."

Kathe glanced back over his shoulder. "Did you know that a Witch Lord's senses are unnaturally acute?"

A flush warmed my cheeks. "I did not."

Zaira laughed. "You should stay away from the Tallows, then. Parts of it reek like a beggar's armpit."

"I will admit some of us avoid cities due to their, ah, assortment of unique fragrances." He grinned. "Me, I find it highly useful for listening in on secret conversations. But come walk with me, Amalia. We're courting; we don't need to keep secrets from each other."

He slowed his pace to fall back by my side. I raised an eyebrow. "We don't?"

"I did say 'need.'" His eyes gleamed in the dimming light. "That doesn't mean we can't keep secrets for the fun of it."

"Secrets like your intent to use my blood connection to the Lady of Eagles?"

He clicked his tongue. "I don't know that I intend to *use* it for anything in particular. But it's certainly something that makes you interesting. Tell me, do you know why we Witch Lords accord the Lady of Eagles such respect?"

"Because you'd be mad not to?" Zaira suggested. "Even I wouldn't spit in *her* tea."

"We show great respect to all three of the eldest Witch Lords. But there's more to it than that." A certain edge entered his voice, and he kicked at a pebble in the road. "She's managed something no one else has been able to do, even among the sixteen of us that call her a peer."

"Oh?" I asked.

"You've seen that we use rivers and streams to spread our blood claim throughout our domains," he said. "Water flows one direction, but magic doesn't necessarily follow the same rules. Her power, understanding, or control is good enough to make it flow upstream. It's a trick I've never managed; I'm not sure anyone else has."

"So she can exert her power in any domain her blooded rivers touch?" I considered the map I'd seen of Vaskandar, trying to remember the borders of Atruin. The image came clear in my mind, and I suddenly understood. "Grace of Majesty. Eyrie Lake."

"Yes." He sighed, a sound full of resigned exasperation. "You see how it is."

"What?" Zaira demanded. "You're both pox-rotted impossible, do you know that? What's your fuss about this lake?"

"It lies at the heart of Vaskandar," I told her. "Within the Lady of Eagles' domain. Half the waters in Vaskandar must drain down into it, one way or another. So if she can reach her power upstream..."

"She has her fingers in nearly every domain in Vaskandar," the Crow Lord concluded. "It's not the same as if it were her own domain, of course, but her influence is there, webbed through half a continent. That's why no one dares stand against her."

And why Kathe and Ruven seemed so interested in me, no doubt, if her blood in my veins might give them a way to touch that web.

Zaira glared around at the darkening forest, as if imagining it on fire. "And to think I used to tease Halmur that all he could do was make flowers bloom or be friends with the seagulls. I can't believe you want to go to a party with seventeen of these demons."

"Ah, yes, the Conclave." Kathe raised his brows. "Do you still want to go?"

"Yes." The word surprised me, bursting out with more confidence and less reservation than I expected given the events of the past two days.

"There will be, as the Lady Zaira says, seventeen of us demons there." He punctuated this with a modest bow. "The rules of the Conclave would protect you, as an invited guest—but then, our rules also protect travelers on the roads. With mixed results, as you have seen."

"Are you advising me not to go?" I asked.

"Oh, no." He stopped, turning to face me with a swirl of his cloak, all the mischief of a Hell full of demons dancing in his eyes. "The Conclave will be *far* more interesting if you attend. And Lady Zaira, too, of course, since I understand you cannot be separated. So much the better! I'll lay bets with the Fox Lord about whether you make it through the Conclave without setting anyone on fire."

Zaira smirked. "There's no way to lose a bet like that."

"Precisely." Kathe extended a hand to me, the gesture gracious and diffident, but a challenge in his gaze. "So, my lady, will you join me at the Conclave?"

I glanced at Zaira. "It's your decision as much as mine."

Her eyes narrowed. "I'm going back to that cursed castle one way or another. I still have to get Terika out."

"Then I would be delighted to accept your invitation." I put my hand in Kathe's, pulse quickening at my own audacity. Graces only knew what my mother would think of this.

His wiry fingers closed over mine. Power hummed under his skin. "I look forward to it with glee, my lady."

We linked arms and resumed walking. Kathe's warmth against my side was incredibly distracting. I couldn't help the thrill that raced through me at his closeness, and the smooth, hard muscle of his arm in mine. And demons take it, why shouldn't I enjoy this? It did Marcello no favors if I resolved to be miserable throughout our entire courtship. This was only a game to Kathe, after all, and games were supposed to be fun.

So I returned his smile and let the stiffness go from my back and shoulders as we walked.

The few flakes in the air thickened to a flurry, laying a deep hush on the forest and kissing my skin with tiny drops of ice water. I was too tired to keep myself from shivering.

Kathe tilted his head to regard me from the corner of one eye. "Do you need to stop for the night?"

"I can't afford to," I said grimly.

A howl rose up from the woods, piercing through the distance and the muffling trees. I sucked a breath between my teeth.

"Here it comes," Zaira muttered.

"No," Kathe said. "Wolves know better than to start a fight they can't win, and Ruven won't have a deep enough claim to force them yet. Chimeras are another matter."

Another howl rose from a different direction, somewhat closer. It was a wild, haunting sound, from a world older and truer than the fragile folly of cities. I could barely make out the road in front of us, a paler path through the many layers of darkness and the soft shroud of falling snow; it was easier to follow the bright gap of sky above, forming a clouded river between the treetops.

Grace of Mercy, it was cold. My shivers spread until my whole body shuddered with them. Kathe blinked down at me in alarm.

"Are you well? Ah, wait, you're cold." He nodded, as if human feelings like being cold and tired were something he'd known once but forgotten until now. "I believe it's customary for me to offer you my cloak at this point."

"Zaira must be just as cold as I am." She walked an arm's length away, giving me more room than usual; it occurred to me with something between panic and excitement that she might be attempting to afford me some degree of privacy with Kathe. I realized I'd instinctively pressed closer to his side for the heat he gave off.

"Oh, take the cloak," Zaira said. "I don't really feel it. I've got my fire to keep me warm."

"All right, then. Thank you."

I braced myself; Kathe settled his cloak around my shoulders, still warm from his body. Its feathers tickled my neck. No matter how the rest of me was doing, my face was certainly hot now.

"There." Kathe sounded pleased. "I think I'm getting better at this courting business."

The strangled sound of Zaira struggling to suppress laughter didn't help my floundering search for a reply.

"You said we could negotiate as we walked," I managed at last. "I do appreciate you seeing us safely back to Highpass. I think we've burned rather enough of Vaskandar for one week, given the war hasn't even started."

"Ah, yes. I'm doing you a favor." His voice took on a slight edge. "So of course I must want something."

"If you don't, that's quite all right," I assured him.

"Oh, I do, Lady Amalia. We all want things from each other." He turned his gaze up at the gap in the trees, so the moonlight dripped silver on the lines of his face. "Child to parent, lover to lover, ruled to ruler... It doesn't matter. Always, the people around us want something from us."

"What is it *you* want?"

He was silent awhile. Another howl rose up from the woods, like the voice of night itself, but he didn't seem to notice. Finally, he said softly, "There was a man, once, who didn't seem to want anything from me."

His voice had changed. It was tentative, faraway, like the fragile feeling of old papers crumbling under your fingers when you lift them from an undiscovered box in the attic. I didn't dare speak.

"He was one of my Heartguard. They are all close companions, and I like to find ways to reward them. Presents, kindnesses, glory, whatever it is each of them most seems to want." Kathe shook his head. "But Jathan devoted himself wholly to my service. All he seemed to want was the next task. He was young and eager, an arrow drawn and quivering to fly." He fell silent.

"Did you ever find out a way to reward him?" I asked.

Kathe shook his head. "I heaped all manner of gifts and praise on him, until I risked making the rest of the Heartguard jealous. He received everything graciously, but none of it was what he truly wished most. I could tell." He sighed. "Finally, I thought perhaps he sought greater responsibility and trust, since he threw himself into his work so much. So I sent him to Sevaeth on a delicate diplomatic mission, to work out a minor disagreement I had with the Lady of Thorns."

"What happened?" I asked, because his pause demanded it. But I knew full well the answer couldn't be anything good.

"She took insult that the emissary I sent was not a mage. She thought one of my Heartguard was too far beneath her." Kathe's voice went hard as a sword blade. "She killed him. She murdered my friend like she was tearing up a letter."

"I'm sorry," I said, sickened.

"The Lady of Thorns is too powerful for me to attack directly. But I do not forget." His mage mark shone in the darkness for a brief instant, like a night predator's eyes. "For two years, I've sought a way to destroy her. And somewhere along the way, I think I've realized what Jathan wanted all that time." He let out a long breath. "To make me happy. That's all."

To my own surprise, my eyes stung. I pulled Kathe's cloak closer around me. After a moment, I swallowed and managed to ask, "Did he?"

"Did he what?"

"Make you happy."

Kathe cocked his head, considering. After a moment, he laughed. It was a strained sound, but a true one. "Yes. Yes, he did."

We walked in silence a little longer, the night shadows of the forest shifting around us. The flurry tapered off, and stars like chips of ice began to show through the shredding clouds. Patches of fallen snow that had made it through the heavy pine boughs gleamed through the tree trunks like pieces of sky fallen to earth.

Finally, Kathe said, as if we'd never stopped talking, "So maybe it's all right if we take time to figure out what we want from each other. Maybe that's the fun of the game." His voice was light and full of mischief again, with no trace of hurt remaining.

"You're right," I said. "There's no need to rush."

Thank the Graces he didn't ask for anything. In that moment, I would have given him far too much.

I'd stayed up all night before—at parties, working on projects for my university classes, and reading particularly good books. But this walk felt a thousand times longer than any of those endless evenings.

After the past two harrowing days, I'd come out the other side of exhausted to a place where I could keep going forever, weightless as a worn ghost of myself. But I ached in a dozen places, and I had never felt so stretched and strained, as if whatever fabric held me together had thinned to the barest gossamer web.

Growls and awful cries rose from the forest, and every village we passed through had all its doors locked and shutters closed.

"They're afraid," Kathe murmured, frowning at an inn with its sign taken down and its windows covered, meager light leaking around the shutters. "They can feel the change happening. Ruven's magic threading through the earth, working its way into their flesh and their minds through the bridge of his father's blood."

My insides went cold at the thought. Zaira made a revolted noise.

"I'd run for the border, if I knew that snake was getting his fangs into me," she said.

"They can't." Kathe shook his head. "They're his. Even if they left, they'd still be his. It's not something they can run from."

"As your people are yours?" I asked, lifting a brow.

"Yes." He sighed. "Some of us take it as a responsibility, and do our best to care for our people. Like the Lady of Eagles—you saw her domain. I've told my people they can leave if they wish, and I like to think they stay because I've made my domain a good place to live. But they're magically tied to the land, and to me. I don't honestly know whether they are capable of choosing to leave."

"Like the brats who grew up in the Mews." Zaira glared at the handful of darkened buildings huddled by the road. The circle of the forest gathered close around them; there was barely room for a few paltry fields lying bright with snow beneath the moon before the pines loomed overhead again. "They don't even realize they're prisoners."

Kathe shrugged. "Everyone is a prisoner, Lady Zaira. But I try to leave the cage door open."

We walked in tired silence for a while, through the black forest. As hints of sunlight grew at last from bare traces of gray, I could pick more and more details out of the darkness. I watched Zaira from the corner of my eye, mulling over what she and Kathe had said.

Finally, I dropped back to walk by her side. "You don't have to go back to the Empire, you know," I said quietly.

She grunted. "I need reinforcements to get Terika out of that damned castle."

"I mean after that." I shrugged uncomfortably. "I'm sure the Lady of Eagles isn't the only one who'd be glad to welcome you. You'd be nobility here."

"I won't lie, I'm thinking about it." Zaira glared around at the rough-barked pines. "Do they have any cities in this backwater country?"

I tried not to show how my heart sank. "Ah...not like in the Serene Empire, no. The Witch Lords' power comes from the wilderness, and they don't tend to allow cities to spring up. Towns, perhaps."

"Huh. That's the rub." She shook her head. "Can you picture me living in this cursed forest? Or even on some happy little farm, kept like sheep?"

"I admit it doesn't seem like your natural environment."

"I'd fit in like a demon in the gardens of the Graces. I'm a city girl. What I *want* is to be able to live in Raverra, however I like, without being stuck in the Mews or chained to some prissy rich brat." She paused. "No offense."

"None taken."

"Or maybe Ardence. Ardence was nice." She sighed. "But my own castle, where I'm the one making the rules...Well, it's tempting."

"The people here certainly treat you with reverence," I forced myself to admit. The idea of losing Zaira to Vaskandar twisted a knot of pain under my breastbone, but I'd interfered more than enough in her life already.

But Zaira shook her head. "No," she said quietly. "They're just afraid of me, like everyone else."

I wasn't sure what to say to that. I gave her shoulder an awkward pat, trying to convey my sympathy through the quick touch. "Well, even if you're terrifying, you're still a good friend."

Zaira laughed. "Thanks. And you're all right, even if you're annoying."

She caught my hand in a quick squeeze that warmed my frozen fingers in an instant.

"Anyway, we've got to get out of here before I make any moving plans." Zaira blew a great, steaming cloud of breath. "That's step one. Step two is saving Terika. Step three is my favorite: punch Ruven in the face so hard he's peeling pieces of skull off his castle wall."

"Those are good goals," I said.

Chapter Twenty-Six

The fortress of Highpass watched over a dirt track that made its way through mountain meadows and a tough scrabble of low pine forest across a broad shoulder of mountainside. It was a difficult and minor pass, too rough for horses, but it was still good enough for fit soldiers to manage on foot; and so the stone fort brooded over the road with a full complement of cannons, its walls marked with artifice wards, enjoying a clear vantage over the long path up the mountain from Vaskandar.

When it came into view at last, rearing blocky and gray over a sweep of snow-blanketed meadow as the sun peeked over the shoulder of the mountain beyond it, my eyes stung with more than the mountain wind. Finally, we were back safe in the Empire. Nothing was trying to kill us; warm beds and warm food waited for us inside. It seemed impossible, like walking into a memory of a place that no longer existed.

But we were coming back without Lienne and Braegan and the other soldiers whose names I'd never learned. They should have been marching home by our sides, triumphant and weary, not left behind in Vaskandar to fall to the teeth of chimeras. The empty space around us felt thick with their ghosts.

Zaira let out a long breath of relief. "The Empire and I have our disagreements, but damn me to the Nine Hells if I'm not glad to be back."

I squeezed Kathe's hand, impulsively. "Thank you for escorting us. I'm not sure we'd have made it without you." Twice, passing through Sevaeth, he'd stared down a pack of whiphounds, and once a mountain lion. I had little doubt he'd used vivomancy to keep them from attacking us. Zaira could have dealt with them, but that would have likely left her unconscious, and I could never have carried her up the mountain to reach the pass.

"If your gratitude extends to offering hospitality, I will admit to some weariness." His shoulders strained against the soft fabric of his tunic as if he yearned to unfold wings, and the golden light of dawn caught on the sharp planes of his face. I could read the tiredness in the lines of it as he gazed toward the castle, and he seemed thinner, somehow. I felt an unexpected, almost tender pang of concern.

It occurred to me to wonder why he'd been in southern Atruin, and how fast he'd had to travel to get there. This might not have been his first night without sleep. I lifted his cloak from my shoulders and handed it back to him; his vivomancy might fortify him against the cold, but I suspected he was not entirely immune to it. My fingertips slid across his as I passed the cloak to him, and a tingle like rushing seafoam ran up my arm.

"Of course," I said. "Highpass is a fortress, not a palace, but what comforts it has to offer are yours."

We were still some distance from the rune-scribed arch of the open gates when a scarlet-uniformed figure ran out between the startled guards, setting their bayonets to swaying like reeds in the wind. Even from this far away, I knew him: Marcello. The warm glow that flooded me went beyond reason; the familiar line of his shoulders and the windblown waves of his dark hair renewed me like a drink of fresh water.

He caught up to us in the dawn-stained snow and swept me into a quick, tight hug, without so much as glancing at the others. Then he released me, staring at my face as if memorizing every line of it.

"You're all right. Thank the Graces. You're all right."

Every exhausted inch of my body wanted to melt into his arms. To put down the past few days like a burden and let him hold me. That brief moment of warmth had felt so good, so safe, so *right*. But Kathe watched me over Marcello's shoulder, his yellow-marked eyes unreadable, weariness or sorrow pulling at his face.

"Yes," I said, trying to keep my voice light and courteous. "We're fine. We made it home."

"Istrella and I arrived early yesterday morning, as the commander of Highpass and Princess Brisintain were starting to prepare forces to go after you." Marcello pushed a shaking hand through his hair. "I hadn't even known you were gone. Then just as we were about to cross the border, we got your second message, that you were safe and on your way home. But I couldn't..." He broke off, shaking his head. "No one else who went with you came back alive."

Grief pulled at me like a receding wave, eroding my strength to stand. "They gave their lives for us, Marcello. I wouldn't be here without them."

Marcello nodded gravely. "We'll make sure they're remembered as heroes."

Kathe was still waiting silently, his yellow-ringed eyes on us. I gestured to him, clearing my throat. "Lord Kathe was the one who saw us safely home."

Marcello regarded Kathe warily. "Then I am in your debt, Lord Kathe." He bowed, his back stiff.

Kathe smiled, but there was an edge to it. "Not at all, Captain. If I didn't enjoy the Lady Amalia's company, I wouldn't be courting her."

"Yes, yes. Can you glare at each other later?" Zaira pushed between them, heading for the fortress. "I'm so starving I can hardly stand."

The commander of Highpass welcomed us with stern relief into a fortress mobilized for our rescue, ordering a disturbing number of ready soldiers to stand down at last. I headed straight for the courier lamps to inform my mother that I was safe and report all of my disturbing news: Ruven's ascension to a Witch Lord, his capture and control of the missing Falcons, the activation of the volcano enchantment, and my own invitation to the Conclave as the one morsel of hope in the buffet of despair. She received this information with terse grace; for every pause in the rapid flashes of the courier lamp, I could picture her turning to Ciardha or the lamp operator to issue orders and relay messages to the doge. I had no doubt she would walk out of the lamp room with all the gathering power of a storm surge, pulling events into motion around her.

La Contessa's only personal message to me was brief: *I'm glad you're safe. We'll talk later.* A sense of foreboding settled over me at those last words; it took no great exercise of the imagination to guess that I had not handled matters as she would have done over the past two days.

I tried to shake off thoughts of looming disaster, be it volcanic or maternal, while I bolted down warm food, then washed off the remnants of Vaskandar and chased out its chill with a hot bath. Finally, exhaustion aching in my bones, I limped to the guest room the commander had assigned me, planning to collapse into bed. Matters of war and empire, volcanoes and Witch Lords, could all wait until I'd had some sleep.

But Bree waited for me at the door to my room, her ankle

splinted, leaning on a crutch. She flung her free arm around me, squeezing so tight I thought my ribs would break.

"Grace of Mercy, I thought you were dead, too." Her voice caught. She held me out at arm's length. Lines of worry creased her brow that I'd never seen there before; her hair looked as if she hadn't brushed it since we'd found her in the forest, with bits of leaf still stuck in it. "I went after Terika because I couldn't stand losing her when I was supposed to be protecting her. But look what happened."

"Terika's alive," I told her. "We only know her location because we went into Vaskandar. And I learned important information. It wasn't for nothing."

Bree let out a long breath. "That's good to hear. But I still feel terrible. This is the first time I've made a decision that cost lives." She shook her head; shadows of strain and exhaustion lay on her face. "Now their blood is on my hands, and we didn't even rescue her. But it would have felt even worse to just leave Terika to die."

"I don't think there was a right answer," I said, grief roughening my voice.

"It's awful, Amalia." Bree rubbed her face. "I'm glad I'll never be queen."

I nodded, a lump in my throat. My mother had to make life-and-death decisions all the time as a member of the Council of Nine. I knew I wouldn't be able to avoid them forever, myself. "How are the villagers, and Terika's grandmother?"

Bree brightened. "The alchemist was able to mix the antidote. They're recovering."

"Good." Relief swept over me. At least something had turned out well. "We have a lot to talk about, Bree. But for now, I'm going to bed."

The finest bed at the fortress was lumpy and hard compared to my silk-sheeted feather bed at home. But after nights with little or no sleep, it felt like sinking into clouds.

The next morning, a brisk knock at my door interrupted my breakfast. I answered it to find the commander of Highpass, his bushy eyebrows creasing his forehead into a frown beneath his balding dome.

"Lady Amalia," he greeted me. "I'm sorry to interrupt you, but perhaps you can help me with your, ah, guest."

It took me a moment to realize he must mean Kathe. I rose. "Is everything all right?"

"Well enough. But I'm afraid he's spooked the guards on the north tower. No one wants to go near him." He shook his head. "They're mostly Callamornish, and downright superstitious about Witch Lords. If you could just talk to him—show them he's not going to murder everyone..." Captain Edhras trailed off and gave me an expectant look, as if hoping for confirmation that Kathe was, indeed, not going to murder everyone.

I sighed. "I'll be right there."

Kathe perched on the parapet, seemingly oblivious to the long drop below him, the wind catching his feathered cloak and ruffling his hair. He made a strange and striking figure, which might have been enough to rattle Callamornes who'd grown up with Witch Lords as the villains in every story, but what I suspected truly pushed them over the edge were the crows.

He held out his hands as if greeting the mountains. Crows perched on his palms, his arms, his shoulders, and the parapet around him; they fluttered in the air, looking for places to land, or took off again and flew toward Vaskandar. He muttered to them quietly in some strange, rough language, a distracted smile on his face, and slipped them tidbits from a pouch at his waist.

There must have been dozens of them, strutting and flapping their dark wings and watching everything with their bright round eyes.

I wasn't sure how to approach him, myself. I waited several paces off, feeling rather as if I might be interrupting a conversation. A crow on his shoulder cawed at me, then pecked his ear.

Kathe turned, crows rising from him all at once with a thunder of wings. He grinned and hopped down from the parapet.

"Lady Amalia. I'm glad you're awake. This place is deadly dull."

"Well, it *is* a military fortress preparing for war," I pointed out. "Everyone is probably too busy to entertain guests."

"Luckily, I'm an expert at entertaining myself." He offered me his arm. "Will you walk with me?"

I was getting used to the strange, electric tingle when I touched him, but the sheer absurd audacity of walking arm in arm with a Witch Lord still hadn't worn off. The wind tangled my hair as we strolled side by side along the parapet, with the mountains rearing in snow-mantled grandeur all around us.

"I gather you have some attachment to that officer who greeted you yesterday," Kathe said, his voice neutral. "I seem to recall him from the party, as well."

I jumped. I couldn't help it. "Captain Verdi is a good friend," I said.

Kathe clicked his tongue. "Come now, Lady Amalia. You can do better than that."

"It's the truth." But not the whole truth. A warm flush crept up my neck to my ears. "We never courted. His family is patrician, but his rank is insufficient." It was none of Kathe's business that we'd kissed, or that hardly a day passed when I didn't spend at least a little time wishing I could kiss him again.

"Ah, I understand." Kathe sighed. "You can imagine the difficulties of trying to court as a Witch Lord. I can't show interest in anyone from my own domain; even if they seem eager, it feels like an abuse of my rank. Courting someone from another domain requires permission of their Witch Lord. And if you're hoping for an heir, well, you have to consider bloodlines and magical potential on top of everything else."

"It sounds rather complicated," I said.

"This boy of yours." He gave me a gleaming sideways glance, and I suspected him of enjoying my discomfort at the phrase. "Does he understand that for one of your station, courtship is not a matter of the heart?"

I resolved not to let him rattle me. "Courtship is a political game for those of our rank, Lord Kathe. But I would argue that the heart must become involved in order to take home the prize."

"Oho?" He cocked an eyebrow. "Surely you don't mean to imply that *all* marriages among the nobility are love matches."

"No." I knew too many aristocratic couples in Raverra locked in arranged marriages with spouses they did no more than tolerate. "But perhaps they should be."

He spun away from me, a hand going dramatically to his chest, as if I'd struck him with an arrow. "Do you mean to tell me that if I wish this courtship to be successful, I must actually earn your *love*, of all things?"

I laughed. "Isn't that what courtship is technically for?"

His eyes narrowed in calculation. "That will make this rather harder."

A chill came on me, half excitement and half foreboding, borne by the mountain wind. "Why, Lord Kathe, I would nearly think you were serious."

"I am rarely serious, my lady. But that doesn't mean I'm not in earnest."

Mirth lit his face, but an intensity lay behind it, keen as an arrowhead. He meant it.

I couldn't shrug this off as a joke, but I couldn't give him assurances either. Kathe played his games to win, and my future was a stake on the table.

I clasped my hands behind my back to keep them from worrying at my hair or sleeves. "Are you so intent on gaining access to the Lady of Eagles' bloodline, then?"

"It's intriguing, I admit. But I'm looking at the larger picture." He stepped to the parapet and gazed up at the crows now circling overhead. "They're clever creatures, you know. They're curious, they're good at solving problems, and they work together. They notice and remember, but they're so common no one sees them. My crows have already spread throughout Vaskandar and half the Empire. If you see a crow anywhere in Eruvia, there's at least a chance it was born in Let. You are La Contessa's daughter; you must be able to see the advantage they give me."

"Spies," I whispered. "They're perfect spies."

He nodded, grinning. "Most Witch Lords turn their eyes inward, to their own domains. I look beyond. I have ambitions, Lady Amalia. I don't want to take over more land, or rule Eruvia—I want to *know* things. And to be able to make things happen, when I wish it."

I leaned back against the parapet, dazed by the scope of possibilities. "No wonder my mother wanted to cultivate you."

"You see? I have a lot to offer. But I don't have the experience at this sort of game a Raverran does." He gave me a deferential nod. "I don't have the web of human connections and agents you do. And I know little of the Serene Empire. But together—well, I can see in your eyes you understand what we could do together."

It shouldn't have been tempting. I was a scholar; I achieved my fulfillment from hiding in my room with a good book or fiddling around with artifice designs. My ambitions tended toward writing papers on magical theory that might someday be cited by great scholars. But for a moment I saw the world through my mother's eyes—the imperial intelligence services, Cornaro wealth and influence, and Kathe's virtually invisible crows casting a net across the entire map, north and south of the Witchwall mountains. Add to that whatever magical leverage my blood connection to the Lady of Eagles' network of waters through Vaskandar might give us, and it would be almost trivial to become the secret powers behind every throne in Eruvia.

It wasn't something I'd ever wanted. But it was a great and terrible prize, one worth winning, too powerful to simply shrug off and ignore.

"I do understand," I said slowly. "I may understand even better than you do."

"Precisely." His eyes gleamed with appreciation. "So yes, Lady Amalia. Consider yourself warned. This courtship is no sham; I am your honest—or at least your *genuine*—suitor."

Graces preserve me, but I couldn't help feeling a stirring at his impish smile, and the casual grace and energy of his every small movement. And if a woman existed who wasn't at least a bit curious about what it would be like to kiss a Witch Lord, I was not that woman—at least, not when the Witch Lord was Kathe.

My mother hadn't started out in love with my father; I knew that. They'd liked each other, and found each other attractive, and had seen what an alliance between their countries could do. And they'd grown to love each other deeply and truly, over time. Was that a love any less to be coveted than the summer storm passions that led to half the so-called love matches I'd seen, here and gone within a year?

The spark in Kathe's eyes anticipated an answer. There was a thirst in me to take up his challenge, and I saw no reason to deny it.

"Very well." I put my hand in his, returning a wry smile. "Then I will be certain to entertain your suit with all the seriousness it deserves."

He raised my hand to his lips, the vivid yellow rings of his mage mark piercing above it, and brushed a whisper of a kiss across my knuckles. "I can ask no more, my lady."

I watched from the parapet as Kathe strode off through the pass toward Let. He'd said he needed to return to see to matters in his own domain before the Conclave but would make arrangements for me to arrive there safely. He moved at a pace a normal human couldn't possibly keep up for long, but with an easy roll to his step suggesting that perhaps in this regard, a Witch Lord wasn't an ordinary human. A strange, possessive pride uncurled in my chest as I looked down on him: this creature of grace and power, of wings and lightning, was offering himself to me, through some wild twist of fate and scheming whimsy. If I wished it, he could be mine.

And I his. There lay the difficulty.

Marcello found me still standing there a while later, alone, watching the crows circling and cawing against the blue sky.

The scent of leather and gunpowder reached me first, borne on the mountain wind. I turned to face Marcello, and the concern in his warm green gaze cut a path through my heart like a deep wake in the Raverran lagoon.

Grace of Love. I needed him like water, like sunlight, like home. I could imagine a future with Kathe, grand and exciting—but I couldn't imagine a future without Marcello.

If I wanted to become my mother's true heir and serve the Serene Empire, I would need to stretch my imagination. And that knowledge tore a great aching rip in my heart.

"How are you?" he asked, and in his voice I could hear days of worry to match my nightmarish nights in Vaskandar.

"Glad to be back in the Empire. Anxious about the volcano

and the Conclave." I hugged my arms against the chill on the wind.

"Would you like my coat?" he offered, his hand going to his buttons.

"Thank you, but I don't think that would be wise." His warmth and scent enveloping me would hurt too much, right now.

Marcello nodded and leaned against the parapet at my side, leaving exactly the right amount of space between us for a close friend. No more, and no less.

He was too good. He would make a wonderful father, damn him. In a flash that took my breath away, I could see it: Marcello, with lines of silver in his hair, shepherding our children upstairs to play a game while I received the doge and the Council in the drawing room. Marcello helping our tiny daughter, raven-haired like her father, climb into a boat by herself for the first time. Leaning back into Marcello's arms to rest, cuddled up with him before a merry fire with a good book and a cup of mulled wine. Laughing with him after only a glance, crinkles of age and mirth around his green eyes, because we'd known each other for so many years we didn't need to say the joke aloud.

It was a future so real I could reach out and touch it, living and breathing before me in Marcello's strong shoulders and sincere green eyes. This was what I stood to lose. This was what I would sacrifice, if I played my games too long.

I swallowed a hot, messy knot in my throat. What kind of idiot was I, to think of something like that? I might as well sit around stabbing myself in the face with a table fork.

"Your button kept me company in Vaskandar," I told him, slipping a hand into my pocket to feel its familiar curves. It had felt wrong to leave my room without it, after all we'd been through together. "I'm not sure it talked me out of any bad ideas, but it made me feel like you were with me."

"Then take it with you to the Conclave," he said. "I don't like the idea of you going back there alone."

"With Zaira," I corrected him. "Zaira is like at least ten people, in a variety of ways."

He laughed. We stood in silence, side by side, then, watching the wind blow withered leaves across the melting remnants of snow in the meadow below. Mount Whitecrown reared up above the shadowy lesser mountains in the distance, its glaciers forming stark streaks of white against the clear blue sky. Only one small puff of cloud clung to its southern face, near the summit, drifting up and away on the wind.

Out of a fold in the mountainside, another wisp of white cloud peeked, slowly rising into the air.

I grabbed Marcello's elbow. "Look," I whispered hoarsely.

That wasn't cloud. It was steam.

With all the slow grandeur of a sleeping dragon rising from its bed of centuries, the volcano was beginning to awaken.

A tense mood settled over the castle as Mount Whitecrown continued to emit innocent-looking, fluffy puffs of steam. It might well not mean anything; Mount Whitecrown was an active volcano, after all, and didn't sit with the proper immutable stillness one might reasonably expect from a mountain. But I kept glancing out windows at its snowy peak, ghostly with distance, all too aware of the magical forces even now building up a terrifying pressure within its fiery heart.

It was hard to focus on my books that evening. I'd left Zaira and Bree drinking together in Bree's room, throwing knives at a crude drawing of Ruven's face. I needed to take advantage of this moment of rare quiet and solitude; I only had a week to prepare for the Conclave. I'd had a long follow-up conversation over the courier lamps with my mother, half explaining my rash actions in Vaskandar and half trying to convince her that I needed to go back. She'd seemed to see the opportunity but had warned that the doge and the Council of Nine would need to agree if I were to attend with any authority to negotiate for Raverra.

I was staring at Lavier's *Chronicle of Vaskandran Expansion* without comprehension when Istrella knocked on my door, then bustled in without waiting for a reply, carrying a tray piled high with a tangle of beaded artifice wire and two steaming mugs.

"Hello," she said cheerfully, kicking the door shut behind her. "Mind if I show you what I'm working on?"

"Of course not." I pushed my book away with some relief. "Is that chocolate?"

"Coffee!" Istrella plunked the tray down on the table between us. "I remembered how much you like it."

I stared dubiously at the sloshing cup of evil black liquid. "It smells nice," I said politely, and nudged the cup away. "What have you got?"

The tangle of wires and beads on her tray appeared to be two separate devices: one a crystal that probably stored energy, from the look of the runes carved into it, and the other a complex little wirework basket wrapped around an irregular lump of copper.

"Oh, are you not going to drink the coffee?" Istrella sounded relieved. "That's just as well, really. I don't think I made it right."

"I'm not that fond of it anyway," I admitted.

"I know," she said. Then she added, in a strange tone, "Last chance!"

I glanced up from her device to her face, startled. Her eyes bugged earnestly at me, as if she were expecting something. "I'm sorry," I said, "last chance for what?"

Istrella sighed with evident exasperation. "Never mind. Here, hold this, and I'll show you."

She plunked the device with the copper lump into my hand,

trailing loose wires. I scarcely paid attention; I was staring at the shadows under her eyes. "Istrella, is something wrong?"

"Oh, nothing really." Quick as a wink, she twisted the dangling wires together with more loose wires that hung off the power crystal, connecting the two halves of the device. In my hand, the copper lump hummed with energy; the vibration traveled up my bones and all through my body.

I couldn't move.

Every nerve buzzed with a heavy numbness. Every muscle locked precisely in place: not with tension, but exactly as it had been when she'd connected the wires. My body felt far too normal, far too relaxed, for the white-hot alarm building in my chest.

Istrella peered anxiously into my face. "Still breathing? Heart still beating?"

I couldn't move my lips to reply. All I could do was stare at her in horror.

"Oh, good! I wasn't sure this would work." Istrella sank back into her chair with apparent relief. "I had to throw it together overnight when I got the command. I was hoping you'd figure out the coffee hint, but you missed it, like all the others. You and Marcello can be really oblivious when you're distracted, you know."

Hells. She was under Ruven's control. She'd been under his control since Lady Aurica's dinner party. That assassin hadn't been trying to kill her at all; she'd knocked her out and given her the potion.

Istrella was the traitor.

Chapter Twenty-Seven

Istrella picked up my coffee cup in both hands. "I'm sorry about this," she said anxiously. "I know you don't like coffee. And I know you don't like Prince Ruven. I feel terrible about the entire business."

I tried to scream for help, but the only sound I could make was a breathy wheeze. I stared at the coffee cup with more revulsion and terror than if it had been full of blood and Black Malice. I didn't need my ring to know it was tainted with Ruven's poison.

There could be no greater torment in the Hell of Nightmares than falling under his dominion. I'd rather jump into a pit full of vipers, or take a bath in Zaira's balefire. Panic exploded in my brain, cascading like a spilled oil lamp setting off a room full of powder kegs.

Istrella leaned across the table with the cup, her tongue between her teeth in concentration, her brows furrowed with worry.

I struggled to move, but it was as if some invisible wall lay between my mind and my body. The hum of Istrella's device filled me, and I sat just as I had been, cupping the copper lump in my open hand. There was nothing I could do to fight her; I was going to become Ruven's tool, and betray my friends and my Empire.

Blisteringly hot coffee sloshed over my lips and dribbled

down onto the table. I couldn't even flinch at the scalding pain. But not a drop made it onto my tongue.

Istrella blinked. "Oh, right. Your mouth is closed."

Is she doing this on purpose?

Istrella fumbled at my lips, prying my teeth apart with her slim fingers. "I am so sorry," she said. "Really, I can't tell you how much I'd rather not be doing this. I mean, I literally can't. If I try, I'll probably start babbling about the research I did into human nerves to create this device instead, which is actually quite interesting."

No matter how hard I strove to struggle and thrash, to make even the tiniest movement, the only thing I could control was my breath. And now Istrella was tipping the coffee cup toward my lips again, her hands trembling as she fought against her compulsion.

I blew out all my breath at once, as hard as I could.

Hot coffee sprayed over my lips, my chin, Istrella's hands. She yelped and jumped back, dropping the cup. It shattered, splashing coffee everywhere; the table jerked as Istrella bumped into it.

The lump of copper fell out of my hand.

I leaped to my feet at once and made a grab for Istrella, my heart still pounding violently in my chest. She let out a squeak of surprise and bolted from the room.

I ran after her, chasing her down the keep's stone corridor. "Istrella! Wait!"

"You know how it is!" she called back over her shoulder. "Sometimes you just have to run!"

I was gaining on her, despite the tingling that lingered in my nerves. She rounded a corner only a few steps in front of me—

And ran directly into Lord Caulin, the Chancellor of Silence.

Whatever he did was so quick I couldn't follow it. He stepped neatly to the side, moving with swift precision, and caught Istrella in his arms as she suddenly collapsed. His calm expression never wavered.

"Istrella!" I cried.

"She's quite all right," Lord Caulin said. He lowered her carefully to the floor and offered me a deep bow. "This is most fortuitous, Lady Amalia. I've just come from Raverra with new evidence about the traitor. I'm here to place this Falcon under arrest."

"What is the meaning of this, Lord Caulin?" Marcello demanded as he strode into my sitting room, anger in every tautly controlled line of his face.

I had insisted that Istrella be brought to my rooms rather than a holding cell; Lord Caulin had insisted on guards. This had led to Istrella awakening groggily in a chair at my dining table, with two soldiers standing watch on either side of her, just as her brother burst in.

Relief and anxiety swept over me at the sight of him, both from a single source: there was no way Marcello would let anything happen to his sister.

But he had no idea who Lord Caulin truly was, or how much danger Istrella was in. And I couldn't tell him.

Lord Caulin spread his hands disarmingly. "Good evening, Captain Verdi. As I was just telling the Lady Amalia, my investigation has finally borne fruit, and I regret to inform you that it incriminates this Falcon."

The harsh laugh that erupted from Marcello held nothing of humor in it. "My sister, the traitor? Your investigation couldn't be farther off base if it led you to the bottom of the ocean."

Istrella grimaced, blinking as if she couldn't quite pull her vision into focus, her artifice glasses askew on her forehead.

"Oh, dear," Lord Caulin sighed. "Do you want to tell him, Lady Amalia, or shall I?"

Marcello spun to stare at me, green eyes wide with shock.

"She's under Ruven's control," I told him, my voice wound tighter than a violin string.

"What?!" Marcello stepped back as if I'd struck him.

"No, I'm not," Istrella piped up. "I can't possibly imagine what you're talking about. Surely if I were under a malevolent Witch Lord's control, my dear brother would have noticed the many hints I would have tried to give him over the past few weeks."

Marcello flinched.

"The evidence is rather conclusive," Lord Caulin sighed. "The Mews clerks helped us assemble a list of people who might have accessed all the relevant papers, and we compared it to those physically present at Durantain with the necessary knowledge to alter the wards. That left only a few suspects, so naturally we searched your sister's tower."

"You'd better not have disarranged my projects!" Istrella cried, nearly lunging to her feet. One of the guards stopped her with a hand on her shoulder. "Some of them are very delicate! And dangerous, for that matter."

"Yes, well, two of the searchers will likely take a few days to recover from their injuries, but no one died." Lord Caulin flipped the idea away, with a motion like turning a page. "We discovered signs that your Falcon had been feeding the seagulls at her window, and, more damningly, found crumpled-up drafts of letters outlining Falcon leave schedules on the floor nearby. She clearly had been passing messages to the Witch Lords via the birds."

Istrella sighed. "I was hoping you'd find those," she told us, "but nobody ever comes in when I tell them not to come in. You people need more native curiosity."

Marcello had gone pale as if he might faint. "You disabled the wards at Durantain," he whispered. "When you told us about the weaknesses in the wards, you were trying to warn us."

"Well, I probably would have noticed those regardless," Istrella said. "They were inexcusably sloppy."

"You see?" Lord Caulin shrugged. "She admits it."

"She's under the effects of a potion," I snapped. "I saw the same thing in Vaskandar. If we search her room, we'll probably find it."

Istrella glanced at me in alarm, then suddenly snatched a flask from her pocket and began drinking great gulps from it. The guards beside her hesitated for a surprised moment, and then one knocked it from her hand. The remaining liquid spilled across the floor.

So much for that evidence. "Do you have any more?" I asked her urgently.

Istrella looked a bit woozy. "If I did, do you think I'd have swallowed all that down? Ugh, it tastes terrible."

Lord Caulin hooked a finger over his lips and stared at the flask, his dark eyes glittering. "If there *is* a potion, this is most interesting." He paced over, picked up the flask, and slipped it into an inner pocket. "Either way, we need to learn more, which means taking this Falcon back to Raverra for interrogation and examination."

My insides went cold. If Istrella vanished into the care of the Chancellor of Silence, I held little hope we would ever see her again.

"And why would you want to know more about the potion?" I demanded, seeking an angle to block him.

Lord Caulin blinked, his face a mask of mild-mannered innocence. "Why, to find a way to counter it, of course, Lady Amalia."

I didn't believe that for a moment. From what I'd heard of Lord Caulin, he wouldn't hesitate to use a potion like that if he had access to one.

Marcello straightened, a fire in his eyes to match Zaira's. "It doesn't matter. Istrella was controlled against her will; she's innocent. You can't arrest her."

"Ah, but I'm afraid I can." Lord Caulin offered an apologetic smile. "The doge granted me the authority to apprehend the traitor when he placed me in charge of this investigation."

"With due respect, my lord, I don't care." Marcello bit off each word. "Istrella is a Falcon, and I am her captain and her Falconer. It's my duty to protect her, and I don't take orders from anyone but Colonel Vasante."

"I assure you, the doge himself—" Caulin began silkily.

"Do you have written orders from Colonel Vasante?" Marcello pressed.

"My orders were verbal, Captain. However—"

"From the doge, then? Or perhaps the Marquise of Palova?" Marcello's face was hard, his tone relentless. Istrella watched him with bright eyes.

Annoyance flickered across Lord Caulin's bland face. "Let me assure you, Captain Verdi, I have the authority."

I could imagine his frustration. Caulin and I both knew his true rank, but to Marcello, he was a mere legal adviser overstepping his bounds. And the secrecy of Caulin's position prevented him from shattering that illusion.

Time to tighten that vise. "It seems to me that Captain Verdi has precedence here," I said. "The doge granted you authority to arrest a traitor. But Istrella isn't a traitor; she acted under the effects of an alchemical potion. I can bear witness to that. Without a guilty party, you have no power to arrest anyone."

Lord Caulin considered me from narrowed eyes. I kept my face impassive, hiding the racing of my heart. I could almost see him calculating how much it would tip his hand to push further, and who would win if I pushed back.

With Istrella's life in the balance, I was willing to push as hard as necessary. Marcello stood at my side, stern and clear-eyed, back straight and proper in his Falconer's uniform. *There is no enemy more implacable than an honest man*, my mother had once told me.

Caulin looked back and forth between us. At last, he sighed. "Very well, Lady Amalia. I bow to your wisdom. But perhaps when you visit Vaskandar for the Conclave, you can attempt to learn more of this most interesting potion."

"Oh, I assure you, I intend to," I said. I neglected to add that it would take some of the potion itself to compel me to tell him the recipe.

"Then I leave the Falcon to your care." Lord Caulin nodded stiffly to Marcello. "I recommend you quarantine her until this potion's effect fades."

Caulin bowed to me and left, taking the guards with him. Once he was gone, Marcello's shoulders slumped, and he blew out a long breath of relief.

"Well, I'm glad that's over with," Istrella said, settling her artifice glasses properly on her forehead. "Amalia, I'm really sorry." She opened her mouth and then pressed her lips together, staring at me intently, as if she wanted to say more.

"It's all right," I said. "I know you didn't have a choice."

She shuddered. "I can't speak to that. But on an unrelated note, how long does it take a potion to wear off? If, say, you drank something really horrible by mistake. I'm just curious." Her voice quavered slightly.

"For most potions, only a day or two," I assured her. "You'll be fine."

Marcello knelt down beside Istrella's chair and hugged her, his eyes squeezed shut. "I'm so sorry, Istrella. I should have figured out something was wrong."

"Nothing's wrong." Istrella's voice was muffled by his shoulder. "But yes, you should have. I could never get your attention."

"Since this promotion, I've been so busy, and I've had so

much on my mind..." He held Istrella's shoulders at arm's length then, and met her eyes. "But I should never have let that distract me from being a good brother for you. I wish Colonel Vasante had never made me a captain."

"Don't be silly." Istrella frowned at him. "I can't count the number of times I've gotten involved in a project and forgotten all about you for weeks. That doesn't make me a bad sister. Does it?"

Marcello hesitated. "Ah...no."

Istrella nodded decisively. "See? Don't feel bad about being a captain."

"Thank you, 'Strella." He managed a smile for her. I wished I could hug them both and tell them it was all right.

"Feel bad about being so obtuse." She poked him in the forehead. "If you were better at picking up on my hints, I'd never have managed to get Amalia paralyzed."

"Paralyzed?" Marcello swiveled to look at me, wide-eyed.

Istrella brightened. "Yes! I'm really proud of the device I made, actually. Do you mind if I show you?"

Marcello put his face in his hands, his shoulders shaking with what I hoped was laughter.

We saw Istrella settled in the improvised workshop in her room. Marcello lingered in the doorway as I said good night.

"I'll have to keep a watch on her," he said, his voice low and worried. "At least until the potion wears off."

"You were wonderful, standing up for her like that," I said warmly. "She's lucky to have you for a brother."

"Even though I missed all the clues she was trying to give me?" He grimaced. "Looking back, she's been acting oddly for a while, but..."

"Istrella *always* acts oddly, so it's hard to tell," I said, finishing for him. "I feel foolish for not having seen it, myself. Especially after the flare locket she made for Zaira malfunctioned and knocked out Bree's entire escort of soldiers. I'll bet that was a trap to try to take out Zaira, if she used it the next time an assassin attacked." I frowned. "I should get on the courier lamps to Durantain and the fortress where she worked on the defenses the other day, to have them check for sabotage. Though hopefully Istrella will be able to tell us herself about anything else she did soon enough."

"If you could, that would be wonderful. I shouldn't leave Istrella alone. And not just because she's under Ruven's control." Marcello ruffled a hand through his hair, as if he could push the worry out of his head.

"Agreed." Choosing my words carefully, I added, "I wouldn't want Lord Caulin to come try to arrest her again."

"Thank you for backing me up against him. I know I can always count on you." He caught my eyes, then, and his were a deep and impossible green I could fall into for days and never hit bottom. "No matter what happens."

My breath came up short. We were standing too close. I hadn't noticed, with all my worries about Istrella; we'd fallen back into old habits from our days in Ardence. But now it was too much, and I took a step back, flushing, my fingers rising up unbidden to fidget with a lock of my hair.

"Of course," I said. "No matter what happens, I'll always be your friend."

But I knew, with unbearable certainty, that nothing could be quite the same between us. Not while I courted Kathe, or any other political prospect, and certainly not if I married him. In every interaction with Marcello, we would always be handling this invisible, heavy thing between us, all full of broken edges with which we could unwittingly cut each other.

"Marcello," I said. "I need to tell you something important."

His throat jumped. But he nodded, slowly, his eyes never leaving mine.

"Don't wait for me," I said.

His face crumpled in pain as if I'd punched him. He looked away.

Hells, this was terrible. I'd rather he stabbed me. I'd nearly rather stab *him.* My eyes burned, but I blinked back the tears; I couldn't cry, not now, or he wouldn't believe me.

"So...Does this mean you're choosing the Crow Lord?" he asked, his voice harsh.

I swallowed. "I'm choosing duty." I tucked my hands into my sleeves to keep from reaching out to him. "I'm becoming who I need to be."

He turned back to me, then, and his eyes shone wetly. "But I love who you are."

I closed my eyes. "For Graces' sake, Marcello."

"I'm sorry," he whispered.

His hand touched my hair, light as the brush of a butterfly's wing. I almost thought I imagined it.

And then he closed Istrella's door between us.

Chapter Twenty-Eight

"Lady Amalia."

There hadn't been the slightest whisper of sound behind me as I stood on the windswept battlements the next day, brooding over Marcello. But the voice was so familiar, with its tone of respectful confidence smooth as silk and strong as steel, I didn't jump or startle. I turned to face her, apprehension tightening my gut as to what her mission might be.

"Hello, Ciardha. What brings you to Callamorne?"

She stood elegant and ready as always, a vision of grace and lethal poise. She dipped me a bow. "La Contessa originally sent me to ensure that you returned safely from Vaskandar, among other things. She was somewhat nonplussed at your impulsive action in crossing the border."

I winced. I'd had that conversation over the courier lamps. "So she's informed me."

"But it would seem you need no assistance in such matters, which leaves the rest of my mission."

"The rest of it?"

"La Contessa sent me updated orders. I am here to help you prepare for the Conclave, Lady." She produced a terribly official-looking document on thick vellum, scribed with the ornate writing reserved for important writs and bearing a prominent imperial seal. "The Council of Nine and the doge himself have granted you the authority of a Serene Imperial Envoy, to negotiate with the Witch Lords on behalf of the Empire."

I stared at the document in disbelief. The words were a jumble of fancy letters to my stunned eyes, but the seal was unmistakable: the rearing winged horse of Raverra, surrounded by nine stars, pressed firmly into a circle of blue wax. "The doge and the Council trust me with *this*?"

Ciardha's mouth quirked. "As to that, with all deference, you are the only Raverran noble attending the Conclave whom they have available to trust. But they are most impressed that you secured an invitation." She rolled up the writ. "I suggest you gather those whose advice you value, Lady. We have much to discuss."

"So. We need to stop Ruven from triggering the volcano, free the captured Falcons, and influence the Conclave against war."

I scanned the faces gathered around the table in the briefing room we'd taken over: Ciardha, Marcello, Bree, Zaira, and Istrella, who had fully shaken off the effects of the potion. As soon as she could speak freely, she'd given us the full details of everything she'd done while controlled, quivering with righteous anger at Ruven for using her against her friends. ("Though it's just as well he made me sabotage those wards in Durantain," she'd added. "If I hadn't examined them for flaws, something worse would have gotten in eventually.")

This was real. My hands trembled in my lap. The doge and the Council had entrusted me with the future of the Serene Empire. I was going to the Conclave, to face the Witch Lords and help determine the course of history. And all these competent, brilliant people looked to me to lead them.

I'd been less scared staring down the assassin's pistol. If my plan wasn't good enough, Mount Whitecrown could cover half the Empire in ash, killing thousands and spreading Ruven's influence like a sickness. If Zaira and I failed to convince enough Witch Lords not to join in the war, the Serene Empire could face an invasion brutal enough to shatter it to pieces. I had my hand on the quill of fate as it wrote the next chapter of Eruvia's history, and it was up to me not to spill red ink all over the pages.

I cleared my throat. "The circles we need to disable completely surround Mount Whitecrown," I said. "The Lady of Eagles is taking care of the ones in Atruin. I estimate there may be two or three at most on our side of the border, where the southernmost skirts of the mountain cross into the Empire, and the rest will be in Kazerath."

Marcello frowned over the map and diagram I'd sketched. I couldn't tell if he was avoiding meeting my eyes, but he looked tired and worn, and my throat ached at the sight of him. "Getting into and out of Kazerath will be dangerous," he said, all business. "There are a lot of troops in that area."

"I don't think you need to get every single one," Istrella said thoughtfully. "So long as you modify more than half the circles to slowly release the pressure rather than building it up, it'll drop below the danger point over time. Of course, if anyone triggered an eruption before the pressure decreased enough, then *boom*!" She made exploding noises and hand gestures, with great enthusiasm.

"I can take a group to handle the circles on the west side," Marcello offered. It did not escape my notice that this would put him as close as possible to Ruven's castle, where Zaira and I would be attending the Conclave. "We'll just need someone reliable to handle the east."

"Did I hear someone say 'reliable'?" my cousin Roland asked, striding in the door.

"Roland!" Bree leaped to her feet, wincing at the sudden

weight on her ankle. She had access to the best alchemical bone-mending potions in Eruvia, but healing still took time. "What are you doing here?"

"I took some sage advice and asked the queen for permission to come here, to see if you needed any help." He settled down at the table, giving me a warm, grateful glance. I returned an encouraging smile.

"And she said yes?" Bree's tone conveyed disbelief.

Roland folded his hands and rubbed his thumbs together. "Well, she didn't say no. Though I'm strictly forbidden to take one step closer to the Kazerath or Sevaeth borders. But I do want to help." Frustration tightened his voice. "I couldn't stand it if someday, when my grandchildren ask me what I did in the war, I have to tell them I stayed home safe and sound in Durantain while everyone else fought to save their country."

"You can take an artificer to disable the circles on the east side of Mount Whitecrown, then, along the Atruin border," I said. "That shouldn't put you in any more danger than riding here from Durantain."

"Excellent." Roland's eyes lit with excitement. "I'll be glad to finally be doing something."

"Looks like I'm the one stuck at home this time," Bree grumbled. "Grandmother's ordered me back to Durantain, so I don't get tempted to try to fight on this ankle before the bone finishes mending."

"It's almost as if she knows you," Roland said dryly.

Marcello turned to me, meeting my eyes at last, his demeanor stiffly courteous. "Will you need guards to protect you at the Conclave, as well?"

I hesitated. "I don't think I can bring anyone besides Zaira."

Marcello made a strangled noise. So much for his professional face.

"I know, I know." I spread my hands. "But I'm going there as the Crow Lord's guest, under his protection. And if anything attacks us there that Zaira and Kathe can't deal with, a few guards or a hundred won't make any difference."

"They'd only hold me back." Zaira tipped her chair, hands behind her head. "I'm much more effective if I'm not surrounded by people I'd rather not set on fire."

"La Contessa has spoken to Colonel Vasante on the matter," Ciardha said smoothly. "The colonel is sending Jerith Antelles and his Falconer to stand by at Highpass in case you face any difficulties in getting out of Vaskandar."

A strange mix of relief and dread settled over me. "So she deems this a two-warlock situation." There were only a scant handful among all the Falcons.

"La Contessa has complete faith that you will handle the situation diplomatically, Lady, and that no such fail-safe will prove necessary," Ciardha said. "But La Contessa also believes in preparing for contingencies."

Istrella brightened. "I can make you some artifice devices, as well, to defend yourself in case of an emergency." She rubbed her hands. "If I had more time, I could arm you like a small battalion, but I'm sure I can come up with something fun in the time we have."

I attempted not to show my alarm at the notion of carrying something Istrella considered "fun" into a delicate diplomatic situation in enemy territory. "Ah, well..."

"It's the least I can do, after I tried to poison you." Istrella strained at the edge of her chair. "Please, let me make it up to you. I insist!"

"All right, then," I agreed weakly.

"What about Terika and the other Falcons?" Marcello leaned his elbows on the table, concern coloring his voice.

"We'll get them out," Zaira said firmly. "We'll be right there in the castle for the Conclave."

"Exactly. You'll be at the Conclave." Marcello made a face, as if the words tasted bitter in his mouth, but he knew better than to argue. "You won't be able to run off in the middle of it. Who will get all those Falcons safely back to the Empire? They're artificers and alchemists, without any devices or potions. They'll have no way to defend themselves."

Bree jabbed a finger at the map. "You can meet them halfway. Take a small but well-armed force across the border on that smuggler's footpath Zaira found near the castle. Amalia and Zaira can sneak them out to meet you and hand them off. You'd just need a way to signal each other when the time was right."

"I can make something like that!" Istrella offered. "I make courier lamps all the time. It'd be a fun challenge."

"Taking even a small, stealthy force across the border would be incredibly dangerous," I said dubiously.

"The Witch Lords will be busy with the Conclave," Roland said. "It's certainly risky, but at least there'll be a distraction."

Ciardha lifted a hand to silence us, listening. I didn't hear anything, but a moment later, a knock came at the door. She glanced to me for confirmation, then answered it.

It was Lord Caulin.

He gave Ciardha a wary nod, bowed to my cousins and me, and ignored the Falcons altogether, earning him a scowl from Zaira. "So sorry to interrupt, Your Highnesses, Lady Amalia."

I forced a smile, which was better than Marcello managed. "What is it, Lord Caulin?"

"Only that I must return to Raverra and would like a quick word with you before I depart, my lady."

"Of course." I sighed. "Everyone, please excuse me. Lord Caulin, shall we go for a walk?"

Lord Caulin and I strolled through the fortress corridor as if we were old friends, but tension pulled my spine straight and stiff. Whatever he had to say to me, I was certain I wouldn't like it.

"Lady Amalia," he began after a while, his voice soft and courteous, "the arrest of the Falconer was only my secondary business here."

That was an ominous start. "I am most curious as to your primary business, then, Lord Caulin."

"The doge asked me to speak to you regarding the most unfortunate matter of the captured Falcons."

A series of narrow windows looking into the courtyard plunged his face into shadow, then light, then shadow again as we walked.

"We're making plans to rescue them," I said.

"Good, good. And if you need any assistance at all, don't hesitate to request it. The doge considers their retrieval of the highest priority; the Falcons are the pillar of the Serene Empire's power." He paused, licking his lips. "Of course, just as crucial is the widespread understanding that Falcons belong to the Empire alone."

Here it comes. "I'm glad His Serenity takes the matter seriously," I said.

"Very seriously." The corridor ended in a stairwell; Lord Caulin stopped and regarded me closely, his dark eyes assessing. "Do you think you could bring someone to the Conclave with you? As a servant, perhaps?"

"No," I said firmly. "That would jeopardize my chances of negotiating alliances at the Conclave, if they let me in at all. It's a rare honor that they've invited me; I'm not going to flout their rules in their faces."

"No, no, of course not." Lord Caulin stroked his chin. "It will have to be you, then."

"What will have to be me?"

He dropped his voice so low I could barely hear him. "Lady Amalia, we all devoutly hope and pray to the Graces that you'll be able to bring those Falcons back to the Empire. But if you can't, His Serenity wishes to grant them at least the mercy of death."

I stared at him. "You want me to kill them."

"Only if your attempts to bring them home fail. We would far rather have them safe and sound back at the Mews, of course."

Anger churned in my stomach, growing like a foaming wave rushing in to shore. "What if they would rather be captives than dead?"

"We may not have another chance to retrieve them. It's so difficult to get people into Vaskandar, and it's even harder with war in the offing." He smoothed the lace at his cuffs. "We can't let them languish there, giving the whole world the impression that anyone can steal a Falcon and get away with it. And they're being compelled to create devastating weapons against the Serene Empire. This must be resolved quickly, for the safety of the Falcons and the Empire alike. You are the only one who will have a chance to do so. One way or another."

"You're asking me to murder them." I pushed the words out through my teeth.

"No, Lady Amalia. Not I. And not asking." He shook his head, as if he regretted the need to clarify such unpleasant matters. "His Serenity is giving you an order. If you cannot get them out, you are to ensure they do not survive."

He passed me a velvet bag; I took it, instinctively, too stunned to refuse it. "That contains a vial of Black Malice," he said. "Put a drop in their food or drink, or dip a dagger in it and give them the slightest scratch. The Empire is relying on you."

"I am no assassin, Lord Caulin," I said indignantly. Outrage swelled up in my chest like a great wave.

"I know." He sighed. "But you are what I have to work with."

"This order is a violation of the trust the Falcons place in us. We're supposed to protect them!"

"Perhaps. But it is an order nonetheless." He smiled apologetically. "And with help from the Grace of Luck, you'll bring them home, and it will never come to pass. No one but you or I will know it was even a possibility." He lifted a finger. "And, of course, this discussion is a secret between us. Do not speak to anyone about it; that's another order from the doge."

"No one?" I sharpened my tone into a weapon. "Are you telling me the doge wishes me to keep this a secret from my mother, and the Council of Nine?"

"Not the Council, of course." He waved a hand, but a frown crossed his brow, as if it vexed him that I'd asked. "The doge can have no secrets from *them*, by law. But do not mention it to anyone in the military—not Captain Verdi, or your Falcon, or Colonel Vasante herself. We need to retain their confidence. They must gain no hint that we're considering such an option. Do you understand?"

I made my tone as cold as possible. "I believe you have conveyed your message, Lord Caulin."

"Good." He nodded, seeming pleased. "In that case, Lady Amalia, my mission here is complete, and I bid you good day. If you have any questions, do not hesitate to contact me, or the doge himself."

He bowed, deeply and formally, and seemed unperturbed when I did not return the gesture. I watched him walk away with my hands clenched at my sides, the velvet bag full of death hanging from my fist.

Chapter Twenty-Nine

I tried to smooth out my face before stepping back into the meeting room, but I suspected the others noticed the fury pulsing in my temples.

Zaira raised an eyebrow. "What did the little weasel want to talk to you about?"

"Stupidity," I growled. "Secret stupidity I'm not allowed to repeat."

Zaira shrugged. "Nothing secret about the Empire being stupid. And why would you want to repeat idiocy anyway?"

"Excellent points." I took a deep breath. "What did you come up with while I was gone?"

I sat down at the table with them and plunged myself into planning with renewed fervor. There was no way in the Nine Hells I was going to carry out that order. Kill Terika and the rest? I'd rather throw myself on Ruven's nonexistent mercy. But if I refused the order, it would be treason, and Ruven could keep using them against the Empire.

We *had* to succeed.

When we finished and everyone started off to dinner, I lingered behind and caught Ciardha's eye. She closed the door, once the others were gone, and turned to me.

"Something troubles you, Lady."

"Do you know what Lord Caulin spoke to me about?" I asked.

A faint divot formed between Ciardha's brows. "No, Lady. I was unaware he was coming here until I arrived."

"Really." That was definitely strange. "He had an order for me from the doge. One I'm not fond of. Does my mother know about it?"

Ciardha's frown deepened. "La Contessa did not speak to me of any orders I would expect you to deem offensive."

"I suppose the decision could have been made after you left." I gnawed my lip.

But Ciardha shook her head. "I spoke with La Contessa in our personal cipher over the courier lamps this morning. She mentioned nothing of this order."

She would have found a way to warn me, even if she couldn't tell Ciardha outright for some reason. My mother must not have known about Caulin's scheme.

"Can the doge give an order like that without consulting or informing the Council of Nine?" I wondered.

"I don't know the nature of the order, Lady," Ciardha reminded me.

I twisted a lock of hair between my fingers. "I was commanded not to talk about it with anyone but the Council. But perhaps you can use your cipher to suggest to my mother over the courier lamps that she look into it. I don't think she'd like this order, either." She might be ruthless sometimes, but she practiced a sort of pragmatic benevolence: treating people poorly was rarely good politics. There were more problems with murdering Falcons than just the moral ones—though one would think those should be enough.

Ciardha nodded slowly. "I am but a humble retainer, and I do not claim to know the mind of the doge, Lady. But if he's giving you orders without telling the Council, logic would seem to suggest he doesn't think La Contessa would like it, either."

"I am not going to let the doge use me as a tool to get around my mother," I said crossly.

"You are a Cornaro, Lady," Ciardha reminded me, her eyes gleaming. "You do not let anyone use you as a tool at all."

The next morning, Ciardha found me in my guest room and handed me a message from my mother, translated from their personal cipher:

This could be a delicate matter. I will investigate, but it will take time. Be wary of verbal secret orders. Try not to do anything rash.

I looked up at Ciardha. "What does this mean?"

"I do not pretend to fathom the mind of La Contessa, Lady. But I would suggest it means someone is being underhanded."

"But in Raverra, someone is always being underhanded."

Ciardha nodded. "As you say. And yet La Contessa feels this situation requires special handling. I notice that she warned you to be cautious."

"Yes." I couldn't keep the annoyance out of my voice. "Everyone is always warning me to be cautious, as if they expect me to act on some foolish impulse and stick my hand in a fire."

Ciardha's eyes danced. "With respect, Lady, is that not precisely how you came to meet Zaira?"

I opened my mouth, then closed it. "Well, yes. But still, I don't need to be reminded to be careful all the time, like a child."

"La Contessa knows you are no child."

I'd like to think she knew. She'd certainly been treating me more like an adult since Ardence, leaving the drawing room door open and letting me see the inside of some of her plans. *Be wary of verbal secret orders. Try not to do anything rash.* It was such a short message, and in cipher; would she have wasted time with an encoded message nagging me to take basic precautions?

"She thinks this could be a trap," I said slowly.

Ciardha nodded, holding my eyes. "I don't know the content of this order, Lady. But if it puts you in a difficult enough position you felt the need to ask about it, there is a chance someone is trying to force you into actions that could be used against you. To gain power over you, or leverage over La Contessa."

I puffed out a long breath through my lips. Refusing this order could be treason. Following it could destroy my ability to work with the Falcons and, even more important, to pass the Falcon reform law. Even setting aside the moral repugnance of the command, either path could put me in an untenable position.

"And we don't truly know whether this is the doge's idea, or Caulin's, or perhaps even some other adviser or member of the Council who has the doge's ear," I said.

"Indeed, Lady."

I handed the paper back to Ciardha. "I suppose you'll want to burn this?"

Ciardha bowed. "Of course, Lady."

As the Conclave approached, I plunged into my books, researching everything I could about the mysterious event. Apparently the Witch Lords tended to call a Conclave every couple of years, but there was no set schedule to it; some years might have three Conclaves, while other times Vaskandar might go nearly a decade without one. It depended, essentially, on how much the Witch Lords felt they had to discuss with each other. My books claimed the whole affair was steeped in tradition and ceremony but, frustratingly, had no details on what those traditions or ceremonies might be, since none of the authors knew anyone who'd attended one.

"I can't even pack for it," I complained to Zaira over dinner.

"Do I wear Raverran court dress? Something more practical? Do they require ominous hooded robes?"

"The blood of your enemies, more like it." Zaira grinned wickedly. "Mind you, I wouldn't mind seeing your crow beau dressed in nothing more than that. Or your great-grandma, for that matter."

"I don't..." My mind wouldn't even form the latter image, but it was disturbingly easy to imagine Kathe lounging on the Wolf Lord's throne, wearing scarlet streaks and a mischievous grin, licking blood off his fingers. "I'm not going to respond to that."

Zaira waved her spoon at me. "But you're going to think about it," she crooned.

"Anyway," I said hastily, fighting off a blush, "I was thinking I should send Kathe a message asking him for more details, but then I realized they don't have courier lamps in Vaskandar."

"I'm going to wear whatever I damn well please, and anyone who doesn't like it can eat balefire." Zaira shrugged. "I'd lay odds they're going to do the same. These are Witch Lords. They're mad as magpies, and they don't respect anything but themselves."

"Kathe does," I objected.

"Maybe. I'm not convinced." She eyed me closely. "You trust him too much. Just because he told you a sad story."

I poked my own spoon into my potato soup. "It was a *true* sad story. He's never been anything but honest with me."

"He's using you."

"He's been honest about that, too."

Zaira shook her head, taking another spoonful of soup. "All right. But when he knifes you in the back, don't give me big surprised-and-hurt eyes about it. Everyone has sad stories. That doesn't mean they're nice people."

I sighed. "I know he's not nice. But we have to trust him at least a little. He's our protection at the Conclave."

Zaira snorted. "No. *I'm* our protection at the Conclave. If you rely on him, you're going to regret it."

Zaira's words echoed in my mind as we stood together on a dirt track that ran alongside a stream through a narrow, mossy ravine. Mist filled the chasm today, dripping off the moss and swirling above the river. I peered into the hazy distance, where the looming stone walls turned to hulking gray ghosts crowned with the jagged suggestion of pines, watching for any sign of the escort Kathe had promised us. In theory, our safe passage to the Conclave was guaranteed as invited guests, but I saw no reason to take chances. Not when the Empire itself was counting on me.

Fortified towers watched over us, guarding the road, such as it was; artifice circles graven into the walls of the ravine could collapse the whole thing on the heads of any army foolish enough to attempt to invade the Serene Empire this way. It was no surprise that Kazerath had not chosen to position troops here. And the lack of enemy forces, in turn, made it a good place for us to cross the border and head back into Vaskandar for the Conclave. If there was such a thing as a good place to enter Kazerath; I couldn't quite bring myself to be sanguine about returning to Ruven's domain.

Marcello shifted, his hand resting on his pistol. He'd brought along a complement of soldiers to see us off; he saw no reason to take chances, either.

We still hadn't talked about anything but business since I'd told him not to wait for me. The space he'd left between us was big enough for two people to stand in. Shadows gathered in new hollows beneath his eyes; I could tell by the way he'd hovered near Istrella over the past week that it was still eating at him that she'd been controlled and he hadn't noticed.

And now he had no one to talk to about it. Guilt pricked my breastbone. Honesty was all very well, but in retrospect, I'd picked terrible timing.

He met my eyes at last. Pain and worry clouded his. "Promise me you won't do anything foolish, at least," he said, his voice catching.

"I like to think I'm not in the habit of doing foolish things. Calculated risks, perhaps." I kept my tone light, trying to extend a safe bridge across the ice between us, which was full of brittle places and dangerously melting patches. "Besides, I'm in excellent hands."

I waggled my fingers at him, adorned with the unfamiliar burden of seven new rings, all gifts from Istrella.

Worry pinched a divot between his brows. "Yes, about that. Do you know what all of those do?"

"More or less." I examined the runes etched into the bands, running them through my memory again. Left index finger, defense against magic; right middle finger, to incapacitate without killing; left ring finger to wound or kill; and so on. "She was so excited she could barely explain them, but I asked her questions about anything I couldn't work out on my own. They're good for one use each, to be thrown at one's enemy. I feel quite dangerous."

He grimaced. "Maybe *too* dangerous. She can't have had time to test those."

"Life continues to be an adventure."

Zaira nudged me with a sharp elbow. "Here he comes."

Sure enough, the vague outline of a lone figure appeared through the mist, gray and insubstantial at first, making its way toward us. But even before I could pull details beyond a soft outline from the shrouding fog, I knew him from the way he walked right at the edge of the dropoff into the river, as if he were incapable of falling.

Marcello tensed. "He came by himself? Where's the escort?"

"He's a Witch Lord," I pointed out. "Between him and Zaira, we'll be more deadly than a thousand musketeers."

He turned to face me as Kathe approached, words struggling to make it past his lips. "Amalia..."

Graces. When he said my name like that, so full of suppressed emotion, everything I'd been so sure of crumbled into doubt. "I know, Marcello," I said quietly. "I know."

He swallowed. "Try to come back in one piece."

"I'll be all right." I slipped a hand into my pocket and pulled out his button; it lay gleaming in my palm. "I've got you to keep me from doing anything too reckless."

He stared at the button a moment; when he looked up, it was with a faint, wry, tender smile. But he said nothing.

Zaira clapped Marcello's back, breaking the moment like a thrown rock shattering the stillness of a pond. "I'll take care of her. We'll bring everyone home—Terika, Namira, all of them. You just be ready to come pick up the package when we call for you, like a good delivery boy."

Marcello blinked. "I think that's one of the nicer things you've called me."

"Don't get used to it."

Kathe finished materializing from the mists, the edges of his cloak feathers and the dyed tips of his hair coming into sharp focus at last. His eyes sparkled, and he gave us a broad grin. "Good to see you both again."

I offered him a slight bow, which he returned with a flourish. "I'm honored you came to collect us yourself, Lord Kathe."

"I could do no less for you, Lady Amalia. Are you ready?"

I stared off between the steep chasm walls, along the rushing gurgle of the river. If I could peel back all the layers of gray with my eyes, I could reveal the ancient forest that waited on the far side, gathering patches of shadow and snow beneath its boughs.

Once I stepped past that border, I'd be in Ruven's domain. His presence would wind through every living thing: staring from the eyes of a fox, reaching in the branch of a tree. The last time we'd entered Vaskandar, we'd barely made it out alive, and our enemies hadn't known we were coming. This time, I carried far heavier burdens: the writ of the doge and the Council declaring me a Serene Imperial Envoy, and the tiny vial of Black Malice in a velvet bag.

Zaira caught my eye. "We can do this. We're a good team, remember?"

I nodded, feeling grateful. "Just like in Ardence."

Zaira snorted. "Let's hope it goes more smoothly than Ardence." She punched my shoulder, which I took as a sign of affection.

"We're ready," I told Kathe.

We stepped forward together into the mist.

Chapter Thirty

"We have to time our arrival carefully," Kathe said, glancing out the tavern window at the mist-damp trees across the road as if he could somehow discern the hour from the general cloudy grayness. And for all I knew, he could.

We'd stopped for lunch at a lonely tavern near the foot of the hill on which Ruven's castle crouched. The place seemed to have been built to serve the castle's staff and guards. The proprietress, a hard-faced and silent woman in her fifties with a scar like finger marks across her mouth, served Kathe with an unflinching reserve that suggested she had seen the worst many times and was braced to do so again at any moment. She'd sent the other server, a young boy, from the room with a jerk of her head when we walked in.

"Why is that?" I asked, nervously turning one of Istrella's rings on my finger. *Left index, for defense against magic.*

"Precedence. We enter the Conclave in order of seniority, from youngest to oldest." Kathe's mouth quirked. "Ruven is spared the indignity of going first by virtue of being the host, and thus not needing to make an entrance at all."

"And where do you fall in the order?" I asked.

Kathe's eyes crinkled, his mage mark gleaming yellow. "We

haven't played a game in a while. Why don't you guess how old I am?"

That was right. Kathe was a Witch Lord, and thus more or less immortal. He could be hundreds of years old, for all I knew.

I analyzed the sharp planes of his face. No marks of age creased his brow, and only the faintest of laugh lines flanked his eyes. Silver would be hard to pick out from the moon-blond roots of his hair, but I doubted I would find any. His skin lacked the rounded smoothness of lingering childhood but bore none of the sunken wear of middle age either. If I were forced to guess his age based on appearance, I might place him somewhere in his twenties.

But the Lady of Eagles didn't look much older, and she predated the Empire. It was the power of life itself that infused the Witch Lords, giving them an endless bounty of vitality that maintained them eternally at their prime. They probably *all* looked somewhere in their twenties. Clearly I would have to rely on other clues.

"You're too ambitious to be one of the oldest," I said. "You would have carved out your place or died trying by now if you had centuries behind you."

He chuckled. "Is that the most precise answer you can give? I thought you were a woman of learning."

"Give me a moment." I frowned at him. Older than Marcello, certainly; Kathe had reached an age where he'd stopped trying to prove himself to anyone. Younger than my mother? Graces, I hoped so.

"Eight," Zaira laughed. "He's tall for his age."

"Only at heart." Kathe grinned back at her.

I slapped the table. "Forty."

Kathe lifted his eyebrows. "Is that your final guess?"

If he was a hundred years old, I'd probably mortally offended him. If he was nineteen, that might be even worse. But I nodded. "Yes."

"Not bad." He lifted his mug to me. "I'm thirty-seven, as it happens."

"An old man," Zaira waggled her eyebrows. "Well, they do say experience counts where it matters most."

I kicked Zaira's ankle under the table. "So where does that place you among the other Witch Lords?" I asked.

"Ruven is the newest," Kathe said. "Then the Aspen Lord of Ordun. He's a relation of yours—a son of the Lady of Eagles. He moved in and took over the Oak Lord's domain when he perished in the eruption of Mount Enthalus a few years ago, ousting the Oak Lord's heirs. Then a couple of others, and then me. I've been the Witch Lord of Let since my mother died twenty years ago."

A strange thought struck me. I hesitated to ask, but Kathe's expression remained serene. I traced my uncertainty on the tabletop with a finger. "If she was a Witch Lord, and immortal..."

"How did she die?" Pain sharpened Kathe's gaze, tightening the skin around his eyes. "There are some powers greater even than life itself, I fear. One of them is the sea."

I drew in a sharp breath. "She drowned?" It was a fear every Raverran understood, the finality of the strangling darkness below the lagoon's sunny green surface.

Kathe lowered his gaze to his hands. "She loved to explore new places, which is rare for a Witch Lord. It's hard to think of a ship as dangerous, when there is so little that can harm you. And when hers went down, in a storm far out at sea, the life she held was enough to keep her alive in the crushing deep, unbreathing, trapped, for a long time. Too long a time."

"That's terrible," I whispered, horror filling me up and spilling over like cold, salty water.

"When it takes so much to kill you, there is no such thing as a clean death," Kathe said softly. "My mother could have kept herself alive much longer. Perhaps weeks or months. She might even have managed to escape the wreck in which she was trapped, somehow, and make her way back to shore. But she would not drain the life from her domain to sustain her own. She let it go." He opened his hand, lifting it with a sort of slow, wondering grace. "And in that moment, every seed in Let sprouted in my heart. Every sleek, furry thing in its burrow, every bird testing the currents of the sky, every tree with its roots gripping deep into the earth and its hair shaken loose in the wind. Every child in the cradle, and every dog dreaming by the hearth. I held all of Let within me, pulsing through my veins with my blood." Kathe closed his eyes. "It's quite a strange thing, to lose so much and gain so much in the same instant."

His voice had remained calm, though my own heart ached with each beat. "I can't begin to imagine," I said huskily. But I could—or at least, I could picture a seventeen-year-old Kathe, bowed in agony under the sudden twin burdens of an entire realm in his mind and his mother's horrifying death.

"It wasn't my best day," Kathe admitted. "But it was twenty years ago." He glanced out the window again, and rose. "Time to get into position, I think. The Aspen Lord has arrived, and the others are on their way."

I stood as well, Kathe's story still weighing on my mind, and threw a few coins on the table for the proprietress. Kathe lifted his brows, as if the concept of currency were surprising, but said nothing. I knew they had money in Vaskandar; I supposed Witch Lords weren't accustomed to paying for anything.

I stepped gingerly in the road, avoiding the puddles that filled the deep wheel ruts left by a convoy of supply wagons that had passed earlier, on the way to the army encamped at the border. I'd worn a finer coat and breeches than I normally would while traveling, to make a good impression at the Conclave, and I didn't want mud stains on my pristine white stockings.

Lichen stood out brightly against the damp-darkened tree trunks around us, and trails of moss swayed from the branches, sucking up mist. Sodden snow hugged the shadows and hollows on the rolling forest floor, with more fog lifting up off them to add to the unreal cloud huddled close around us. The air felt raw on my face and hands. I reached into my pocket for my gloves and touched the comforting round rim of Marcello's button.

"I know," I whispered. "I can't believe I'm going back there, either."

I couldn't see the castle with its towers like reaching black claws, or even the hill it crowned. But I knew the road up to it was near. We couldn't be more than a few miles from the spot where Zaira had let her bitter flames rage through the forest.

Zaira lifted her determined stare toward the invisible castle, as if the black rings of her mage mark could pierce the fog.

"Terika," she muttered. "On my way."

Kathe had sent our baggage ahead to the castle with porters, so we walked along the road unencumbered. A light of anticipation entered his eyes, and as he walked power seemed to accrue to him, as if he gathered it close with each step—or as if he slowly shed the cloak with which he normally disguised the full impact of his presence, like a bird dropping its dull winter molt one feather at a time to reveal a blaze of splendid color.

It was hard not to feel like an afterthought, trailing behind him.

A thought occurred to me, and I sidled up to Zaira. "*Exsolvo*," I whispered.

"Ahhh." Her shoulders eased, and her spine straightened; a greater spark kindled in her eyes.

"Sorry," I murmured, guilt pinching my chest. "I should have done that the moment we crossed the border."

"Cursed right, you should have." She stretched her arms over her head. "But better now than later. I don't want to walk into the nest of vipers with my hands tied."

"You can ask me anytime, you know, for any reason," I said. "Or I can just leave you unleashed all the time if you prefer." I hesitated a moment. "Even back in the Empire."

Zaira's brows lifted. "What about the law? I thought you were a good little citizen who'd go down with a sinking boat before you moored it in an illegal spot."

"The law allows me to unleash you when we judge the situation to be dangerous." I took a deep breath. "I'd say our experiences to date suggest that the situation is *always* dangerous. Wouldn't you agree?"

Zaira gave me a long, narrow look. "Must be nice, being a high enough rank you get to decide what the law means. Why now?"

"What do you mean?"

"Why tell me this now, and not, oh, two months ago?"

The heat of shame raced up my neck to my ears. "I should have. I hadn't thought of that particular, ah, interpretation of the law yet. And I didn't realize you might want your power unsealed even when you had no reason to burn anything."

"Hmph." Zaira flexed her fingers. "I suppose there's also the little matter that we were in a city full of thousands of innocent, flammable people then."

"Well, that too."

She poked my ribs with a bony finger. "But you're a milk-faced, simpering idiot about obeying the law. You don't have to follow laws if they're stupid."

"Technically, you do," I objected.

Zaira snorted. "Do you think your mamma obeys every little law all the time?"

"Well, she's on the Council of Nine, so she can authorize..." I trailed off, thinking of several things she *couldn't* authorize without convening the full Council that I was fairly certain she did on a regular basis. "No," I admitted.

Zaira gestured grandly. "The law is like a corset. Lace it too tight, and you might look proper, but you stop breathing."

I wasn't sure I agreed with that analogy, but I suspected that legal arguments with Zaira were doomed to prove personally unsatisfying, so I made a noncommittal noise.

Kathe paused, his head cocked as if listening, and then turned to me. "I should warn you."

That was ominous. "Yes?"

"It's traditional to make a dramatic entrance," he said. "I've been too busy to come up with anything clever in advance, so I'm going to make something up as I go."

I swallowed. "All right."

"I can help you make it *very* dramatic," Zaira offered.

A wide grin started to spread across Kathe's face. But then a thought seemed to strike him, and it faded. "Hmm. It's poor manners to damage your host's home."

"Oh." Zaira sighed. "Never mind, then."

Graces help me, the company I kept was going to kill me. "Are there any other traditions we should be aware of?" I asked.

Kathe started walking again, his stride brisk; Zaira and I had to stretch our legs to keep up. "Let's see. The Conclave has three phases. First there's the Arrival."

"I'm guessing that's what we're about to do now," Zaira said, as we came to the place where the road branched and began winding up the hill.

"Yes, but it also includes what I suppose you Raverrans might call a reception." He frowned, as if he wasn't sure that was the right word. "Everyone attends and can simply talk. There is no official business designated to attend to, so usually one uses it as an opportunity to sound out possible strategies and alliances. It's the least formal part of the Conclave."

The idea that the reception could be the *least* formal event seemed odd to me, when I was used to them being court events with grand balls and a certain amount of pomp, but I nodded. "So would you say the dress is evening wear, but not court dress?"

Kathe blinked. "Uh…I suppose I'd wear something warm, since castles are often drafty."

Zaira snickered and mouthed, *Blood of your enemies.*

"Anyway," Kathe went on, seemingly oblivious to my blush, "the second phase is the Reckoning, when we have a chance to resolve grievances and favors." He caught my eye. "That's possibly the most important phase. Grievances and favors are a form of currency among the Witch Lords."

"Oh? We trade favors all the time in Raverra, but our grievances are usually resolved more, ah, unilaterally."

"If someone has a grievance against you, you owe them a debt." He waved a hand at the claws around my neck. "For instance, the Lady of Thorns attacked you with her whiphounds, even though you wore my safe conduct token and stayed on the roads. That gives me a grievance against her. A minor one, since you weren't permanently damaged, but a grievance nonetheless."

"A *minor* one?" I objected. "A dozen good people were killed!"

"But they didn't carry my token. They had no safe passage, and they weren't mine. I am owed no grievance for them." He frowned. "And they weren't mages. It's foolishness at best, but I have had it made clear to me that the lives of nonmages count for less." By the strain in his voice, he was thinking of his friend Jathan.

"So you can claim a favor to compensate you for your grievance?" I asked. "Is that how it works?"

He nodded. "Yes, or I can hold myself unsatisfied. A sufficient accumulation of grievances is cause for war. And anyone who has unsatisfied grievances piling up against them will find it hard to make or keep allies. Usually favors from another Witch Lord are valuable enough to let small matters go."

I had no doubt that Kathe held himself unsatisfied in the not-so-small matter of Jathan's death. But I didn't bring it up. "I can see where the results of the Reckoning might affect who allies with whom later on."

"Yes. Very much so. Certain Witch Lords tend to accumulate favors, and they can often call them in to sway the Conclave. Watch out for the Lady of Spiders and the Elk Lord; they both are highly influential in this way. If you can win one of them to your side, others will follow."

I recalled the maps in my books. "Their domains are expansive, too, aren't they?"

"Yes, and they're old, especially the Elk Lord. Many defer to him." Kathe lifted a finger. "Don't expect me to help you much at the Conclave. I have my own matters to attend to; I won't be spending favors on your behalf. But I see no reason not to arm you with enough information to fight your own battles."

"I'm used to that." My mother had said almost the same thing when I'd started my efforts to gain support for my Falcon reform law.

"I imagine you are." Kathe glanced toward the trees; something fluttered among the leaves there. "After the Reckoning comes the Kindling, where we decide the matters of substance for which the Conclave was called. At this Conclave, the only question for the Kindling is whether to go to war with the Serene Empire. That's when everyone's candles are counted, and then the Conclave is closed."

I was about to ask what he meant by counting candles, but Kathe nodded sharply, as if answering a question.

"Best to start gathering them now, I think," he muttered, and lifted a hand.

A crow flew to it from the trees and perched on his wrist,

keeping its wings spread slightly for balance. Another followed, landing on his shoulder.

"For our entrance, feel free to walk beside me or behind me, whichever you wish," Kathe said. "I can ask them not to land on you, if you want."

By the time he'd finished the sentence, another crow had flown to his other shoulder; more watched from the trees. Black wings flashed among the green leaves, and crows glided ahead along the road, swooping to the next tree one after another, weaving a pattern in the air.

"I'm not certain they'd go with my outfit," I said wryly, gesturing to my bronze and chocolate brocade coat, its sleeves thick with embroidery.

"Very well. And you, Lady Zaira?"

Zaira watched the crows warily. "I'd rather not have their cold scaly claws on me, thanks."

Kathe grinned. "Ah, now I know the perfect way to annoy you, if I ever feel the urge to find out what balefire tastes like."

"I don't recommend it," Zaira growled. "No one's ever asked for a second helping."

Kathe laughed. More and more crows kept gathering; the trees swayed and rustled with hundreds of feathery black bodies, and their shining dark eyes watched us curiously from the branches. They swept past constantly, one after another, sometimes brushing close enough to ruffle my hair.

It would be easy to fall in behind Kathe and let him lead the way into this dangerous place, the lair of my enemy. But that would send a message that I gave him precedence. I gathered my courage and stepped up beside him, offering my arm.

He took it. The crow on his near shoulder cocked its head at me and opened its beak, silently laughing.

When we stepped out of the trees at the crown of the hill, the three of us side by side, the mist had lifted enough to reveal the castle's black towers stretching jagged and forbidding overhead. The orchid-colored leaves on the great tree glittered with frost, and all the vines on the castle had burst into purple blooms, unnatural against the gleaming, pristine white of the thin coating of snow covering the lawn. The wolves guarding the door were gone, replaced by human musketeers in black uniform doublets with violet trim.

I barely had time to take it all in before the crows exploded out of the forest with us.

Their wings made a great thunder, buffeting up a wind that whipped my hair this way and that. They rose around us in a cloud, trailing behind and above, claiming the air itself for their lord with their fine, glossy shapes, like slices of black laughter. There must have been hundreds of them; they cast us into shadow, blocking out the sun. The guards cringed away, throwing up their hands to shield their faces.

It was all I could do to keep pacing along grandly at Kathe's side, my arm through his. Zaira muttered a curse under her breath but fixed a murderous smile on her face.

Kathe strode between the guards with an amiable nod to each. "Good afternoon," he greeted them cheerfully.

And we stepped out of the thundercloud of crows into the majestic gloom of Ruven's castle.

Chapter Thirty-One

The crows didn't follow us into the castle. I supposed that would have been rude. They broke off in a double wave as they reached the gates, swirling up to the sky like huge black wings unfolding.

The castle swallowed us with its quiet, oppressive presence. The air within felt heavy and dead, like that in a tomb. Every inch of my body remembered that this was a trap and screamed at me to leave before the doors swung shut behind us once more.

But at the same time, some inner chamber of my heart quickened with excitement. *The Conclave.* No Raverran had ever attended before, but here we were, about to witness the most secret inner workings of Vaskandran power. A gathering of all seventeen Witch Lords was something to fear, but surely it must also be a thing of wonder and deep mystery. Really, when I got home, I should write a paper or two about this for the Imperial Library.

If I got home. If I didn't fail at my task here, and doom the Empire to ruin so profound that no one would write papers for the Imperial Library ever again.

Guards lined the foyer, Ruven's human soldiers taking the place of his father's wolves; somehow, instead of being reassuringly normal, this only increased my sense of wrongness and dread. They stood stiff and formal in a double line to channel us straight through into the great hall. The throne room's black ribs arched far over our heads, the light falling vine-patterned through its high windows. The throne stood empty, the wolf pelts removed; purple velvet cushions now softened its dramatic black points and curves.

A handful of figures waited for us in the hall, clustered loosely around a stone bowl that stood on a pedestal, like a garden birdbath. They gave each other a wary space, each radiating power enough to suck the air from the room. One bore a crown of golden leaves and wore a long, high-collared coat in white and silver; I guessed this was the Aspen Lord, my great-uncle. Another had brilliant red-orange hair in a long ponytail and wore an artful patchwork of close-fitting leather in different shades of brown and russet.

But the one who caught and held my attention was Ruven. He had changed.

It wasn't his floor-length black coat, with its jagged, asymmetrical purple embroidery; that was the same as always. It wasn't his sleek blond hair, or the smile of wicked amusement curling his lips, or even his arrogant stance.

It was his presence. His violet mage mark struck like lightning when he met my eyes. He filled the great hall, his power hanging in the air like a miasma of sickness. The absolute certainty of control lay upon him like a mantle.

Graces preserve us. By killing his father, we'd unleashed the worst demon in the Nine Hells.

He spread his arms wide in welcome. "The Crow Lord of Let. Welcome to my home. And what fascinating guests you bring!"

Kathe offered him a bow so short and stiff it barely qualified as a twitch. "I'm delighted to meet the newest Witch Lord. I believe you already know the Lady Amalia Cornaro and Lady Zaira."

"Of course." Ruven's gaze landed on Zaira, and the air grew heavier. "You have some gall, Let, bringing my father's murderer to his castle as your guest."

The other Witch Lords exchanged glances; the redhead raised his eyebrows at Kathe, and one woman whispered to a companion behind her hand.

"Why, thank you," Kathe said. "I do try to be shocking whenever I can."

"As it happens, I've been wanting to thank the lady." Ruven flashed a bright smile at Zaira, all teeth and poison. "I owe you my ascension to my father's domain. You have conferred upon me the great gift of immortality. I must consider what I can do to best show you my gratitude."

I would not have thought a curtsy could convey murderous intent before I met Zaira. "If you need suggestions," she said sweetly, "I can think of a wide variety of things you can do."

Ruven turned to me. "And Lady Amalia." He placed his hand on his chest. "It wounds me deeply to learn you are now courting another Witch Lord. Alas! I fear I moved too slowly."

I raised my eyebrows. "Alas indeed, Lord Ruven. I fear courtship prospects are generally rather soured by preparations for war."

"Then it's fortunate I am nearly done preparing," Ruven replied, his eyes narrowing like a pleased cat's. Dread settled in my stomach, and I sent silent, urgent wishes to Roland and Marcello to hurry up with their sabotage of the volcanic artifice circles.

Kathe cleared his throat. "Where are my manners? Tradition first. The Truce Stones."

He stepped up to the basin on its pillar. It reminded me of

the Lady of Eagles' blooding stone; it seemed just as ancient, the gray stone worn smooth at the rim from years of handling. And indeed, a tiny pool of dark liquid stained the center of it. But the symbols that ringed the rim were unquestionably artifice runes—not of a style I recognized, and worn with time, but an artifice circle nonetheless. Graven lines stretched inward from the runes at the edge to form a diagram in the center.

Excited, I approached with Kathe, peering closer. "This is some kind of binding, isn't it?"

The Aspen Lord nodded, interest lighting his eyes, which were gold as his mother's in an angular face. He was shorter than I'd have expected for a man titled after a tree but radiated quiet strength. "I had heard you were a scholar, Lady Amalia. The Truce Stones are an ancient artifact of Vaskandar, created by the original Witch Lords with the assistance of a great Ostan artificer. This is the central stone; the others are placed to encircle the castle grounds."

I frowned at the basin, tracing the lines with my eyes and trying to muddle out the meaning of the runes. "I see reflection patterns. A defensive ward?"

"It's to make us play nicely with one another," Kathe said. He unsheathed a bone dagger and drew it across the back of his arm. Red beads of blood rose up; he let them drip into the basin to mingle with what was already there. "We blood the stones every day, starting with this one. Now if we hurt anyone whose blood is mixed with ours while within the ring of the Truce Stones, the harm rebounds upon us. Or so it's said, anyway."

I stopped myself from reaching out to touch the runes. They might not like me poking their artifact. "That sounds about right. I think your own blood would turn against you, somehow."

"Really?" Kathe seemed interested. "Sounds nasty."

"It is," the Aspen Lord said, his voice deep and resonant. "My mother has seen it happen. She warned me it would be folly to break the Truce. While the punishment is not enough to kill a Witch Lord, it would leave you quite vulnerable to a return attack, and the Truce would no longer protect you."

"What happens if you accidentally step on someone's toe?" Zaira asked, eyeing Ruven. I could see plans to trip him into another Witch Lord forming in her head.

"The harm must be deliberate and serious to trigger the vengeance of the Truce Stones. A mere jostle or even a slap would not qualify." The Aspen Lord lifted his head. "Someone else is coming."

A strange sliding, rumbling sound reached my ears first. Then the wide-open castle gates framed a wondrous sight: a living carriage, growing with vines and flowers that twisted and turned into new beautiful shapes as it rolled along with no horses to draw it. Roses and ivy trailed behind it like a queen's train, and butterflies surrounded it, flashing colors like bright jewels. When it stopped, the woman who stepped out wore a gown of leaves and flowers, bright against the rich, deep brown of her bare arms, and a crown of laurel and live dragonflies above the long, dark fall of her many-braided hair.

Zaira made a soft, appreciative sound. Beautiful though the lady undeniably was, however, ice threaded its way up my spine; she moved with the predatory grace of a mantis, and I had no doubt she was far more lethal.

"The Lady of Laurels," Kathe murmured. "I suppose I'd best step aside and give her a turn."

The three of us drew back to make room. I watched in awe as one Witch Lord after another arrived, each bearing an aura of potency and majesty, attended by nature itself like the Graces in the most romanticized paintings. The sense of power in the hall became oppressive, until I felt like I would faint from the sheer accumulated weight of it; but Zaira stood loose and easy, unaffected. She was their peer, after all, terrible as any of them.

I was out of my depth, as a mere mortal. And the eldest hadn't even begun to arrive.

We weren't the only guests to accompany the Witch Lords. The Lady of Bears rode up to the gates mounted on a great black grizzly the size of an ox, dressed in fur and leather armor; her three sons came behind her on their own ursine mounts. A rumble like thunder hung around them, below the threshold of hearing. It was all I could do not to back up until cool stone pressed against my spine to get away from them. The three sons jostled each other as they dismounted and followed their mother into the castle, rough and noisy, acting like boys despite the gray thickly striping the eldest's hair and beginning to streak the middle one's beard.

I'd heard of the Lady of Bears; she was one of the Witch Lords who'd invaded the Serene Empire during the Three Years' War, seeking domains for her sons. My generation had grown up on terrible stories of the atrocities of that war—whole villages falling to snakebite, or smothered and buried alive under an avalanche of vines; soldiers ripped apart and devoured by packs of wild animals, or caught on the piercing branches of trees and then stung to death by valley-filling swarms of hornets—and it struck me with a lurch of horror that she was probably personally responsible for many of them.

The Lady of Bears greeted Ruven with warm enthusiasm. "This fight will go better with you on our side. Never could trust your father not to get cold paws. Unless you're out now that you've got your own domain?"

Ruven returned a sharp smile. "Don't worry. I'm as dedicated to the war effort as always. I am most eager to expand my borders, and more than ready to do so."

The way he said it set a deep chill of foreboding into my bones.

Not long after the Lady of Bears, a pair of women arrived together, one of whom was all too familiar. The Lady of Thorns swept into the hall, her shimmering green robes trailing behind her, three pale braids shining down her back. I drew in a long, measured breath, unclenching my teeth; this woman might be a monster who had attacked my family and likely murdered my father, but I was here as a diplomat. The mantle of a Serene Imperial Envoy demanded I set aside my personal animosity.

Her companion was ancient and stooped as the Lady of Thorns was young and tall. She leaned on the lady's arm, every movement made with the careful frailty of extreme age. Thin wisps of white hair clung to her mottled skull, and her flesh hung loosely on her gaunt face, but her gray eyes stared clear and piercing from their pits, marked with bloodred blazing circles to proclaim her power.

"The Lady of Thorns and her daughter," Kathe whispered, his arm tense in mine.

I caught myself before asking if he'd meant to say her grandmother. It was hard to accept that the fresh-faced Lady of Thorns was older than the crone she supported, who must be close to a century, if not past it. But by the tender care with which the Witch Lord escorted the old woman, I had no doubt of where her desperation to conquer more land came from. Whatever her flaws, her love for her daughter was real.

A touch of pity mingled uncomfortably with my anger as the Lady of Thorns greeted Ruven and then settled her daughter in a chair at the edge of the hall to rest. It wasn't until she finished the blooding ritual and turned to greet the rest of the Witch Lords that her eyes fell on me.

Hatred flashed across her face at once.

"You," she hissed, stepping toward me. "Lochaver vermin."

It was hard not to recoil at the sheer force of her fury. But I drew myself up. "Is that what passes for manners in Sevaeth?"

"I owe no respect to a common, powerless insect such as you." She gave Kathe an acid glance; he grinned at her benignly.

"The Lady Amalia is my guest," he reminded her. "Protected by the rules of the Conclave. I urge you not to get ahead of yourself."

His choice of words didn't escape me, and I gave Kathe a narrow look.

"Then I have no choice but to allow you to live for now," the Lady of Thorns said with disgust, "even though you profane this place with your presence."

I mustered all my cold politeness, learned from years of watching my mother devastate her enemies in court. "I haven't any notion where this hatred of my family comes from, my lady, but it demeans you."

"Demeans me?" The Lady of Thorns seemed to swell, and the force of her power fell upon me like the shadow of a massive tree; the room grew colder and darker. "It is your grandfather who did the demeaning. He was my *ally*, little worm. We planned to take Callamorne together, to split the new domain between Vandrin and my daughter. But he betrayed me when he saw his chance to seize the entire kingdom for himself." Her lips peeled back from her teeth. "She would be free of the grasp of death forever if it weren't for his treachery. And you are the fruit of that betrayal, you vile, common creature."

I caught myself before taking a step back from her in shock. "You think my grandfather took Callamorne as his domain."

"Of course he did. You don't think he married for *love*, do you?" The fury on her face twisted to poisonous amusement. "A son of the Lady of Eagles, marry some powerless clod for love?" Her laugh echoed from the high ceiling.

"You might be surprised," Kathe said, his voice deceptively

light, "at how much the mage-marked can care for people with no magic whatsoever."

The Lady of Thorns seemed to miss his allusion to her killing of Jathan entirely. If she even remembered it. *If it even happened*, Zaira's skeptical voice said in my mind.

"My grandmother rules Callamorne in her own right," I said stiffly. "I never knew my grandfather, but from everything I've heard, he would never usurp her sovereignty like that."

"You are a fool. Of course he claimed Callamorne as his domain. Who would give up such an easy chance at immortality?" The Lady of Thorns shook her head. "I had to kill him to clear his claim from the land my daughter needs to live. Just as I must kill every last one of his spawn; she's too frail to challenge even a passive claim." Her lips spread in a cruel smile, and her eyes pierced mine, the rings of her mage mark shining venom-green. "That's why I sent a snake to make your father's horse throw him on a treacherous mountain trail and snap his foul neck."

A hot rushing wave seemed to crash over me. I had never felt such an overwhelming, physical need for violence in my life. Words had always been my preferred weapons, but in that moment, my own two thumbs seemed quite enough, if I could gouge them into her hateful eyes.

A hand closed on my arm, stopping me before I could move. Not Kathe—Zaira. I tried to shake her off, but I couldn't; her fingers were too strong.

I whirled on her, ready to snap, but her eyes stopped me: grave and somber, and all too understanding.

Revincio, she mouthed. The corner of her mouth quirked.

The word hit me like a bucket of cold water. I took a deep, ragged breath and gave Zaira a nod of thanks.

Then I turned back to the Lady of Thorns.

"Duly noted," I said in a voice of glacial ice.

It was what my mother said to her opponents in the moment she decided the time for diplomacy was over and the next step was their utter and complete destruction.

But of course, the Lady of Thorns didn't know that. She turned to Kathe, dismissing me. "And you, Crow Lord. Giving your attention to a powerless wretch whose existence pollutes an ancient line is beneath you. I expect better of you."

"You need to learn to think beyond the impulse of the moment. I have my reasons." He winked at her, for all the world as if they shared a secret joke and he didn't hate her at all. "As you know."

The Lady of Thorns nodded slowly. "Have it your way, crow. I'll not break the rules of the Conclave. But protect her beyond it at your own peril."

Kathe shrugged. "The Lady Amalia doesn't require my protection."

With my blood still burning from my burst of fury, it was easier to appear confident that this was the case. The Lady of Thorns made a contemptuous noise deep in her throat, turned from us without another word, and swept back across the hall to her daughter.

"You handled that quite well," Kathe complimented me.

I didn't trust myself to speak. I'd suspected the Lady of Thorns had killed my father, and I knew she'd only confirmed it to my face to provoke me into attacking first so she'd be within rights to kill me. But knowing she wanted me to feel this anger didn't keep it from shaking my bones.

Zaira faced Kathe, hands on her hips. "What was that wink about? What game are you playing?"

"Merely keeping her on her toes," Kathe said airily. "I've cultivated a reputation for being clever and unpredictable, so when

I say vague and mysterious things, everyone assumes I'm up to something. The Lady of Thorns is the type to play along so she won't look like a fool."

"Well, I don't care if I look like a fool, and I think you *are* up to something."

"Of course I am." Kathe's eyes widened in pretended shock. "I'd be very disappointed in myself if I weren't. Anyway, it got her to go away, didn't it?"

Zaira's eyes narrowed. "I don't trust you."

"Good." Kathe smiled benevolently. "You shouldn't."

I forced myself to turn that over in my head instead of thinking about my father as the next Witch Lords arrived. Of course Kathe had his own plans and schemes; we were allies, yes, but uneasy ones. And I still knew very little of this extraordinary and dangerous being at my side.

When Kathe was busy talking to the red-haired Witch Lord, Zaira leaned in and whispered to me, "He's going to stab you in the back."

"Perhaps," I said. "But so long as I have something he wants—*holy Hells!*"

Another Witch Lord had entered the hall. Her silver-gray hair trailed loose and free down the back of a Raverran-style corseted gown—though its lines were slimmer than had been in fashion for fifty years. I'd just realized that what I'd taken for beading on the bodice and skirt was in fact a patterned arrangement of thousands of live spiders.

Zaira turned to see what had elicited my reaction. "What? It's... Hells have mercy, are those *real*?"

"Unfortunately," I managed. I wanted to look away, so very badly, but I couldn't. The Witch Lord stepped up to the basin, greeting the others cordially, and the spiders on her skirts swarmed over one another, forming new patterns.

"All right, that's impressive," Zaira admitted.

"*Impressive* is a word that one might use."

Kathe had said the Lady of Spiders was one of the influential Witch Lords I should try to sway to my side. I was going to have to talk to her. Up close.

I swallowed. Maybe she'd wear a different dress tomorrow.

Chapter Thirty-Two

The last few Witch Lords made less extravagant statements with their entrances. They carried such a weight of power with them that they needed no eye-catching fancies to impress their fellows. These were the surviving original Witch Lords from the earliest days of Vaskandar: the Elk Lord, with a crown of great branching antlers and a regal bearing; the Lady of Eagles, who gave me a small nod of recognition as she entered, fierce and overwhelming as I remembered in her winglike mantle; and at last the Yew Lord, thin and sharp as a knife-cut in the flesh of time, with deep, sunken eyes I could believe had seen the dawning of the world itself.

Ruven spoke words of welcome to us all, but they sounded muffled beneath the sheer force of magic in the air. Then he offered his guests rest and refreshment and clapped his hands; servants cringed up to each group of guests, terror in their faces, to show us to our rooms.

Kathe's guide urged him in a different direction than ours did. He raised his brows at me. "It would seem guests are lodged in a different wing than Witch Lords. Will you be all right?"

It only made sense. The best guest rooms would all go to the Witch Lords themselves. But still, my nerves prickled; I half expected our room to be a dungeon.

"We'll be fine," I assured him. "You don't need to protect me, remember?"

"I should hope not." Amusement sparkled in his eyes. "If anything, Lady Zaira could protect *me*."

"If I felt like it," Zaira said.

Our guide led us down ominously familiar corridors, then up the stairs past the second floor where Ruven had locked us on our ill-fated previous visit. He conducted us to the third floor, which we hadn't seen last time, and down a hallway covered in some climbing vine with dark, triangular leaves and bloodred berries. I hoped the lattice on the outside of the castle reached this high, in case we had to escape.

Zaira's eyes darted down each side corridor and lingered on every doorway. "He'll have moved Terika out of that big bedroom, with all these guests," she muttered, dropping far enough behind the servant to be out of hearing range. "We'll have to find her again tonight."

I had been so overwhelmed wondering how I could possibly conduct diplomacy with the bizarre visions I'd just seen arriving at the castle that I'd almost forgotten our other critical mission. "She's probably with the other captured Falcons now. We can go looking for them after everyone goes to bed."

Zaira's expression went grim. "If these demons even sleep."

There were no chimeras at our door this time, nor were we locked in. I supposed even Ruven wouldn't quite dare mistreat the guest of another Witch Lord. So we had no need to creep along the side of the castle, which was just as well, given that our windows were higher up. Still, it felt strange to simply open our door and step out into the dim corridor. The enshrouding vines and flickering oil lamps gave it a starkly shadowed, ominous appearance.

"No luminaries," I murmured. "No courier lamps. No wards."

"They can probably see in the dark, they can send birds to carry their messages, and no one in their right mind would attack a Witch Lord," Zaira replied. "I doubt they miss the conveniences of the Empire."

"*You* attacked a Witch Lord," I pointed out.

"And given that I don't remember it, I'm fairly sure I wasn't in my right mind at the time." Zaira glanced up and down the corridor. "I'm betting he'll have the Falcons in one of the towers, to keep them out of sight. Come on. And don't skulk—we're invited guests, and no one said we couldn't walk around the castle at night."

"I'm not skulking," I said.

"But you were about to."

Whether Witch Lords slept or not, the dim corridors of the third floor were empty. The Witch Lords would have no reason to come up here, after all, and the other mortal guests were in bed. We found mostly bedrooms presumably occupied by fellow guests of Witch Lords, as well as a solarium overlooking the valley that must have a spectacular view during the day; now its windows showed only black emptiness. A covered easel tucked in a corner of the solarium reminded me of the redheaded boy we'd glimpsed on our last visit, and I wondered if he'd been allowed to keep his room on the second floor with so many important guests in the castle.

We discovered five different stairways ascending to the cluster of towers that crowned the castle. One and only one of them bore an artifice lock freshly carved into the door.

"It's got to be this one," Zaira said, stopping in front of it. "Can you open it?"

I examined the circle. "This isn't a standard door seal," I realized. "Usually they open to a physical key or a password. But the runes for this one dictate that it will open to 'the blood of the master.'" Another case of Ruven mixing imperial artifice with Vaskandran vivomancy. Now that I'd seen the Truce Stone basin, I wondered if perhaps he'd gotten the idea before he'd come to Raverra and Ardence on his journey of literary larceny, and if *Interactions of Magic* hadn't been his primary goal there from the start.

"So do we have to cut Ruven and splash his blood on the door?" Zaira sounded entirely ready to pull out her knife and go find him.

"That might tip our hand a bit early." I frowned at the door. There was no definition for the term *master* in the artifice diagram, which made no sense. It was as if the enchantment expected the door to already know who the master was.

Of course, if it was made from a tree grown in Kazerath, it *would* know its master. Sprinkling Ruven's blood on the door wouldn't unlock it, even if we could somehow get some; the door wouldn't recognize us.

Or would it?

I closed my eyes. If I drove out all the distractions—the pulse of my own anxious heart, Zaira's breathing, the overpowering hum of magic emanating from the seventeen Witch Lords gathered in one place—I could faintly pick out the tracery of vines on the ceiling, a dim presence in my spatial sense of the corridor around me. I knew, somehow, that a spider had built its web in the corner where wall met ceiling, waiting for some lost fly to wander into its grasp. My awareness of the life in the corridor didn't extend far—barely beyond arm's reach—but it included, ever so weakly, the dead wood of the door before me.

This sense of mine wasn't magic, any more than it was magic when any normal person touched a luminary and felt the warmth of the crystal, or caught the scent of strange herbs in their wine and identified a potion hidden there. It was like the connection I could dimly sense between Zaira and me, created and anchored by the jess I'd placed upon her. The magic was there already. But because I was connected to it, I could feel it.

The Lady of Eagles' rivers had fed this tree. Her life had become a part of its life, and the door remembered.

I laid my palm on the door. The wood felt warm and welcoming to my touch. It knew me.

I pushed it open, revealing a dim stairway spiraling up into darkness.

"How did you do that?" Zaira demanded.

"It worked because I'm descended from the Lady of Eagles." I stared at my own spread fingers. "No wonder the Witch Lords want this," I whispered. No seal in Vaskandar would keep me out. Much of the country would recognize me on a deep magical level as the blood of its master.

"Do you think Ruven realizes you can walk through all his wards?" Zaira asked warily.

"I don't know. He might, if he's given thought to it. We should be careful."

No lamps lit the winding stone stairs, and only occasional windows let in the thin starlight. As we climbed, the darkness around us felt full, not empty, as if all manner of things might be hiding in it. And I supposed something was: this was Ruven's domain now, and his power flowed through every part of it.

The Wolf Lord had known when we crept around his castle. Ruven might be too new to his role to recognize our steps falling out of place, among all the other lives moving about all the land in Kazerath, especially with the power of all seventeen Witch Lords gathered below us, unstable and dangerous as the fires within Mount Whitecrown itself. But then again, he might not.

The low murmur of subdued voices came from above, too muffled to make out words. Zaira froze ahead of me on the steps. I barely made out that her shadowy outline had stopped before running into her.

She started moving again, silent as falling snow. My huffing from all the climbing sounded impossibly loud by comparison. I did my best to quiet my breathing and followed.

Lamplight trickled down the stairwell; soon it became apparent that it leaked from under a door at the top. A woman's deep, mature voice came from within.

"I'm not sure we can risk drawing their attention. Some of them make him look like the Grace of Mercy, if you believe the rumors."

"That's Namira," Zaira whispered. "I'm going in."

I loosened one of my artifice rings and nodded.

Zaira flung open the door on a wide, round room that took up the entire level of the tower. Oil lamps and candles lit a simple living area, with chairs around the hearth and a large dining table; a couple of cots were crammed in against the far wall, and open stairs led up to another floor.

The cots stood empty, the blankets neatly made. Half a dozen people sat around the table, leaning conspiratorially together, the flickering lights throwing their faces into shadow: old and young, male and female, some of them all too familiar. When the door flew open, they recoiled in surprise; a few sprang to their feet.

Terika was among them. She froze, gripping the table, her eyes wide. The missing artificer Namira sat beside her, expression rapidly changing from shock and alarm to a broad grin. The other four I didn't immediately recognize, though at least one or two of them looked familiar from around the Mews.

We'd found the missing Falcons.

"Don't be alarmed," I said quickly, to the ones I didn't know well. "We're here to help you."

"We don't need help," Terika said, her voice raspy with emotion. Her gaze locked on Zaira as if no one else were in the room.

"Of course not," said a thin young man with perfectly groomed brown ringlets and tired eyes. His voice dripped sarcasm. "We're so very happy here."

Namira stood and offered me a bow. "Lady Amalia, Zaira, I can't tell you how glad I am to see you."

"Terika," Zaira said urgently. "Your grandmother is all right. They made her the potion, and she's fine."

Terika closed her eyes and swallowed. "Thank the Graces. Thank you for telling me. And now, please..." she trailed off, shaking her head.

Zaira's voice took on an edge. "What's wrong? You don't look good."

She was right. Terika's face was pale as paper, and she looked as if she might faint.

"Everything is lovely. We're all fine." Terika drew in a shuddery breath, and a spark came into her eyes. "You shouldn't have c...co..." She swallowed the word she couldn't say and tried again, her knuckles white on the table. "You shouldn't have... combs."

Zaira blinked at her. "Of course I came." She stepped forward. "It almost killed me to leave you last time, Terika. We're getting you out of here."

Terika shook her head violently. All the others murmured, "No, we're fine, we like it here."

Terika forced words out past a fixed smile, sweat beading on her brow. "You're in d...daisies, Zaira. Right now. Do you understand me? You're in daisies, and you need leaves. Now. Everything is so, *so* wonderful."

The Nine Hells lay in her eyes. My skin crawled with unease, as if I'd gone to the Lady of Spiders' tailor. Something wasn't right. The other Falcons exchanged frowns and confused glances, seeming unsettled as well.

Zaira stepped forward. "We're in danger. Right. Don't worry; we're invited guests. That viper already knows we're here, and he can't do anything about it. I'm going to get you out of this cursed place." She reached toward Terika's hair, tenderly.

Terika let out a wail and threw herself into Zaira's arms.

But then Zaira staggered back, a hand clapped to the side of her neck, mouth gaping.

A bloody knife gleamed in Terika's hand.

"You shouldn't have come back, Zaira," Terika said, tears spilling from her eyes. "Now I have to kill you."

Chapter Thirty-Three

The room erupted into consternation. Some of the Falcons scrambled back out of the way; Namira lunged to try to grab Terika's arm, but Terika dodged, her eyes still fixed on Zaira.

"Terika, what are you *doing*?" Namira cried.

I steadied Zaira by the elbow. "Are you all right?"

Zaira just stared, one hand half extended, the other pressed to her neck. I'd never seen her struck so utterly silent. A few drops of red stained her fingers, but the cut didn't seem serious.

But then, it couldn't be; Zaira's enchanted corset stays and hairpins stopped the sudden, forceful impacts of musket balls or dagger strikes. A tiny nick, however, wouldn't set off the shield, which had to let through the thousand gentle touches of daily life.

My stomach dropped. Terika was an alchemist. If she were going to kill someone, she'd use poison.

"Zaira!" Terika cried, anguish in her voice. And she lunged at her again, knife flashing.

Zaira didn't even try to step out of the way. Terika's knife came down for her heart, but this time she'd moved fast enough to trigger the shield; the air an inch from Zaira's chest rippled and chimed, and the bloodstained blade rebounded.

I threw myself between them, even as Namira grappled with

Terika for the knife. The tired-eyed young man leaped in to help her, and they twisted it from Terika's grip.

"Don't touch the blade!" I warned them. "It could be poisoned!"

The young man threw the knife away from himself across the room, as if it were a stingroach. It clanged off the stone wall.

In the distraction, Terika wriggled free of them and threw herself at Zaira again, knocking her down. Zaira stared at her in shock from the floor, lifting empty hands between them, as Terika pulled something from her pocket.

I dove and grabbed her wrist before she could shove a tiny glass vial into Zaira's face.

"Careful, Amalia!" Terika cried. "That vial's totally harmless!"

Namira swore and started prying Terika's fingers off the vial with both hands, while I kept mine clamped around her wrist. Terika made a grab at Zaira's knife with her other hand, but Zaira scrambled away across the floor, still staring in wordless shock.

Then the other Falcons all jumped in and helped hold Terika down. She struggled against them, her honey-brown curls shaking.

I dropped to my knees beside Zaira. "Are you all right?" I asked.

She held up trembling fingers before her eyes, staring at the blood on them. Some kind of darker substance smeared through the red.

"I feel...strange," she said, her voice higher than usual. "Demons have mercy. Didn't see that coming."

Terika went still. "She needs an—" The word stuck in her throat, but her face was pale and desperate. "Quick, she needs a dose of...It's...Hells take it!"

"Check the knife," I called. An old woman with a crown of white braids retrieved the knife and sniffed it gingerly, holding it up to the light.

Zaira slumped against the stone wall behind her, drifting slowly over to the side. "Whoo. Seeing some strange stuff now."

I steadied her, taking her weight as she went nearly slack against me. Fear tasted coppery in the back of my throat. "Terika," I said urgently, "do you have access to alchemical supplies and equipment here?"

"Yes," she said from where they still held her pinned to the floor. "We make things for Ruven, because we love working for him *so much*. Hurry!"

"Do you make things for yourselves as well? Do you have anything in stock?"

"Why, yes!" she shouted it more loudly than was remotely necessary. "I'm so glad you asked! I keep a stock of assorted useful potions and antidotes in my pillowcase upstairs. For no particular reason!"

A young boy dashed up the stairs and came rushing back down a moment later with an entire pillow. Zaira had started shivering in my arms, and her eyes roved wildly as if they were tracking things only she could see.

"*Revincio*," I muttered, because the last thing we needed was a hallucinating fire warlock burning down the castle.

The white-haired woman tore through the pillowcase, pulling out one vial after another until she came to one holding a bright blue liquid. "Ferroli's Tincture of Purity?" she snapped to Terika.

"Of course not," Terika said eagerly. "Why would I ever make Ferroli's Tincture? It's not as if I was expecting anyone here to be poisoned!"

"Right." The woman hurried over to Zaira, squeezed open her jaw, and dumped the vial into her mouth, over Zaira's incoherent protests.

Zaira spluttered, but the old woman clapped a hand over her mouth to make sure she couldn't spit out the tincture, with grim practicality. In a moment, a sizzling sound came from the cut on her neck, and there was a smell of fresh lemons. Terika let out a sigh of relief.

The old alchemist nodded decisively, shaking scraggly white tendrils free of her braid crown. "That should do it. Powerful stuff, Ferroli's Tincture."

Sure enough, Zaira shook her head and clambered to her feet, her eyes sharp again.

"Ruven ordered you to do this, didn't he?" she said to Terika. Rage filled her voice as she dusted herself off. "Hells take his rancid soul."

"Sorry," Terika panted, smiling apologetically up from where three Falcons held her pinned to the floor. "It's really good to see you, though."

Zaira nodded, swallowing. "Good to see you, too."

After a few attempts, we found that if we sat Terika on the far side of the room, with no weapons or dangerous objects to hand, and put the rest of us between her and Zaira, she could consider the situation impossible enough that she wasn't forced to attempt to kill Zaira anymore. She waved forlornly at Zaira, who stuck out her tongue in return, and then they degenerated into making bizarre faces at each other across the room. I murmured the release word, once I was sure Zaira was back in full possession of her faculties.

"Now," I said, settling into a chair and attempting to gather the attention of the assembled Falcons, "we want to rescue all of you. But before we go any further, I have some questions."

"We don't need rescuing," Namira said with a weary shrug.

"Yes, we're *so very happy* here," the young man sighed.

"I know. But first tell me, out of curiosity, is there anyone to whom you might feel obliged to report this conversation, under any circumstances?"

Namira shook her head. The young man said dryly, "Well, if you suggest treason against the Serene Empire, I might feel obliged to report it to Colonel Vasante."

"Well said, ah..."

"Lamonte Clare. I'm an artificer."

The older woman with a white braid coiled on her head offered me a nod. "And I'm Parona da Valisia. An alchemist, as you've seen."

"And I think you know me," Namira said. Then her voice took on extra intensity. "I would *absolutely love* to talk to you about a project we've been working on lately, if I ever get the chance."

"Is it a project of, ah, explosive proportions?" I asked.

"Why, yes." She sat back, satisfied. "So it is."

"I would love to speak about that, as well. And it's my hope that soon, we may be able to." I worried at a loose thread on my jacket sleeve, thinking. "Do you have any orders to eat or drink specific things, or at specific times?"

Parona straightened, eyes shining. "No. Only that we must eat and drink, and not starve ourselves."

"Perfect. Then if you don't mind, Zaira and I will bring you food and water, which we hope you'll take advantage of over the next few days."

"That sounds lovely," Parona said eagerly. "Not that Lord Ruven isn't an excellent host, of course. But I could use a change of fare."

"Then hopefully we can talk more freely in a couple of days, when the potion has worn off."

"What potion?" Namira said, her voice flat. "I don't know what you're talking about."

"Right. That potion." I glanced at Zaira; she and Terika were blowing sneaky kisses at each other over the heads of the Falcons separating them. I suppressed a smile. "We're here for the Conclave, and we'll be looking for an opportune moment when everyone is distracted to sneak you out. In the unlikely event anyone changes their mind and decides they'd like to leave after all, of course."

Lamonte chuckled weakly. "I'm sure no one will take you up on that, but I suppose it's good to know one has options."

"Is there anything else you can tell us now?" I asked.

The Falcons exchanged glances. "Do you know how we came to be here?" Namira asked.

"More or less. Ruven's people faked your deaths, mostly." An unpleasant thought occurred to me. "Ah, do you all know what happened to your Falconers?"

Terika's face sobered, as she no doubt recalled Lienne. Parona said grimly, "I think we can guess."

"I didn't have one," said the youngest of them, the boy of about twelve who had run to grab the pillow, ducking his head shyly.

"Oh?" I looked into his eyes; they bore an indigo mage mark, hard to make out in the dim light. "Are you not from the Serene Empire, then?"

He glanced nervously at Namira, but she put a reassuring hand on his shoulder. "You can tell her, Selas."

"I'm from Ardence," the boy admitted. "My sister and I were in a small orphanage there. The old man who ran it couldn't see colors, so he didn't know I was mage-marked. But then a few years ago a man showed up and claimed to have an indenture contract for me, and took me away to here."

Zaira stiffened and swiveled to face him. "An indenture contract! Was his name Orthys, by any chance?"

Selas hesitated, then nodded. "I think so."

"*That* stingroach," Zaira growled. "I almost wish he were alive just so I could kill him again."

"So Orthys sold you to Ruven?" I prompted.

Selas nodded. "Lord Ruven said I could have anything I wanted and be treated like a prince, so long as I did artifice for him. But I didn't have any training, so I couldn't do much." He winced and made a shrugging motion with one shoulder. I glimpsed the mark of finger-shaped burns through the neck of his shirt and felt a slow rage welling up in my chest. "Then I tried to run away, to get back to my sister, and he kept me locked up after that. Until about two months ago, when he started giving me the..." the boy stopped.

"Yes?" I prompted.

He glanced at Terika, and his face lit up in a smile. "He gave me the *lotion*." He mimed drinking. "So now I love it here. I don't want to leave. I don't miss my sister at all." He grimaced and shook his head.

Orthys had a history of selling mages to Vaskandar. There weren't nearly enough people here to account for all of them, though I didn't think he'd gotten many who were actually mage-marked. I frowned. "Were there any others like you? Mages who Orthys brought here?"

Selas hesitated. "Well, there's a boy who was here before me, but he really *does* like it here. Ruven spoils him, like he used to do me before I tried to run away. He's the one who makes the... the lotion."

I frowned. "So he works for Ruven willingly?"

"We all do," Namira said, with a forced smile. "But this boy especially. If you see him around the castle, don't trust him, despite his years. He's the reason we're all here."

"There were a few others, too," Selas said, his voice going so quiet I could hardly hear him. His shoulders hunched up around his ears. "He didn't have the lotion recipe back then, so they didn't have to..." His words hitched, and he tried another tack.

"They all eventually displeased him. I... I made sure not to displease him, so I'm still here."

"Grace of Mercy," I breathed. "I'm sorry. We'll get you out of here as soon as we can."

Namira gave the boy a quick, fierce hug. "None of us are going anywhere, of course, because we want to stay with Lord Ruven," she murmured. "But thank you. We appreciate the sentiment greatly nonetheless."

Zaira flexed her fingers. "I keep thinking I couldn't possibly want to punch him with a fistful of balefire more than I already do. But he keeps proving me wrong."

"I'm not in the habit of letting anger dictate my actions," I said. "But nonetheless, I pray the Graces give you the chance."

There was no dancing at the Arrival reception. There were drinks, thank the Graces, and a rather paltry selection of things to nibble. Witch Lords and their guests prowled the throne room, coming together for brief conversations before moving on, restless predators circling one another. Human servants moved through the hall, refreshing drinks and carrying messages, but no chimeras slinked around the edges. I hadn't seen any since we'd arrived. It occurred to me that Zaira might have killed most of the chimeras in Kazerath when she unleashed her balefire on the Wolf Lord.

I'd decided that if someone had a gown of actual spiders, one could wear whatever one pleased to the Conclave. Thus, I'd settled on a richly embroidered coat and breeches in sapphire velvet over a silver brocade bodice, with modest but beautifully crafted lace at my throat and wrists. It was one of three potential outfits I'd packed for formal occasions at the Conclave, and the most comfortable—and also the most Raverran, with winged horses worked into the coat collar as well as plenty of Raverran blue on display. If my presence could remind some of the Witch Lords that there was another major power in Eruvia besides Vaskandar, so much the better.

I was used to Zaira dropping me like a soiled handkerchief the moment we entered a party; usually she made herself the center of attention at once, laughing and flirting. But this time it was Kathe who circulated among the gathered Witch Lords and their guests, a sharp-edged smile on his face, while Zaira hovered by my side. She looked bold as ever in a gown layered with all the shades of fire, from red to gold, but I knew her well enough to spot the extra stiffness in her back and wariness in her eyes.

She handed me a glass of wine a servant had passed her. "Check this, will you?"

My ring stayed cool and dark. I passed it back. "No alchemy. It could still be poisoned, but honestly, Ruven has a great deal at stake here, hosting a Conclave as a brand-new Witch Lord. I doubt he'd risk disaster by murdering a protected guest."

Zaira raised an eyebrow. "Didn't stop him from ordering Terika after me."

"That's different. We can't admit he did that, because it would reveal we were snooping around and tip our hand that we're in contact with the captured Falcons. And he could blame it on Terika if we did. It was a clever trap."

Zaira glared across the room at where Ruven chatted with the Lady of Laurels, gesturing with long, elegant fingers. "I don't like this. I hate being in a place I'm not confident I could burn my way out of."

I slipped my hand into my pocket and held Marcello's button for reassurance. "Well, we can't just stand here. We have to go talk to them. We need a sense of who's backing the war, who's against it, and who hasn't picked a side."

At that moment, Kathe sauntered up to us, arms linked with the redheaded Witch Lord. The latter fixed eyes the color of sunlight through leaves on us, ringed by a jet-black mage mark; I had the unsettling sense he was assessing me on levels I couldn't perceive, seeing things no human could. His close-fitting sleeveless coat was cut like a country woodsman's but consisted of hundreds of delicate and beautiful shapes of beasts and birds, all crafted from different shades of leather and stitched carefully together. I could have stared at it for hours if that wouldn't have been painfully awkward. I had to force my eyes back up to his, and found him smirking at me.

"Lady Amalia, Lady Zaira," Kathe greeted us cheerfully. "May I introduce my friend, the Fox Lord of Kar."

We exchanged bows and curtsies all around. I reviewed the map in my head; Kar lay to the north of the Lady of Bears' domain. If she was bent on invasion, as seemed likely given her involvement in the Three Years' War, an alliance with Kar would be useful indeed.

"I'm delighted to meet any friend of Kathe's," I told the Fox Lord. "How long have you known him?"

The Fox Lord laughed. "My lady, nobody *knows* Kathe. When he was born, his own mother asked, 'Who are you?' "

Zaira flicked a glance to me. "See, I say if you don't know someone, you can't trust them."

Kathe cocked his head. "You don't strike me as a woman who trusts *anyone*, Lady Zaira. Which is wise; trust is for fools."

The Fox Lord slung an arm over Kathe's shoulder, showing pointed teeth. "Precisely. Trust your enemies, if you have enough of a hold over them. But never trust your friends." He smoothly snatched a beer glass from a passing servant and clinked it off Zaira's, then took a long swallow.

"And who are your enemies, then?" I asked, smiling in what I hoped was a charming fashion. "Not the Serene Empire, I hope?"

"Why make an enemy of the moon, or the sea?" The Fox Lord shrugged. "My domain shares no borders with the Empire. I have little opinion on it. It's the bear at my door that concerns me."

"Do you fear its appetite?" I asked.

"I don't *fear* anything human. And while we may not seem like it, most of us do still qualify." He winked. "But it's no secret where the bear will turn next if she can't bite off a piece of your Empire. So forgive me if I hope for her to succeed. A hungry bear on one's doorstep is unsettling to anyone."

"Ah, but what if you had a friend to help protect you from the bear?" I suggested.

"We've already established that you can't trust friends." The Fox Lord's eyes gleamed. "People who distract bears so their friends can get away usually wind up mauled, I believe."

A man in a shining robe of many iridescent colors turned from another conversation to approach us. His slicked-back hair fell in a long braid nearly to the floor, lending further harshness to a face of jutting angles and pale gray eyes. A black snake circled his collarbones like a living torque, its tongue flickering inquisitively toward me. Even though I didn't mind snakes, I had to suppress a shiver; something about the man set me instinctively on edge.

"Crow Lord, I need you to settle a bet," he said to Kathe, in a voice both soft and penetrating.

Kathe spread his hands. "I am the most neutral of arbiters."

The newcomer's lips thinned in amusement. "Perhaps not in this case. The bet is about you."

"Oh?" Kathe's brows lifted. "I fear I can't tell you my secrets just to settle your bet, though I admit I'm curious what aspect of my life the Serpent Lord might find worthy of a wager."

"No secrets, I should think." The Serpent Lord's pale eyes flicked between Kathe and me. "The Lady of Thorns claims you're not truly courting this Raverran. She says it's a stunt to insult her."

Kathe shook his head. "I'm wounded that she would think me so petty."

"And I am offended that anyone could believe I would stoop to be used in such a ploy," I said.

The Serpent Lord turned his flat gaze to me. "So you are truly courting the Crow Lord?"

I knew of this one. He was one of the Witch Lords who had invaded Loreice during the Three Years' War. This was no matter of idle curiosity; he was testing the strength of the Empire's connection with Let, to see whether he and his allies truly needed to worry about a threat at their backs if they went to war.

I stepped closer to Kathe, taking his hand. "Of course!"

"I believe my good neighbor in Sevaeth is merely jealous," Kathe said. "After all, everyone knows her own courtship of the Lady Amalia's grandfather failed."

That was news to me. I'd realized they were allies but hadn't known the Lady of Thorns had wanted more from the relationship. That must have given extra sting to the reversal when my grandfather had abandoned their alliance to marry the queen of Callamorne.

"That only lends credence to the idea that your courtship is a mere show," the Serpent Lord pointed out. "Why would the Lady Amalia Lochaver Cornaro, of three royal bloodlines, court *you* when her arguably less auspicious ancestor rebuffed a Witch Lord of greater power?"

"I can think of several reasons," Zaira said, looking Kathe up and down appraisingly.

Kathe clicked his tongue. "If the Lady of Thorns cannot see what I have to offer, I suggest she give it deeper thought."

There was another layer to his words, slow and carefully chosen. Damn him, how many games was he playing?

The Serpent Lord shook his head. "How am I to know this is a true alliance you parade before us, and not some shallow scheme? You don't *act* like you're courting."

Kathe caught my eyes; his vibrant yellow mage mark encircled bright gleams of mischief. He angled toward me, lifting a questioning brow. "Well, my lady? How seriously are we courting?"

Hells. My pulse quickened with a mix of nerves and anticipation. I had to remove any doubts the Serpent Lord might possess. If he thought this was some whimsical gesture on Kathe's part, without any substance to it, all his allies against the Empire might ignore Let at their backs and bring their full force to bear on the border after all. Thousands of lives might depend on what I did now.

I'd been wondering what it might be like to kiss him. It seemed I was about to find out.

Chapter Thirty-Four

I gripped Kathe's arm as if to keep him from escaping; lightning coursed under my fingers. My heart buzzing like a hummingbird's wings, I leaned in and brushed his lips with mine.

His mouth responded, nimble and pliant, with startling expertise. The energy that I always felt in him seemed to jolt through me, down from my lips all through my body. I redoubled my own efforts, with sudden urgency; for a flickering instant, I tasted his tongue.

He ended the kiss before I did, his lips curving against mine in a smile.

I realized I'd closed my eyes.

I pulled back slowly, to give my head time to stop swimming, and gave the Serpent Lord a challenging stare. I didn't dare look at Zaira; I'd blush from head to toe if I did.

"Well?" I demanded. "Is that proof enough for you?"

The Serpent Lord gave us a curt bow. "My apologies. I will let the Lady of Thorns know she has lost her bet."

He withdrew. I could feel a flush creeping inexorably up my neck. My lips still tingled.

The Fox Lord put his hands behind his head, grinning. "Well! I see Raverra is willing to commit to its alliances after all, Lady Amalia. Good to know."

"We take care of our friends," I said, striving to recover my dignity.

"Extravagant care." Zaira gave him a saucy wink. "Exquisite care. Like you've never been cared for before."

My face burned. "Zaira, please."

But the Fox Lord only grinned wider. "And here I thought Raverrans had no sense of humor. I like you, warlock." He tapped his chin, adopting a musing expression. "I was skeptical about your offers of friendship. But perhaps I might consider a different relationship with the Empire."

"Then you're in luck," Zaira said. "The Empire is a right strumpet and will court anyone."

The Grace of Mercy wasn't hearing prayers that day, because no crack opened in the ground beneath my feet to swallow me up.

The Fox Lord laughed. "Perhaps if you can convince me Raverra won't toy with me and discard me like a duchess's sixth husband, I might find a way to embrace the idea of some form of cooperation."

"I look forward to persuading you," Zaira said, and blew him a kiss.

"And on that note," Kathe said, sweeping into a bow, "I fear I must make my apologies, my lady. The Arrival only lasts so long, and tradition dictates each Witch Lord must greet every other personally. I've only made it a quarter of the way down my list."

"Me too," the Fox Lord admitted. "But we'll speak more tomorrow. It was fun to meet you both."

Kathe lifted the back of my hand to touch his secretive smile. "Lady Amalia, as always, a pleasure."

"Likewise, Lord Kathe."

Don't stare after him, I reminded myself as they walked away across the throne room. I pulled my eyes away to meet Zaira's amused expression.

"I had to do it," I said quickly. "For the Empire."

"Mmm," she said. "Looked like a terrible sacrifice."

I tugged at a loose lock of my hair. "I told Marcello it might come to this."

"You were never courting Marcello," Zaira pointed out. "You kissed the man you're courting. If you feel guilty, the person you need to explain things to is yourself."

"You're right, I suppose." I reached for my flare locket, out of some protective instinct, and my fingers snarled in Kathe's claws. "I wasn't prepared to . . . to . . ."

"To kiss him?"

"No," I confessed. "To like it quite so much."

Zaira burst out laughing. "Grace of Love's sweet tits, woman, if you kiss a man and *don't* like it, he's doing it wrong." She shook her head. "Come on. Let's get you a drink."

"Yes," I agreed. "That sounds lovely."

A glass of wine slowed my pounding heart back to its normal pace and erased the lingering taste of Kathe from my lips. My eyes kept pulling to him, across the room, where he stood at graceful ease talking to the Aspen Lord. I leaned against a pillar and hid my face behind my cup, thoughts still racing.

Of course I'd liked it. I liked *Kathe*. His clever wit excited me, but even more intriguing were the glimpses he occasionally let slip of his true, hidden self. Here was a man whose society had handed him absolute power and demanded no accountability in return, and yet somehow, against all odds, he seemed to have turned out to be a good person. Mostly.

And there was no denying he was an advantageous match, even for a Cornaro. What was holding me back?

My hand slid reluctantly into my pocket, fingertips brushing the familiar lump of Marcello's button. With Marcello, I never had to dance around the truth, or wonder what he was hiding from me. There were no games or bargains; if I needed something, he gave it freely. I had no fears that he would betray me, or use me to achieve a goal and then cast me aside. Kathe was an exciting and dangerous journey, but Marcello was home.

If you were going to marry a man, it should be the one you could imagine growing old with, not the one you could imagine lapping up your enemies' blood.

Of course, one could argue that only a lack of imagination prevented the two from being one and the same. My parents' courtship had begun in politics, after all, but it had ended in love.

I shook myself like a wet dog. *Well played, Kathe. Well played.*

"Are you cooled off?" Zaira asked, smirking. "Ready to go back to work?"

"Oh, hush. Who do we need to talk to next?"

Zaira shrugged. "You're the one who knows Vaskandran politics. Point me at someone to flirt with or insult."

"It's good to know one's strengths, I suppose." I scanned the room. The Elk Lord was deep in conversation with the Lady of Eagles; I didn't dare interrupt *that* discussion. The Lady of Thorns had her head together with the Serpent Lord and kept glaring in my direction, which I didn't like one bit. I found myself staring at Kathe again, appreciating the lines of him, and jerked my eyes elsewhere.

Ruven stood near a side doorway, speaking to the redheaded boy we'd seen on our last visit here. That must be the alchemist Selas had spoken of who served him willingly. The boy was telling Ruven something, gesturing enthusiastically and staring up at him with open adoration. Kathe smiled indulgently and patted the boy's head, as if he were a dog.

"Just not the lady covered in spiders," Zaira was saying. "I'm not sure I could—holy Hells, she's right behind you."

I spun, squeezing my wineglass too tight, to find the Lady of Spiders standing far too close for my comfort, a dead-eyed smile stretching her round face. I choked back a yelp. Spiders formed elegant patterns on her bodice, all different sizes, legs scuttling and waving as they crawled past one another to keep the fronds and curlicues of their design curling and shifting as if in a breeze. A large, black spider centered her neckline, long legs spread. Tiny spiders gleaming with bright colors climbed her long silver hair, forming more patterns there.

It was beautiful. But I had never wanted to scream so much in my life.

I scrambled away a step before I caught myself and managed a bow, trying to recover my poise. Zaira backed up behind me, her hands clasped and white-knuckled; I suspected she was having trouble holding back her instinct to set the whole horrifying dress on fire.

"Oh, hello, my lady," I said breathlessly. "I didn't see you there."

The Lady of Spiders grinned. I suspected she found our reactions more than a little amusing. "You should be more alert," she said in a smooth, deep voice quite different than the cackle I'd been expecting. It resonated with power. "There is at least one here who has no intention of letting you leave the Conclave alive."

I glanced toward the Lady of Thorns. I could almost feel her malevolent intent from here. "I know."

"Your position is weak," she said, running a lock of her own hair through her fingers. "The Witch Lords in the south of Vaskandar want to annex territory from the Empire, either to give their children domains of their own or to keep from being conquered themselves. The Witch Lords in the north don't care either way, or will support the war due to favors and grievances owed. You will see. If they held the Kindling now, at least ten candles would burn for war. And the rest would be indifferent, rather than opposed."

Ten Witch Lords wanting war. My heart sank. The Vaskandran ambassador had said only three joined in the Three Years' War, and that had been bad enough.

"What about you?" I asked, keeping my voice as calm as I could. "Will you light your candle for war? I've heard that many will follow your lead."

Her lids drooped in apparent satisfaction. "What I do will depend on which course most amuses me."

"Would seeing the whole border on fire amuse you?" Zaira asked, showing her teeth. "Because that's what will happen if there's a war."

The Lady of Spiders chuckled, deep in her throat. "It might."

I resisted a sudden impulse to brush at my arms to make sure no spiders were crawling up them. "Well, at least some Witch Lords seem set on an invasion, so you'll probably get your balefire regardless. What else amuses you, if that's truly your deciding factor?"

The Lady of Spiders tilted her head. "Secrets. Mysteries. Surprises. Things raw and new, and things buried and forgotten. I have lived a long time, little ones, but there is always more to discover."

I perked up. "Are you a scholar?"

"No."

Such a flat dismissal. *Ah well.*

Zaira frowned. "What sort of secrets and mysteries?"

The Lady of Spiders held out a hand, as if in invitation. A spider crawled onto her palm. "The ones humans hold deep in their hearts, and treasure past all reason. The ones you have to break a soul open and suck out the marrow to find."

Zaira gave me a *What the Hells do I even say to that* look. I couldn't stop a nervous laugh.

"I could help you," the Lady of Spiders said then, her voice gone sweet and slow as molasses.

"I'm certain you could," I replied warily.

"Both of you are interesting." She savored the word on her tongue, in a way that set my stomach to squirming. "I would love to crack you open and find out what dwells inside, in the dark places you keep from the light of day."

"I prefer to stay in one piece, thanks," Zaira said, her voice somewhat higher than usual.

"If what I found there amused me enough, I might see fit to weave my web in your favor. My candle remains as yet uncounted."

I tipped the last drops of my wine into my dry throat. "What, ah, would this cracking process entail? You're speaking metaphorically, one hopes."

"Hope is a fragile thing, Lady Amalia. Spider silk is much stronger." Her smile widened, a rift of darkness in her face that seemed fit to split her skull in half. "Think on it. If you become desperate enough to accept my offer, come to me."

"Is desperation a requirement?" I asked, my voice coming out unevenly.

"Oh, yes." The Lady of Spiders tipped her head in a gracious nod. "Do enjoy the evening. I like to see young people with a spark of life and pleasure in their faces. So fleeting, so transient."

"You have a good time too." Zaira waved weakly. "Terrifying people, or whatever it is you do for fun."

The Lady of Spiders laughed as she glided away.

"Well, I know what I'm having nightmares about tonight," Zaira said conversationally, watching her go.

I nodded. "Me, too."

When we returned to the Falcons' tower prison late that night with more food and fresh water, we found them gathered tensely around the table, waiting for us. Terika, seated at the far end, started to lunge to her feet when Zaira stepped in the door; Lamonte and Namira, on either side of her, each put a hand firmly on her shoulder and pushed her back down.

Namira gestured to a couple of empty chairs. "Why don't you sit," she said. "We're finding our tongues a little freer, after a day eating what you've brought us, and we have a lot to talk about."

We put down our baskets of food and settled into our seats. Zaira blew Terika a kiss. "Still not safe to come near, huh?"

Terika sighed and shook her head. "Old commands he didn't repeat are fading, but recent or repeated ones are still in force."

"She has no weapons or poisons, though," said Lamonte, "so if she's forced to attack you, it should be comically ineffective."

"Does he give you verbal orders, then?" I asked, leaning my elbows on the table. "Is that how it works?"

Parona's nose wrinkled with disgust. "I mix the cursed stuff, and I'm not sure how it works, myself. It contains some very strange ingredients, like sand and blood."

My stomach turned. "Ruven's blood. And sand is ground stone. Graces preserve us—he's making you part of his domain. That's how he can control you."

The Falcons grimaced or shook their heads; some drew back in revulsion.

"You should know he's made me create far more than he's using on us," Parona said urgently. "He must have a huge stockpile by now. I'm concerned about what he may be planning."

"That doesn't sound good," I said. The idea of Ruven with enough potion to control dozens or hundreds of people made my palms clammy. Getting all the Falcons out of his hands had become even more important.

I thought of the redheaded alchemist boy, and the vial of Black Malice in its little velvet bag, and felt sick.

"Will the potion have any lingering effects on us?" the boy Selas asked timidly.

"It seems to be temporary." Istrella hadn't shown any after-effects once the potion wore off. "But we may want to have a vivomancer look at you when you get safely back to the Mews, to be sure."

The Falcons exchanged glances around the table. Namira cleared her throat. "About that."

Zaira chuckled. "I thought this might be coming."

A dizzying gulf opened in my chest. "You don't want to go back to the Mews."

"Some of us do," Parona said, folding her hands primly on the table. "I have unfinished work to attend to. And I've been a Falcon my whole life; at my age, it's a bit late to start a new career."

"And I've heard of your plans for a reform law." Lamonte fixed me with a commanding stare. "I'm a gambling man, and I'm willing to take my chances that you'll get it passed. I don't want to be a fugitive; I'm engaged to be married. I want to go home to Loreice and start a family in peace."

"All *my* family and friends are at the Mews," Namira said. "And I'm not going to leave Raverra to fend for itself when war is threatening. But there are some of us who might prefer to consider other options."

"I've never *been* to the Mews," Selas said, looking worried. "And if I become a Falcon, it's for life. I don't know."

"You never were a Falcon," I said carefully. "Since you aren't in the Serene Empire, there is no law that compels you to go to the Mews if you don't want to." I didn't mention that he was exempt from Lord Caulin's order, too.

The boy looked relieved. "I'm not sure," he admitted, "Mostly I want to get out of here, and see my sister again. But I'm glad I have a choice."

"And what about me?" asked the only Falcon who hadn't yet spoken, a portly man in his twenties with an impressive mustache. "No one ever gave me a choice. Forgive me if I'm being forward, my lady, but I'm rather disenchanted with an Empire that tells me what I must do with my life and who I must be." His voice, timid at first, gained strength. "I never had a chance to pursue my dreams, learn a craft, travel, make a home, find someone to marry...all the little things that make a life. I want those things, my lady." He lifted his bare wrist. "My jess is off. I don't want to stay in this miserable castle, but I do want to fly."

I swallowed. It seemed I wouldn't avoid Lord Caulin's trap so easily. "And what is your name, sir?"

"Harrald Callo, my lady. I'm an artificer." He straightened his sleeves, as if making himself presentable. "My parents were farmers, but they thought they might try to send me to a university, before the Falconers came for me."

I had my orders from the doge. The velvet bag with its vial of Black Malice sat in my room, full of death, waiting. But all this man wanted was to find out who he truly was. Who he could have been, if the Empire hadn't laid out another fate for him.

My duty as a Serene Imperial Envoy was clear. But there was also my duty as a human being.

"The law is unambiguous, for now," I said slowly. "I'm working to change it. But right now, it doesn't give you a choice."

Harrald's shoulders slumped. "I see, my lady."

I leaned toward him across the table, holding his eyes. "But it's going to be very difficult getting everyone back across the border. If you got separated from the group, it seems highly unlikely anyone would find you."

His brows lifted. "I see," he said in an entirely different tone.

"Atruin is a good domain," I observed. "The Lady of Eagles protects her people and treats them well. Her border is only a short distance from here. I've also heard good things about Let, to the north."

"Is that so?" Harrald leaned back in his chair, sounding almost cheerful.

I nodded. "The mage-marked are given high status in Vaskandar; I'm sure any domain would welcome a mage-marked visitor. And I might be able to arrange introductions or possibly safe passage for travelers. Generally speaking."

"Well." He beamed. "Perhaps we should talk some more about that."

"There's something else we need to talk about," Namira said, leaning her elbows on the table. "Mount Whitecrown."

"Wait." I lifted a hand, despite the dread growing in my stomach over where this might lead. "Terika hasn't said whether she's going back to the Mews yet."

Zaira rose slowly to her feet.

"Neither have I."

Chapter Thirty-Five

I closed my eyes.

This was it; the moment I had been afraid of. I should have been happy for Zaira, that she had a choice, and glad that she trusted me to not try to stop her from making it. But all I could feel was a sick, endless dropping sensation, as if something priceless had slipped from my fingers and tumbled over a cliff.

"All right, then." I opened my eyes again, smoothing my expression as much as I could. "Do you want to go back to the Mews?"

Zaira snorted. "That's easy. No. That place is deadly boring."

I stared at her, stricken.

"But that's not the question." Zaira crossed her arms. "The question is whether I'm going back there anyway."

I nodded. Of course. Silly me. If I threw up on her shoes, it would serve her right.

Zaira turned to Terika. "What do *you* want?"

Terika let out a nervous laugh. "Honestly? Right now? To be with my grandmother. Even knowing she's all right, well, she's getting old. I want to spend time with her, while..." She swallowed. "I want to see her more."

"That can be arranged," I assured her quickly. "We could get you stationed at Highpass. You could see her every day."

Terika's face lit up. "That would work."

"Highpass is even more boring than the Mews," Zaira groaned.

"Good Graces, I wouldn't want to make you live there," Terika grimaced at the idea. "You could visit often. And I could visit you. I'm sure we could figure out a way to be together. I don't want to miss out on time with *you*, either."

"Ugh." Zaira made a face. "Sentimentality."

Terika grinned. "I'm like a sticky burr. You're not getting rid of me so easily."

Namira laughed. But my insides still twisted with apprehension. For all I wanted Zaira to be free, and wanted her to make her own choice, it was hard not to pray to the Graces with all my might for her to choose the Mews.

Zaira caught my eyes. "And you? What happens to you if I run off to your grandma's domain and build my throne of skulls, or whatever mages do for fun here?"

I drew in a shaky breath. "I'm more concerned about the consequences for the Empire. Without your balefire—"

"I'm cursed well aware of what my balefire can do in war," Zaira said sharply. "I'm asking about *you*."

"All right." I spread my hands on the table. "I don't know. They probably wouldn't execute me." But my mother's cousin Ignazio had proven that the Cornaro name was no protection against the consequences of treason; he would spend the rest of his life in an imperial prison. Certainly my political career would be over. "Perhaps they might let me retire in disgrace to some little villa full of books." Once, that would have sounded wonderful. Now, the prospect brought a clammy sweat to my palms. "My Falcon reform act would fail. And... I would miss you a great deal."

Aside perhaps from the prospect of imprisonment for treason, none of that came close to balancing the scale against Zaira's freedom. Even Falcon reform could be taken up by someone else. I stared down at my hands. I knew there was more I could say, things that might convince her to stay—but this had to be her decision. Never mind that if she decided to leave, the Empire could lose its war—and I might lose my title, my freedom, and most of all, my friend.

A heavy silence fell over the room. I didn't dare look up. I was afraid of what I'd see on Zaira's face.

At long last, she let out a sigh. "Your grandma did say it was a standing invitation."

I lifted my head, hope leaping in my chest.

Zaira shrugged. "You think I'd let you fight that festering bastard Ruven without me? That human disease has one cure, and it's balefire."

"We're not at war yet," I pointed out, to hide the wave of dizzy relief that swept over me.

"I'll bet you a ducat I can fix that for you."

Namira cleared her throat to get our attention. "If we don't do something about Mount Whitecrown, you won't need balefire to reduce everything around us to ashes." The reminder set a cold stone in my belly.

"Are you the one who created the artifice circles?" I asked.

She gestured modestly to the other artificers at the table. "We all worked on it, but I was the lead, yes."

"I found one of your circles," I said eagerly. "I figured out you'd left gaps in the design on purpose. We have people looking for the others and modifying them to slowly release the pressure."

Namira let out a long sigh and slumped in her chair, passing a hand across her close-cropped gray curls. "Thank the Graces. That's a start."

"What else do we need to do?" I asked.

"You need to destroy the control circle." She reached behind her and plucked a notebook, quill pen, and inkwell off a desk, then began sketching. "I'll draw you a map to it. If Ruven uses the control circle, he can trigger an eruption with whatever pressure is built up; it might be smaller, but it'll still be destructive. He can choose the direction it will blow, too. If you destroy the control circle, then so long as the other circles maintain the containment and continue to ease off the pressure gently, the volcano might not erupt for a long time."

"How about never?" I asked.

She raised an eyebrow. "It's still an active volcano. Artifice can't change that."

Zaira frowned. "What happens if that stingroach triggers it before we get there?"

A grim expression settled over Namira's face. "Then," she said, "everyone had better take cover."

The Reckoning was held the next day, in the castle gardens. The snow in the open castle grounds had melted overnight, though it still lingered under the shadows of the surrounding forest; the revealed grass grew lush and vivid green as if it were May instead of November, no doubt thanks to Ruven's magic. If the Witch Lords felt the wintry chill that clung to the mountain air, they didn't show it. Even my fur-lined velvet coat couldn't keep me from an occasional shiver.

In contrast to the reception last night, where the Witch Lords had moved quickly from one greeting to the next, making their rounds, the Reckoning was a day for lengthy private conversations. They went for strolls around the grounds together, or found isolated spots in which to stand a breath apart. At a glance, one could take them for couples enjoying a romantic turn in the gardens—and indeed, Zaira felt obliged to speculate extensively about pairings that would make a good match.

"Oh, those two would shred the sheets," she chuckled, eyeing the Fox Lord talking to the Lady of Otters. "I wouldn't mind joining the party."

"Ah," I managed, my face burning.

"And there's a sweet couple." She nodded toward where the Aspen Lord stood in serious conversation with the Elk Lord. "Wonder if he keeps the antlers on."

"Um."

"Now, those two make a pretty picture," she sighed, turning her attention to where the Lady of Laurels bent her head in close attendance to the Lady of Eagles. "All those long legs and flowing hair—"

"Zaira, she's my *great-grandmother,*" I protested.

Zaira grinned. "Pity you didn't inherit the good looks."

Someone had placed pedestals around the garden holding wooden bowls full of red or blue stones. At first I thought they were sweets, since the Witch Lords would occasionally pluck one out, or scoop a handful, but a closer look showed them to be polished crystals.

"What do you suppose those are for?" I asked Zaira, curious.

She shrugged. "Decorations, maybe?"

As we watched, Kathe dipped his hand into one, coming up with a red stone. He tossed it in his palm as he sauntered over toward the Lady of Thorns.

"There's got to be some significance to them," I muttered.

Zaira elbowed me. "Maybe they're money. Look." I followed her gaze to where the Lady of Laurels now passed a couple of blue gems to the Lady of Spiders, thankfully across the garden. My skin crawled just thinking about her, and I quickly glanced away.

"It's hard to imagine the Witch Lords all paying each other off, though." I remembered what Kathe had said about what counted for currency at the Reckoning. "They must represent grievances and favors. The exchange must be purely symbolic, a ritual to seal a deal, since there's no way to keep a proper accounting of them. But they're trading favors owed for political support, and giving up grievances in return for more favors."

"And we're broke."

"Well, yes." I straightened. "But we can still try to persuade people the old-fashioned way."

Zaira grinned and waggled her eyebrows.

"With *words*," I clarified, my ears burning.

The sense of power surrounding the Witch Lords was less palpable and oppressive here, where they were spread out across the gardens in the open air, so it was less frightening to approach them. Zaira bantered some more with the Fox Lord, trying to coax him into an alliance with the Empire; I had a polite exchange with my great-uncle the Aspen Lord, in which I discovered he was quite firmly remaining neutral, following his mother's lead. The Lady of Thorns kept staring murder at me across the garden, until I half expected to break out in a nosebleed from her pure hatred alone. And Kathe had a long talk with the Holly Lord, a well-muscled and young-looking man who seemed to be dressed mostly in elaborate tattoos and a crown of dark leaves with red berries. I found it hard to look away from those two.

I spoke to the Lady of Lynxes, a slip of silken grace with cropped hair and fierce eyes who barely came up to my shoulder, by a trellis shrouded with drooping purple blooms.

"I've heard you're also seeking a domain for your heir," I said, after managing to keep my smile through introductory pleasantries while feeling rather like a mouse being sized up for dinner, The Lady of Lynxes' intense, predatory presence was alarming, far out of proportion to her size. "That must be a tricky situation, when your domain is surrounded by fellow Witch Lords."

The Lady of Lynxes walked a blue stone between her fingers,

then up over the backs of her knuckles. "I need two domains, as it happens. One for my wife, and one for our daughter."

"Even more difficult, then," I said sympathetically.

"Hardly." The Lady of Lynxes flicked the stone into the air; it spun end over end, until she caught it with a snap. "They're both strong enough to be Witch Lords. My daughter is a monster." She grinned proudly, showing teeth sharpened to a point. "And Sevaeth is big enough to make two domains."

"You have your eye on Sevaeth then?" I asked. "Does the Lady of Thorns know that?"

"Oh, yes. She's not fond of me. But she hates you even more."

"It seems that we might benefit from an alliance, then," I suggested. "If we both are enemies of Sevaeth."

The Lady of Lynxes opened her hand; her palm was empty, the stone vanished. "I hunt alone. When you're done fighting each other, she'll be weak, and easy prey. That's when I'll strike."

"So you're staying out of the war, then?"

"Not at all." She chuckled. "I'm lighting a candle for it. If they don't get enough backing, they might not go to war, and then she won't be weakened. I want a nice, even fight, long and drawn out, with heavy casualties."

"Charming," I murmured.

So much for the Lady of Lynxes. At least the Lady of Thorns knew she was a threat and would likely hold some strength in reserve to deal with the inevitable attack from the north. Still, it was hard not to feel a growing anxiety. I had yet to definitively convince anyone against the war, and the burden of the trust the Empire had placed in me pressed heavier on me with each polite refusal.

Mount Whitecrown loomed above the castle as a constant reminder of the consequences of failure, its glaciers scraping the sky. Every few minutes, it released another innocent puff of steam to float off southward, casting a wisp of ominous shadow over the Empire.

I looked about for Zaira and spotted her sitting alone in the grass near a row of tall bushes, plaiting flower stems together. I started over, annoyed—How could she sit there daydreaming at a time like this? But she gave me an intent stare as I approached, though her fingers kept idly fiddling with the flowers, and I realized several things at once.

Zaira had grown up in Raverra, where space enough for a garden was a luxury reserved for the rich. There was no way she knew how to make flower chains. Nor was she the type of person to sit alone at a social gathering playing with plants.

She was up to something.

I closed my lips on the greeting I'd been about to call out and approached more quietly, settling down beside her. She gave me a pleasant nod, but whispered through her teeth, "There. Through the gap in the bushes."

The dense line of slender evergreen shrubs walled off a small, private garden; I glimpsed a fountain and beds of orchids beyond. The Lady of Thorns and her daughter sat on the edge of the fountain: the latter bent and wasted, shoulders drooping with exhaustion or illness, and the former fresh as a spring daisy, her arm protectively around her elderly heir.

Ruven stood talking with them. They were too far away for me to hear what he said, but I could see him gesturing expansively as he took a cup of tea from an offering servant.

"Something's wrong," Zaira said softly, without moving her lips. "Look how Ruven's standing. He's ready to—*ah*."

Ruven's gesturing hand dipped, quick as a striking snake, to seize the servant's wrist. The man froze in midcringe.

I shifted uncomfortably. "We should help him."

"The only way to help the poor bastards working here is to

get them out of Kazerath. You tell Ruven to stop now, and he'll torture him more just to spite you."

The servant didn't seem hurt, simply immobile. Still holding his wrist, Ruven extended a hand to the Lady of Thorns' daughter, with a genteel flourish as if he were offering to help her into a boat. She put her gnarled, trembling hand in his, her eyes down on her lap.

The servant remained frozen halfway through an uncertain bow. He didn't move, didn't make a sound—but something changed. His pose became unnatural, somehow—he held that shape not because it was his own, but because it contained him, like paper dolls crumpled up and stuffed into a bottle.

The Lady of Thorns looked away, her lip curling in disgust.

I rose. Zaira caught my arm. "What are you doing?" she hissed.

"We should stop him. Distract him, or—"

Zaira shook her head grimly. "It's too late."

Ruven released the man, and he collapsed to the ground. By the way he fell, limp and loose as a bag of sticks, I knew he was dead.

"Hells," I whispered, shaken. "Why did he do that?"

"Look at that bloody-handed crone," Zaira growled softly.

The Lady of Thorns' daughter moved less stiffly as she released Ruven's hand. More color bloomed in her cheeks. She was no less old, but she wore her extreme age more gracefully, as if it weighed on her less.

Her mother smoothed her thin white hair and spoke to Ruven, the diffidence of her posture conveying gratitude.

Ruven snapped his fingers at someone I couldn't see, and a servant girl emerged, lips pressed tight together. She picked up the dead man's feet, averting her face, and began dragging the corpse toward an unobtrusive side door into the castle. She moved without hesitation, as if she'd done this before.

"He's feeding her lives," I breathed. "To keep her from dying of sheer old age. That's the hold he has over the Lady of Thorns. He's the only one who can do it, because he's a Skinwitch."

Ruven made a florid gesture that ended with his palm up, as if he expected something. The Lady of Thorns dropped a handful of blue stones into it, gave Ruven a deep bow, and turned to lift her daughter to her feet.

We hurried to put a stretch of green lawn between us and Ruven before he emerged from his secluded nook. But that space was an illusion; he was in the grass under our feet, the looming shadowy pines beyond the gardens, the sickly-sweet purple flowers that bloomed unseasonably all around us. He could blink an eye and wither every one, then make them blossom again.

"I wish we could get the entire population safely out of Kazerath, somehow," I muttered to Zaira.

"I know a simpler way to free them from Ruven." She flexed her fingers into claws.

I spotted the Elk Lord pausing by a bowl of blue stones, the great spread of his antlered crown dipping as he selected a few. I'd been waiting for him to be alone all morning.

"I should talk to him," I muttered nervously.

"You do that. I'm going to go see what that brat is up to." Zaira tipped her chin toward a stone terrace that looked out over the gardens. The red-haired boy stood at an easel, painting.

"Ruven's willing alchemist," I breathed. "We can't let him keep making that horrible potion. If we can talk him out of it somehow..."

"I'll let you know it goes," Zaira said. "Good luck with old branches-for-brains."

Zaira headed for the terrace, leaving me to approach the Elk Lord on my own.

I took a deep breath and strode toward him. He watched me come with eyes knowing as the night sky, gleaming from a deep brown face carved into stark lines of wisdom. It was hard to push through the thickening cloud of power around him to get closer; he was old, older than the tall pines girdling the hill, and his quiet presence made me feel an urge to stop and put down roots like a tree.

When I'd drawn close enough for conversation, I bowed. "My lord. Amalia Cornaro, of the Serene Empire. I'm honored to meet you."

He regarded me impassively. "No one from your Empire has attended a Conclave before. You bring change on the wind of a crow's wingbeats."

I suspected that was exactly Kathe's hope. But without knowing how the Elk Lord felt about change, I merely smiled. "Some changes are more dangerous than others. Such as the upheaval of war."

"War." The Elk Lord sighed, and gazed out toward the mountains. "When you are as old as I am, Lady Amalia, you gain a perspective on the patterns of history. They unfold as clearly before you as the rhythms of conversation. War is not change. Not in Vaskandar."

"I may lack your years of experience, but I am a student of history," I said. "I know of Vaskandar's cycle of violent expansion."

"Then perhaps you can see the problem that makes conflict with your Empire inevitable." The long folds of his embroidered leather robe stirred as he began to walk. I scrambled to stay at his side; his legs must have come up to the bottom of my rib cage, given how his casual stroll outpaced me. "We have run up against the Witchwall Mountains like a rising flood against a seawall. The peace cannot hold. The Witch Lords must either fight you or each other."

"Surely there must be some other solution. War hurts us all."

"Not while we have would-be Witch Lords hungering for domains and immortality." The Elk Lord shook his head, the great span of his antlers sweeping the air. "No, as much as I find it distasteful to back a Skinwitch, we must have this war."

I leaped on the opening. "But if war is a part of Vaskandar's natural cycle, isn't a Skinwitch a greater threat to stability? You've never had a Skinwitch ruling a domain before."

"That's true," he conceded. "I will admit to some concern. The Skin Lord of Kazerath could become a problem."

"He's planning to trigger an eruption in Mount Whitecrown, to spread his influence with its ashes," I pressed. "That certainly tampers with the order of things."

"We reshape the land all the time. A few ashes will not be enough to affect the blooded claims of other Witch Lords." The Elk Lord frowned. "This is a matter of some concern in that it shows his recklessness, however."

"Can you truly justify using your substantial power and influence to support one such as he?" I spread my hands, trying to match his philosophical demeanor. "What may come of it?"

The Elk Lord stopped. He turned to look down at me, and the weight of his gaze fell on me like a mountain, ancient and uncaring. "What he does is counter to the workings of nature," he said. "He is like a mad creature that eats its own filth. But whether he poses a threat to any but his own people remains to be seen."

"If you know him at all, you know he will."

"I do not know him," the Elk Lord said. "Nor do I care to." He returned his gaze to the mountains, in a clear dismissal. "If he oversteps himself, we will take care of him then. We do not require assistance from the Serene City."

I bowed, biting back my frustration. "Then I hope you deal with him handily when the time comes."

I stomped off, grinding my teeth. I wasn't making nearly enough progress. But then, my mother always said the doge never admitted it when you changed his mind—he wouldn't concede a single point but later would repeat the ones you'd made to him as if he'd always held that opinion. Like as not the Witch Lords, as fellow rulers, were the same.

"Ah, Lady Amalia," a familiar voice purred, far too close. "I hope you are enjoying your stay in my home."

I whirled and found Ruven at my elbow. Now that I faced him, his presence was so strong it nearly choked me, pressing poisonously on everything around him. From his cruel smile to his sleek blond ponytail, every inch of him radiated an absolute assurance of dominion.

"I prefer your hospitality this time," I managed.

He chuckled. "It pleases me to hear you prefer Kazerath when it is mine."

That wasn't what I'd meant, but I seized on the opportunity. "You do have your own domain, now," I observed. "So surely you have no further reason to seek war with the Serene Empire."

"Ah, my lady, you know me better than that. I am not a man of such small ambitions." He reached out a hand, idly; a servant passing a tray of tiny apple cakes veered from his course, eyes wide with alarm at his silent summons, and presented it to his master. Ruven selected one, then waved the servant on his way.

My shoulders unlocked; I'd been afraid he'd called the man over to do something terrible to him, just to make me uneasy. By the gleam I caught in Ruven's eye, he knew it.

"Consider this," Ruven suggested, turning the tiny plate on which the apple cake sat in his fingers. "When I was a young boy, and it first became apparent that I was a Skinwitch, my own late father wanted to put me down, as he worded it, like a mad dog."

I winced. I wasn't sure what was worse; that the Wolf Lord had said such a thing, or that I couldn't help but feel his instincts might have been correct. "That's terrible."

"Oh, I do not tell you this for your sympathy. What need

have I for that?" Ruven shook his head. "You miss the point, my lady. I am surrounded by sixteen powerful peers who are only waiting to see if I can be useful or if I must be destroyed."

"You don't seem the type to make himself useful," I hazarded.

Ruven dropped the uneaten apple cake on the grass and ground it under his boot. "No," he said. "I am not."

"So you want power enough that they can't threaten you." I couldn't keep a thin thread of contempt from my voice. "You're doing all this because you're afraid."

The ground shifted and groaned beneath my feet, as if it might swallow me up. The sense of pressure in the air increased until I could hardly breathe. Something in the forest let out a howl that sounded disturbingly human.

Ruven smiled, his violet-ringed eyes full of death. A sliver of black ice slipped down the back of my neck. He was going to kill me right here—or worse, melt the flesh from my bones and leave me grotesquely alive. I'd made a terrible mistake.

"We all dwell in fear, Lady Amalia." His voice was soft, caressing, but it resonated through my bones. "It is not an enemy, but a teacher. You would do well to learn its lesson."

Then the weight of his power was gone, as suddenly as if it had never been. Ruven, smiling, offered me a courteous bow. "Enjoy the rest of the Conclave."

I stared after him as he moved off to talk to the Serpent Lord. My hand slipped into my pocket, my fingers closing around Marcello's button.

"The Hell of Madness itself has nothing on that man's mind," I whispered to it.

Chapter Thirty-Six

Not long after my talk with Ruven, Kathe sauntered up and offered me a glass of wine. "I saw this going past and thought you might like a reprieve from beer," he said.

His lips quirked in a smile, and I found myself staring at them; suddenly all I could remember was our kiss. Like swallowing liquid lightning. I took the glass from him with a grateful nod, hoping he couldn't tell what I was thinking.

"Thank you." My ring remained dark; I took a sip of the full-bodied red wine, chasing the taste of his lips from my memory. "I could use a drink. Your fellow Witch Lords are difficult to sway."

"Try offering a trade deal to the Lady of Gulls," he suggested. "She'd love to see more Raverran ships stopping by her island."

"I will. Thanks." I sighed, rubbing my tense neck.

He shifted closer to me, his feathered shoulders rustling. "I won't be able to help you publicly as much as I'd like," he said in a low, sober voice. "I'm working on something, and I need Ruven's allies to be willing to talk to me. But I want you to know that's all a game; I do support you here."

I raised a brow. "I thought your support for me was a game as well?"

He laughed. "Some games I play for fun. Others I play to win."

"And which one is our courtship?" I asked, with my best approximation of a teasing smile. I found myself unexpectedly invested in the answer.

"Both, of course." He raised his eyebrows. "Now, if you'll excuse me, I need to put some ideas in the Lady of Laurels' head for later."

Feeling greatly daring, I offered him my hand. With languorous care, he lifted it to his lips; his eyes never left mine, the vivid yellow circles of his mage mark burning into me. After the kiss we'd shared, the touch of his mouth on the backs of my fingers seemed to light up every nerve in my body.

He released my hand with a roguish smile. "When the Conclave is over, you and I must take some time to court properly, without matters of war and death distracting us."

"If we have no matters of war and death distracting us after the Conclave," I said, "I will be pleasantly surprised."

Kathe laughed and offered me a parting bow, cloak swirling. "Then perhaps I'll have to work on becoming even more distracting than death."

I watched him go, admiring the easy grace of his stride. He was well on his way.

But I still couldn't be sure what he was up to. Not knowing what other games Kathe was playing could prove a disadvantage at best, and dangerous at worst.

"He's pretty, but he's no good for you," said a fluid voice near my ear.

I turned, my mouth dry, to face the Lady of Spiders. Gold-legged spiders with ruby abdomens formed an elaborate net in her hair, webs strung between them in lacelike patterns. The spiders on her bodice wove an ever-moving knotwork design, clambering over and under each other with horrifying precision.

I let out a high, nervous laugh and backed up a step. "Perhaps, my lady."

"Have you considered my offer? There is much I could give you in return." She fingered the silver strands of her hair. Fat, jewel-hued spiders crawled out of it and lined up along her knuckles, like rings. "His secrets. Ruven's secrets. The Lady of Thorns' secrets. Sooner or later, I learn what each and every one of them holds coiled inside."

That might even be worth it. The thought sent horror walking with eight legs down my spine.

But then I thought of everything she might learn in return. My dependence on the elixir I needed to survive. All the spy codes and signals my mother was teaching me, and the secrets I'd heard attending sessions of the Council of Nine. My shameful fear that I hadn't earned my admission to the University of Ardence as a scholar but been handed it as a Cornaro. The pure, breaking terror I'd felt at being locked in the close, stifling darkness of a coffin.

I swallowed. "Ah, I'm afraid I will have to decline."

The Lady of Spiders smiled, and it was a terrible, knowing smile. Whatever secrets lay behind her eyes had left them dead and wise and full of crawling shadows.

"For now," she said, her voice deep and oddly lulling. "There will come a day when you need something, Amalia Cornaro. When you need it so desperately, you are willing to pay my price. And then you will come to me."

I tried to smile, but I couldn't manage it. I could only stare at her.

"Until then. I look forward to it."

She passed on her way, trailing a writhing gossamer train. I downed the rest of my wine in three long gulps.

I found Zaira still on the terrace, facing off with the red-haired boy, her hands on her hips. He scowled at her and clenched his paintbrush as if it were a weapon.

"So you don't care that he uses the potions you make to enslave your fellow mages?" Zaira demanded of him.

The boy threw his hands up. "I don't make it anymore! That old lady does. And I don't see what the fuss is. They should be *thankful* to Lord Ruven. He saved them from the Mews."

"That's like saying you saved someone from a bad marriage by feeding them to a shark!"

I paused at the edge of the terrace, entirely uncertain of how to join such a volatile conversation. They didn't seem to notice or care that I was there.

The boy stepped toward Zaira, more aggressively than I would have recommended. "Don't you speak ill of Lord Ruven! He treats me like a prince. The Falconers are monsters. They tried to take me from my home, and when Lord Ruven sent people to rescue me, a Falconer *shot* at me!" He brandished his paintbrush at her. "He would have killed me if Lord Ruven hadn't saved me!"

Hells. I knew who this boy was.

"Emmand," I blurted. The child Marcello had failed to save, four years ago. The one the assassin had kidnapped.

He turned at the sound of his name. "Who are you?" he snapped.

"Someone who knows the truth." I came closer, holding out my hand. "Emmand, the Falconer was trying to save you. He wasn't shooting at you; he was shooting at your captors. The people who 'rescued' you sold you to Ruven for dream poppies."

"I know what really happened," Emmand scoffed. "I was there."

"They killed your parents."

Emmand went still. "They did not. My parents sent me to Lord Ruven to protect me from the Falconers."

"Who told you that?" Zaira's voice oozed cynicism. "The kidnappers? When you asked where your parents were, after they murdered them?"

The boy threw his paintbrush down on the hard stone of the terrace. "That's not what happened! Lord Ruven is my patron. He's only giving the others the potion temporarily, until they see reason and stop trying to rush back into captivity. Then he'll help them find good homes, like he did with the others."

The others. I exchanged glances with Zaira, remembering what Selas had said.

Zaira let out an exasperated sigh. "Brat, you're living in a world less real than that painting. Ruven is a lying bag of pig vomit, and you've eaten up everything he fed you."

"Don't you dare speak ill of him!" The boy quivered with rage. "Go away and leave me alone! I want to paint in peace."

"Fine." Zaira turned from him with a contemptuous swirl of skirts. "You keep poisoning good people for the man who had your parents killed, if that makes you happy. I don't waste time talking to bridge posts, either, and they at least listen better than you."

I fell in by her side. "This has not been my day for convincing people," I murmured.

"That's human nature. You can warn a brat not to stick his hand in the fire, but he still has to try it himself and get burned." Zaira kicked a loose bit of shale down the terrace steps. "What's next?"

I glanced around the gardens as we descended to the grass. Everyone was absorbed in deep discussions; no one was paying any attention to us. There was at least one vital thing we could accomplish today.

"We go find that control circle," I said. "It's time to put an end to Ruven's volcanic ambitions."

The map Namira had sketched for us showed the control circle at the crest of the next hill toward Mount Whitecrown; a saddle-shaped ridge connected it to the hill upon which the castle sat. A path at the edge of the gardens led off into the pines in the direction of the ridge. At the beginning of the path stood a knee-high Truce Stone, its designs worn with age, the hollow in the top stained with fresh blood.

We waited until Ruven was busy talking to the Yew Lord; distracted and with the power of sixteen other Witch Lords around him overwhelming his magical senses, it seemed unlikely he would detect two mere mortals wandering astray in his domain. Zaira checked thoroughly to make sure no one was watching us, and then we stepped beneath the trees.

The cold, shadowy air beneath their boughs immediately swallowed the murmur of conversations behind us. The scents of fresh pine and decaying leaves overwhelmed the perfume of the purple flowers in which Ruven's mother had shrouded their family castle. A squirrel scolded us from a bare, gray tree branch, and I heard water flowing somewhere. The oppressive, expectant atmosphere I'd come to expect from the Vaskandran forest was muted—perhaps because Ruven's attention was focused elsewhere.

Our boots crunched in the inch of snow on the trail. There was no way to avoid leaving footprints. We'd have to hope the Conclave kept Ruven too busy to come wandering down this path.

"Hells take this whole country," Zaira grumbled. "I can't wait to get back to Raverra, where there are about six trees altogether, none of which are trying to murder me."

"And where people want simple things, like money and political influence, not immortality or magical dominion," I agreed.

Zaira shrugged. "That doesn't bother me as much. Power is power, and that's what all these bastards want in the end."

I supposed that was true. Even Kathe—and my mother. "It's what they want the power *for* that makes the difference," I said.

Zaira shook her head. "I don't give a flea's tiny bollocks what lofty reason someone has for wanting power. What matters is how they use it. That bitch back in Ardence—Savony, the old duke's steward—wanted it for the sake of her city, and the Lady of Thorns wants it to save her dear sweet daughter; and either of them would climb over a mountain of corpses to get it. I'll take a principled rogue over a ruthless idealist any day."

"You have a point," I conceded. "But still—What's that smell?"

A sharp odor came and went on the wind, faint with distance or time, but still pungent enough to wrinkle my nose. I couldn't make out if it was decay, animal musk, or some combination.

"Death." Zaira's mouth set in a grim line. "Over there."

She jerked her chin ahead, to where a steep bluff beside the path fell down perhaps thirty feet into a wooded gulley. The wind shifted, and I caught a whiff of the unpleasant scent again.

"Come on." Zaira held her sleeve across her nose and drew her dagger. "Let's take a look."

We crept cautiously to the edge of the dropoff. Lichen-crusted rock fell away below us to a large patch of barren ground where heavy animal traffic had beaten down anything that might have tried to grow there. Game trails cut thin, converging lines through the white-floored woods to this spot, and paw-prints churned up the thin coating of snow into muddy slush.

Directly below us lay a scattered pile of well-gnawed human bones.

Some were newer, still held together by enough lingering scraps of sinew to be called a carcass. The shredded remnants of clothing still clung to these skeletons, or lay in faded tatters, trampled into the mud. But all the meat was off their bones, even their faces gnawed away; the wolves had taken the good parts.

"Grace of Mercy!" I recoiled from the charnel pit, grabbing Zaira's arm.

"Ruven's dumping ground." Zaira shook me off and crouched by the edge, staring down. "No doubt that servant we saw him kill will wind up here soon enough."

I steeled myself to creep closer and take a second look. "There must be dozens of bodies down there." If you could call them bodies at this point.

"And some of them were children." Zaira jammed the words through her teeth. "That rotting piece of demon dung."

She was right. A few of the oldest-looking bones were too small to have belonged to adults. My stomach clenched against a heave.

They all eventually displeased him, Selas had said.

"Graces rest their souls," I breathed. "They must be the other mage children Orthys sold him. From before he had the potion. The ones who refused to obey."

Zaira's breath hissed in. I expected a barrage of fluent cursing, but she stood and whirled to face back along the path.

"Going for a walk in the woods?" she demanded.

I rose and turned, more slowly. The Lady of Thorns advanced toward us, her gown running eerily silent along the snow, as if she'd told the ground itself to make no noise. Her lips curved into a smile in her too-young face, her eyes narrowing to dangerous venom-green gleams.

"How convenient," she purred. "Ruven won't need to bother himself to remove the body."

Chapter Thirty-Seven

I loosened one of Istrella's rings: left index finger, for defense against magic.

"The rules of the Conclave forbid harming invited guests," I pointed out, forcing more confidence into my voice than I felt.

The Lady of Thorns raised her eyebrows. "But we are no longer at the Conclave. Didn't you see the Truce Stone? Those rules don't protect you once you stray past their bounds."

She laid her hand casually on a tree trunk. A new branch shot out of it, sharp as a spear and bristling with thorns, straight at me.

I ripped off Istrella's ring and threw it.

It bounced off the branch in a shower of sparks; the thorny spear stopped as if it had struck a wall. The last few feet of it splintered and fell to the ground, unable to hold together without vivomancy to sustain its unnatural growth.

The ring lay shining in a pile of kindling shards, expended. I had six left.

"You're making a mistake." I couldn't keep my voice even. My blood raced in my veins like the tide rushing in through a ship's cracked hull. "If you kill me, there will be consequences."

The Lady of Thorns sneered dismissively. "I'll owe the Crow Lord another grievance. It's worth it to see a Lochaver dead.

Your Empire cannot reach here, little fool, and nothing else protects you."

Zaira stepped forward. "Excuse me, Lady Itchweed. Your mind's gone soft as the free porridge at the Temple of Bounty if you think there's no one standing right here who can stop you."

"You?" Genuine surprise widened the Lady of Thorns' eyes. "You would defend this common insect who dares to chain your power? I'd expect you to thank me for killing her."

"It so happens," Zaira said, "she's my friend."

The words kindled a warmth and light in me bright as balefire. I would have battled all the chimeras in Vaskandar for her with my bare hands in that moment.

"Thanks," I murmured.

Zaira shot me a sideways glance. "Ugh. Don't let it go to your head."

The Lady of Thorns grimaced with revulsion. "Please, spare me the sentiment. The powerless can be pets at best. Very well; I'll pay you a grievance, too."

She touched another tree. This time, a shower of dry leaves flew off it at me, edges gleaming razor-sharp. I flinched away, raising my arms to protect my face.

Heat blasted me as the whole cloud of leaves burst into blue flame in midair. Sparks of balefire rained down to the ground mixed with ash. I caught myself before stepping away; the edge was at my back, with nothing but a long tumble down to the pile of bones below.

Tiny lightning-pale flames leaped up from where the sparks had fallen. Zaira grinned. Blue fire flickered deep within her eyes.

"I killed the Wolf Lord in his own domain," she said. "Last I checked, this isn't Sevaeth. Want to try me?"

"You wouldn't dare." But she took a step away from Zaira.

"You killed the Wolf Lord because he underestimated you. Since then, every Witch Lord in Vaskandar has been planning how to thwart your balefire if necessary. I'm no arrogant fool who will insist I could defeat you easily—but I assure you, it would be trivial to kill your so-called *friend* before you could destroy me."

I took her point all too well. I'd nearly wound up a casualty in Zaira's battle with the Wolf Lord, and neither of them had been trying to hurt me. I loosened another ring, fingers fumbling with desperation; this one Istrella had told me I should throw at an enemy when I needed to get away from them.

"Threatening each other solves nothing," I said, trying not to let fear crack the foundations of my voice. "We all have goals to accomplish at the Conclave, and all of us cast away our chance to accomplish those goals if we start a fight now. Do you really want to risk your daughter's future over a petty grudge, Lady of Sevaeth?"

The Lady of Thorns gave me an assessing stare. The full force of her presence hit me, all wasp venom and the too-strong scent of violets, and my knees wavered.

"Yes," she said slowly. "We do have a great deal at stake, and much to accomplish. And what, precisely, were *you* trying to do, out here in the forest while everyone else was at the Reckoning?"

Hells. Ruven had included the Lady of Thorns in his volcano scheme; she might be well aware of where this path led. I couldn't let her know we knew about the control circle. Then they could find a way to stop us from destroying it—and worse, they might realize we'd freed the captured Falcons from Ruven's dominion.

"To uncover Ruven's treachery." I flung an arm dramatically at the boneyard below us. "Now we know his true measure. The other Witch Lords may not be so eager to ally with him when they know he's a murderer."

The Lady of Thorns laughed. "Is that all? Oh, you silly child.

Everyone knows he's a murderer. No one cares. He may do what he likes in his own domain." She shook her head. "Run back under the wings of your Crow Lord, little Lochaver. Everything you do here is a waste of time. And when the Conclave is complete, and I have what I want, I will wring the life from you and bend your bones into a crown for my daughter."

She gestured down the path toward the castle, dismissal in the contemptuous line of her arm. I couldn't help but notice that she angled her body to block the path onward toward the control circle.

I exchanged a look with Zaira. She shrugged minutely, the blue spark extinguished in her eyes. There was no point pushing this now; we could try to destroy the circle again later.

"Very well," I said. "We'll see, when the Kindling is done and the candles counted, whether what I do here is worthless."

Zaira closed her hand into a fist, and the balefire licking and spreading up from where the sparks had fallen winked out. She made it look effortless, but I saw how the skin next to her eyes tightened. She'd been struggling to keep it under control all this time.

"Glad you decided not to open the gates of the Hell of Death today," she said. "But if you change your mind, I'm standing right here with the key."

We started back down the path toward the castle together. My back itched and crawled with the knowledge that the Lady of Thorns had a clear shot at it, long after we left her out of sight.

When we emerged onto the manicured lawn, with the castle's dark claws looming above us, we found Kathe waiting for us. He'd been lounging against a slim ornamental tree, watching the path, but straightened when we stepped out of the forest.

"You seem to have survived," he observed.

Zaira glared at him. "You knew the Lady of Thorns went in there after us."

Kathe shrugged. "I assumed she hadn't just taken a fancy to go for a walk in the woods."

"Weren't you worried she'd kill your sweetheart?"

Kathe spread his hands. "Here I am, waiting to make sure all turned out well! But you didn't need me. I'm not surprised. You are far more dangerous than I am, Lady Zaira."

Zaira gave him a long look. "I'm not so sure about that."

"I'm honored." Kathe bowed. "Now if you'll excuse me, I don't want the Lady of Thorns to see that I was waiting here for you. And I recommend you not place yourselves in her path again, either."

He winked at me, then strolled back toward more populated areas of the gardens, whistling.

Zaira grabbed my arm and tugged. "Come on. He has a point."

"I feel a bit better knowing he was watching for us," I said as we walked.

"Are you stupid?" Zaira stared at me, incredulous. "How do you think the Lady of Thorns knew where we were?"

"I assume she saw us go into the woods."

Zaira shook her head. "No one saw us. I was careful."

"Then perhaps she saw our footprints. How should I know?"

Zaira jabbed a finger into my chest, rattling the claws at my throat. "Your crow friend always knows where you are, because of this little trinket. Remember? *He* told her."

"Or Ruven did," I pointed out. "This is his domain. Perhaps I was wrong, and he could feel us moving around in it after all."

"If Ruven knew you were heading for his precious control circle, he'd have showed up himself. Why are you defending that feathery scoundrel?"

I sighed. "I like him," I admitted.

"You can like someone and still recognize they'd knife you and throw you in a ditch to make a smoother path for their carriage." Zaira shook my shoulder. "We're in a right pit of snakes, here. You can't afford to have a blind spot."

"All right. I'll try to be more wary."

Zaira snorted. "No, you won't. But I'll keep doing it for you."

It was hard to get back to politics when my heart still raced from our encounter with the Lady of Thorns, especially when she returned to the gardens herself a few minutes later. She paid me no mind as she glided among the other Witch Lords, talking and occasionally exchanging colored stones, her train running along the grass behind her like a snake's belly; every now and then her eyes raked across mine, hatred flaring in them even as the rest of her face didn't so much as twitch.

It was unsettling, too, to glimpse Ruven up on the terrace with Emmand, exclaiming delightedly over the boy's painting and patting his head. Emmand stood proudly, gazing up at Ruven with worship in the tilt of his chin, gesturing with his brush at the mountains he'd been painting and talking with obvious excitement. Could he truly not know that all the other children Ruven had "rescued" lay in a charnel pit so close by, nothing but cracked and scattered bones?

I did my best to convince various Witch Lords of the benefits of keeping cordial relations with the Serene Empire and the perils of siding with Ruven. Zaira worked the gathering separately, in her own way, flirting and joking with the Fox Lord and the Lady of Otters and anyone else who seemed willing to be charmed. They accorded her a certain respect, as a mage-marked warlock; many of the Witch Lords seemed willing to engage with her as an equal in a way they wouldn't with me.

None of it seemed to be enough. The tide was coming for the Serene Empire, and I was trying to shift it by moving pebbles.

Near the end of the Reckoning, as the sun slipped behind the mountains and cast the gardens into gray and violet shadows,

Kathe came and slipped his arm through mine. A grin pulled at his lips. His warmth along my side felt entirely too enjoyable; I entertained the notion of pulling him closer.

"How goes it?" he asked. "Are you making progress?"

"I can't tell," I said reluctantly. "No one will commit to anything. I've dangled all sorts of bait that should be enticing, like preferential trade deals and custom artifice devices, but all anyone will say is that they'll consider it." I couldn't help but feel the Council had been wrong to place its faith in me; my mother would have had half of them sworn allies of Raverra by now.

"When you're a hundred years old with the weight of mountains and forests behind you, I suppose you don't like to be rushed." Kathe scooped a few blue stones out of a bowl as we passed. "I find it gives an advantage to those of us willing to be more nimble."

"What about you? Have you accomplished what you hoped?" Perhaps I could lead him into divulging a little more about his plans.

Kathe stopped and faced me. We stood beneath a slender tree with spreading branches heavy with unseasonable flowers; the breeze shook petals down like intermittent flurries of snow. In the dusky light, Kathe's mage mark gleamed yellow like a cat's eyes.

"I have an idea," he said. "I'll tell you what I'm trying to accomplish here if you tell me the same. One goal at a time, in even trade."

I raised an eyebrow. "Another game?"

"Of course." He tossed and caught his handful of blue stones. "Society is so full of rules. We may as well make it a game whenever we can."

"All right, then," I agreed.

"I'll go first, since I'm a generous fellow." He inclined his head modestly. I laughed, and he returned a wicked grin. "I'm here to collect favors and show everyone how useful I can be, to build my power base for the future."

I'd seen my mother do the same, many times. "That's the tactic of someone who either has few resources and needs to gather them, or is already in a position of advantage and is consolidating to make themself unassailable," I noted.

"How perceptive!" He widened his eyes. "I wonder which it could be?"

I had my suspicions. "You love it when the others underestimate you, don't you?"

"My lady, you see far too clearly." He sighed. "I must practice longer before I dance with a Raverran. But it's your turn."

"Very well," I said. "One of my main goals is to attempt to strip backing from Ruven and the Lady of Thorns so they go into this war with as few allies and as many enemies as possible, of course."

"And a goal of mine is to support you, naturally—mostly because I like the idea of the Lady of Thorns being without allies," he confessed. "I'm collecting favors from her and piling up grievances against her, both for myself and for others. She has very little influence with the other Witch Lords at the moment, and a great deal of debt. Partly due to her own reckless desperation to protect her daughter from the ravages of time, and partly due to my efforts."

"Well, thank you," I said.

"I didn't do it for you." Kathe pocketed his blue stones and spread his empty hand. "I should let you think I did, so you'd owe me a favor. But honesty is the basis of any successful courtship, is it not?"

"Of course." I put irony in my voice to match his.

"Your turn, my lady. I'm sure you have more than one objective at the Conclave." He grinned at me. A falling petal caught in his black-tipped hair.

My other major goal was to rescue the captured Falcons. If I told Kathe, he could be instrumental in helping us; having a Witch Lord for an ally would make it much easier to sneak them out of the castle and safely to the border. But he'd made it clear that information was the currency with which he intended to make his fortune, and his quarrel was with the Lady of Thorns, not Ruven. If he betrayed us, Terika and the others might join the pile of bones in the forest.

He'd told us himself not to trust him.

Hells take it. I was already trusting him by coming here as his guest. All he had to do was withdraw his protection to leave Zaira and me in a terrible spot.

"Ruven is using a combination of alchemy and vivomancy to control a handful of captured Falcons against their will," I said. "I'm here to free them."

Kathe raised an eyebrow. "To free them, or to take them back into the Empire's captivity?"

I winced at the question. Lord Caulin's order gave me no room for interpretation, and neither did the Serene Accords. My duty to the Empire was clear. To allow a Falcon to fall into the hands of an enemy nation went against the very heart of the order the Serene Empire had built, undermining the strength by which it protected the peace of Eruvia. I knew what the doge would command me, even without Lord Caulin's poison weighing down my conscience: to do everything I could to bring back the missing Falcons. And I suspected my mother would advise the same. After all, if I cared about their welfare, the best course would be to pass my Falcon reform act, and my chances of success were higher if I was politically impeccable.

But if I disagreed with my mother on one thing, it was this: there was a time to be wise, and there was a time to stand on principle. And when people's lives and happiness depended directly on my actions in this moment, it was definitely the latter.

"To free them," I said, my voice rough with the weight of the words. "In fact, I wanted to talk to you about that. If any of them want to stay in Vaskandar rather than return to the Mews, would you let them settle in your domain?"

"Of course." He rubbed his hands. "Alchemists and artificers are quite rare in Vaskandar. I'd make them very welcome."

"And would you give them complete freedom?" I asked sharply.

Kathe's expression softened, his brows coming together. "Freedom is an elusive thing, my lady. I'm not sure anyone in Vaskandar, or the Serene Empire for that matter, can be truly free."

"You're evading the question," I accused.

"No, I'm trying to give you an honest answer." He plucked a falling petal out of the air and turned it in his fingers. "Anyone with the mage mark is effectively a noble in Vaskandar. They have status above mages without the mark, who in turn are above those with no magic at all. So your Falcons would be at the highest levels of Vaskandran society. *But*." He let the petal go, and it fluttered to the ground. "After a few years living in Let, eating the food and drinking the water, they would become a part of my domain. I can't prevent that. I'm not a Skinwitch, so I couldn't control or twist them the way Ruven could, but at a fundamental, magical level, they would be mine. And in Vaskandran law and tradition, they would also be mine, to do with as I please." He shrugged. "Is that freedom?"

"I don't know whether it's any more freedom than the Mews offers," I admitted. "But I can at least explain, and give them the choice."

Kathe nodded. "I'll send a message to one of my Heartguard who's stationed nearby, and tell him to be ready to escort your Falcon friends safely to Let under my protection if any choose to remain in Vaskandar."

This went directly counter to the doge's order as Lord Caulin had relayed it, and probably violated the Serene Accords as well. The knowledge of treason settled in my gut like a stone. I could feel my mother's stern gaze on me all the way from Raverra. "Thank you, Kathe."

"Oh, it's my pleasure. As you may have noticed, many Witch Lords would do a great deal to gain a mage-marked alchemist or artificer." He tilted his head. "Which means Ruven will do anything he can to keep them. Do you have a plan for getting them out of the castle?"

"Ah... We're hoping to sneak them out unnoticed," I said, waving a vague hand. No need to let him know about Marcello waiting in position at the border.

Kathe shook his head. "My lady, hope is a terrible basis for such a key move. You are too skilled a player to make such a mistake."

"I hadn't planned out that part yet," I admitted.

"You'll need a plan, and a good one," Kathe said. "Ruven may be new to this, but once you get them away from the background noise of all the Witch Lords at the castle, he'll feel them traveling across his domain. He might not notice right away, but I wouldn't personally want to bet on him not noticing at all. They're important enough that he's bound to be watching them."

"What would you suggest, then?"

Kathe grinned. "Do it during the Kindling."

"The final phase of the Conclave."

"Yes. Even if he knows they're moving, he *can't* leave then, or he forfeits the question of war. He'll be tied up in ceremony and politics, and any response he can manage from afar will be highly distracted."

It made sense. If Ruven even noticed us with the Kindling going on, he'd have to choose between stopping us, or abandoning his war movement and destroying his own credit with his fellow Witch Lords. Either way, we won.

Assuming Kathe was telling the truth. Trusting him was a gamble; but by coming here under his protection, I'd already cast those dice.

"That seems like good advice," I said. "Thanks."

"You'll have to send them alone, or with Zaira." Kathe tapped my breastbone, lightly, just under the hollow of my throat. "You need to be at the Conclave for the Kindling, yourself."

"I do?" That complicated matters.

"Of course. It's when everyone gives their final arguments for and against the question proposed—in this case, going to war with the Empire. You could skip the opening ceremonies, and possibly even the initial lighting of the candles—there will be two pedestals, one for those who will join in the war, and one for those who are opposed to it. Each Witch Lord with a stance in the matter will light a candle and place it on one of the pedestals. Some will leave their candles unlit, staying out of the matter."

It hit me, then, like a falling mountain, that this was real. Tomorrow, the Witch Lords would make their choices, and something so small as a tiny lick of golden fire at the tip of a candle could spell the fate of the Serene Empire. And if Zaira was off on her own perilous mission, leading the Falcons to safety through the night-dark forests of Vaskandar, only I would stand for the Empire in that room of ancient blood-bound power, with no weapon but my words to protect my people.

I fiddled with Marcello's button in my pocket, to give my restless fingers something to do. I would give a lot, right now, for the unwavering faith he seemed to have in me. "Is that when guests can speak?"

"That's during the arguments, which come next after the candle lighting. This is the part you can't risk missing." Kathe clasped my arm, his face serious. "Any Witch Lord or invited guest with a stake in the matter may speak, and anyone may move, snuff, or light their own candle after each speech. Sometimes Witch Lords will place their candles in one spot at the beginning, then move it after a particular speech to show support for the speaker, or to win favors from them."

"So it's a last chance to persuade people."

"The last and most critical chance, yes."

I squeezed Marcello's button so hard it dug painfully into my skin. The idea of getting up in front of seventeen Witch Lords and making a speech was so terrifying I'd almost rather fight them. At least a fight would be over quickly.

But this was what everyone was counting on me to do. My mother and the doge, who had entrusted me with the position of Serene Imperial Envoy; my grandmother and the people of Callamorne, whom I'd told that I stood with them. Domenic and Venasha in Ardence, which lay in the path of a potential eruption of Mount Whitecrown. All the Serene Empire, which had held peace and order in Eruvia for three hundred years and was not ready to fall.

This was why I had been born a Cornaro. To win the day with words, that it need not be won with swords and fire.

I drew myself up and nodded decisively. "Then I'd better give a good speech."

Chapter Thirty-Eight

"We'll have to split up," I told Zaira, back in our room that night.

She stared at me as if I'd gone mad. "Have you noticed we're in an enemy castle with an all-powerful mage who wants to kill you?"

"It had not escaped my attention." I flopped onto the edge of my bed and started pulling off the gold-accented riding boots I'd been wearing all day. "But all the Witch Lords will be busy, and I'll be in the castle under Kathe's eye and within the Truce Stones." And trying to move the ancient, icy hearts of seventeen Witch Lords to mercy, but that was another matter. "If Marcello can get into position in advance to meet you on the road and take them the rest of the way, you may only be gone for a few hours."

"And she can murder you in a few minutes."

"She's not going to kill me in the middle of the Kindling, when they're performing solemn ceremonies and making serious arguments. I'll be fine." If I didn't die from the sheer terror of making my speech. This would be my last chance, my very last chance to prove myself worthy of the Council's trust and save the Empire. "I'm more worried about you, coming back to the castle alone at night through Ruven's forest when he wants you dead."

Zaira shrugged. "So long as the Witch Lords are busy, there's nothing else in this cursed place that can stop me. I can burn a path all the way to the border if I need to."

It was true enough, though that might leave the Falcons she was trying to rescue in more danger than if they stayed in Ruven's clutches. But her control was getting better, and while I wasn't much inclined to gamble where balefire was concerned, I'd lay a wager she'd be twice as good at taming her flames when Terika was nearby.

"Shall I contact Marcello and tell him our plan, then?" I asked.

"It's a terrible plan." Zaira kicked off her own shoes; they flew across the room, one after the other, and thunked into the wall. "But all right. Go ahead."

I went to my trunk and rummaged in the folds and layers of my petticoats. My finger snagged in a silken loop: the drawstring of Lord Caulin's innocuous little velvet bag.

I ignored the dropping feeling in my stomach and pushed it aside. To the Nine Hells with Caulin's order. I was no assassin. Their jesses were off; unless they chose to come home to the Mews, they weren't Falcons anymore.

At the bottom of my trunk, I found the pieces of the device Istrella had made for us out of her limited supplies at Highpass: a haphazard jumble of coiled wire, a serving platter engraved with a runic circle, a musket ramrod wrapped in wire and crystals, and a single chunk of quartz she'd sent soldiers scouring the mountainside to find. I rewound some of the wire, set the quartz at the center of the platter on a table by the window, attached the assembly to the ramrod with more wire, and pointed the ramrod out the window at the mountains. It took some work with a compass to get the angle exactly right.

"I thought courier lamps couldn't work without the relay network," Zaira said, coming over to peer at what I was doing. "If this will work, why do we have those cursed poles all over the Empire with mirrors on them?"

"Without the relay mirrors, courier lamps can only work if they're in direct line of sight," I replied. "You could never send a message farther than you could see a signal fire, so there's not much point. But we worked out a place for Marcello to make his encampment where, in theory, there's a direct sightline from the shoulder of Mount Whitecrown to this castle."

"In theory."

"Well, I suppose we're about to find out."

I tapped the quartz crystal with two fingers. Within it, a spark flared to life.

"Is it working?" Zaira asked.

"It's trying to send, anyway. We'll see in a moment whether Marcello is receiving."

I tapped again and again, sending a simple signal. The spark within the lamp flickered on and off with each tap. If anyone was out in the garden at night, they couldn't help but see it.

For a long time, I waited, staring at the darkened crystal. Then, at last, the light flared within it again, pulsing a single word back: *received*.

Triumph flooded through me. By the gift of the Graces, it had worked. Istrella was amazing. *Marcello?* I tapped out.

Here. Is all well?

Of course he was worried. Dear Marcello. A tender smile curved my lips. *All is well. This is Amalia.*

I tapped out the details of our plan, painstakingly slow. I'd seen my mother's fingers flash on the courier lamps at home, setting the lights to flickering so fast I could hardly read them, but I didn't possess her practiced skill. I had to think about each letter or common combination, remembering the precise pattern of flashes to convey it.

Marcello was even slower; imperial officers had to know the

lamp code, since even without courier lamps it could be used to pass signals with mirrors or lanterns, but he probably hadn't used it often in practice. I had to note each pulse of the lamp to make certain I didn't lose the thread of his halting sentences as he reported that they'd successfully altered all the volcanic artifice circles that they could safely access.

His stumbles and hesitations warmed my heart; they made the flashes of the lamp human. As if somehow, across the miles between us, our fingers touched through this bridge of light.

Be careful, he signaled at the end. *I'm thinking of you.*

I miss you, I sent, my fingertips lingering on the crystal.

When it went dark, I stared out the window into the night for a long time.

It was full night, the castle swathed in wintry darkness, and the Kindling was due to start soon. I'd been running key lines and phrases from my planned speech through my head all day, whispering them under my breath, repeating them in my mind with every step. Time had continued its relentless advance with each muttered syllable, sweeping me closer to the moment when I had to try to save Raverra with my fragile net of words.

I wasn't certain I'd ever dreaded anything more in my life. If I failed to sway my audience, it could mean the end of the Empire.

Finally, the time to make our move arrived, as a hushed and expectant excitement for the Kindling built in the sleepless castle. As all eyes turned to the throne hall, we crept up the winding stairs to the Falcons' tower room.

When we opened the door, we found Terika standing tensely waiting, with no one holding her back. The others stood poised and ready to pounce on either side of her, but no one blocked her line to Zaira.

"So, does this mean you can get close to me without trying to murder me?" Zaira asked.

"I think so?" Terika spread her hands. "I'm not armed, so if I'm wrong, the worst that happens is we have an embarrassing scuffle before these nice people pry me off you."

Zaira approached her cautiously. Terika stood there, beaming. Soon, only a couple of feet separated them.

"About damn time," Zaira said gruffly, and threw her arms around Terika, burying her face in her curly hair.

"Oof!" But Terika squeezed Zaira back just as hard, eyes shining. And then Zaira kissed her, with joyful enthusiasm, while Terika laughed through the kiss.

Namira chuckled. "Very nice, lovebirds, but I'm given to understand we're on a tight schedule."

Zaira made a rude gesture, but Terika grabbed her hand and kissed it, then turned her attention toward the others. She kept Zaira close to her side, though.

I cleared my throat. "Yes, well, the opening ceremonies of the Kindling have begun, and we need to get you all out of the castle as quickly as possible." I scanned the room; everyone was here, from an eager-faced Parona to a determined Lamonte and a frightened-looking Selas. Some of them had small bundles of possessions ready to go at their feet. "We can take you to an imperial military escort that will see you back safely to the Empire, and thence to the Mews. On the way you will be passing by a certain gentleman who can provide safe passage to the domain of Let, under the protection of the Crow Lord, who I incidentally happen to know has promised to host any random traveling mages who show up in his domain and not hold them against their will." I tried to speak casually, but my mouth was dry. This part was treason, plain and simple. "We'll be moving too quickly to spend any time looking for any Falcons who stray from the group at that point, I fear."

Parona gave me a narrow look. "With all respect, Lady Amalia, do you have the permission of the doge or the Council to mention these fascinating details to us?"

"Ah, no." I laughed nervously. "I'm fairly certain they'd disapprove, in fact. But I'm not going to drag any of you back to the Mews against your will."

Parona crossed her arms. "Then nobody mention she made this offer. It never happened. Do you hear?"

The others nodded. Zaira and Terika stood with their arms around each other, grinning.

"There are some things you should know if you're considering not returning to the Mews," I said seriously. *Like the fact that I have a vial of deadly poison meant for you.* But that was one thing I still didn't dare mention. "First of all, if you stay in one domain for long, you'll become a part of it, bound magically to the Witch Lord who rules it. Second, if you're already a Falcon, well, it's against the law." I swallowed. "There are powerful people in Raverra who will be frightened or angry at the idea of a Falcon in Vaskandran hands, and while it shames me to say this, they may take steps to recapture or harm you. I recommend lying low, pretending to be dead. And if you ever choose to come back to the Empire, you may want to have a convincing story ready about how you tried to get back to the Mews but were recaptured or lost."

The Falcons met my gaze with somber faces. One or two nodded their understanding. I still couldn't believe those words had left my mouth. I tucked my hands behind my back to hide their trembling.

"Do any of you plan to go to Let?" I asked. "I don't want to leave anyone behind who doesn't want to be left."

Harrald raised a hand. "If it's all right, my lady, I might like to see what life is like in Let. I've never had a choice before, and I want to explore it, not throw it away."

Grace of Majesty damn me for a traitor. I'd hoped, on some level, they'd all choose the Mews. I swallowed a knot in my throat and nodded. "Very well. Anyone else?"

Selas looked up at Namira. She squeezed his shoulder, encouragingly. He hesitated, then nodded. "I might want to go to the Mews, in the end," he said. "Especially if I can't see my sister in Let. But I don't want to decide yet, and I like the idea of being a noble here. And since I was never a Falcon, I'm not breaking any laws if I stay in Vaskandar for a while, am I?"

I shook my head. "No. You're not. Just remember that if you stay in Let for more than a year or so, you'll become part of the Crow Lord's domain. Hopefully the Graces will smile on me and my law will pass the Assembly, and then you can come back to the Empire and take as long as you need to make your choice."

Lamonte made a skeptical noise, but he nodded. "I'm betting on it. Don't make me regret my gamble, Lady Amalia."

"I'll do everything I can to make it pay off."

"And let us ensure that the Lady Amalia continues to be in a position to put forward this law," Parona said sharply. "So far as any of us are concerned, Harrald became lost from the group as we escaped. None of us know where he went. Are we all clear on this?"

The rest of the Falcons nodded.

"Thank you," I said.

Parona waved a dismissive hand. "We'd wind up in trouble ourselves for letting him go, too. It's common sense to keep this quiet."

"Now, if we're ready," I said, "we should go. We don't have much time."

The dark stairs swallowed us like a chimera's gullet as we groped our way down. I winced at the amount of noise eight people made on the twisting steps. When we stepped out into the dark-ribbed, narrow hallways of the main castle, I blinked in the guttering lamplight.

I could feel the power gathered below us, in the throne hall, all seventeen Witch Lords unfolding their full presence as the ceremonies of the Kindling began. It was like walking across a thin crust of earth over the boiling heart of a volcano. *Please, Grace of Luck, Grace of Mercy, don't let us draw their attention.*

We took a servants' staircase down to the first floor. I could hear muffled voices rising in the throne hall, and the subdued ones of servants from the kitchens. We headed through a whitewashed hallway that led past the kitchens, silently as we could manage, toward the unobtrusive garden door I'd seen the servant drag that poor man's body through the previous day.

A small figure stepped out of the kitchens, a loaf of bread in hand, and froze in front of us. He moved with too much confidence for one of the common folk of the household, and the flickering light of the candle in the nearest wall sconce picked out a bold splash of red in his hair.

Emmand. *Hells.* He was bound to sound the alarm.

He sucked in a gasp. "What are you doing?" he demanded.

Selas stepped forward, gripping Namira's hand. "We're leaving. And you're not going to stop us. Have some decency, Emmand."

"I can't let you make this mistake," Emmand said, drawing himself up. "I'm going to tell Lord Ruven." He sucked in a breath.

"Wait!" Selas made a grabbing motion toward him, desperate. "Listen to us, first! We used to be friends, Emmand." A pleading note entered his voice.

Emmand paused, eyeing Selas warily. "What is there to say? You're being stupid, turning your back on everything Lord Ruven wants to give you."

I ran my thumb across one of Istrella's rings: right middle finger, to incapacitate someone without killing them. But I had no idea if it would be enough to knock Emmand out, or what would happen if I missed. Namira shifted as if she might jump at him, then stopped. The last thing we needed was for him to start screaming and bring all the guards in the castle down on us.

If we could handle this quietly, it would buy us time. And we needed that more than anything, to get the Falcons to the border before Ruven could stop them.

"I understand you're happy here, Emmand," I said, trying to keep my voice gentle, "but they're not. Do you truly want to imprison them against their will?"

He hesitated, clutching the bread so tightly that crumbs showered to the floor. "Lord Ruven wouldn't want me to let you go. He treats me like a prince. Like a son."

"How nice for you," Zaira snapped. "Too bad for those other brats who didn't bow down to him, eh?"

I stared at her in shock. Normally Zaira was surprisingly good with children, gentle for all her gruffness. But her face was taut with anger—outrage on behalf of the ones who had died.

"He found them all good homes," Emmand said stubbornly. "Are you all really so tame you'll go quietly back to the Mews with this Falconer? Lord Ruven knows that the mage-marked are meant to rule, not to serve."

The Graces can't save a fool from believing what he wants to believe, my mother had said once. I shook my head.

Terika and Namira exchanged glances. "I have sleep potion," Terika whispered. "But if I use it on him, I might get some of us, as well."

"No need," Zaira growled. She stepped right up to Emmand, until she stood nearly on his toes; he backed away before her, eyes fearful, but she jabbed a finger into his chest and matched him step for step. "You go into the woods, on the path that leads from the back of the garden. Bring a light, and follow the smell.

You'll find the rotting bones of all those other brats who saw Ruven for what he really is. The only homes he found for them were in a wolf's belly."

"That's not true!" Emmand's face paled, and his voice dropped to a hoarse whisper as he squeezed his loaf of bread to his chest. "Lord Ruven would never do that. Not to someone with the mage mark. Our lives are precious to him!"

"You keep believing that, if you can." Zaira's voice held contempt enough to wither all the purple flowers choking the castle gardens. "Or you can go get one glimpse of the charnel pit in the woods, and know that maggot for the murderous wretch he is. I don't care which. Now get out of our way, brat, or I'll burn you to cinders."

Emmand backed a few steps, staring at Zaira. Then he dropped his bread and fled into the kitchens without another word.

"Come on," Zaira said. "He's bound to call the guards on us."

A deep crease persisted between her brows. As we moved through the corridor, I murmured. "Are you all right?"

"That brat couldn't have started out as such a waste," she muttered. "Ruven did that to him. I've never wanted to smack a kid before, but by the Hells, I was tempted."

We made it to the door and threw it open. The wide night waited beyond, stars shining sharp as glass shards in the black sky above. The air smelled clean and cold, and despite the icy chill of it, for a moment all I wanted was to burst out into the freedom of it with them.

"I should get back to the Conclave," I said, my insides twisting at the thought of what I had to do. "Will you be all right?"

Zaira nodded. "I'll take care of them."

"And I'll take care of her," Terika said, throwing an arm over Zaira's shoulders. Zaira snorted, but Terika added seriously, "If she has trouble keeping control. As I said, I have sleep potion."

I gave her a nod of deep respect.

A hissing wail rose from the forest—an angry, inhuman sound. Pine branches rustled in the wind. Ruven must have noticed his prisoners were gone.

"Keep to the road," I urged Zaira.

"I'm not an idiot." She shooed me off. "Go save the Empire. I'll get these Falcons handed safely off, then come right back to keep you out of trouble, as usual."

They slipped out into the night. Terika squeezed my hand, briefly, in passing. Namira gave me a grave nod. And then they were a cluster of black silhouettes hurrying across the moon-silvered lawn.

Grace of Luck bless them, and let them make it to safety.

I had my own battle to fight. Just me and my carefully curated words, as well as I could utter them with dread seizing my lungs, between the Empire and ruin.

But that had always been my role. I was a Cornaro. Others protected the serenity of the Empire with magic and muskets; we used our minds.

I stepped back into the castle, chin lifted, and went to wage my war.

Chapter Thirty-Nine

When I slipped into the throne hall to stand among the crowd of guests and onlookers at its edge, I found it completely transformed. All my anxiety vanished, drowned in pure wonder.

Delicate vines grew up the inside walls and covered the ceiling; pale, luminous flowers bloomed among them, casting an eerie light. Fireflies danced in the air, and moths fluttered about, wings glowing with pale luminescence. Each Witch Lord must have added some living light to the room as part of the opening ceremonies; mushroom rings sprouted from the marble floor, shedding a faint green glow from under their caps, and lichens spread lovely patterns of light across the ceiling. The Lady of Spiders had kindly contributed a swarm of arachnids to crawl along the walls, each with a gleaming spot on its back in the shape of a skull. The air I drew into my lungs tasted fresh and damp, and the place felt like an enchanted forest.

The only warm light came from the flickering pillar candles at two of three pedestals arranged in a triangle around the Truce Stone basin at the center of the throne room. The third pedestal held unlit candles, and as I watched the Serpent Lord reached out to kindle one.

A hand seized my arm. A crawling sensation radiated from the painful grip, as if worms invaded my skin.

"What have you done?" Ruven hissed, bending his face near mine.

On either side of me, the Lady of Thorns' daughter and one of the Lady of Bears' sons drew aside, giving Ruven space. The Kindling ceremony carried on.

I tried to shake free of Ruven but found I couldn't move my arm. "You know what I've done. You left us a present in hopes we'd try it."

"But not *now*!" Pain shot through my arm, to punctuate his words. I drew a sharp breath through my teeth. "My lady, normally I admire your audacity, but this is too much. Where have you taken them? Why can't I reach them?"

A surge of triumph stretched a smile across my face. "Because they're not yours anymore. They never were."

Ruven's mouth twisted toward a snarl, but he visibly mastered himself, smoothing it back into his usual expression of amusement. "So you've stolen them back. Well played, my lady, well played." He leaned even closer, until his lips nearly brushed my ear. I couldn't pull away, with his magic wound through me. "But you made one mistake. You came back here alone."

"You won't do anything to me during the Kindling." I tried to keep my voice calm, though my heart raced and stumbled like a three-legged racehorse. "You would never dare disrupt such an important ceremony, especially since it's your first time hosting the Conclave."

His smile spread wide. "Ah, but you forget that I can kill you while you stand here, silent as a fall of snow, and leave you standing in place until the Conclave is over." He laid a hand along my cheek. "So discreet, even a Raverran would approve."

I tried to reply, but I couldn't move. I couldn't breathe. He'd stopped my lungs. *Graces help me.*

I stared desperately across the shimmering ghostly lights of the throne hall toward Kathe, but he watched the Serpent Lord place his candle on one of the pedestals, seemingly enthralled by the ceremony. My pulse pounded like thunder in my ears, and my chest burned with the need for air.

"But wait." Ruven let out a sigh, and I could breathe again. "I forgot the little matter of your connection to the Lady of Eagles."

I sucked in a deep gasp and yanked my arm away from him. "You vile wretch," I rasped.

"It might not even be an issue," he murmured contemplatively, "but best not to risk it, yes? I lose nothing by waiting." He swept into a courtly bow. "Enjoy the Kindling, my lady. We will finish our business once the Conclave is over."

He turned and sauntered off, leaving me clutching at my flare locket, my fingers entangled in the claws at my throat.

Kathe caught my eye across the hall and ambled over, grinning, careful not to disturb any of the people watching the Kindling. I couldn't repress a flare of anger at the cheery unconcern on his face.

"You seemed to handle that well," he greeted me.

"He nearly killed me! Where were you?"

"Shh." He lifted a finger to his lips, his voice barely above a whisper. "We must respect the ceremony. And I judged you had it under control."

"Then you're a terrible judge," I said.

"Look." He directed his gaze toward the center of the throne hall, where the Lady of Bears placed her candle on one of the pedestals. "That one is for those who support the invasion. The other is for those who stand against it."

I counted the slim golden flames with despair. The Lady of Bears had lit the fifth candle for war. Only one candle burned alone for peace. But the remaining eleven still stood unlit on the third pedestal, so there was hope yet. "You said it's customary for some candles to move during the course of the Kindling, right?"

"Yes. You'll see. And I do plan to speak out against the war, for what it's worth." His eyes glittered with interest as he watched the Lady of Gulls light her candle. She might have been an image of one of the Graces, with a slim, rippling white gown and a white-winged crown. Hers was an island domain, off the northern coast, and on Kathe's tip I'd spoken to her at some length of the benefits of trade with the Serene Empire. She caught my eye and nodded before placing her candle with Kathe's.

I sighed with relief. "Well, that's a bit better. I'm glad my efforts here haven't been entirely in vain."

But then the Elk Lord lit his candle and moved with solemn stateliness to set it on the pedestal for war. I gripped Kathe's arm for support, stricken, as two more Witch Lords immediately followed suit, casting glances at the Elk Lord.

"The Lady of Otters is his daughter," Kathe murmured, "and the Willow Lord his neighbor. They will always follow his lead. It's a shame you couldn't convince him."

Eight candles lifted their flames for war. Only two against it. Grace of Wisdom help me—if three Witch Lords had been enough to plunge the Empire into three years of hard-fought war, eight could destroy it utterly.

Seven candles remained unkindled. The Lady of Otters and the Willow Lord took their places in the loose ring of spectators, and silence fell over the throne hall.

The Yew Lord stood forward, the oldest of the Witch Lords and the officiant of the ceremony. His sunken eyes stared out above a beard like a trail of moss, and his deep brown hands rested on a staff formed of delicately braided wood in different colors. His ancient presence drank the silence in, until it became a deep, still pool that held us all.

"Are there any others who would light a candle before we begin?" he asked. His voice sliced the air with a keen profundity, a blade of sound and air.

No one stirred.

"Then let any speak who would seek to sway the Conclave." The Yew Lord stepped back, releasing the room's attention.

My heart thundered like an unleashed storm. This was my final chance to tip the balance. The words of my prepared speech jumbled together in my head, merging to become the meaningless roar of the ocean.

Ruven strode forward into the void the Yew Lord had left, spreading his hands in welcome.

"My friends! Thank you for answering my late father's call and coming to this Conclave. My house is honored by your presence." He bowed to the assembly. "It is a great tragedy that I must take over my father's place in this Conclave as the Witch Lord of Kazerath. But it is all the more reason we must show strength against the Serene Empire. We cannot allow them to think us weak, that one of theirs slew a Witch Lord! No, we must put the common rabble in their place." He smiled, as if the idea delighted him. "I am grateful to those of you who give me your support at this vital moment. I will repay you as you deserve—and as the first Skinwitch to become a Witch Lord, I remind you that I can repay my favors in truly unique ways." He caught the Lady of Spiders' gaze; to my horror, she smiled at him. "Thank you, my fellows. That is all."

With a swirl of his black leather coat, he marched back to his place. He had hardly taken it when the Lady of Spiders glided forth, moving to the cluster of unlit candles at the third point around the center.

"To an interesting future," she said, and lit her candle. She lifted it to Ruven like a toast, and placed it with his. On her way back to her place, she gave me an amused look that said clearly, *You should have taken my bargain.*

The Lady of Laurels sighed then, kindled her own unlit candle, and moved it to stand beside that of the Lady of Spiders. She cast a resigned look in her direction that I took to mean she was discharging a favor.

Ten candles for war, and only two for peace. "Graces preserve us," I whispered.

"I'm hardly one of your Graces," Kathe said, "but I'll see what I can do."

He strutted out to the center of the room, nodding to a few particular faces. Then he addressed them, turning slowly to take in the entire room.

"Crows are creatures of opportunity," he said, "and the opportunities in alliance with the Serene Empire are limitless. War locks us in the cycle of the past; but some of us are bold enough to fly forward into the future." He caught and held the gaze of a few Witch Lords in turn; I couldn't tell which ones from where I was standing. "Some old legends say crows have the gift of prophecy and can foretell death." He shrugged, grinning. "When all debts are paid, and all battles lost and won, I think I know who will still be standing. I've spoken to some of you about this. Time will tell soon enough if I'm right."

It was an odd speech. I scanned the faces of the other Witch Lords; they reflected a variety of reactions, from thoughtful consideration to puzzlement. The Lady of Thorns smiled, seeming deeply satisfied.

Her face struck a deep chill in my chest. Why would she react like that to Kathe's words? Didn't she know how he hated her? Unless his hate was a sham, and he was playing me for a fool.

It was an unbearable thought. Not after all the trust I'd placed in him, and how I'd grown to like him. Not after I'd kissed him, and hurt Marcello to keep courting him. He couldn't have been lying all this time.

Kathe returned to his position by my side, in a rustle of feathers.

"I'm afraid I'm not all that influential yet," he sighed, as the Holly Lord stepped forward and lit his candle for peace. I held my breath, hoping for more, but none followed.

Three to ten. This didn't look good. I was going to have to give a speech to charm the demons back to the Nine Hells. I wiped clammy hands on my breeches.

The Lady of Bears stomped to the center of the hall and issued a call to battle, urging her fellows to avenge Vaskandar's defeat in the Three Years' War, and then delivering an unsubtle threat to her neighbors if they didn't comply, with a glare at the Fox Lord. When she finished, the Fox Lord grimaced and, with apparent reluctance, lit his candle and moved it to stand beside that of the Lady of Bears.

Eleven straight golden flames leaped up, proud and martial, on the war pedestal. Eleven candles to count out the Empire's doom.

Hell of Despair. The speeches had only moved one or two candles each. Even if I laid out all Ruven's crimes, what of it? The Witch Lords already knew he was a monster, and they were willing to back him anyway. I was some upstart foreigner, without so much as a trace of magic. They had no reason to defect en masse at my words, and that was what it would take to protect the Serene Empire from a devastating invasion beyond our power to resist.

Kathe nudged my ribs. "My lady. If you wish to speak, now is the time."

Now is the time. My moment had come. I held history in my hands; if I dropped it and broke it, no one would come clean it up.

But this was something only I could do. The Serene Empire had put its trust in me. I had to try.

"Right." I took a deep breath. "Here I go."

Fireflies swirled around me as I walked forward. My boots

called echoes from the stone. I could feel the weight of seventeen domains on me, through the Witch Lords' combined gazes—all those miles of forest and mountain. All those thousands and millions of lives, animal and human alike, staring out with mad intensity from seventeen pairs of mage-marked eyes.

If any of them remembered what I said here, my words could last a thousand years. To speak in this place, surrounded by the flickering candles of their solemn ceremonies, under the soft glow of lichen constellations that hadn't been there this morning, was pure audacity. Who was I to dare?

I knew the answer. I'd given it to Ruven, back in Ardence.

I wasn't here as myself, mere Amalia: scholar, heir, and Falconer. I was here as a Serene Imperial Envoy. I was the voice of the Empire.

We were no different, I realized, as I scanned their outlandish figures, shaping antlers and wings. It was their domains that made them powerful. But my domain was far greater than any one of theirs. The only difference was that they took from the lives in their domain to achieve their own power and immortality, while the Empire, at its best, used its power to protect and sustain the lives within its bounds.

I faced them all and bowed.

"Thank you for hearing me." My voice rang out, strong and confident under the eerie lights that swirled like giddy falling stars above us. "I stand here as the guest of Lord Kathe of Let, to speak for the Serene Empire."

I reached out toward the Witch Lords, as their eyes gleamed at me in the dim hall. "We have a history of conflict. But history is a book in which we write new pages every day. The Empire holds out its hands to any who would take them. Instead of turning our might against each other, to the diminishment of both, let us work together to see what our combined power can do."

Kathe tipped me a mocking salute, grinning. I suppressed

a return smile. He was more than eager to see what we could accomplish together already.

"As for those who insist on standing against us..." I gestured to the eleven candles that still burned for war, trying not to think about what that number meant. "I suggest you take a close look at who stands with you. Yours is the power of life, the greatest and most sacred force on this earth. But Lord Ruven has twisted that power to enslave the mage-marked and murder children. And perhaps even worse, he has turned it against the land itself." This was my strongest card: that by backing war, they backed Ruven. "He seeks to rend Mount Whitecrown asunder with its own fire, turning his power of life into one of destruction."

I yearned to go into detail, explaining how he'd done it and the many levels on which it was a terrible idea. But everyone else's speeches had been quite short. I had best come to a conclusion if I didn't want the Yew Lord to cut me off. "Ask yourselves," I said, dropping my voice to the greatest depth and power I could muster, "whether this is what you want for the future of Vaskandar. Ask yourselves if you wish to feed this monster and let it grow unchecked on your borders."

Silence followed my words. My bootheels clipped holes in it as I walked back to my place, staring straight ahead, hands trembling. I could feel all their eyes still on me.

For a moment, everything was still. The silence hung dread in my heart—would not one single Witch Lord move their candle?

Then Ruven's laugh rang through the hall. "My dear lady, come now. That was a pretty speech, but I am hardly a monster."

From the back of the hall, like a miracle of the Graces, a young voice rang out: "Yes, you are!"

Everyone turned and stared. Emmand stood there, his thin chest heaving as if he'd run all the way there. Dirt streaked his face, and he held his fists clenched at his sides.

Terrible knowledge haunted his eyes, and his face seemed

green in the unearthly light. He must have listened to Zaira and found the bones. Hope lifted its tired head in my heart.

"Ah, young Emmand," Ruven said, flashing brilliant teeth. "You are lost, perhaps. You have no place in the Conclave."

The Yew Lord struck his staff against the stones, and silence fell over the hall with the weight of ten years of snow.

"The boy bears the mage mark," he said into that silence. "He may speak, if any Witch Lord will vouch that they wish to hear what he has to say."

The Lady of Eagles lifted two fingers, like the lazy stirring of a wing to catch the breeze. "I am curious. Speak, boy."

Emmand bowed, trembling so violently I could see him shaking from across the room. He wouldn't meet Ruven's eyes. "My lords and ladies, I beg you, forgive me, but I must tell you what my Lord Ruven has done."

I would never have thought I could admire this boy, who had made a potion used to rob my friends of their free will. But it took an uncommon courage to stand before the people you respected most and admit you'd been wrong. I held my breath, silently urging him on.

"Emmand," Ruven said, the picture of blithe unconcern save for the daggers in his eyes, "what nonsense is this, foolish boy?"

"It is forbidden to interrupt," the Yew Lord said, his voice rolling through the room with the force of thunder. Ruven bowed and said no more, but there was murderous intent in every line of him.

Emmand fell to his knees, as if he couldn't bear to stand in the presence of all seventeen Witch Lords anymore. With his head bowed, in a faltering voice, he began, "Lord Ruven has been capturing mage-marked and using a mix of alchemy and his own Skinwitch powers to force them under his dominion. He collects and uses them like toys, and if they resist, he—"

Emmand made a choking sound. His hands went to his throat.

"Yes?" the Elk Lord prompted. "Go on."

But Emmand clawed at his throat, his eyes bulging, and shook his head. He pointed an urgent, trembling finger at Ruven.

Hells. He couldn't breathe. Ruven was killing him.

I whirled to face Ruven. "Release him!" I demanded.

Ruven's eyes narrowed with lazy malice. "My dear lady, he's mine. Part of my domain. Why should I?"

"Because," the Elk Lord said sternly, "he is no common serf. He is mage-marked."

"And he's just a boy," the Lady of Otters added, shaking her chestnut hair indignantly. "If this is how you treat a mage-marked child who is your own ward, Kazerath, I shudder to think how you would treat an ally."

Ruven shrugged. "If you insist." He sliced his hand through the air. Emmand gasped in a ragged breath and collapsed on the floor, chest heaving. His fingers clawed the stones as he pulled breath after breath into his starving lungs.

It was the only sound. Aside from Emmand's labored breathing, no whisper broke the silence. I held my own breath, barely daring to hope for the outrage that surely even Witch Lords must feel at this. Only firefly lights marked the time, flickering in the air.

Then the Elk Lord swept into the center of the room. His eyes flashed, and the antlers in his crown spread menacing shadows against the walls. Glowing moths and fireflies danced around him, turning him into something from a prophetic dream.

"You have transgressed against the laws of nature," he told Ruven, seeming to swell until he loomed above the rest of us, his presence filling the hall. "To claim noble mage-marked as slaves through a corruption of alchemy is a base trick that undermines our most sacred and ancient traditions. You must blood and mark a domain to claim the life within it. And you must respect the power that the mage-marked bear, for it is what places *you* above your own people."

Ruven's lip curled in a furious sneer. But with a glance at the Yew Lord, standing ancient and watchful with his hands about his staff, he refrained from saying anything.

"I had planned to back this war, as a necessary outlet for the pressures that drive our cycle of expansion," the Elk Lord said. "But the Lady Amalia is correct. I cannot condone any war that stands to advance this Skinwitch's power. War I may deem necessary, but *this* I cannot support." He gestured toward Emmand where the boy lay curled on the floor, softly weeping.

The Elk Lord strode to his candle and picked it up with careful reverence. Maintaining an aura of grace and ceremony, he placed it on the opposing pedestal, joining its light to the three slender flames already there.

As he returned to his place, I held my breath. The Lady of Otters came forward at once, moving her candle to stand beside her father's, with a glare at Ruven. The Willow Lord followed suit, with less enthusiasm and without the glare.

And then the Fox Lord stepped to the center of the room. "I am disgusted," he said simply, with a scornful glance at Ruven. Turning his back on the Lady of Bears, he, too, moved his candle to stand for peace.

When he left the center of the room, instead of returning to his former place, he came to stand by my side. "So," he whispered, out of the corner of his mouth, "what you said earlier, about the Empire helping its friends."

I gave him my most brilliant smile. "We have a lot to talk about."

Seven candles now shone for peace. It was far better than three—but still not enough. The hope that had swelled in my chest began to fade.

Ruven stood straight and still, staring at the candles. A menace gathered around him, pooling like poison, an animosity fit to wither the light from the air.

He laughed, but it held a bitter edge. "Do you truly place so much stock in the words of an excitable child and a foreign woman with no magic? And why should any of you care what I do in my own domain?"

"Perhaps we should not." The Lady of Eagles' voice filled the room with the relentless and unanswerable force of rising floodwaters. "But I care what you do in *my* domain, Lord of Kazerath."

Ruven went still. The Lady of Eagles crossed the hall and stood before him, her mantle billowing behind her in the breeze of her passage. Her golden eyes bored into his, until he looked away.

"I have one last grievance to claim," she said.

Chapter Forty

The Lady of Eagles' voice went soft as wings bent to stoop for the kill. "You trespassed on *my* mountain, Skin Lord."

"I am sorry, my lady." Ruven bowed his head. "I acknowledge your grievance. I will make amends."

"You will." She held out her hand. Red stones rained from it, striking at his feet with a great cacophonous clatter. "In recompense for your insolent trespass, I claim my price from your domain itself. Kazerath will cede to Atruin its half of Mount Whitecrown, so the mountain in its entirety is mine and mine alone. I will blood this claim tomorrow under the morning sun, and you will give up all right to it."

A hissing murmur ran through the room. For a Witch Lord, this must be the steepest price one could exact for a grievance—their domain was their power, their life. And it wasn't a small area; Mount Whitecrown's ridges and shoulders spread for miles.

Ruven's jaw worked and clenched. But then he forced his teeth into a smile. "As you will it, Lady of Eagles. Your grievance is true. I do not contest this claim. Tomorrow morning, Mount Whitecrown is yours."

A chill pierced deep into my chest at those words. He'd given up too easily. He must think that by tomorrow, he wouldn't need it.

The Lady of Eagles turned to face the rest of the Witch Lords, apparently satisfied. "I take no stance in this war," she declared. "My candle remains dark. But I suggest you listen to my descendant, and think carefully before binding your fates too closely to this transgressor."

Unexpected pride leaped in my chest at the words *my descendant.* She paced back to the edge of the room. Murmurs rose in her wake.

One by one, Witch Lords came forth and snuffed the candles that stood on the pedestal of war. Soon, only four remained: those of the Lady of Bears, the Serpent Lord, the Lady of Thorns, and Ruven himself. The ones whose intent to invade had never been in doubt.

A giddy euphoria swelled in my belly. The Conclave had gained Ruven no allies whatsoever and had likely made him some enemies. I would have to thank Zaira for convincing Emmand and make certain the boy was all right; it was Ruven's treatment of him that had turned the tide.

Kathe seemed to read my mind. "That boy will need protection," he murmured. "I think I'll offer to take him in."

"Oh, good." I let out a relieved sigh. "I don't want to leave him to Ruven's mercy."

"Speaking of Ruven, I think you've finished him, politically." Kathe rubbed his hands gleefully. "The bear and the serpent may use him as a distraction while they wage their own war on the Empire, but afterward they'll drop him like a dirty boot. With both the Elk Lord and the Lady of Eagles taking a stance against him, he might as well be carrying plague."

The Yew Lord raised a hand, and the clamor of conversation fell silent. "Does anyone else have words to speak before I call an end to the Kindling?"

Ruven took a step forward. "Only that I will remember who stayed with me," he said. "And as to those of you who deserted me—it hardly matters." Satisfaction narrowed his eyes. "I never needed you."

Apprehension twisted my gut. "He's talking about the volcano," I whispered.

Kathe frowned. "I think you're right. Can you stop him from triggering the eruption?"

"Only if I get to the master circle before he does."

"Go, then." He angled to block me from Ruven's view, his movements casual. "The Yew Lord will call an end to the Kindling soon. You need to hurry if you want a chance to beat him there."

I squeezed his hand. "Thank you, Kathe."

He flashed a grin at me. "Save your thanks for when I've done you a favor. This is all for my personal amusement."

Feeling bold, I blew him a kiss before I turned to slip out of the hall. He laughed and pretended to catch it.

Before I left the throne hall, I cast one last glance over my shoulder, but Kathe wasn't there anymore. I scanned the gathering; most of them were focused on the Serpent Lord, who was giving some final speech. Kathe, however, was talking to someone, and pointing in my direction.

He was speaking to the Lady of Thorns.

She looked straight at me and smiled.

I raced across the darkened garden, my heart aching with each rapid pulse. The full moon washed the grass in silver but made the tree line into a flat black mass of jagged shadow. The air felt cold and alive on my skin.

Surely Kathe couldn't have just betrayed me to the Lady of Thorns. He *hated* her. Never mind that I only had his word for that. But this was one of his games, for certain—and he might not hesitate to sacrifice a piece to win.

It didn't matter. Just like it didn't matter that it was madness to be out here, ready to plunge into Ruven's own forest alone at night. If I didn't destroy that control circle before Ruven activated it, Mount Whitecrown would erupt, and even a small eruption could wipe out our border defenses in a critical pass, kill thousands of people, and cover vast swaths of the Empire with ash carrying Ruven's claim of dominion. There was no time to wait for Zaira to return. The Kindling could be over in minutes, and I had no doubt he intended to trigger the eruption tonight.

Still, I paused before the forest's edge. The trees towered above me, blotting out the paler sky and its scattered stars. The remaining snow had melted during the day, and the path seemed to disappear immediately into absolute darkness.

If Ruven realized what I was doing, those trees could wake into violent motion and kill me with the casual ease of a courtier spearing a cream puff with a dessert fork.

There was no sense in agonizing about it. I was the only one here, and this had to be done. I took a breath and plunged into the forest as if it were a deep, black pool.

Layers of darkness and light shifted around me. Moonlight streamed down through gaps in the branches, bright enough to read by, but it only made the shadows gathered beneath the trees darker. I stumbled on a tree root, barely catching myself on the smooth bole of a young sapling.

"Last time, I asked what you were doing in the forest," came the rich, lovely voice of the Lady of Thorns. "This time, I frankly don't care. All that matters is that you're alone."

Hell of Disaster. I spun, pulling off one of my rings. The band of skin-warmed metal dug into my palm. "Isn't your presence required at the Kindling?"

"This is more important." She stepped closer, the dappled light falling over her as she moved between shadows. "My daughter cannot claim Callamorne while you live. For her to survive, little Lochaver, you must die."

She brushed a hand along the trunk of a towering pine that loomed over us both. There came a great crack, and I barely jumped out of the way before a branch crashed to the ground where I'd just been standing.

I threw my ring at her. Despite my sloppy, panicked throw, it left my hand with astounding speed and force, as if I'd fired it from a musket. It traced a hot, glowing path through the air, missing the Lady of Thorns by mere inches. She jerked back in alarm from the ember-edged hole it punched in the tree beside her.

"So the little mouse bites," she purred. "Very well; I am warned."

She seized a bramble bush by the path's edge. Dozens of thorny tendrils stretched toward me, lashing and coiling. With a yelp of alarm, I yanked off another ring and tossed it at the writhing mass that reached for me.

The ring bounced off one of the whipping vines. Frost crystals puffed from it, like the flurry of a snowball's impact; a blue glow flared in its runes, then fizzled out. *Like a pistol with damp powder.*

I scrambled away from the grabbing thorns, then closed my eyes and opened my flare locket. My eyelids reddened from the blinding flash, and the Lady of Thorns cried out in anger. I turned and ran, shadows sliding over me. But I didn't make it far before I tripped on a root and fell sprawling on the path, my hands skidding on the pine needles under me.

I staggered to my feet, shins smarting, heart bursting with fear, and tried to keep running. But my ankle was still stuck in the root.

I twisted around to see the problem, and more roots buckled and burst up from the path all around me. I shrieked and reached for another ring, but a root caught my arm, yanking it away. More coiled around me, painfully tight, until I could hardly move at all.

The Lady of Thorns stood down the path, rubbing her eyes fiercely with one hand. Her other hand rested on the trunk of a great, ancient tree.

"This may not be my domain," she said, "but I am still more than a match for your little toys in this forest. Life is all around you, city girl—even in the ground beneath your feet."

I struggled to get a hand free, to twist out of the crushing grip of the roots that held me, but they tightened further against every move I made. Panic clawed inside me, a frenzy to escape, giving me strength, but the tree was far stronger.

Graces help me. I had no way left to fight her. If I couldn't somehow convince her not to kill me, I was going to die.

"I'm still under Kathe's protection!" I called. "If you kill me, you'll have to answer to him."

The Lady of Thorns laughed. "Really! Is that true, Crow Lord?"

An oddly shaped patch of shadow detached from a tree behind her and stepped forward into the moonlight. Silver gleams caught in Kathe's eyes, and the hint of a breeze ruffled the feathers on his shoulders. He crossed his arms on his chest and unfolded a slow, wide grin.

"I'm here to fulfill my promise to you, my Lady of Thorns," he said, his voice light and casual. "Carry on."

Chapter Forty-One

My heart plunged as if he'd chucked it off a cliff into Ruven's boneyard. "I trusted you, Kathe."

"A wise man once said to trust your enemies, if you have enough of a hold over them, but never your friends." Kathe shrugged, rustling feathers. "It seems he may have been right."

"Now that we've settled that..." The Lady of Thorns closed her fist against the tree trunk.

The roots that held me clenched tight around me, with crushing force. I cried out as my limbs twisted; then the breath drove from my lungs, taking my voice with it. Sharp pain flared through my chest as a rib cracked.

The Lady of Thorns screamed.

I fell to the ground in a tangle of suddenly brittle roots, gaping in astonished confusion. She doubled over as if in agony, clutching at her own body: chest, stomach, and arms, as if everything hurt. The Lady of Thorns slumped against her tree and let out another horrible scream, while Kathe watched with narrowed eyes and a satisfied smile.

"What... have... you... *done*?!" she cried, her voice raw and breaking.

"I?" Kathe placed a hand innocently on his chest. "Oh, hardly anything. Only moved the Truce Stones a little further out beyond the garden."

The Lady of Thorns clawed at herself. "My blood! It's burning!"

"It's turned against you." Kathe put a friendly hand on her shoulder, as if to comfort her. "Because you broke the truce and harmed the blood of the Lady of Eagles."

I kicked the withered roots off and dragged myself to my feet. Every breath sent a stab of pain through my side, and my limbs ached with strains and bruises. But whatever the Lady of Thorns felt was clearly far, far worse. Another scream tore its way out of her throat, and she dropped to her knees.

"And you know what that means," Kathe sighed. "While your blood rebels against you, I'm afraid it can't serve as a conduit to draw life from your domain."

She bared her teeth at him, with the desperate snarl of a wounded animal, and gripped the bark of the tree that supported her. Its branches lurched toward him, jerky and erratic. But Kathe shifted his toe to casually touch one of the roots, and the tree froze in place.

"Why are you doing this?" the Lady of Thorns demanded. "We had an agreement! You promised!"

"I'm keeping my promise." Kathe drew a long bone knife from his belt. "And as for why I'm doing this, do you remember a man named Jathan?"

"No," she gasped, folding in on herself in a fresh wave of pain.

"Good," Kathe said. "He didn't understand why he died, either."

His knife flashed down, white in the moonlight. With a sickening thud, he buried it in the Lady of Thorns' back.

She sprawled in the path, twitching weakly, as a dark stain spread across her gown. Beneath her, the ground parted, roots pushing the dirt away and leaving a shallow, crumbling ditch.

She clawed at the roots, her fingers digging into the earth, and some began to writhe in random desperation. But a thousand tiny rootlets sprouted up and rushed over her like the tide, pulling her down into her own grave. She let out a choked, despairing cry as they dragged her under.

Kathe fingered the leaf of a vine and watched impassively as it spread rapidly along the ground, leafing and branching to cover the last traces of where the Lady of Thorns had lain. In seconds, only the hilt of his knife stuck up from the vine-covered ground.

He set his boot on it, expressionless, grinding it further in.

I stared at him, balanced between horror and awe, my breath frozen in my throat. *Grace of Mercy.* He'd killed her, murdered her, gotten his vengeance at last.

And used me as bait to do it.

"You scoundrel," I gasped. I put a hand to my rib; pain flashed under the light pressure, and I dropped it again. "She almost killed me!"

"I watched very closely to make sure she didn't." Kathe yanked his bloody knife from the earth, wiped the blade clean on a patch of tree moss, and walked over to me. His mage mark gleamed yellow in the darkness. "How badly are you hurt?"

I scrambled back a step, holding up a hand like a shield between us. "Don't come any closer! Your trap could have gotten me murdered."

Kathe stopped and bowed, with no trace of mockery. "I acknowledge your grievance. I am deep in your debt, Lady Amalia."

"What did you promise her?" I demanded. "To finish me off?"

"No." He laughed, the sound setting the leaves to quivering. "I promised to help make certain her daughter got her own domain. And now she has her mother's, and can escape the doom of old age at last."

"Was your plan to use me against her from the start?" Fury strained my voice raw. "Did you court me only to lure me here as bait for your enemy?"

"Of course not. Any more than you courted *me* only to threaten your enemies. I'm fond of accomplishing multiple purposes at the same time." He glanced up the path. "I owe you a better apology, but we need to hurry. I sent a crow with a message for Zaira letting her know you might need help, and it's leading her to you now. But Ruven will take the most direct route to the control circle; this is his domain, and he needs no path."

"Wait." I steadied myself against a tree. Graces, everything hurt, but there was no time to think about that. "If you want to prove you're not my enemy, send a message for me."

"Certainly." He lifted an arm, and a crow fluttered to it at once, its dark wings spread for balance. "Where?"

"To Jerith Antelles, at the border. I need him to summon a wind."

Kathe tilted his head. "A wind?"

"In case we can't stop Mount Whitecrown from erupting. To blow all the ash back into Kazerath."

Kathe nodded. "That I can do." He gazed into the crow's eyes a moment, then flung it back into the air. It cawed a protest, but flew off into the night.

"Good." That was as close as I was willing to come to thanking him. I started hobbling up the path, moving stiffly as I worked to settle all my new aches and pains. I needed to get to that control circle as quickly as possible. Even if Jerith got my message in time and was able to turn back the ashes, an eruption would at minimum clear Ruven a smoldering path into the heart of the Empire and kill thousands.

"Will you let me help you?" Kathe asked, falling in behind me. His voice was uncharacteristically quiet, almost humble. Did he feel honestly guilty? Or was he just trying to win his way back into my good graces?

I wasn't certain I cared. "No," I said shortly. My cracked rib flared with pain each time I took a breath.

The trees tossed their limbs, then, as if a wind shuddered through them. A great tramping and rustling came on the path behind us, followed by shouts and howling. A chill settled over me, deeper than the night air alone.

"Ruven knows," I breathed. "He's sending forces after us."

Kathe stopped in the path. "I'll hold them off. You keep going."

The approaching racket grew louder. I hesitated. "It sounds like a lot of guards, and chimeras as well. This isn't your domain. Can you handle them?"

He laughed. "Of course I can."

"Why are you doing this?" I asked. "Because you owe me?"

"No." His voice went soft, and a little sad. He looked away. "Because I like you. Sometimes, it's all right to do something for a person you like, and to not want anything in return."

I stared at him. My fingers curled around the claws at my throat. "You're a strange and infuriating man, Kathe."

He grinned. "I know. Now, go. The crow I sent to get Zaira is close; she'll catch up to you in a moment and can see you safely the rest of the way."

I couldn't help but remember Braegan, and all the other brave soldiers who had given their lives to hold off the whiphounds so Zaira and I could escape. No matter what Kathe had done, I didn't want to leave him to guard my back alone.

But he was a Witch Lord. If he said he could handle Ruven's guards, I had to believe him. "All right."

I hurried along the path. The trees around me swayed and rustled but kept their branches to themselves. Perhaps Ruven didn't realize Kathe and I had split up; he must be distracted, racing to reach the control circle before me, and Kathe certainly had a more noticeable magical presence.

The shouts and howls intensified, far behind me, and took on the sound of desperation and terror. I swallowed and kept going, uncertain whether the fear in my heart was for Kathe, or for what he was doing to Ruven's guards to make them scream that way.

A figure stood in the road ahead, a deeper shadow standing sentinel in the moon-splashed path. I slowed, wary. "Who's there?"

"Demons have mercy, I can't leave you alone for one hour, can I?"

"Zaira!" It was all I could do not to run up and hug her. "Thank the Graces. We have to hurry; Ruven's on his way to the control circle."

"I know. This feathery little Demon of Madness told me." Zaira gestured into a tree; a mocking caw answered her. "And let me tell you, it's creepy as the Hell of Nightmares to have some bird swoop down in your face at night and start *speaking in words*."

The crow cawed again. Zaira pointed a menacing finger at it. "Shut up, you. It's not funny."

I caught up to her and kept huffing along. She fell in by my side. "I'm glad you're here," I said. "Kathe stayed behind to hold off Ruven's guards and chimeras, but I can't guarantee some won't slip around him."

Zaira grunted. "I guess I was wrong about him."

"No, you were right." The admission hurt almost worse than my cracked rib. "He used me as bait to kill the Lady of Thorns."

"Huh. Well, no loss there. Maybe we were both right." For a moment there was only the sound of my labored breath as we hurried along the trail. Then, "Are you two still courting?"

Good Graces. I'd just been betrayed and almost murdered, and we were running to save the Empire from a horrific volcanic eruption, and she asked *that*?

Of course she did. "Technically, yes."

She laughed. "He might be pretty, but you know what? I'll still take Terika."

"How is she?"

"Everything went smoothly. Marcello took over at the meeting point, and the road seemed clear. Ruven's got other things on his mind."

"Like us," I said grimly, and pushed faster.

We broke out at last onto the open hilltop where Namira's map had marked the control circle, under a thick scattering of crystal-dust stars. A cold wind swept across the rocky dome, whipping my hair off my neck.

A man stood at the far end, on the hill's highest point, arms upraised. The wind caught in his long coat, billowing it around him. *Ruven.* He'd beaten us here.

And between him and us stood perhaps two dozen backlit human figures, pointing swords and spears at us. The moon behind them cast their sharp-edged shadows toward us across the stone.

"Right, then." Zaira raised her hands, and balefire blossomed on them, beautiful and hungry.

The blue flame lit the features of the forces arrayed against us, and Zaira swore.

They weren't soldiers. They were the old and the young and the infirm: Ruven's own people, gathered from the villages and farms below, those who had been passed over for the army. Their eyes stretched with fear, and they held their weapons uncertainly. Tears streaked some of their faces.

The old innkeeper who'd taken care of the babies in his common room stood among them, grimacing apologetically. So did the barkeep with the scar on her face, from down the hill, and the serving boy she'd sent away to keep him from falling afoul of a Witch Lord. One girl couldn't have been more than twelve, though she held her spear better than most of them, her mouth set in a determined line.

At the end of the row stood Emmand, a fresh hand-shaped burn on his cheek, as if Ruven had slapped him for speaking against him. His face twisted in bitter misery as he pointed a dagger at us.

"Demon piss," Zaira swore, dropping her hands. "I can't fight these brats."

"Stand aside," I called. "We don't want to hurt you."

"We don't want to fight, either, my lady," the innkeeper replied, his voice breaking with fear.

"We have no choice," Emmand said, wincing in pain as his words pulled at his burn. "If you try to get past us, we're going to attack you."

"Ruven, you coward!" Zaira roared. "Lining up children and grandfathers to protect you? You're lower than a plague-ridden sewer rat!"

Ruven didn't respond. Around his feet, an elaborate artifice circle flared with scarlet light.

"We don't have time!" I pulled off the ring on my right middle finger—the one that was supposed to incapacitate without killing. Istrella had said it might take out one or two people, but we needed it to do more than that. But it didn't have enough power.

Luckily, we were standing on a massive outcropping of volcanic rock. Power was easy to come by.

I desperately scanned the rocky ground in the dim light and bent and seized a chip of dark rock. *Obsidian.* I jammed it through the ring, wedging it as far as it would go, pressing the rock up against the runes.

And then I threw it.

The old innkeeper dodged, and it struck the stone between him and the twelve-year-old girl. But as it bounced and settled on the rock, its runes blazed to life. A webwork of glowing lines shot out from the ring, spreading and branching and connecting under the villagers' feet. They cried out and tried to scramble away, but their feet stayed rooted to the rock, caught in the shining web. Zaira and I had to back away quickly so the lines of light wouldn't catch us, too.

"Impressive," Zaira said. "That Istrella is crazy as a kitten on catmint, but she's good."

"Obsidian is an excellent power source," I said. "This should hold them for a while."

The controlled people strained toward us as we passed by them, but Istrella's enchantment held them fast. The little girl threw her spear; it clattered to the stone behind us.

"Stop Lord Ruven," Emmand called. "Hurry! Don't let him finish!"

We raced across the hilltop. As we approached, Ruven dropped his arms, turned to face us, and stepped out of his circle. A smile of pure pleasure curled his lips.

"Too late," he said. "It's already done."

Chapter Forty-Two

Beneath my feet, I felt the undeniable hum of magic. My bruised legs wavered under me, and a cold, dread certainty settled in my stomach.

Too late. Thousands of people in the border fortresses and the villages below, already dead and not even knowing it. All our border defenses, fortifications, and carefully laid artifice traps, doomed to fall. Mount Whitecrown loomed above us, a serene black outline against the starry sky; no one could guess the magical forces Ruven had unleashed upon it, set irrevocably in motion, ready to rain ash and ruin upon us all.

"No," I breathed. "There must be some way to stop it."

Ruven spread his hands. "My lady, you are the expert on artifice here. But I have been assured that there is none. I'm afraid your efforts have been in vain."

"Not quite in vain," Zaira said. Cold fury suffused her voice. "I get to do something I've always wanted."

Fire blazed up in her eyes all at once, blindingly bright, filling them end to end. And without any further warning, a wave of flame roared from her—all the anger at Ruven she'd kept pent up all this time, unleashed at last in a devouring inferno. All her rage for Terika, for the servants with burn marks on their skin, for the children whose bones he'd fed to wolves. It exploded from her at last in a terrible blast of light and fury, and it swallowed him whole.

Or it seemed to. A tower of blue-white flame raged where he had stood, clawing up higher and higher, toward the belly of the sky itself. It washed the entire hilltop in light; the villagers cried out in fear and tried to shrink from it, but Istrella's binding still held them fast. Heat seared my face, and I threw up a sleeve to shield myself as best I could.

"Die," Zaira ground through her teeth. "Die, die, die, damn you."

A shrill, agonized cry came from the flames, and I flinched at the sound. But then it descended down through a wild howl to something far more chilling.

Graces protect us. That was laughter.

It was the sound of madness. A sharp-edged laugh, true and free, full of surprised mirth.

And then he stepped out of the column of balefire, trailing flames and still laughing. Blue fire wreathed him, clawing at him with unanswerable power and hunger; smoke rose off him, and his flesh rippled as it kept trying to sear and shrivel, but he kept repairing it even faster.

"So this is how my father died." He held out his hands and stared at them. Fire leaped up from his arms, charring away the leather of his coat, but he remade that, too. "Alas for him, he was not a Skinwitch. It would seem I do not share his weakness."

"Burn," Zaira hissed. "Burn, you cursed demon." Blue tendrils of flame danced all along her hair, her shoulders, her back and arms; it poured from her eyes and her hands and raged all around Ruven. But he stood there, undaunted.

"I must thank you," he said. "You have given me proof that what I hoped is true. With all the life in Kazerath to fuel my power, I can strengthen and rebuild my own body even beyond the capacity of balefire to destroy it. I alone, in all this world, am truly, unequivocally immortal."

My stomach twisted. This was our doing. He was right; if balefire couldn't kill him, nothing could. Graces protect us all.

"My fire will never go out, so long as you have life left to fuel it," Zaira rasped. Her voice was harsh, wicked, and beautiful, speaking with the tongue of the flame itself. "Let it eat all the life in Kazerath, then, until you have nothing left to feed it but your own."

Ruven shrugged. "If you wish. We can start with these."

Behind us, someone screamed.

I whirled in time to see the talkative innkeeper drop, convulsing in a brief moment's agony before he went still. A bent old woman followed.

"Stop!" I cried. "Stop killing them, you monster!"

"It's not I who's killing them," Ruven said. "It's you, warlock."

Zaira didn't answer. Her gaze stayed fixed on him; her eyes were fire. She was lost to her flames.

Emmand crumpled to the ground next. His final wail, a lost and broken sound, tore at my heart. Tears started in my eyes, but the heat of the balefire sucked them dry before they could fall.

Graces curse it. All we were doing was killing innocent people.

"*Revincio!*" I cried.

The night went dark. Zaira tumbled to the hard rock, like a puppet with its strings cut. Sounds of fear and grief came from behind me, and the terrible stench of burned human meat lingered in the air.

The breeze stirred Ruven's coat. A ripple shook down the length of it, and it was smooth and whole again, minus the embroidery. His ponytail streamed on the wind, growing back to its full length. He smiled at me.

"And here we are at last, Lady Amalia. Just the two of us."

My hands formed tight fists, my nails cutting into my palms. "They were your own people. Emmand looked up to you. Do you have no shame whatsoever? A good ruler's life is lived as a sacrifice for the sake of those they rule."

"What a dreadfully dull way to live." Ruven shook his head. "Shame is a symptom of weakness, my lady. It is not for those who stand astride the world, such as we do." He held out a hand toward me. "Come. We have perhaps an hour before Mount Whitecrown erupts. I'm directing the blast to the south, into the Empire, but still, best to not be too exposed when it happens."

He didn't cast so much as a glance at Zaira, lying crumpled at my feet, the wind stirring her hair. Afterimages of balefire still danced in front of my eyes. I wrestled to contain my anger.

"You have quite some nerve, to behave solicitously toward me after all this. Do you truly expect me to believe you care for anything but my bloodline, when you cast the lives of your own people away so easily?"

Ruven's eyes widened. "But, my lady, you are so much more than your bloodline! No, no, you do not understand how highly I value you." He shook his head. "This won't do at all. Why, for instance, I still have a stockpile of the excellent potion that boy used to make for me. Just think of the possibilities, with the Cornaro heir under my dominion!"

I did, and my stomach twisted.

"There was another man who thought an alchemical trick was sufficient to subvert the Council of Nine," I said coldly. "He paid dearly for his error."

Ruven chuckled. "I never can intimidate you, can I, Lady Amalia? You are not so easily cowed. Ah, it's no wonder I admire you." The hand he'd stretched out dropped to his side, and he shook his head. "I look forward to many more wonderful conversations with you as my guest. But first, there is one small matter to take care of."

I didn't like the shift in his tone. I slid one of my last rings into my palm. "And what would that be?"

"Your warlock." He sighed. "I'd hoped to control her, but I fear my father was right about her after all. She's simply too dangerous to live." He reached for Zaira's windblown hair, like a curious child hoping to catch some in his fingers.

I slapped my ring down on the volcanic rock at my feet. A circle of golden light instantly blazed up around Zaira and me. Ruven pulled back from the ward, like a cat with an unexpectedly wet paw.

"This will last at least three hours," I lied. "Your guests are waiting for you in the castle. Do you truly wish the other Witch Lords to come and find you here?"

Ruven's eyes narrowed. "Very well. Stay up here in the open for the eruption if you wish. You are still in my domain; I don't need to be here in person to exercise my power upon you. The land itself will detain you for me. I'll be back for you once my guests and the mountain are both settled—if you survive."

He turned, his black coat swinging behind him like a wave of deeper shadow in the night. "Enjoy the view," he called cheerfully. "I can think of no better display to celebrate my ascension."

I waited tensely, counting the heartbeats as he paced off across the bald crown of the hill. The trapped villagers cringed away from him as he passed, lit from below by the fading lines of light beneath their feet, but he didn't so much as glance at them. Emmand's corpse lay stretched toward him, sad and still, his hand flung out on the rock.

Once he was gone, I counted a few minutes longer. Then I reached for the ring lying next to Zaira on the cold stone, but the protective circle sputtered out before my fingers touched it.

"One moment," I muttered to Zaira's unconscious form, and I ran to the control circle, ignoring the stab of pain in my side as I moved.

A faint red light still shone from the graven lines in the rock, making it easy to examine the design Namira had carved there at Ruven's command. It was a complex circle, with patterns inside patterns and long arcs of runes spelling out terms and rules with careful precision. This was the work of a master. *Grace of Wisdom, grant me insight.*

My heart descended into the murky forest below the hilltop as I studied the design. Ruven was right. It had already discharged the magic that would drop the containment and create a sudden release of the pent-up pressure in the mountain; that was done. And the artifice circle included no way to reverse or undo it. Mount Whitecrown would erupt, with whatever force remained to it after our efforts to decrease the pressure, and it would erupt within a few hours. There wasn't even time to evacuate.

The only section of the circle that seemed to still be active was the second stage of the enchantment, which would open a path for the eruption and point the force of the blast down the passes into the Serene Empire, toward Ardence. A single rune indicated the direction, painted on rather than graven, so Ruven could choose his target himself when he triggered the eruption. That second phase hadn't taken effect yet and could still be altered. But this wasn't pure artifice; it was designed to connect to and work with Ruven's vivomancy. Without his blooded connection to Mount Whitecrown, merely moving the targeting rune would do nothing.

A blooded connection to Mount Whitecrown. The door and the Truce Stones had recognized my blood as that of the Lady of Eagles. It was worth a try.

I placed my hand on the warm stone, feeling the carved lines of the artifice circle beneath my fingers, and closed my eyes.

I knew the stone. The planes and angles of this wind-worn slab of rock occupied a comfortable space in my mind. My awareness didn't reach beyond to the hill below me, or the trees at the edge of the open space, but this rough, grainy rock beneath my fingers I knew. And I could wrap my mind around the enchantment worked into it, and feel how the magic connected to the rock, and to something else as well. Something massive and ancient, with a terrible fire rising up within it, raging with a power beyond that of any Witch Lord.

But it knew me. Half the mountain belonged to my bloodline. All the awful majesty and destructive fury—it recognized me.

I could do this.

My eyes snapped open. I memorized Ruven's painted rune, then rubbed at it with my sleeve. It was still wet and smeared off easily enough, ruining the deep blue velvet.

I drew my dagger and cut my finger, freeing a trickle of blood.

And froze. *Hells.* I had to redirect the eruption somewhere. There were villages and fortresses all around Mount Whitecrown. Whatever I chose, someone would die.

The artifice design offered four possible locations for the direction rune, corresponding to four vents or weak points in the mountain.

I pictured the map of the border that I'd pored over in Highpass, with all the little forts and passes and villages marked carefully in different colors. I had to balance innocent villages against vital alliances, and key defensive fortresses against the lives of people I knew and loved.

One option aimed back into Kazerath, toward Ruven's castle, and it was tempting to direct the blast there. But not only would that likely kill Zaira and me, as well as wiping out a few villages whose twinkling lights I could spy in the valley below, it would mark the end of any budding alliances I might have built with the friendlier Witch Lords. And I doubted it would do more than inconvenience Ruven himself.

The currently marked one certainly wasn't feasible; it would destroy our border defenses on a critical pass, killing hundreds or thousands of soldiers, and likely wiping out the town that supported the border fortresses at the foot of the mountain, which would add thousands of civilians to the death toll. A third option would force the blast westward, into a river valley scattered with villages and packed with both Vaskandran and imperial troops facing off across heavy fortifications. While the angle seemed more likely to keep the devastation mostly on the Vaskandar side of the border and might decimate their forces there, it would lead to heavy loss of life, including many civilians—and I stood a strong chance of killing Marcello, Terika, and the escaping Falcons as they crossed the mountain's western shoulder on their way back home.

The final option was to skew the eruption eastward, along the ridge of the Witchwall Mountains. The terrain in that direction was too rough for farms or villages. But I might well catch Roland and his crew in the blast, since they were positioned on the eastern flank of the mountain, altering artifice circles.

There was no way around it. People were going to die. I had to choose whom to kill: Marcello and Terika and the other Falcons, Roland and his soldiers, or Zaira and myself.

My belly clenched with nausea, and a soft whimpering sound escaped my throat. This was terrible. I'd almost rather Ruven had dragged me back to the castle as his unwilling guest than kneel here, my friends' faces vivid in my mind, and choose which of their lives to snuff out forever.

But this is what my mother does. This was what the Council of Nine did, every day. Choosing between good and evil was easy. Choosing the lesser evil, and knowing that your choice damned people to death, was the part that hacked off pieces of your soul.

This was the task I'd been born to, and that I'd taken up willingly when I accepted my role as my mother's heir. This was part of the duty I'd accepted when I came to the Conclave as a Serene Imperial Envoy.

I took a deep breath, reached out a trembling hand, and sketched a new target rune in the eastern quadrant.

Please don't be there, Roland. Grace of Mercy, protect him, I beg you.

There would be few civilians, if any, in the rugged stretch of the Witchwall Mountains that bordered Mount Whitecrown's eastern flank. The imperial border fortresses in those passes lay farther south, and should be protected by the next line of peaks. The headwaters of the River Arden might become even more choked than they had been by the eruption of Mount Enthalus three years ago, but we already had plans in the works to mitigate that issue, and I could apologize to Domenic later. It would be a red stone I owed him, a minor grievance; easy to make amends.

Only Roland and his handful of soldiers would have to die.

Only my cousin, so serious and brave, who had finally talked our grandmother into letting him go to the border, on my advice. The cousin who had played with me in the halls of Durantain castle when I was small, and helped me up into the branches of the apple tree in the garden. Roland, who would give his life for me in a heartbeat; who would give his life for anyone. Roland, heir to the throne of Callamorne, who would never see what a good king he would have made despite all his doubts.

I rose, legs trembling. My eyes were dry.

He might still make it to safety. The eruption might be minor enough to spare him, if our alteration of the other circles had had time to do its work. But that wouldn't change the fact that here, in this moment, I'd been willing to kill him.

This was what it was to be a Cornaro.

Chapter Forty-Three

The power of the binding ring must have faded while I was working on the control circle; Ruven's villagers had fled, taking the bodies of the innkeeper and the old woman with them. Emmand, friendless, lay where he had fallen.

I shook Zaira's shoulder, with increasing vigor. I needed her awake. Not just to spare my cracked rib the pain of carrying her down the hill, but to save me from the dark spiral of my own fears. She stirred at last, groaning.

"Come on," I urged. "I don't know how long we have until the eruption."

She blinked her eyes open and lurched to a sitting position, one hand on her temple. "Hells on a stick, my head hurts. Please tell me I imagined the part about not killing him."

"Ruven is disgustingly alive," I admitted. "And I couldn't stop the eruption, but I..." I swallowed. "I redirected it. It's probably safe here, but we can't take chances."

"Fine." Zaira let me help her to her feet. Her eyes lit on Emmand's still form, and she froze. "I didn't kill him, did I?" Panic stretched her voice raw.

"No," I said. "You didn't. Ruven did."

She averted her eyes as we passed him, mumbling, "That poor little bastard."

As we plunged once more into the darkness of the forest, the ground under my feet trembled, and the trees shook their leaves in a rising whisper. I thought for a moment it was Ruven moving the land against us but then realized the truth.

"An earthquake." The words took on a corroded edge of dread in my mouth, tasting like old iron. "Just a small one. Mount Whitecrown is getting ready."

"You're sure we're safe here?" Zaira asked, face pale in the speckled moonlight.

"If the magic works as it's supposed to, and nothing unexpected happens, yes. But this is the first time anyone's tried anything like this. So, no. Not at all."

Zaira hurried a bit faster.

The blood rune I'd sketched on the control circle seemed to have given me a lingering sense of Mount Whitecrown, and the volcano pressed at my awareness with overwhelming urgency. The forces built up within the mountain could move the earth far more than that little tremor, and the fires raging within it dwarfed even Zaira's inner inferno. I supposed that was one good thing; if Mount Whitecrown dominated my senses even with such a weak connection, Ruven must be blind to anything else. He might well not realize we were escaping, and I doubted he could pinpoint where we were.

Kathe met us partway back to the castle, limping up the path, a crow riding on his shoulder. Seeing him clearly injured sent an unexpected pang through me. I almost ran to him; much as I hadn't forgiven him, I didn't want him to get hurt on my behalf. But I caught the wild gleam of his mage mark through the darkness and held myself in check.

"Are you all right?" I asked, trying to sound like I didn't care.

"Better off than you." He lifted his face to catch the moonlight, seeming to strain to listen. "What's happening? Something is stirring, all across the land."

"Mount Whitecrown. We were too late. It's going to erupt." I caught my breath, wincing at the sharp stab of pain from my rib. "I've redirected it away from...from most people, I hope, but you should still take cover."

"As should you." He glanced behind him. "I've taken care of the immediate pursuit, but there's an uproar at the castle. Ruven is sending more forces after you, and the new Witch Lord of Sevaeth is after your blood as well, Lady Amalia. She blames you for her mother's death."

"But I didn't kill her!" I protested.

"I, ah, may have neglected to correct her assumption that you were responsible," Kathe admitted. "Suffice to say it's not safe for you at the castle anymore. You need to get out of Kazerath as quickly as possible, while Ruven is still distracted with the Conclave and this coming eruption. If you're still here in the morning, he'll be able to bring his whole domain to bear on capturing or killing you."

"We'll head to the border by the shortest route, then. Maybe we can catch up to Marcello." It meant running toward Mount Whitecrown, which seemed foolhardy in the extreme, but in all I'd rather take my chances with the volcano than with Ruven.

"I have to get back to the castle." Kathe reached out and put a hand on my shoulder, warm and gentle and strangely hesitant. "I should have told you about the trap. I'm sorry." The words fell strangely off his tongue, as if it might be the first time he'd spoken them.

Sorry was a start, but anger still simmered in me like chocolate too hot to drink. "Yes, you should have. I might even have played along." His crow half spread its wings, muttering deep in its throat, and I caught its beady eyes. "Wait! Can you send a message?"

"For you, my lady? Anything."

"To my cousin Roland." I caught both his arms in my urgency.

"He's in the path of the eruption. Warn him to run and take shelter, please."

"I'm not sure he'll have enough time for a warning to do any good," Kathe said dubiously. "But all right."

He stroked the crow's beak, whispering to it in some strange guttural tongue. The crow made a noise of protest and flapped its wings. He soothed it, stroking the feathers of its chest, and finally it fluttered off, cawing.

"Will it be all right?" I asked, feeling suddenly guilty.

"That depends on the size and nature of the eruption. I've told him to be quick and careful, and not to get himself killed."

I felt a bit odd, worrying over a crow. But there'd been enough death already, and more was coming. I squeezed Kathe's arms. "Thank you."

"Now, hurry." Kathe leaned forward, hesitated, and placed a quick whisper of a kiss at my hairline. "I'm heading back to the castle, to do what I can to make sure the other Witch Lords know that the volcano is Ruven's fault, and that the Lady of Thorns' death is... well, that it's no loss."

"We may need to have a talk after this is over." I sounded like my mother, letting a younger me know the only reason she wasn't reprimanding me right now was because guests were watching.

Kathe laughed. "I suppose we should. Good luck, Lady Amalia. Don't die."

"I'll try not to."

The ground shuddered again under our feet as Zaira and I fled through the cold silver night. Through the gaps in the trees, we could glimpse a pale gray light rising in the east, washing out the farthest stars. A breeze picked up, growing stronger, swaying the highest tree branches to point deeper into Kazerath; I hoped it was Jerith, raising up a wind to protect the Empire from falling ash.

So much now depended on factors out of anyone's control. How big an eruption could magic trigger, if the volcano wasn't naturally ready? How much pressure had Ruven's enchantment built up, and how much had our sabotage released? How much of the mountain would be blasted skyward when it unleashed its fury? How precisely could the control circle direct such a terrible and untamable force? They were the sort of questions I would have enjoyed discussing over a pile of books with Venasha and Domenic, had they been purely theoretical. But now they chased each other around my head with bleeding-sharp edges, answerless and echoing.

We stayed on the road, taking a trader's path that led up over a low point in Mount Whitecrown's long shoulder toward the closest mountain village across the border in Callamorne. Ruven must have been busy, because the trees seemed content to behave like a normal forest; they hadn't been grown and nursed on hatred of us, like those in Sevaeth. We occasionally heard large things moving in the woods, or an ominous howl or growl in the distance, and we passed close enough to an army encampment to smell the smoke from it; I released Zaira's power at the first sign of danger, but the road remained safe. For a while, it looked as if we might make it to the border unmolested.

But as the road began to climb the base of the mountain, we found our path blocked by a line of some dozen soldiers. The graying light was bright enough to pick out gleams from the row of muskets pointed at us.

"If I burn them all, you're going to have to carry me," Zaira muttered.

"Maybe we can bluff our way through," I replied, without much hope. The pain from my rib and general exhaustion dulled my wits; I wasn't sure I could have bluffed my way out of a boring meeting, let alone mortal danger. But I had extreme doubts that I could drag an unconscious Zaira up a mountain with a broken rib, either.

"If I see one spark of balefire, I'll shoot," the man in the center of the line called, sighting grimly along his musket. "Come with us back to Lord Ruven's castle, and no one will be hurt."

Hells. They knew who we were. This was no random mountain patrol; Ruven had sent some scouting party in the area to stop us.

"You're making a mistake," I warned, trying to sound sure and dangerous. "Get out of our way, while you still can."

"I can't do that, my lady," the officer said, and by the tension in his voice, I knew he meant it. "Now, if you won't come with us quietly, I have orders to—"

I never found out what his orders were. A light flashed on the dark road behind him, and a loud crack split the air. It sounded like a flintlock pistol, but even as the soldiers whirled to face their attacker, it was followed by a deep chime, as if someone had rung a massive bell. The air rippled with a wave of magic.

As the wave hit them, the soldiers went suddenly limp. Their muskets clattered to the ground. Their bodies followed, boneless and oddly graceful.

I slapped my hands over my ears and scrambled backward. The wave had nearly petered out by the time it reached us, but still it shuddered through me with numbing force, and my legs buckled under me. I fell to my knees but was able to rise again at once, the tone still echoing in my head. Zaira clutched my arm for balance, her free hand pressed to her temple.

"What in the Nine Hells was *that*?" she growled.

The scent of gunsmoke teased its way along the path. Marcello stepped from the shadows ahead, pistol in hand. Brass bands marked with glowing runes spun lazily around the barrel, which was encased with crystals and wire. Sweet relief swept through me at the sight of him.

"I left my pistol where Istrella could get it," he said. "Now I have no idea what it'll do each time I fire it."

"Where's Terika?" Zaira demanded.

"Safe on our side of the border." Marcello glanced at the stunned soldiers, who were already stirring weakly. "Come on. I've got more people up the road, but we'd better run."

We'd made it past the Kazerath boundary stones and a set of imperial guard towers and could see the walls of a border fort well enough to pick out the cannons on the battlements in the rosy light of dawn, when the mountain shook hard enough to throw us off our feet at last. I caught myself on my hands and knees in the dusty road, beside the stream course the trader's path followed; the great trembling in the earth traveled up my arms and rattled my bones. Marcello let out a startled cry, and fearful oaths rose from the imperial soldiers who'd joined our escort on the way.

In the bones of the mountain, something broke.

Hell of Disaster. Here it comes.

There came a deep and terrible rumbling, greater than a thousand thunders. I grabbed onto Marcello, who sprawled in the road beside me, and lifted my eyes to the sublime glacier-mantled peak of Mount Whitecrown. Immense and remote as the sky itself, it reared above us, past the green-swathed ridge that rose immediately overhead.

Gray ash unfurled skyward from the far side of it, blossoming greater and greater, reaching and spreading in awful immensity. The colossal dark cloud reared up like a living thing, some demon more terrible than all the Hells rolled together, here to bring the Dark Days upon us once more. The noise was terrible, as if the sky itself might crack open and crumble down on us. And still the mountain shuddered.

The ground should not buck like a tipping boat. The sky should not hold so much billowing darkness. My senses tried to reject it all in horror, but it was real.

My heart seized with guilt and terror. *Roland.* Graces protect him.

Marcello's arms went tight around me, sending a stab of unheeded pain through my cracked rib as we clung to each other. Zaira let out a steady stream of profanity, her usual creativity lost to emphatic repetition. Still the ash cloud loomed larger above us, opaque and unreachable as death, spreading faster than spilled blood as it unfolded across the blue sky. But it bent and leaned, pushed by the wind that tugged our hair and clothing, and the top of the terrible plume began reaching toward Vaskandar.

We were alive. And the Empire was safe. Our efforts had worked; no deadly flows of ash, rock, or lava had poured down the south side of the mountain onto the fortresses, villages, and encamped armies there.

But I had just killed my cousin.

I could feel it, deep in my blood—the same way the jess gave me a vague sense of where Zaira was, and the same way I recognized the blooding stones in Atruin. I was dimly aware of the bloody rune I'd painted on the control circle, of the mountain's fiery heart to which it connected me, and of the gaping hole in Mount Whitecrown's side from which the towering ash cloud continued to rise. I knew of the path of devastation down the side of the mountain—the hot flow of gas and ash and pulverized rock that had blasted down ancient pines and wiped a clean swath down Mount Whitecrown's forested flank to the river below.

And I knew the lives that had winked out there, like snuffed candles, one-two-three.

Roland.

A sob tore out of me, no more possible to repress than the eruption itself. Marcello and Zaira stared at me like I was mad—they didn't know. But I couldn't explain, not now. I was crying so hard I could barely gasp in enough breath.

Treat strong emotions like cards: keep them close in hand and show them to no one, my mother's voice admonished me in my memory, but it was too late. Grief shook me harder than the earthquake, and a bewildered Marcello folded his arms around me and stroked my hair while the tears ran down to my chin.

Chapter Forty-Four

The great column of gray ash loomed behind us like the accusing finger of some massive demon as we made our way down out of the mountains and back toward Durantain. Poor Jerith might have to keep his wind going for days; I was glad Balos was there to take care of him.

Imperial scouts had confirmed what I already knew. The eruption had been a small one, compared to others in the violent history of the volcanoes of the Witchwall Mountains; the effects of the blast had been limited to the eastern flank of Mount Whitecrown itself. But a deadly flow of hot ash and lava chunks had swept a gray streak down the mountainside, exactly where I'd aimed it.

Prince Roland and his handful of soldiers had not survived.

I tried to tell myself it was a victory. We'd stopped Ruven from taking out our border defenses and claiming vast swaths of territory with his falling ash. The Lady of Eagles seizing the entire mountain for Atruin would ensure that he couldn't try again. We'd saved thousands of lives, and lost no known civilians to the eruption.

But all I could think of, during the journey to Durantain, was what I would say to my grandmother and Bree. I was so nauseous with dread I could barely eat.

We arrived to find the city already in mourning. Black bunting draped shops, homes, and statues; nearly everyone I saw in the street wore black mourning ribbons at the very least, and every corner shrine had at least a dozen candles lit. The knots in my stomach twisted tighter. *You see? They did love you, Roland. And they still do.*

People had laid countless flowers at the foot of the statue of Queen Galanthe making her stand on the Ironblood Bridge; they rose up the base and to the statue's knees, so my grandmother's bronze image waded through a sea of lilies and roses. My eyes stung as we passed it. Marcello reached out and squeezed my hand.

My grandmother and Bree met us at the castle gates. The utter misery of loss in Bree's eyes hit me like a blow to the face. She threw her arms around me, and all the words of the apology I'd practiced froze in my throat.

"I'm so glad you're all right." Bree's voice sounded strained and raw in my ear.

I hugged her back, tentatively. "Bree, I..." *I'm sorry. I'm so, so sorry.* But I couldn't say it.

She squeezed me until the breath huffed out of my lungs and my rib stabbed pain through my side. "Don't say anything. I can't bear to talk about him yet. I'm still angry at him for being at the border when I was stuck back here. It should have been me." My hair grew damp where her cheek pressed against it. "He should have stayed home. He didn't have to die."

"No," I whispered. "He didn't."

I met my grandmother's eyes over Bree's shoulder. The deep, wrenching sorrow in them was matched only by the weariness that dragged at her features. She knew this pain. She had lost a husband and a son already. This new wound I'd inflicted on her was a terrible one, but she had survived its like before, and she would again.

Those wise, grieving eyes read the anguish in my face. Her lips pressed together, and she gave me a slow nod.

"Come inside the castle," she said. "You must be tired."

Graces, yes. I was as tired as I'd ever been.

During the process of welcoming us into the castle, as servants in the courtyard took our horses and unloaded our baggage, my grandmother drew me aside. Her grip on my arm was gentle, but her fingers were hard as iron, and the lines of her face had gone grim as she studied me.

"What is it?" she asked. "What don't you want to tell Bree?"

For an instant, I almost fell apart again, like I had with Marcello when the volcano erupted. But I stuffed the unsteady surge of emotion back down where it belonged, mostly, and kept my eyes dry, at least.

"I had to choose where to channel the eruption." I forced the words out, soft and low, and made myself meet my grandmother's intense, grieving gaze. "There were no good options. I thought...I thought Roland would want me to pick the way the fewest people had to die."

The queen closed her eyes. Her hand tightened on my arm. But then she released a long breath.

"That he would," she agreed quietly. "He would never have forgiven you if you had chosen otherwise."

"I killed him, Grandmother." My voice trembled.

"No." Her eyes snapped open. "That vile murderer Ruven killed him. You did what a ruler has to do." Her gaze pierced me like a well-honed rapier. "You did what I do, every time I send soldiers into battle. The Graces called for a sacrifice, and you made it."

"I chose who would make it, you mean."

"That *is* your sacrifice." She dropped my arm, and gave me a grim nod. "And now you've accepted it. You are truly prepared to rule."

"Sometimes," I said bitterly, "I'm not certain that's a good thing."

We headed to our rooms early that evening, after a somber dinner. The absence of the usual lively bickering between Roland and Bree cut fresh wounds into my heart; to see the wrong cousin talking seriously with my grandmother about how to reassign troops to account for the changing situation in Vaskandar rubbed salt in them. Bree knew it, too, and kept drinking more and more despite the queen's disapproving gaze, until finally my grandmother suggested pointedly that we'd all had a long day and perhaps we should go to bed.

Zaira's rooms adjoined mine, and I stopped at her door to say good night. Zaira stood with the door in hand, paused in the act of closing it between us, and frowned.

"We're back in the Serene Empire," she said.

"So we are," I agreed.

"You never sealed my power."

I shrugged. "Do you want me to?"

Zaira fell silent, her dark eyes thoughtful. She ran her hand up and down the edge of the door, the jess shining on her wrist.

"Keep my power sealed by default when we're around people," she said at last. "I don't want some brat to bump into me from behind in a crowded street and startle me into murdering half a dozen passersby. I'll let you know when I want you to release me."

I nodded. "All right. Now, then?"

"Why not," she sighed. "Now."

"Revincio."

She shook herself, like a wet dog, and grimaced.

"Like putting a corset back on?" I hazarded.

"A bit." She sighed. "But then, corsets have their uses." She grinned and put her hands on her hips, pushing out her chest.

I cleared my throat. "I suppose they do. Well, good night, Zaira."

"Good night, Amalia."

I froze in the act of turning away. I swiveled to stare at her. "That's the first time you've ever called me by my given name."

Zaira frowned. "No, it isn't."

"I . . ." I swallowed. There was no point arguing with her.

She'd called me a hundred insulting nicknames, and even Cornaro once or twice; but there were precious few people I'd ever heard her call by their given name at all. As if somehow speaking a name might make the person real, a part of her life she couldn't dismiss and forget in an instant.

My throat felt tight and hot. "Perhaps not," I said. "But thank you, anyway. And good night."

The warm feeling in my stomach barely lasted two minutes. I had my hand on my own door latch, eager to finally get some rest, when Lord Caulin rounded the corner.

"Lady Amalia," he called down the hallway. "I'd hoped to catch you before you went to bed."

Irritation replaced my goodwill. "You have only done so by the barest technicality."

He offered me an apologetic bow and approached anyway. "The doge has asked me to congratulate and thank you for your exemplary service to the Serene Empire. Everyone is most impressed with the results you obtained at the Conclave."

I waited, my hand still on the latch. I'd already spoken directly with the doge over the courier lamps from the border fortress, and he'd expressed his gratitude then. There was no way he would bother so senior an adviser as Lord Caulin to track me down to deliver such sentiments a second time in person.

Lord Caulin licked his lips. "So marvelous, that you managed to bring home the captured Falcons, as well. But we did notice in the reports we've received that one of the names on our list of missing Falcons is not among those who returned to us."

"You mean Harrald," I said shortly.

"Yes, I believe that was the name." He smoothed imaginary dust from the front of his jacket. "I know we discussed this matter earlier, before the Conclave, and I was curious what had happened to him."

I fixed Lord Caulin with my coldest stare. "And I am curious why we even had that discussion without the Council of Nine being consulted first."

Lord Caulin's smile faltered. "I imagine it was a matter of expediency, my lady."

"Of course." I held his gaze until he glanced away. "To answer your question, I don't know precisely what happened to Harrald. He was with us when we sneaked the Falcons out of Lord Ruven's castle. But it was dark and dangerous work getting them through the forests of Kazerath undetected, and he was no longer with the group by the time Captain Verdi took charge of them." All true, as far as it went.

"I see." Lord Caulin sighed. "A pity. I suppose there isn't much chance he survived, alone in the forests of Vaskandar at night. You had no chance to make sure of him?"

"Lord Caulin. With all due respect, you do not command me." I let my voice drop to the deep register my mother used for uttering her most serious warnings. "I answer to the doge and the Council of Nine alone. You gave me a verbal order without the approval of the Council. Do you have a writ to show me, with the imperial seal?"

Lord Caulin's face went still. "No, my lady."

"Because the doge didn't want evidence that he went around the Council," I said flatly.

Lord Caulin's eyes narrowed. "I would not dare make guesses about such things, my lady."

"Oh? I would. In fact, I would go so far as to guess that if I stood the doge and my mother in the same room and asked him to confirm the order you gave me, he would deny it ever existed. Even if it meant leaving *you* in a rather awkward position, Lord Caulin."

He said not a word, mouth clamped shut. Thoughts moved in his dark eyes, but I couldn't read them. Lord Caulin was no fool, to show me his hand now, when the wrong move could lose him the game.

"Despite this," I said, softening my voice, "I did all I could to return every Falcon home. Because I am a loyal servant of the Serene Empire. And now, Lord Caulin, I must bid you good night."

They held a memorial for Roland in the Temple of Mercy, since his body lay somewhere under ash and lava rubble on Mount Whitecrown. The crowd filled the temple and the square outside it, overflowing into the streets beyond. My mother had taken a fast coach up from Raverra to attend, changing horses at the imperial post stations, arriving just in time for the ceremony. She stood by my side, her face grim and pensive; I suspected she was remembering my father's memorial in this same temple.

I stayed silent as one person after another spoke of what a good man he had been, and what a tragedy it was that his life had been cut so short. I tried to focus on Roland, on everything I loved about him, from the stern look he gave Bree and me when I followed her into trouble as children to how free he looked when you surprised him into a laugh.

But I couldn't forget that I'd killed him.

Afterward there was a feast in his honor in the great hall—swept clear of all remnants of the thorn tree, with a slightly paler patch of stone where they'd replaced the floor—and nearly everyone got roaringly drunk, in the Callamornish tradition. I wished I could, but too much queasy guilt lay in my belly.

This was only the beginning. I would have to make life-and-death decisions all the time, on the Council of Nine. This was a growing pain, part of becoming what I needed to be.

No. I forced my attention to Bree's face, smiling somehow through her tears as she told the table a story about Roland from when they were children. Tonight was about Roland, not about me. Time to remember him as he was, not to dwell on the death I'd given him.

So I listened to the stories, and told some of my own at last, and drank a little of the beer, though not enough to take the edge off my sorrow.

Late into the night, when nearly everyone had gone home and only the most devoted or inebriated remained in the great hall, Bree rose and grabbed my hand. She was drunk enough she almost fumbled it but got a firm grip on her second try.

"Come on," she said. "Come out to the courtyard with me."

"What for?" I asked, rising obediently.

"To rail at the stars."

I followed her out into the great, empty yard, built for military drills rather than pleasure. No gardens adorned the clean-swept expanse, but the stars spread bright above us. We stared up at them together a moment. Bree let out a long, miserable sigh.

Then she slapped me across the face.

I staggered back, shocked and smarting. Bree glared at me, tears in her eyes.

"I heard what you did," she said. "Grandmother told me."

Oh, Hells. "Bree, I'm sorry. I'm so sorry. Any other way would have killed hundreds or thousands of people."

She took a step toward me, her fists balled at her sides. "Then you find a different way! You're supposed to be the smart one, Amalia. The one who can always think of something."

I raised a hand to my stinging cheek. "I wish that were true. But I didn't have time, or...or I just wasn't smart enough. I'm no artificer, Bree. The eruption had to go somewhere, and so I picked the direction where the fewest people would die." A pleading note had entered my voice. "I wish to all the Graces that Roland hadn't been one of them."

Bree shook her head. "Listen to you. This isn't an equation for you to solve, Amalia. You can't weigh lives against each other like fruit at the market."

"What would you have done, then?" The words leaped past my lips on a spark of anger. "Let the volcano erupt how it would, and risk killing everyone?"

"I would have kept trying, and to the Nine Hells with the chances." She set her jaw in a way I knew well from when we were children. "Because that's what you do. You keep trying to save everyone. You don't give up and say, 'Oh well, I guess my cousin has to die.' Otherwise, you're just a coldblooded monster."

I stiffened. "I suppose I am," I said. "But that was what I needed to be, at the time."

Silence fell. Bree stared at me, her eyes black pools of shadow under the swollen moon.

"Get out," she growled at last.

I hesitated. "Bree..."

"You killed my brother. Go away, before I hit you again."

I turned, a deep ache cutting into my chest, and walked away.

I made it halfway across the courtyard before the muffled sound of sobbing began behind me.

I looked back. Bree was sitting on the ground, her face in her hands, the moonlight spilling over her like a blanket of consolation.

Coldblooded monster.

I straightened my shoulders and walked back into the castle.

Chapter Forty-Five

I was in councils with Bree all the next day, but she never met my eyes. We talked with my grandmother, my mother, the Serene Envoy to Callamorne, and various generals and advisers about the new situation on the border. Sevaeth had withdrawn many of its forces, and while Kazerath hadn't moved its troops, they showed no signs of preparations for immediate attack. At the very least, they were rethinking their strategy after the Conclave and the diminished eruption. We had gained a reprieve, it would seem; and with snow likely to close the passes within the month, the reprieve might well last until spring.

After the last strategy discussion finally dispersed, my mother pulled me aside in a tapestried alcove outside the council chamber—the sort of small space with padded benches where people might wait before being called in to a meeting. It was the first moment we'd had alone together since she'd come to Callamorne. All yesterday through the memorial and banquet we'd been on display, and all today we'd been in council.

She read my face as if it were a book, her brows pinching a faint divot between them in the warm, flickering light of the alcove's oil lamps. And then she folded me in her arms.

I breathed in the familiar scent of her perfume, her auburn

hair tickling my nose. I could almost be a little girl again, whose most wrenching decision was which book to read at bedtime.

"It's hard," she said softly. "I know. But you'll be all right."

I didn't have the heart to tell her that was exactly what I was afraid of. La Contessa had made her peace with deciding the lives and deaths of others long ago.

"You did well at the Conclave," my mother said then, releasing me, her mouth stirring in a faint smile. "That should secure you quite a reputation. Amalia Cornaro, with the iron nerves to negotiate successfully with Witch Lords."

"This isn't over," I fretted. "There are still at least three, possibly four Witch Lords bent on invasion. And Mamma, I've been wanting to ask you—what is Lord Caulin up to?" I dropped my voice. "He ordered me to *kill* any Falcons who I couldn't get out of Vaskandar."

La Contessa's eyes narrowed. "And you disobeyed?"

"Of course. I'm not a murderer." I thought of Roland, and my breath caught for a moment. But there was a difference between killing and murder. I held that distinction close, though I was well aware some of my academic colleagues might ably debate the point for hours. "Is that going to cause problems? Was that order really from the doge?"

"That is a very interesting question, and one I suspect Niro would not give me a straight answer to if I asked." My mother rolled her string of black pearls between her fingers. "There is a shift happening in the Council of Nine. The Assembly is on the verge of finally completing the election of Baron Leodra's successor, and it seems likely that Lord Caulin will win his seat."

"Unfortunate." I shook my head in disgust.

My mother shrugged. "He has some useful qualities. He'll be better than Leodra was. But he is not compassionate. He sees the Falcons as resources—weapons of war—and he urges the doge and Council to hold them close." She leveled a frank, penetrating gaze at me. "He will be your opponent, because of your Falcon law. If he learns you disobeyed the order, he'll use it against you. As he would have if you had complied."

I let out an uneven breath. "I was afraid of that."

"You're a full player of the game at last, Amalia." My mother brushed a lock of hair back from my neck, a gleam of ironic amusement in her eyes. "Congratulations. Now things will get difficult for you."

Graces help me. My vision of a perfect future—relaxing with a good book and a glass of fine wine in my personal library, with Marcello leaning warm against me—blurred with the haze of endless political struggle. The Serene City was never going to let me rest.

"What do I do?" I asked, trying not to sound like a nervous child.

"Gather your resources." My mother's voice was wise and hard with decades of experience. "Build your power. Collect allies—people with influence, certainly, but competency and loyalty are far more important. You're off to a good start there."

I thought of Marcello, Zaira, and perhaps even Kathe—he was terrifyingly loyal, in his own way, though I couldn't trust him to express it in a manner I would find comfortable. "Yes," I agreed. "I am."

"Keep those people close," my mother said softly. "You'll need them."

The following morning, Zaira and I set out on an errand that would take us away from Durantain for a few days. We had a full escort of soldiers, including Marcello. I'd already said good-bye to my grandmother, and my mother had departed for

Raverra an hour earlier; I didn't expect anyone to see us off. But as I prepared to climb into my carriage, a voice called from behind me.

"Oy! Amalia!"

It was Bree, striding toward me, a look of determination on her face. I braced myself for another slap.

But she threw her arms around me in a hug. She released me quickly, with a sad smile; I couldn't tell if it was the tracks of dried tears on her cheeks that made it seem stiffer than usual.

"Be careful, all right?"

"I will." I tried to pour all my love for her into my return smile. But my memory still rang with her words from the other night: *Coldblooded monster.* "We won't be gone long."

Bree turned to Zaira, clasping her arm encouragingly. "Grace of Luck go with you."

"Luck won't be enough," Zaira groaned. "There's no escaping this." She glanced toward Terika, who was supervising the loading of her alchemical supplies into our carriage. She had to return to the Mews to get a new Falconer soon, but Marcello had granted her leave for this one trip first.

"Not that I want to," Zaira added.

After a couple of days of smooth travel under sunny skies, we finally came to a small farm tucked into a rock-strewn meadow, near a familiar village high in the mountains. A pair of goats browsed outside a well-kept wooden cottage, and fresh candles stood at a tidy shrine to the Grace of Bounty. Zaira, Terika, and I descended from the carriage and approached on foot; fat brown hens scattered indignantly before us.

Terika clasped Zaira's hand, giving her a bright-eyed glance. "What do you think?"

"It's pretty," Zaira said shortly. She looked as pale as I'd ever seen her.

"Are you scared?" Terika grinned.

"No!" Zaira glared at the polished wooden door before her. "Maybe. A little."

Terika dropped her voice to a spooky rumble. "You should be."

And she threw open the door. "Baba, I'm home!"

I hung back as Terika's grandmother welcomed Zaira into the house with open arms, smothering a smile as Zaira became the alarmed recipient of an enthusiastic hug. I was only here as her Falconer, after all; this moment wasn't for me.

But I couldn't stop grinning at the sound of a delighted old voice from within the cottage, telling Zaira how she'd heard so much about her, and Zaira's surprisingly respectful mumbles in response.

I wandered farther from the cottage to give them privacy, across a lumpy stubble of grass kept short by the hungry goats, each exhalation making a brief, sharp cloud in the crisp air. It was Zaira's life, I reminded myself. Graces forgive me, though, but I couldn't help thinking whom I'd recommend if they happened to find themselves in need of wedding dresses.

"Pssst," a familiar voice called. "Over here."

Kathe. Of course.

I scanned the windswept meadow but saw only birds searching and pecking in the grass for the last seeds of autumn. Then I spotted him in the branches of a low, scraggly apple tree, which he shared with three black crows.

I glanced back toward the road, where our escort waited. The swell of the hill blocked them from sight. But I supposed I was as safe with the Crow Lord as I'd ever been.

"I should have known you'd turn up," I said, approaching the tree.

He leaped down from the branches, landing nimbly as a cat. "Naturally. You can't get rid of crows so easily."

The sun caught on his sharp cheekbones, flaring in the mad yellow rings of the mage mark in his eyes. For a moment, the memory of his kiss came over me strong as a storm wave, and I wanted very badly to try those lips again.

But the twinge in my side whenever I took a deep breath reminded me of the dangers of trusting him. I frowned at him, vexed.

His eyes flicked back and forth over my face, reading whatever was written there. "I should have told you what I was planning, with the Lady of Thorns."

"Yes, you should have."

He bit his lip. "I'm sorry. I was afraid that if I asked you to help, you wouldn't act surprised enough and would give away the plan."

I spread my arms. "If you truly want to convince me to enter into a scheme of world domination with you, you need to show yourself capable of conspiring *with* as well as conspiring *against*."

"We're not used to that in Vaskandar," he said ruefully. "I'll do better next time."

"Hmm." I crossed my arms, considering him. "Can you give me one good reason I should allow you to continue courting me?"

He lifted a finger. "I can do better than that."

"Let me guess. A game."

"Of course." He grinned. "For every reason you give me why we shouldn't court, I'll give you two reasons why we should."

I almost made some tart response, but an edge of desperation showed in the tautness around his eyes. This was the only way he knew how to interact with people, I realized. I hadn't seen him play this kind of game with his enemies. These were his courtship gifts, which he placed before me like a crow presenting some shiny discarded bauble to its hopeful mate.

I sighed. "Very well. For starters, you nearly got me killed, and I have a broken rib to show for it."

"I did." He bowed, sweeping his feathered cloak before him. "And to make it up to you, for my two reasons, I offer you both my full cooperation and that of the domain of Let in your efforts to counter Ruven. Reconnaissance crows, staging troops out of Let, magical assistance, whatever you need."

I stared at him. "Truly?"

"If we're courting." A spark danced in his eyes. "I could do no less for the woman I admire so much. I should add that my efforts would be at *your* disposal, not that of the Serene Empire."

Grace of Majesty. Even aside from the advantages such an alliance would give us in war, that would give me enormous leverage over the doge and the Council. I stopped myself from clutching the claws that still hung at my chest. I couldn't let him see how my breath had quickened.

"But Ruven has no reason to invade the Empire." I forced my voice to be deliberately casual. "He's got his domain. His ploy with the volcano has failed. Your offer of an alliance against him doesn't mean much if he settles down to rule Kazerath like a good neighbor."

Kathe raised an eyebrow. "You don't really believe he'll do that, do you? When he has the capability to put anyone he poisons under his complete control? You know the man. Do you think he'll accept defeat graciously, and be content to rule his inheritance in peace?"

"No," I admitted.

"Especially when he knows that half the Witch Lords in Vaskandar think he should be put down like a rabid animal now." Kathe shook his head. "He's no fool. He knows he has to build his power base quickly, until even the eldest won't want to challenge him directly. The fastest way for him to gain an advantage the rest of us can't easily counter is to try to seize the power of your Empire—its land and Falcons both."

It made too much sense. "But Sevaeth, at least, is surely out of the picture. The Lady of Thorns' daughter is in no position to mount a war."

"Not with the Lady of Lynxes pouncing on her from the north," Kathe agreed. "But that conflict will resolve itself soon enough. If she's smart, she'll let the lynx bite off a piece of her domain, and consolidate her power in the south. Once the dust settles, if she's still around, she's deep in Ruven's debt, and will be his creature." He shrugged. "You still have the Lady of Bears and the Serpent Lord eager for war, too, but frankly, Ruven is dangerous enough on his own. Any other reasons?"

I tapped my chin. "With the Lady of Thorns gone, we don't have a common interest. I don't know if I can trust you."

"What's the fun in courting someone you know you can trust?" He winked. "But if you prefer a boring life, reassure yourself I have as much desire to see Ruven gone as you do. My domain borders his, and I don't fancy a cruel, power-hungry Skinwitch for a neighbor. And for my second reason, you know that I want this courtship to succeed." He grimaced. "I'm aware I'm on my last chance. I can't pretend I'm going to stop liking surprises, but I'll try to keep them somewhat less dangerous."

I held his gaze. "All right, here's another reason. My heart belongs to someone else."

He winced, and for a moment I felt a twinge of sympathy. But then he laughed, setting the crows in the tree above us to flapping in startlement.

"My lady, you and I know courtship is not a matter of the heart."

"Isn't it?" I challenged him, putting my hands on my hips.

"No." His voice went serious then. "But the heart has everything to do with love. And love is a sacred thing, something you give freely and can never take back. It's not a matter for games."

"And courtship is a game." I sighed. "I suppose that's accurate."

"As for my second reason..." He grinned. "I can only ask you to give me time. Most likely either I'll grow on you, or you'll have enough of me and ask your warlock friend to light me on fire."

I couldn't suppress a laugh. Pain flared in my rib, however, and I smothered it, wincing. "Fair enough."

"So, are we still courting, then?" Kathe asked, tilting his head.

I thought of Marcello, waiting patiently down the hill. And Ruven, winding his will deeper through his domain, considering his next course of action, stockpile of potion in hand. Not to mention my Falcon reform law, which I'd need every edge I could get to pass through the Assembly, especially if Lord Caulin was working against it.

"I'm not so rash as to break things off on an impulse," I said. "And a continued alliance against Ruven seems mutually beneficial."

Kathe's mouth pulled into a wry smile. "How dazzlingly romantic."

Warmth flushed my cheeks. "Would you prefer we negotiated these matters by candlelight while boating under the Lovers' Bridge with a bottle of wine?"

"That sounds lovely. I accept your invitation." He reached out and took my hand, bowing over it with amusement dancing in his eyes. "I'll call on you when you're back in Raverra."

I swallowed my protest and let him kiss my hand. The warm pressure of his lips sent a tingling jolt up my arm. "I look forward to it."

And curse him, despite everything, I did.

I made my way down toward the cottage and spied Terika and Zaira through the window. They sat together by the glowing fireplace, leaning against each other and laughing as a tortoiseshell cat attempted to nibble Zaira's hair. Terika's grandmother rocked in a quilt-covered chair nearby, smiling indulgently and knitting. I swerved toward the road; they didn't need me now.

Marcello met me halfway, his green eyes soft and thoughtful. "Can we go for a walk?" he asked.

Graces, he was just what I needed right now. Someone safe, someone comforting, whom I could talk to without worrying about what secrets we were hiding from each other. Someone with whom I could be myself, and not a Cornaro or a Lochaver or a descendant of the Lady of Eagles.

We could always be that for each other. No matter what either of us decided about whom we courted or whom we married. I needed to stop worrying about what would happen in an unknown future and simply be his friend in the present.

"Yes," I said. "I'd like that very much."

We strolled down the road together, away from our escort of soldiers, who huddled in conversation with their coats pulled close and their backs to the cold, and from the cottage where Zaira appeared to be hitting it off splendidly with Terika's grandmother. For a while, we walked in agreeable silence, through the dry, frozen meadow under the bright sun. Then the road ducked into a stand of low pines, breaking our line of sight to the others, and Marcello stopped.

"I can't stop thinking about the Falcons," he said in a low voice. Trouble weighed down his brows. "Emmand, who ran from us when we were trying to help him. Harrald, who didn't want to come back. The captured Falcons who came back to us not because they wanted to, but because the other alternatives were even worse." He swallowed. "I love the Falconers. The Mews saved Istrella and me; it's our home. But it can't be that way for everyone, no matter how hard I try to make it so. And I should have seen that a long time ago."

I rested a hand on his shoulder. "Then help me change things. I'm going to try to push this law through the Assembly when I get back to Raverra. If you can get me Colonel Vasante's support, a lot more people will give it credence."

He nodded, resolve straightening his shoulders. "I'll try."

"Thanks." I sighed. "I hope I can manage it. I'm new at all this."

"You'll do fine," he assured me, smiling. "You're La Contessa's daughter, after all."

You are truly prepared to rule. My grandmother's words blended together in my memory with Bree's: *Coldblooded monster.* They might be the same thing. I winced.

Marcello reached a hand toward my face, then checked it, his fingers curling in on themselves and hovering uncertainly in the air between us. "What is it?"

"I'm afraid." I took his hand and cradled it in both of mine, feeling its warmth and the hard sword calluses on his palm. I needed this now, the comfort of a warm and gentle human touch, and I had nowhere else to turn for it. "I'm afraid of what I might be becoming. I killed Roland. He was my cousin, and I loved him, and I killed him."

"You made the hard choice that needed to be made. It's the same in the military." By the shadows crossing his face, he'd had to come to terms with such choices himself. "Someone has to do it, Amalia."

"I know. There was no way around the decision." I drew in a shuddery breath. "But who am I to decide who lives and dies? The doge would have been willing to destroy an entire city and kill thousands of people to prove a point, last year. I don't want to reckon lives as nothing more than pieces on a board. If I can kill my own cousin, how am I any different?"

"Because you do care." He held my gaze, his green eyes intense. "I know you, Amalia. You won't stop caring, even if you have to make decisions that sacrifice lives. And that's why you're the one who should make them."

"Help me keep caring, Marcello." I squeezed his hand tight. "Year after year, until I'm old and withered and jaded. Don't let me harden my heart, no matter how much I want it to stop hurting. No matter what I have to do."

"I promise," he whispered. "I will."

Above us, a crow called, its raucous laugh scraping at the sky.

The story continues in . . .

Book three of the Swords and Fire series

Coming soon

Acknowledgments

It takes a village to make a book, but a really amazing badass village, like Themyscira. So I have some truly awesome people to thank.

Warmest thanks to Naomi Davis, my agent and fairy godmother, without whom this series would never have seen the light of day. And my profound gratitude goes out to my incredible editors: Lindsey Hall, who edited the first draft of this book, and Sarah Guan, who carried it to the finish line, and Emily Byron, my wonderful UK editor. Thank you all for pushing me and guiding me to make this book the best it could possibly be.

Thank you to the entire Orbit team for being supportive, fun, wonderful, and really good at what you do. I am so lucky to have the chance to work with you, and you all deserve cinnamon rolls and puppies and the magical powers of your choice.

Love and deepest gratitude to my husband, Jesse King, and my daughters, Maya and Kyra, for your patience and support while I wrote this book. With all your help and hugs and understanding, I knew you had my back when writing swallowed my life, and it meant the world to me. And thank you to all my friends and family who cheered me on and helped me out—especially my parents, who in addition to nurturing my dream have had to put up with my shenanigans for decades.

Thanks to my beta readers, who turned around feedback with impressive alacrity and insight: Natsuko Toyofuku, Deva Fagan, Lauren Austrian-Parke, Dan Parke, and Nicole Evans. You gave me sanity checks when I needed them, pointed me in the right direction, and caught my mistakes, all on a tight schedule, and I adore you.

And thanks to you, my readers, for sticking with me. This story wouldn't be complete without you, and I'm so excited to have you along for the ride.

extras

www.orbitbooks.net

about the author

Melissa Caruso graduated with honors in creative writing from Brown University and holds an MFA in Fiction from University of Massachusetts—Amherst.

Find out more about Melissa Caruso and other Orbit authors by registering online for the free monthly newsletter at www.orbitbooks.net.

if you enjoyed
THE DEFIANT HEIR

look out for

MAGEBORN

Book One of the Age of Dread

by

Stephen Aryan

Thousands died when mages sundered the earth and split the sky.

It was a war that devastated entire kingdoms. Now one man believes eradicating magic is the only way to ensure a lasting peace. He and his followers will do anything to achieve his goal – even if it means murdering every child born with the ability.

CHAPTER 1

The air in the tavern was thick with the stench of fear. To Habreel it was sweeter than any perfume. He smiled at the locals' unhappiness and sipped his ale, pretending to be just another traveller passing through the town of Glienned.

A few minutes later there was a stir in the crowd as the door opened to admit another visitor. Glancing in the mirror behind the bar Habreel saw a tall woman dressed in black leather armour and matching trousers approach and sit down on the stool next to him. He could admit to himself, if no one else, that she was a striking woman. Her raven-black hair and pale skin were not unusual, but the slight tilt to her green eyes and high cheekbones made it difficult to pinpoint her nationality. Her array of daggers, eight that he could see from an initial count, would draw attention as much as her features.

Akosh smiled at the barman, who turned a little red under the intensity of her stare. "On the house," he muttered, setting down a mug of ale before scuttling away.

Habreel frowned at her and she raised an eyebrow. "Something wrong?"

"You're a little conspicuous," he said, gesturing at her outfit.

Akosh rolled her eyes and waved at the mirror and their

view of the room behind them. "Look again." The surface of the mirror rippled as if made of water and her image changed, from the leather-clad warrior to a severely dressed woman with a plain face surrounded by a tight bonnet. Every feature of the woman's face was forgettable. Only the colour of her eyes remained the same dark green, but set in a doughy face they were not enough to draw attention. "They see only what I want them to," added Akosh.

Habreel grimaced but said nothing. Magic. He took a deep breath and reminded himself she was a necessary evil. For now.

"Why here?" she asked him.

"Because Glienned is the doorway to Zecorria," explained Habreel, keeping his voice low. It was the first large town any travellers came to when they crossed the border into Zecorria from Yerskania. It was a hub of information and people from all over the world were known to stop here for the night. Anything that happened here would quickly spread across all kingdoms in the west. If they were lucky it would cross the mountains into Seveldrom and perhaps beyond in the desert kingdoms. Tensions between the east and west from the war a decade ago had faded and trade now flourished.

"Is that all?" asked Akosh, running a finger through the foam on the top of her ale. She languidly licked her finger and grimaced at the sour taste.

"And because I've been visiting the town on and off for weeks," added Habreel. "Zecorria is still the most hated nation in the west because of its role in the war. The Chosen and the perversion of the faith. The Warlock. The Mad King," he said, ticking things off on his fingers. "Now I will turn that into strength and other countries will race to unite behind them. Who doesn't like a redemption story?" he asked rhetorically.

"I hear a lot of words, but don't see anything exciting," said Akosh, in a bored voice. Habreel knew she was baiting him but didn't let her get a rise out of him.

"Come then. It's almost time," he said, draining the last of his ale.

Several people outside the tavern were all walking in the same direction with purpose. Akosh and Habreel joined the flow of bodies and soon became part of a large group that was heading towards the main square. By the time they arrived it was a little before midday. Perhaps three hundred people had already gathered, with more appearing all the time.

The sky was a hazy blue and the air was cold enough for Habreel to see his breath. People were stamping their feet and shuffling about to stay warm but no one complained or suggested going inside. None of them wanted to miss this.

In the centre of the square was a wooden platform normally used for travelling theatre troupes and seasonal festivals. Today the mood of the crowd surrounding it was sullen, like that of a public hanging, although there'd not been one of those for decades. Today there was no gibbet but the Mayor still wore a sour expression. "Everyone is so broody," said Akosh, grinning at the faces all around her. "It's delicious."

Habreel said nothing and tried to remain inconspicuous. A few people recognised him but not enough to start a conversation. Today he wasn't the only visitor in the crowd. All of the taverns and shops would be empty. It seemed as if most of the town had decided to show up. Habreel buried his smile but was secretly delighted at the size of the crowd.

Half an hour later the square was packed with people and a low rumble of unhappy conversations flowed around Habreel on all sides.

A shiver of excitement ran through him as everyone suddenly

fell silent. Despite there being so many people squeezed in, they managed to create enough space for the masked Seeker to walk unobstructed through the crowd. No one wanted to touch the hooded figure.

The bulky robe, long black gloves and stylised golden mask completely obscured the Seeker's identity. With only a slit for the mouth and holes for the eyes, it was difficult to tell much about the wearer. A line ran down the middle of the mask from forehead to chin and a swirling symbol, that he thought came from the east, was painted on the right cheek. The locals probably found it intimidating and mysterious. Habreel just thought it was ridiculous.

The only indication that the Seeker was a man came from the width of his shoulders and significant height. To Habreel his stiff gait suggested a history in the military. He wondered how such a person had ended up as a servant of the Red Tower, the school of magic in Shael.

Shortly after the war rumours had sprung up that someone was trying to reopen the school. A few years later people across the west reported seeing masked strangers showing up, offering to test children to see if they had a spark of magic.

Seekers used to be common but it had not been that way for over twenty years. No child would voluntarily declare they had magic and many successfully kept it completely hidden. When a community made such a discovery the hard way, often with a magical accident, it would mean exile for the whole family at best, drowning for the child at worst.

Then came the war and with it the Warlock who soured people towards magic even further. Because of him and his twisted apprentices, thousands had died in a pointless war. Nations had been torn apart with civil war breaking out in Morrinow in the north. In the south Shael was reduced to a shattered ruin that was still in disarray. All of it had happened because of the destructive power of magic and the evil it inspired.

It was a curse, not a blessing from the Maker, the Lady of Light or the Blessed Mother. Those who wielded magic thought it put them above everyone else. Mages claimed the power came from the Source, the heart of creation, but he didn't believe it. History was full of tales where people had been tricked by beings from beyond the Veil, offering them power in return for favours.

Habreel could imagine that wielding such power would be intoxicating, but it was an addictive lie that inspired arrogance and destruction. The war had shown people that magic could not be trusted and, until the Seekers had returned, the old ways of dealing with cursed children had been enough.

Exile or death. It was hard and cruel, but it had worked for a long time. Accidents with magic were avoided and people kept safe.

Now there was a royal decree in many countries which permitted Seekers to visit any village, town or city once a month to test children for magic. He believed in the rule of law, but when it stood in opposition of the will of the people, Habreel knew change was needed.

All eyes were drawn to the Seeker as he moved to stand beside the Mayor on the platform. She flinched at being so close but the Seeker didn't seem to notice. He was looking out at the sea of upturned faces. Habreel thought there was a certain arrogance about his stance.

"Bring them forward," said the Mayor, as if speaking about the condemned. Instead of a line of chained figures several sets of parents reluctantly came to the front of the crowd with their children in tow. All of the adults looked sick with worry, while most of the children were crying. Their ages varied considerably.

Habreel guessed the youngest child was eight or nine years old and the eldest perhaps seventeen. Despite their differences all of them were united by their fear, which pleased him. The good people of Glienned were raising their children to understand that magic was a blight.

"Don't be scared," said the Seeker, who remained blissfully unaware of the mood in the town. "This is a time to celebrate."

The parents stepped forward and many had to shove their child onto the edge of the platform. Even though they were well outside arm's reach of the Seeker, none of the children were willing to go any closer. A couple of the smaller ones tried to run but were firmly held in place by their parents. Eight children. Eight chances of being cursed.

"How exciting," whispered Akosh, her eyes twinkling with delight.

"Can you tell?" asked Habreel. "Do any of them have the ability?"

Akosh grinned and gave him a conspiratorial wink. "That would spoil the fun."

The Seeker started at one end of the line with a slight girl of about ten. She was shaking so badly Habreel expected her to collapse. The masked mage raised one gloved hand towards the child and a few seconds later lowered it.

"No," he said, shaking his head for emphasis. The girl fell to her knees in a flood of tears. Her parents cradled her, openly weeping in relief.

This gave the Seeker pause and he stared at them with concern. His mask roamed across the many faces in the town square and Habreel saw a noticeable shift in his posture.

"He knows," he murmured. Akosh showed her teeth in an approximation of a smile.

"Did you see the Seeker arrive?" asked Habreel.

"No, why?"

"I wonder if he has a fast horse standing ready. If this continues he'll need it."

Moving more quickly now the Seeker went down the line, pausing briefly in front of each child. Every declaration that the child had no talent for magic was met with relief and often tears of joy. At last there were only two left, the eldest boy and a girl who was keening like a wounded animal. When the Seeker raised his hand in front of the girl her wailing increased in pitch, getting higher and higher. Habreel expected the dogs in town to start howling along.

"If nothing else, she has a future with a voice like that," noted Akosh. The girl's voice had taken on the pitch of a yowling cat on heat.

The Seeker paused in front of the girl and a horrified silence spread over the crowd. Finally the girl's voice either gave out or had become so high-pitched only dogs could hear her.

The Seeker tried to say something but nothing happened. He had to clear his throat and try again. "She has the ability."

At his words the girl's parents collapsed into a tangled heap as if hamstrung. Their wretched cries seemed to fill the entire square. The girl was sobbing, too, begging her mother to take her home, promising she'd be good from now on. Friends were commiserating with the parents, as if the girl was already dead rather than standing right in front of them.

"This is a good thing," tried the Seeker, but no one was listening to him. "It's a gift."

"You mean a curse," snarled the Mayor.

When the girl realised her tears were having no effect on her parents, she grabbed hold of her mother's hand. The reaction was unexpected and surprising. The woman recoiled as if she'd been bitten by a poisonous snake.

"Get away from me!" she shrieked at the girl, staring in horror at her own flesh and blood.

Beside him Akosh was chuckling while doing her best to smother it, but the smile would not stay off her face. She was starting to get some peculiar looks from those around her in the crowd. Habreel elbowed her in the ribs and she tried to turn her laugh into a nasty cough, but it wasn't fooling anyone.

While all of this was happening the Seeker quickly turned to the boy, raised his hand and swiftly lowered it.

"He doesn't have the ability," he said, much to the relief of everyone around the boy.

The cursed girl had fallen silent. Her face was incredibly pale and she stared at her parents with open-mouthed horror.

"Momma," said the girl, pleading with her eyes.

"Maybe we could all leave," suggested the girl's father. "Start a new life somewhere else."

"I have no daughter," hissed the mother, before collapsing against her husband in tears.

When the Seeker tried to lead the girl away she resisted at first but then moved as if in a trance.

"This isn't right," said the Seeker, trying to appeal to anyone who would listen. Habreel could see a few sympathised with him, but they were in the minority and wisely kept their mouths shut. The Seeker was only visiting the town but they had to live here.

"You should take the girl and leave, while you still can," said the Mayor. A low murmur of conversation was starting to flow through the crowd, and the tone wasn't friendly. All of the anger was directed towards the masked stranger.

"More children will be born with the gift," he declared.

"We'll take care of them by ourselves from now on," said the Mayor.

"You don't know how," said the Seeker.

"We managed it for years before the war, long before your kind started showing up again. We'll be just fine." The Mayor received murmurs of support from the majority of the crowd.

At this the Seeker paused, but not for long. He wasn't facing one angry woman. The crowd had let him into the square, but now he must have wondered if they would let him leave so easily.

"You can't do this."

"I am the Mayor of Glienned. I serve the people's will. You should take that child away and never come back. Tell all of your kind, they're not welcome here any more."

At her declaration every person in the square cheered. The Seeker must have realised that to stay would cost more than his pride. As he approached the first row of people the Seeker cleverly used the girl as a shield in front of his body. Everyone recoiled from her as if she had the plague, creating a clear channel through the press of bodies.

As they passed through the crowd, not far away from where Habreel was standing, he saw the girl suddenly lunge at someone. A moment later there was a terrible screeching sound and people began to move backwards in a panic. Something red sprayed into the air and a familiar coppery smell lodged in the back of his throat.

Akosh's reaction was immediate. She pushed forward and he followed in her wake until they were standing in the front row.

The girl lay on the ground, a knife lodged in her throat while the Seeker was vainly trying to stem the bleeding. No one moved to help him save the girl.

"What happened?" asked Akosh, nudging a woman beside her.

"Girl grabbed Tull's knife from his belt," said the woman. "Stabbed herself rather than be taken away." There was a hint of pride in her voice.

"Help me!" said the Seeker but everyone just watched. It didn't take long. The blood pulsing from the jagged wound in the girl's neck slowed and then stopped. Her eyes glazed over and she let out a final breath.

"Leave her be," said the girl's mother, finally stepping forward and taking responsibility. "She doesn't belong to you."

At this distance Habreel could see the horror in the Seeker's eyes. Everywhere he looked in the crowd he was met with the same blank expression. No one was horrified by what the girl had done to herself. The Seeker gently laid the girl down on the street and quickly marched out of sight. Habreel was willing to bet the Seeker wouldn't stop on the road until he was miles away from Glienned.

Once the Seeker had left, the mood of the whole crowd seemed to lift. People began to disperse, quickly going back to their lives as if nothing had happened. Soon only a few remained in the square, including the dead girl and her weeping parents. Habreel and Akosh followed others back to the tavern.

"Well, that was bracing," said Akosh, finally able to laugh out loud without it drawing too many stares. "But it will take more than this to change things. One town refusing the Red Tower will not have much of an impact, even with it being the doorway to Zecorria."

Her tone was mocking but Habreel ignored it. This time it was his turn to grin.

"Did you think I was doing this on my own?" he asked, shaking his head in disappointment. "You have your followers and I have mine. My people are fanning sparks like this all over the west and, any day now, one of them will catch fire."

"You want one of the tests to turn violent," said Akosh, suddenly interested again.

Habreel shrugged. "I dislike violence, but understand that sometimes it's necessary. People are terrified of magic and after what happened during the war, they should be. One mage changed everything. He helped start a war that served no purpose. People lost loved ones and friends in the slaughter and all of it comes back to one mage. In the long run, eliminating all magic from the world will save countless lives. It's been a blight for too long."

"And what if it means killing more children to achieve your goal?" asked Akosh. "Could you do it?"

"I will do whatever is necessary, no matter the cost." He knew what she wanted him to say, but Habreel wouldn't give her the satisfaction. He sincerely hoped he would never have to get his hands dirty, although a small voice in the back of his mind told him it wasn't possible. But they couldn't begin to rebuild without first scouring away those who were already cursed. If it happened, he would find a way to live with it, but in the end it would be worth it to achieve a lasting peace. If a few had to be cleansed to save tens of thousands, then so be it. "Can I count on your support?" he asked.

Akosh's feral smile made a shiver run down Habreel's spine. "Oh, yes. I've not had this much fun in years."